Praise

If you've ever felt like a prodigal longing to return home, you're sure to find yourself in Gohlke's latest. . . . The multilayered beauty of this story will last in your heart and your mind for a long, long time.

SARAH LOUDIN THOMAS, award-winning author of *These Tangled Threads*, on *This Promised Land*

Can prodigals really go home? That question is at the heart of *This Promised Land*. Cathy Gohlke masterfully brings a biblical parable to life through well-crafted characters who must navigate devastating lies, crushing disappointment, and what it truly means to be a family. With poignant truths, *This Promised Land* reminds us that facing the past is often the only way to move forward.

MICHELLE SHOCKLEE, award-winning author of *Appalachian Song*

This story of faith and healing came to me when I needed it most, as timeless stories often do. Gohlke's straightforward yet heartfelt style strikes just the right chord. If you love stories like *He Should Have Told the Bees* by Amanda Cox, you will love *This Promised Land*.

KATIE POWNER, Christy award–winning author of *Where the Blue Sky Begins*

This Promised Land is a memorable, heart-tugging story with well-developed characters who long to build stronger connections and deeper faith and find a way to save their family farm. Authentic, rich storytelling and descriptions bring the era, people, and land to life. I'm confident readers will be inspired by this moving and well-written story.

CARRIE TURANSKY, award-winning author of *A Token of Love*

Cathy Gohlke has once again written a touching epic so authentic it recalls our own families and the hope of new beginnings no matter the past or how old we are. *This Promised Land* will plant its inspirational message into your heart.

TERRI GILLESPIE, award-winning author of *Sweet Rivalry*

With a deft hand, Cathy Gohlke recreates the powerful journey of the prodigal and what it means to be redeemed and forgiven. Readers will connect to the characters' struggle and identify with both the burdens and the blessings of home.

ROBIN W. PEARSON, Christy Award–winning author of *Dysfunction Junction*

Ladies of the Lake touched my heart as it chronicled the enduring power of lifelong friendships. . . . Characters came alive on the pages, sharing joys and sorrows, war and tragedy, betrayal, love, and forgiveness.

LYNN AUSTIN, bestselling author of *All My Secrets*

History buffs looking for deep writing and character development will want to add Gohlke to their lists.

LIBRARY JOURNAL on *Ladies of the Lake*

Night Bird Calling . . . interlaces themes of redemption, friendship, and grace, and its depiction of a small Southern town is reminiscent of writings by Lisa Wingate.

BOOKLIST

Gripping. . . . Gohlke creates a cast readers will love, and the strong themes of the bonds of family forged outside one's kin resonate. The author's fans will love this.

PUBLISHERS WEEKLY on *Night Bird Calling*

This Promised Land

Also by Cathy Gohlke

THIS PROMISED LAND

CATHY GOHLKE

Tyndale House Publishers
Carol Stream, Illinois

Visit Tyndale online at tyndale.com.

Visit Cathy Gohlke's website at cathygohlke.com.

Tyndale and Tyndale's quill logo are registered trademarks of Tyndale House Ministries.

This Promised Land

Cover designed by Libby Dykstra

Edited by Sarah Mason Rische

Published in association with the literary agency of Natasha Kern Literary Agency, Inc., P.O. Box 1069, White Salmon, WA 98672.

Scripture quotations are taken from the *Holy Bible*, King James Version.

This Promised Land is a work of fiction. Where real people, events, establishments, organizations, or locales appear, they are used fictitiously. All other elements of the novel are drawn from the author's imagination.

For information about special discounts for bulk purchases, please contact Tyndale House Publishers at csresponse@tyndale.com, or call 1-855-277-9400.

Library of Congress Cataloging-in-Publication Data

A catalog record for this book is available from the Library of Congress.

ISBN 978-1-4964-8694-3 (HC)
ISBN 978-1-4964-8695-0 (SC)

Printed in the United States of America

31	30	29	28	27	26	25
7	6	5	4	3	2	1

For Natasha

Dear friend, sister in Christ, sister gardener, and longtime literary agent

So grateful for you and for the many miles we've journeyed

Prologue

MID-OCTOBER 1940
WETHERILL PICKERING'S CHRISTMAS TREE FARM
NEW SCRIVELSBY, VIRGINIA

It was late in the season. Harold hand-dug holes while Ginny followed by setting the two-year-old bushes, filling the holes with topsoil and compost, and tamping back earth. They were both hauling water to the upper field for their biggest-ever order of plantings—northern highbush blueberry bushes—when they heard the cough of the rusted green van. Tailpipe smoking, a plume of red dust trailed as the van jerked to a stop in front of their two-story farmhouse down the hill.

Mr. Skipwith, the Pickerings' longtime friend and lawyer, stepped from the car, followed by a broad-shouldered boy half a sandy head taller and dressed in a blue work shirt and dungarees, belted tight at the waist. Even from that distance Ginny saw that the boy looked half man, as if he could own the place.

"That's him." Harold swiped the sweat from his brow on his shirt sleeve and turned the bill of his cap frontward.

"Who?"

"The juvenile delinquent Dad's taking on from Mr. Skipwith."

"The hired boy."

"Don't romanticize. Keep your distance. He's no good."

1

Which intrigued Ginny all the more. "How do you know? What's he done?"

"No idea."

"Then why are you down on him? You don't even know him."

Harold tossed his shovel into the back of their work wagon. "Don't need to. You don't get broadsided by the law and hauled in for community service for no good reason. You mind your business, Ginny Dee. Behave yourself and keep away, if you know what's good for you."

If her older, bossy brother had handed Ginny a gold-leaf-engraved invitation to latch on to the new boy, he couldn't have roused her curiosity more. Ginny pulled off her worn work gloves, stuffed them into the back pockets of her dungarees, and smoothed her auburn sun-kissed braids down the sides of her head. She wished for all the world she could sneak in the back door for a good wash before dinner, maybe even change into that dress Mama was after her to wear half the time. But there was no way and no time.

They unhitched Romeo, the most obliging mule in all of Virginia, and backed the wagon into the barn just as Mr. Skipwith's van pulled back onto the lane. Ginny left Harold quick as she could and snuck in the back door, careful not to let the screen door slam, tiptoeing through the kitchen and heading for the back stairs, determined to change clothes.

Harold followed on her heels, slamming the door behind him.

"Harold? Ginny Dee?" Mama called from the front room. "Come in here and meet Curtis."

Ginny could have kicked Harold in the shins, but he grinned as if he knew just what she'd been thinking, pleased as punch to have thwarted her plans.

"I'll be down in a minute, Mama," Ginny called, almost to the stairs, but Harold grabbed hold of her shoulders and steered her into the front room, much against the will of her feet. Being four years older and fully grown gave him advantages Ginny couldn't match.

Daddy held out his arm to draw them in. "Ginny Dee, Harold,

we want you to meet Curtis Boyden. Curtis will be living and working with us here for the next year or so."

Shy and blushing, Ginny reached her hand out to welcome the new boy.

"Year?" Harold dropped his hands from his sister's shoulders. "I thought we said through planting the blue spruce come spring."

"We'll be needing more help than that," Mama intervened, determined, and brooking no back talk. "And Curtis needs a place to stay near Leesburg."

"How come? For court?" Harold countered.

"Harold," Daddy warned, but it was too late. Cold came into Curtis's eyes.

"Curtis, let's get you settled," Mama directed. "You'll share a room with Harold."

Harold's mouth dropped open. "I thought he was going to sleep in the barn. All the seasonal workers do that."

"It will soon be too cold for that." Mama didn't look at Harold, but Daddy did, and the look was hard. "Come with me, Curtis."

Harold started to follow but Daddy called him back and lowered his voice once Curtis left the room. "Harold, Ginny Dee, you need to understand that from this minute Curtis will be treated as part of our family."

"Family—and in my room? He's a court kid."

"His father died last year and his mother's hospitalized in a sanitarium with tuberculosis. She's not likely to make it. Curtis was charged with stealing food for him and his younger brother. They had nothing to eat. This is the least we can do." Daddy was like that, always ready to help anybody who needed it, kids most of all.

Harold looked away.

"Where's his little brother now? Will he come here too?" Ginny would like a younger brother, maybe trade in Harold.

"A cousin took him in. She can't take both, so Curtis is with us. I expect you both to treat him well. Understood?"

"Yes, sir." Ginny nodded.

"Harold?"

Harold's mouth opened as if he was about to object, but he closed it and nodded. "Yes, sir."

"Good." Daddy laid his hands on both their shoulders. "That's settled."

If only it had been.

CHAPTER ONE

MAY 1992

CAPE MAY, NEW JERSEY

At sixty-five, Ginny Boyden knew the deep satisfaction of paying off years of debt—her car, her mortgage, her husband's medical and funeral bills, even his headstone—all while keeping his secret . . . and hers.

It had required the sale of her home and lean years of renting a single room with kitchen privileges and garden duties, but that was in the past. Finally, it was her turn. With a reasonable cushion in the bank and Social Security about to kick in, Ginny could breathe . . . breathe, and plan.

"That's it, Claire. My final one." Ginny slapped her signed paycheck onto the teller's desktop.

"Fully retired and off to parts unknown?" The bank clerk sighed. "Must be nice."

"Nicer than nice." Ginny smiled. "But all the parts are known. I'll leave as the last red maple leaf falls—for the duration."

"Mm-hmm. I'll see you back by Christmas, that's what."

"No, my friend. You won't." Ginny's brows rose. "No turning back." She wouldn't call it a trip; it was a journey into the future—her future, her first real step in fulfilling her lifelong dream. Ginny turned on her heel and made her way out of the bank, into the sunshine.

She'd leave the week before Thanksgiving, skirting one of those family holidays she'd long dreaded while living alone. Ten days touring formal English gardens out of season, then ten days touring Scotland's Highlands, islands, and gardens—cheaper by far in cold weather. She'd indulge in a short jaunt to Wales and a longer one to explore Ireland's Cliffs of Moher and castle ruins, then back to England and the Lake District for Christmas. Finally, she'd tour London and its museums in winter.

Mid-February she'd reach the village of Scrivelsby, her family's ancestral home, to begin greenhouse work with Logan Longwood, head gardener of Scrivelsby Park. The manor house, Scrivelsby Hall, was long gone, burned out, but the park boasted gardens that Ginny'd learned of and envisioned in her imagination at her mother's knee.

It had taken three years to convince Mr. Longwood to grant her a two-season probationary apprenticeship with lodging in one of the cottages—based, she hoped, on her night school training and community resource and volunteer work as a Master Gardener, her innovative crossbreeding of roses, and her sincerity poured into letters that sped across the Atlantic. She feared it was more likely her desperate persistence, the subtle pressure that her mother was a descendant of the Dymokes—distant relative of Lord Dymoke, Queen's Champion and owner of the park—and the fact that he'd never be rid of her if he didn't acquiesce.

But he'd said yes. That was all that mattered. Despite her age, once her feet hit British soil, she'd convince him of her strength and abilities, her strong work ethic, and her commitment. She'd make herself a valuable contributor, indispensable.

The garden catalogs she'd pored over for all the years of her adult life would have to go. The stacks filled five bins in the small closet of her room. She'd already sold or given away nearly everything not transportable in two suitcases—all but her gardening books and botanical presses. No storage units for Ginny.

Those smacked of baggage and returning.

At the retirement supper, her coworkers had celebrated her and the more than thirty years they'd worked together in the gardening center. Like Claire, they'd teased that her planned move to England was temporary—a flight of fancy and something she needed to get out of her system—and that she'd be back in their midst, eager to rejoin their ranks, before the spring rush.

Ginny knew better. She'd do whatever it took to make her move permanent. She'd volunteer if her application for an extended work visa was denied and camp out at the embassy, begging for extensions on her visa. She'd apply for dual citizenship if necessary. Her coworkers were good friends, but not family. There was nothing and no one to keep her in New Jersey, or even the US, not anymore.

From the bank, Ginny stopped at her post office box. She'd need to close that in a few months and see about having important mail forwarded. She didn't get much mail, so it shouldn't be a problem. Reaching into the box, she pulled out yet another spring garden catalog—always a pleasure—and a long, official-looking linen envelope, clearly not an advertisement.

She turned it over. The name and address did not register at first: *Miss Virginia Dionysia Pickering*—a name Ginny hadn't gone by or seen written out since she was not quite sixteen. The envelope had been mailed to and forwarded from a local Cape May boardinghouse where she'd rented a room decades ago—just after leaving Virginia during WWII, of all things—while she'd saved and waited for Curtis to return from the front before she'd purchased their home.

"I don't believe it," Ginny whispered. The letter could have only found its way to her now because she'd stayed in touch with the family that owned the home all these years—now another generation—and had developed gardens for the old Victorian house as part of her internship in her Master Gardener's program a couple of years ago.

Seeing her maiden name, and the town of her birth, founded by her mother's ancestors, on official letterhead, sent a cramp to her heart, as if a ghost walked over old graves.

Ginny gritted her teeth. She shoved the letter into her purse, locked her box, and hurried from the post office as if someone were following her.

She wouldn't open it, didn't want to know what it said. Anything from New Scrivelsby, Virginia, stank of her past, a past she wasn't about to dredge up now. Not when she stood on the threshold of stepping into her long-cherished dream.

She hadn't yet made her airline reservation for England. There was plenty of time. She wouldn't be traveling for six months. Whatever the letter said would be of no importance by then. She'd simply ignore it.

Back in her room, she shoved the envelope beneath a pile of junk mail and set the stack atop her boxes of seed catalogs to take to recycling. Out of sight, out of mind.

But the envelope niggled at the back of her mind for days, a little spider climbing the wall of her brain, spinning dark and silken threads to tempt her, taunt her.

For three days she stayed busy and tried to forget about it, but in the long night hours, just before dawn, knowing the letter was there, unread—it haunted her.

She wondered if the letter contained bad news, news that might alter her plans in some way. *Never.* On the third night, she turned over, punched her pillow, and stared at the ceiling.

Her parents were dead, and the farm was long gone from her. Every tie she'd ever had to the town of her birth had been severed decades ago. The only person who might still be alive had long ago shut her out, declared her dead to their family.

Why now, Lord? Why anything from there now, after all these years? I'm ready to move on. I need to move on.

Ginny wrestled until the clock's hands teetered on four, then she sat up, groaning aloud. She shoved her feet into her scuffs, dug the letter from her stack of junk mail, and crept down the stairs to the kitchen, taking care not to waken her landlady. She heated a little milk, spooned coffee into the filter for automatic drip, and slipped her fingernail beneath the letter's seal.

May 12, 1992

Dear Miss Pickering,

I regret to inform you of the passing of your brother, Harold Pickering, 69 years, of New Scrivelsby, Virginia, and extend my deepest sympathy.

As your brother's attorney and executor for his estate, I've encountered a question regarding the title for land known as Wetherill Pickering's Christmas Tree Farm which his family is unable to clarify. I hope that you will be able to help.

Please contact me at your earliest convenience.

Sincerely,
Willoughby Skipwith
Attorney-at-Law

Harold dead . . . and with a family. Sixty-nine wasn't that old, but somehow his death didn't surprise her. That he'd married and had children should not have. Not much surprised Ginny. Still, there was no reason she should be contacted. He certainly would not have wished it. She'd been written out of her family's life and will fifty years before. Harold had made certain she understood that.

Could she mourn him? Did she feel anything at all? Ginny wasn't sure.

The name Skipwith rang a distant bell, conjuring images of a suited and portly man sporting only a ring of frizzy gray hair around the perimeter of his skull. A kindly enough man with a gruff exterior. *He can't possibly still be practicing.*

Ginny set the letter down, poured her coffee, and walked out to the screened porch. Cloaked in darkness, she nestled beneath a quilt in the white wicker rocker and waited for the sun to rise, waited for the morning and its light.

It was hard to take in, Harold's dying. No matter that he'd disowned her, had refused her letters, had written words that stabbed Ginny's heart like a knife, he was her brother. Her last living relative, except, of course, for whatever "his family" meant. She closed her eyes. *Harold married, with children—a family?* She knew nothing about him, not since the night she'd left home, except that he'd wanted nothing to do with her.

Losing Daddy, losing the baby, Mama and Harold cutting her off, and finally Curtis coming home forever changed—even after all these years, all of that weighed too heavy. She pushed those memories away.

Black gave way to gray light on the horizon. The first purple streaks across the sky made things seem not so cruel as they had in the dark of night. *Harold's gone. I'm not sorry, and I am sorry. But, maybe, is this an open window?*

Harold could no longer stop her going back. Not that she wanted to "go back," but a trip to New Scrivelsby before leaving the States might be her only opportunity to visit her parents' graves on the farm and say a real goodbye, something she'd given up hope of ever doing.

Closure. Perhaps that's what this is about, putting those final ghosts to rest before moving to England. There's time. My tour doesn't actually begin for a few months. Social Security won't kick in for another month or so, and I probably shouldn't go anywhere until it does, until I know it's going directly into my bank account. Yes, there's time.

Ginny waited until ten o'clock. Surely even legal offices opened by ten. She phoned the number on the letterhead and made an appointment with the woman who answered the phone for Friday at one o'clock. That would give her the rest of the week to work up her nerve and then the weekend to recuperate from the trip—a very short trip.

꧁

With a stop or two along the way, New Scrivelsby, Virginia, was a five-hour drive. During the war, she and Curtis had believed there would be work in Cape May County. After the war, after Curtis had returned so changed, Ginny hadn't cared to move. She'd settled, made a few friends, and found her own work in the gardening center, small pay though it was. And Cape May County was a reasonable distance from New Scrivelsby—far enough that Ginny'd always known her family would not come looking for her, not so far away that she couldn't get back home if she ever needed to, if she ever received invitation or permission to return. She hadn't.

One suitcase holding three days' worth of clothes, two books she'd been meaning to read, a thermos of black coffee, a bag of popcorn, an apple, and a chicken sandwich for the road was plenty. Bare-bones staples, that's all she'd take—as well as the tools needed for the flowers she intended to plant on her parents' grave.

She got an early start, determined to beat the morning traffic. If she drove straight through, she'd likely get there in time to see the attorney before lunch—if he wasn't too busy—visit the family graves, then find a hotel for the night on her way back, maybe stop over near Baltimore. The extra clothes were for if she needed to stay a day or two longer. Not likely, but just in case.

Reaching 70 West, the traffic lightened, and she cautiously invited the ghosts. She couldn't think about her mama, not yet. She'd start with her daddy, and the farm, always the farm.

Daddy—Wetherill Pickering—was known far and wide as a good man, the best of men, with a large and tender heart, if a weak one. Hardworking, God-fearing, smart in a baker's dozen ways, full of grandiose ideas but never a businessman.

Mama possessed those brains for business, as well as grace, beauty, and discipline—her own and the kind that kept her children and occasional farm workers in line. It was Mama who'd insisted Daddy hire help once he'd suffered his first sign of heart trouble.

Ginny remembered the day an acre's worth of blueberry bushes had arrived in mid-October and needed to be planted before frost. Mama'd lamented from the first that Daddy was overstepping himself ordering all those bushes for the fall when they'd never even planted blueberries and didn't know the first thing about them. On top of that news, Daddy said he'd placed a preorder for an acre's worth of two-year-old blue spruce seedlings—five hundred and fifty, slow-to-medium growers, not native—to be delivered early the next spring.

Mama nearly had a fit, but Daddy wouldn't listen. He'd proclaimed that Pickering land was God's idea for soil—gentle slopes with perfect drainage, inches of rich topsoil with just enough sand and no substantial clay, and irrigation brought from a creek with tributaries deep enough to make a Baptist smile. He vowed that with a little help they could dig the old stumps out before the seedlings arrived to transplant. Folks, he'd said, would come begging for those Christmas trees in another five to seven years.

Already he'd cultivated the largest Christmas tree farm within fifty miles—thirty acres of Scotch and white pine, Norway spruce, and Douglas fir, with another twenty cleared and lots more acreage up the mountain in high meadows if he or any future Pickerings ever wanted to expand. Already he'd pushed his bank loan out with an extension, and still the Depression ground on.

It was the only time Ginny remembered her mama challenging her daddy, reminding him the farm was Dymoke land—not Pickering—and that overstepping themselves was not how her ancestors had held on to land in the New World for more than two centuries.

Ginny flicked on the windshield spray and sent the wipers flying to clear her vision, just as her memory raced through the farm's grueling work cycle, year after year—a cycle and anchor she'd hated as a girl and yet missed over the last decades.

Daddy was right about people coming, wanting those trees . . . but what a lot of work, and the outcome always so uncertain.

Hard labor marked November and December, between cutting trees to ship to the city and those to sell directly from the farm. January meant taking down all those signs and props—anything not frozen in the ground—as well as the Christmas lights to store for the next year.

As soon as that was done Mama and Daddy would sit together at the kitchen table and work up the tree orders for the next year. Even now, Ginny could see them sitting there, cups of coffee steaming between them and the ledger book with its long columns—columns that Mama added up because Daddy didn't have the patience. *That was a nice time, that little window when the snow fell and we were stuck indoors.*

As soon as the snow melted, there were stumps left from the Christmas tree sales to dig by hand until they could get the tractor in, and finally to spray to keep the Pales weevils—stem eaters—at bay. By late March or early April, seedlings arrived for transplanting and needed to be in the ground—six feet apart—as soon as possible, all while keeping watch for a late freeze and those thieving gophers eager to eat the roots right back to the trees' stems. Ginny shook her head at the memory.

May had brought new lime-green growth to the trees—"candles" that stood upright on their branches. Those candles were one of the prettiest sights in the world to a Christmas tree farmer. But a late frost could tip them a dry brown, setting the growth back a year and making the tree, though still alive, unsalable for that year.

Fertilizing the trees while trying not to fertilize the weeds came next—what a job—and then the hand removal of cones from the trees. Always so messy. Ginny shuddered. She'd hated that job and all the times Harold had swiped his sappy fingers through her long hair, thinking it was funny. The stuff had been like tar to comb out.

By mid-May it seemed every waking hour outside of school was spent mowing between the rows of trees. In June, they'd sheared and shaped trees waist high or taller. That's how she and Harold had spent their summers—June, July, and August in the heat and humidity of Virginia, feasted upon by mosquitoes, sculpting those trees. So funny that customers thought Christmas trees grew into cone shapes by themselves.

They were still mowing in September, not only between rows but between trees in each row, hoping to make it easier for shoppers to roam the fields come November, and especially to keep the field mice and rabbits from adding the bark of the young trees to their winter diet.

By October, Mama and Daddy roamed the fields while Harold and Ginny were in school. They priced and ticketed each tree, checking for any diseased or stressed trees that might need to be removed—trees that wouldn't hold their needles. Mama touched up any signs that needed a freshening—she had a light hand and artistic bent. Daddy sharpened saws and axes. On weekends they all began hanging lights and lanterns, getting ready for the season. Such a festive time.

Then back to cutting trees to ship in November. Doors opened to customers the day after Thanksgiving. Every day, especially every weekend was crazy busy after that, long hours right up until Christmas morning.

Ginny had to force her eyes wide to keep awake, lulled as she was by memories. *December was the best. Longtime friends and neighbors coming by to choose and cut their tree, often bringing cookies to pair with the hot cider Mama and I mulled. Some folks came from as far away as Maryland or West Virginia to choose their tree—a family tradition—sometimes a second generation.*

Ginny pulled onto Route 15 South. The cycle was relentless, and it had been a hard life, but a good life, for the most part.

Then her daddy had added those infernal blueberries to harvest by the acre for local stores, whatever the pick-your-own visitors missed, and the roadside farm stand to mind. Next came peaches and on and on. Mama had been right. They'd needed more help.

That need was what had brought Curtis Boyden, the handsomest, most dangerous thing Ginny'd ever laid eyes on, out to live on and help work the farm. Even now, despite all that had transpired, Ginny smiled at the memory. That was the year before the war, before Pearl Harbor was bombed, the year before everything changed.

As Ginny pulled into New Scrivelsby the bell in the stone church tower on the corner of Main and Rotherdam bonged noon. She recognized the church, the library, and the diner before parallel parking in front of the two-story white frame building bearing a sign: *Skipwith and Son, Attorneys-at-Law.*

With an hour until her appointment, she didn't want to show up too early and appear anxious, though she was—anxious to know what Willoughby Skipwith wanted, anxious to get the meeting over with. There wasn't time to drive to the farm to visit the family cemetery before the meeting, and she surely didn't want to sit in the lawyer's office while he was out to lunch. Maybe a visit to the church or the library. They were the only places, besides home, that Ginny had truly missed through the years.

Even in that short space she saw that the small town, if you could call it a town, had changed. The post office was gone or moved elsewhere. The old stone building it had been housed in was now a doctor's office. Two small stores of the mom-and-pop variety had been added—a fabric-and-yarn store and a five-and-dime. Only the hardware store remained of the enterprises Ginny remembered. She smiled, thinking of Mr. and Mrs. Reister, who'd owned and run that store, originally the town's general store. They could place their hands on anything you wanted, from a garden hose to the most obscure washer or screw to out-of-season rakes or seeds, at a moment's notice. She wondered if their children ran the store now. It had long been a family business.

She was glad to see that New Scrivelsby hadn't become too new. There were no chain stores or fast-food restaurants. When she'd left, nearly fifty years before, electricity had been new to the town. Now electric lampposts lined the streets alongside mature maples, their limbs decked in spring-green leaves.

Ginny stood outside the stone church, looking up at the bell in the tower, the bell that had tolled for Sunday morning worship and every day at noon and six in the evening, the bell that had tolled each time one of the town's own was laid to rest. She wondered if they still did that. The last time she'd heard it toll for the dead was after her daddy's funeral. *Did they ring it for Mama? Surely.*

Ginny swallowed the dry lump in her throat. She didn't want to think about that, didn't want to remember that she hadn't been there when her mama had needed her, when she was sick, let alone when she lay dying.

I would have come if I'd known, if I'd been allowed. Dear God, You know I would have. Ginny wasn't sure if that was confession or prayer or both. *Coming back was a bad idea. I'm not ready. I'll never be ready.* She pulled her sweater tight around her, even as the sun beat down, and hurried back to her car.

Breathe, Ginny, breathe. Filling her lungs with air, she gripped the steering wheel. Nearly one o'clock. *Decide. You've got to decide whether to leave now or go in there.*

Dear God, this is so much harder than I thought. But I'm here. If I don't do this now, I won't come back. I know I won't. Please. Help me. Come with me. Please.

❧

Ginny grasped the brass door handle. Squaring her shoulders and doing her best to push aside the gawky adolescent she felt inside, she walked into the office of Skipwith and Son, Attorneys-at-Law. Before she could say who she was, a young woman stood from her desk and offered her hand.

"Miss Pickering? Mr. Skipwith told me to expect you." The woman looked half Ginny's age and twice as nervous. "He asked me to tell you he's so very sorry, but he was called away yesterday and won't be back in town or able to meet with you until Monday."

"Monday?" Ginny ignored the use of her maiden name. She was not prepared for the rest. "I've driven all the way from Cape May County."

The woman's brow wrinkled, and she wrung her hands. "He's terribly sorry for the inconvenience. He would have written but knew a letter couldn't reach you in time. He wanted to telephone but we don't have a number for you."

The young woman pulled a set of keys from her desk. "He asked me to give you these. He didn't know if you still had keys to the house or if the locks have been changed over the years. He had me contact the electric yesterday morning. They expect to turn that on today. Mr. Skipwith tried to get someone out to clean yesterday or today but that just didn't work out. He said to tell you he's sorry about that too."

"I don't understand why he would. Have the house cleaned, I mean."

"No one's been living there for years. He said it needs a good going over."

Ginny took the keys, staring at them. *No one? Not Harold?* She didn't know what to say, couldn't formulate questions, let alone the words to ask them.

Finally, "The farm. Mr. Skipwith thinks I'll stay at the farm until Monday? Didn't Harold live there? Doesn't his family?"

The woman looked flustered. "I don't think so. I'm not sure. Mr. Pickering lived with his son and his wife; that's all I know. To tell you the truth, this is my first week. Mr. Skipwith will explain everything when he gets back. He said if he's able to wrap things up today, he'll drive back from Raleigh tomorrow."

"Raleigh? Can he see me tomorrow? Or Sunday? I hadn't planned to stay."

"Well, I don't know. If he telephones, I can ask him . . . You don't happen to have one of those mobile phones, do you?"

Ginny shook her head. She wasn't young enough to be that trendy.

"I can leave a message on his desk, but I won't see him again until Monday. I'm sorry."

Sorry. That's it?

There wasn't anything else to do. Ginny hefted the keys, wondered that they felt so light and cool when they should have weighed a ton or burned the palm of her hand. She shook her head again, still trying to take in this change of plan. *No quick stop and away.* She'd have to stay over, but she had no intention of sleeping in that house.

For all the years she'd longed to come home, now all she wanted was to leave.

The drive on the main road two miles out of town revealed new neighborhoods holding a number of small frame houses. New Scrivelsby had grown, she realized, but modestly. It had always been a small town supported by farmers—dairy farmers, goat and sheep farmers, crop farmers, one or two small horse farms.

The frame houses Ginny had known growing up looked old, weathered. The larger, stone houses looked as if they could stand the test of another fifty years.

She'd wondered about the farm over the years—if Harold had been able to keep it going, if he'd modernized the house, if he'd been successful. She wasn't sure she wanted to know.

She drove a little slower, taking it all in. A right turn off the main road and half a mile down Christmas Road she saw the sign: *Wetherill Pickering's Christmas Tree and Berry Farm*. Seeing her family's name, the name of the farm on a painted board caught her by surprise. It was a new sign since she'd left—of course it would be—but it, too, was weathered, the lettering faded with the words *and Berry Farm* roughly painted over, the letters bleeding through. *Not a good advertisement if you want to attract customers.*

She turned left, into the lane leading up to the farmhouse. Ten-foot spruce trees lined the drive, new since she'd left. *Well, nothing stays the same, does it? I haven't.* The evergreens made a nice entrance to the farm but looked in need of shaping.

Was Harold ill before he passed or did he go down with his boots on— like Daddy? By the looks of things, he let quite a bit go. Wasn't he able to afford help? What about his family?

Ginny reminded herself it wasn't her concern. "Stay focused. You've come to see Mama and Daddy's graves, then you're leaving for a hotel—somewhere. You're not sleeping in the house. You'll see Mr. Skipwith on Monday, if not before, and then you're out of here."

The drive turned. She gasped as the house stood before her. Stone with a clapboard addition eighty years ago, white once upon a time, now in need of sanding and a good coat of paint. The house didn't look half so huge or imposing as she'd remembered it. Not nearly as big as the ramshackle Victorians lining the streets of old Cape May, nor so well cared for. The secretary—what was her name, if she'd even said?—was right. It didn't look as if anyone had lived in the house for years.

Ginny could only imagine what cleaning or repairs it needed. She'd hate to walk inside and see it looking run-down. She didn't want to think about walking inside at all. *The cemetery. You're going to the cemetery. You don't have to go inside. You don't have to stay here. There must be a hotel somewhere, if not in New Scrivelsby then back toward Route 15 or even 70. You are not a prisoner here.*

From the trunk Ginny pulled a light jacket, her spade, a small Radio Flyer red wagon—great for transporting plants over uneven ground—and three flats of her own crossbred flowers she'd brought to plant on the graves of her family, a gift to her parents and the only way she knew to leave a little bit of herself behind.

The afternoon sun had given way to rolling clouds. The temperature dropped steadily, a sure sign that rain was on its way. If she intended to spend any amount of time at the cemetery, she'd best hurry.

Ginny'd always been thankful that the family plot was not right by the house. As a child she'd imagined the horror of looking out her window on a graveyard of Pickerings and Dymokes in the twilight, had never wanted to think about ghosts in their rollicking reunions or skeleton tea parties—all things her older brother had convinced her five-year-old self took place whenever the wind kicked up and the moon rose full over the mountains. Even now, she was glad for the quarter-mile walk and for the sprawling grove of hollies that surrounded the gated cemetery.

A breeze tugged at tree limbs, but Ginny ignored it. Unlatching the black iron gate unlocked a well of emotions. She knew where her father was buried. She'd been here for that. Ginny gulped to see her mother's name written on the stone beside his. Neither grave was well tended. *Harold must have been sick. He wouldn't let Mama and Daddy's graves go like this if he could help it. Surely not.*

Harold's grave wasn't far, just beyond their father's. It was recent but there was not even sod over the rough clay mound. *Harold Dymoke Pickering, born August 12, 1922, died September 18, 1991.* That was all; no epitaph. "Eight months ago. Why did Mr. Skipwith wait so long to write me?" The stone beside Harold's read, *Elaine Pickering, beloved wife and mother, born March 1, 1923, died April 29, 1954.* Ginny's breath caught. *So young.*

The rest of the cemetery had overgrown, as if no one had tended it in years, except for a small section in the far-right corner, beyond the older headstones. It had been cleared of weeds and carefully tended, the stones surrounded by tiny blue forget-me-nots. No names were chiseled on the small monuments, simply three little lambs sitting amid twining vines of ivy, indicating individual plots, likely children. They'd not been there when Ginny was young. *Whose are they? Whose children? Harold's? No, the stones look too recent if Elaine Pickering was his wife.*

The breeze stiffened, whipping Ginny's gray skirt against her thighs. Dark clouds swept low over the mountain, boding a coming storm. The rumble of thunder warned that she'd best get her flowers in the ground pronto.

Ginny pulled just enough weeds to spade holes and fill them with compost. She planted her flowers at the base of each headstone, keeping a running conversation in her head. *The rain will do you good, my beauties. I'll come back tomorrow and get all these straggly weeds out of your way.*

Before she could pack up her garden tools, lightning split the sky. The heavens opened; rain poured in sheets. Ginny dropped her gloves into her wagon. She should have paid closer mind. That's what mountain storms were like—sudden. She'd had plenty of warning. She'd just forgotten. *It's been too long.*

Dragging her red wagon and stumbling as best she could through the downpour, thoroughly drenched and shaking from the steep drop in temperature, Ginny nearly collapsed on the front porch of the farmhouse. She needed to dry off, get warm. She needed a towel or a blanket, something. Anything. She didn't have one in her car, and she couldn't sit in her car soaked; she'd drench the seat.

With trembling fingers, she pulled from her pocket the set of keys Mr. Skipwith's secretary had given her, fumbling the first one into the keyhole. Not a fit. She tried the second, the third. Finally, the fourth slipped into the slot. She turned the key, imagined the old tumblers falling into place, and braced herself.

Stepping into the past should have made the door hinges creak, the ancient lace parlor curtains ruffle, and the floorboards groan. Spiderwebs should have trembled once the outside air made contact. None of that happened. All stood still and silent, as if someone had walked out and shut the door on time.

Just as Ginny remembered, the seven-foot grandfather clock with its brass pendulum stood sentry in the corner of the entryway. The sofa—dusty blue with the 1940s floral pattern—sat in the center of the living room, facing the stone fireplace, the hearth flanked by a matching armchair and her mama's rocker. An old English pastoral scene hung over the mantel, oil lamp sconces on either side, as if electricity had passed the house by, though Ginny knew her father had installed it shortly before his last heart attack. The Victorian rosewood upright piano, its ivory keys yellowed, still sat on the opposite wall, a stack of crumbling sheet music on its lid. Mama's treadle Singer sewing machine stood beneath a window, her work basket overflowing with socks, as if she'd stepped out but would return to darn them any minute.

Ginny swallowed, her breath sucked away and mouth gone dry. Wind howled and the front door slammed behind her; she jumped in the half-light. She hadn't realized she'd stepped farther into the room. She shivered, her rain-sodden hair and jacket shedding droplets onto the floor.

Teeth chattering, she pulled herself together and headed for the kitchen. "A dish towel. That's all I need."

But every step brought some new sense alive, brought a memory to the fore. She moved through the hallway in slow motion. There were the handprints she and Harold had traced on the hallway wall when she was six. There were the marks up the doorframe like rungs of a ladder—measurements of their growing height through the years, carpenter-penciled by their daddy every year on their birthdays, even in their teens, up until the year he died, the year she left.

The kitchen sat tidy, every dish and utensil in its place, covered in a shroud of dust. Cobwebs stretched from ceiling corners to curtain rods. The cast-iron stove looked a shade of gray, so thick was the layer of dust.

A museum. No, not a museum—a mausoleum. This hasn't been touched in years. Is that possible? Nearly fifty years since Mama died? Did Harold just leave it like this? Where was he all that time?

Ginny drew a ragged breath. She walked to the sideboard, just as if she still lived there, and pulled open the drawer where her mother had always kept the tea towels—Helen Dymoke Pickering would never have called them dish towels. She reached for one. Ironed and folded, as if Mama had just washed and sun-dried them as she did every Monday. The idea of taking one to dry herself felt like sacrilege. Ginny closed the drawer, wrapping her arms across her chest. She'd air-dry.

Standing in the middle of the kitchen raised the voice of every ghost in her head. Mama, Daddy, Harold, Curtis—Curtis as he was at nineteen.

"Stop! Stop!" She clutched the sides of her head, pulled her hair by its roots, willing the memories away. "I can't do this. I can't do this, Lord. Why now?" Ginny fumbled through the pockets of her jacket for her car keys. Not there. She'd left her purse in the car. The keys must be there. "I need air. I don't care what Mr. Skipwith wants or needs to know. I'm not staying."

She threw open the front door, startled by the clean, rain-washed scent of earth, of evergreens—fragrances she hadn't inhaled in such strength for years, for decades.

The rain had slowed to a drizzle. *Mama, you'd call this a mizzle. Daddy always made fun of you for saying that. Oh, Mama. I miss you so.* The sharp pang in Ginny's chest drove deep. *Stop. Just stop thinking about her.*

Ginny stepped gingerly down the slick front porch steps. She wasn't about to slip and fall, sprain an ankle, or worse, break a hip and be stuck there. She tugged her car door handle. *Locked!* She tried the passenger's side, the back doors. *You've got to be kidding!* Ginny squinted her eyes and leaned her forehead against the glass. She could see her suitcase through the back-seat window, sitting there full of warm, dry clothes.

Is this some kind of cruel joke, Lord? Because it isn't funny.

She peered through her front window. Her car keys hung tidily from the ignition. *I don't believe it. I'd laugh if I didn't so much want to cry.*

But there was no point in crying, and no point in getting wetter.

Ginny hurried back inside and flicked the first light switch by the door, then the second. She tried the lamp by her daddy's chair. Nothing happened. *Mr. Skipwith's secretary said she called to have the electricity to the house turned on. Either the electric company's not come yet or the storm's knocked it out.*

Well, I should be grateful, right, Lord? It's a roof over my head. It's just for one night. Surely the sun will come out tomorrow, and if Mr. Skipwith or the electrician doesn't come by, I'll walk out to the main road and find a house, ask them to let me use their phone . . . or give me a ride into town . . . I'll call a locksmith . . . somebody.

Ginny sighed and plunked into her daddy's worn chair. Like it or not, she'd be spending the night with old ghosts.

CHAPTER TWO

WANDERING THROUGH THE HOUSE, hunting for candles and matches, lighting the oil lamp, knowing just where every sheet and blanket was closeted felt like reading a book she'd loved as a child but hadn't picked up in ages.

Creepy, spooky, precious, haunting—images and words came to Ginny's mind as she made her way up the steep wooden stairs to her old bedroom.

She stood a long time outside her door, Harold's room across the hallway. The room he'd shared with Curtis. She wouldn't open that door. She wasn't sure she wanted to open her own old door. *Did Mama change it after I left? Erase me from the walls and floorboards? Will there be any remnant of me here?* She couldn't bear the thought of being pushed from her mother's memory and she couldn't bear the thought that everything had remained the same, indicating that she really had broken her mother's heart.

Did Mama hope against hope that I'd come home? Was I really dead to her, as Harold wrote?

Ginny pushed open the door.

A wave of mustiness hit her nasal passages and she sneezed. Her desk still stood on the far side of the room beneath a window that looked out onto the back garden. *I loved watching the birds in the crab apple tree—every season—while the sun set in the west.*

She ran her hand over the bed's posts, its headboard still stationed between the windows. She lifted the corner of the pink-and-lavender patchwork quilt her mama had stayed up late night after night to sew from flour sacks—a birthday gift the year she'd turned thirteen.

"You choose your favorites, Ginny Dee," Mama had said as they'd stood together eyeing the many patterned sacks bulging with flour in the feed store. "Find the prettiest ones for my girl."

Ginny opened the closet door. Her breath caught. She fingered the blush organdy dress she'd worn to the Christmas dance her last year in school, the dance Curtis had accompanied her to. Her heart skipped a beat remembering when he'd stood at the bottom of the hall staircase, his hair brushed back, smart in the navy suit he'd saved every penny to buy just so she'd be proud to walk out with him. He'd looked just a little bit shy and a whole lot dapper, holding the prettiest white gardenia wrist corsage she'd ever seen. Ginny inhaled, remembering the fragrance. She'd loved gardenias ever since.

Remembering Curtis as he was then was like standing outside her life and watching an old film. Before the war had changed him, before it stole the boy she'd loved and replaced him with someone she hardly recognized.

Ginny closed the closet door. He'd hardly known her when he came home, though she'd tried to reach him in every way she knew. She felt the heat burn up her neck and face at those memories, at the things she'd done and the things she'd left undone.

For the last several years of his life, though she'd never admit it to another soul, she hadn't wanted to go see him in the nursing home. She'd made herself do it. When he died—when he passed, as she tried to think of his death—she'd tried to mourn, but she'd done so much mourning for so long that her heart had sealed, grown cold. She wondered now how it was that she'd forgotten what he'd looked like back then—the way he'd stood tall, the laughter and hunger and shyness and love-light in his eyes.

Ginny closed the bedroom door, sealing herself off from the hall-way. She didn't want more old memories creeping up the stairs in the dead of night, poking their heads through her door, beckoning without warning.

It had been too long a day, one she couldn't process. She'd need to think it all through but hadn't the head or heart. Her stomach growled. There was no point in thinking about that now either. Her remaining half chicken sandwich sat in the locked car along with her bag of popcorn, out of reach. Ginny checked her watch. Half past six. She'd not gone to bed that early since . . . well, ever.

She peeked under the bed for mice or snakes or anything else that might make its home in an old, abandoned house. Miraculously, thankfully, there was nothing. She pulled off her shoes, turned back the covers on her old bed, and sank into the lumpy mattress, familiar in its way.

Ginny closed her eyes and welcomed the dark, willing herself to think of nothing. She couldn't have said where nothing ended and remembering began.

She used to listen to Curtis and Harold across the hallway at night. At first there was only silence. Then a few weeks on, their words rose, heated and angry. Later she often fell asleep to the calming cadence of deep, rhythmic tones of friendship, camaraderie, brotherhood, dreams, and secrets shared. Security, contentment, even a restless sort of happiness and anticipation . . . that's what she'd felt then, as if everything was tucked in its place, safe, predictable, not exactly serene but happy, while tingling with possibility. She'd believed in a future for all of them, right there, together.

When Curtis first moved to the farm, he'd refused to get close to anyone, least of all Harold. Harold wanted no one threatening his place as firstborn and only son. Two wary wolves, they'd circled, constantly eying each other, never turning their backs—smoldering embers of a fire that wouldn't die.

But from his first day Curtis worked hard—digging holes, weed-ing, pruning, sculpting trees, turning ground, whatever Daddy put him to—almost as if he had something to prove, as if coyotes chased his tail. Without a word, Mama ladled extra servings of stew or oatmeal or whatever she'd cobbled together onto his plate. He ate like a man half starved. Maybe that's what had softened Harold, at least for quite a while. Through all the years of the Depression not one of their family went without a meal. Farm life was good for that.

Somewhere in Ginny's remembering she turned to dreaming, dreaming that fell true to memory.

Curtis called Daddy "Mr. Pickering" and Mama "Mrs. Pickering." They told him to use their first names, but Curtis wouldn't do it. He'd been with us through Christmas and late into winter, maybe February or early March. It was Saturday, just past dusk. We'd all been working the fields since sunup, the ground having thawed just enough to dig out the old stumps from trees sold that year, getting ready for the delivery of all those blue spruces Daddy'd ordered. We were dead tired, every one of us, and had just come in, leaving our muddy work boots on the back porch to clean later.

Mama had me wash my hands and feet—as we always did after working in the fields—then help her get supper on the table, which I didn't think was fair, given that the men got to sit around the table after washing up, talking and waiting for their meal.

But that day Daddy sat in a chair by the kitchen's back door, pale and quiet. Mama eyed him with a wrinkled brow but kept on with supper, as if that might perk him up. "Supper's almost done, Wetherill. You ready?"

Daddy drew a deep breath. "I need to wash my feet." He didn't speak for half a minute. "I'm just so tired."

We were all tired, but I knew even then that Daddy meant his heart. It was weak and he shouldn't have been working out there so long and hard in the cold. But while I was thinking that and while Harold sat and watched, Curtis took the basin from the back porch and poured water from the kettle on the stove.

"I'll wash your feet, Dad."

Before one of us could think what to do or say, he set the basin on the floor, knelt in front of Daddy, and pulled his socks off. Daddy started to protest but Curtis pushed his hand away and gently, as if he were stroking a newborn calf, washed Daddy's feet. Tears filled Mama's eyes. I glimpsed Harold from the corner of my eye—bearing the look of shame that I, too, felt for never considering such a thing. I didn't want to wash anybody's dirty feet, but Curtis did it, because Daddy needed it. From that day Curtis always called him Dad. From that day Daddy and Mama always referred to him as their son. From that day something in Harold hardened again, as if he saw Curtis as competition for Mama and Daddy's love or admiration.

In Ginny's dream the memory faded. They were back in the fields, turning ground. Everyone looked up. The tractor sputtered, then roared to life on its own, bearing down the field toward them . . . but the motor wasn't right. It wasn't the old red tractor . . . It was the motor of a car or a truck, and Ginny realized she was no longer dreaming.

Headlights swept the curtains of her window. The motor gunned and stopped. A door slammed. *Who could be here this time of night?* Ginny pushed herself up from the bed, nearly tripping over her shoes, and peeked out the window. Headlights, aimed at the house, shone high beams. Downstairs a fierce knocking came on the door. *Thank You, God, that I locked that door!* Locking doors at night wouldn't have occurred to her growing up in New Scrivelsby. It was a habit she'd picked up in New Jersey.

The knocking became a pounding, then an attempted turning, a rattling of the doorknob. Ginny's heart caught in her throat. Finally, boot stomps echoed down the outside porch steps. She couldn't see the person's face, but the man—surely a man, with that strong build—aimed his flashlight at her car. The light wended its way slowly around the car, shining in every window, assessing her belongings. The beam shot across the house front and side. Ginny stood back from the window and closed her eyes, praying—praying for protection, praying that whoever it was would go away. The lock on that front door wouldn't hold if he was determined to get in.

She couldn't hear footsteps on the soft ground, but peeking

around the curtain, she saw the flashlight beam move toward a truck, a truck with writing on its side that Ginny couldn't read, but she could just make out the outline of an evergreen tree against a red cab door. The motor sputtered, the engine revved, and the truck roared to life, slowly edging its way back onto the lane, around the slight bend in the trees, and away.

Ginny checked her watch, its tiny numerals glowing in the dark. Nine forty-five. Not as late as she'd thought. Her heartbeat exited the fast lane, but there would be no more sleeping that night.

CHAPTER THREE

GINNY WOULD HAVE SWORN THAT she'd not slept a wink after that late night storming of the house if it hadn't been for her jump at the sudden knocking—this time more tentative and civilized—on the door below, and for the shocking outpouring of bright sunlight through her window. It took her a moment to gather her wits, to find her feet and peer through the curtain.

This time she saw a car—a station wagon—and before long a well-built, well-dressed man standing in the drive, surveying the house. Something about him seemed vaguely familiar, though Ginny was certain she didn't know him. *Mr. Skipwith?* She envisioned the man she knew fifty years ago, the man who'd brought Curtis to the farm, but also knew that wasn't possible. *Perhaps the "Son" of Skipwith and Son, Attorneys-at-Law?*

Ginny pulled on her shoes, did her best to smooth her skirt and blouse, to run her hands through her hair, though she knew it must be standing on end. Her mouth felt like a half-plowed field, and she wondered if her mascara had landed on her cheeks, but there wasn't time to worry about that. The man outside looked a decent sort, and she needed his help, at least to get to a telephone and call a locksmith or the police or someone—anyone—to unlock her car.

A car door slammed. Ginny feared she might be too late and

hurried down the stairs. Just as she reached the front room, the front door opened. She gasped, jumping back.

"Oh, Miss Pickering, I beg your pardon. I thought when I saw your car and you didn't answer something might be wrong. I didn't mean to startle you." Six feet tall, a decent head of silver-gray hair, and clear blue eyes filled with concern caught Ginny off guard. "You are Miss Pickering?"

Ginny nodded, unable to connect her brain to her tongue. "Mrs. Boyden—Ginny Pickering Boyden. Mr. Skipwith?"

The corners of his mouth lifted in a warm and genuine smile. "Willoughby Skipwith—call me Will. I'm sorry I wasn't in my office when you arrived yesterday." If he'd tipped a bowler hat, Ginny would not have been surprised.

"Your secretary explained." Ginny wanted to sound all business, but she felt like a disheveled middle schooler. "I wouldn't have stayed overnight, but I locked myself out of my car."

His eyes widened, seeming to take in her appearance for the first time. "Well, that's something I can help with right away." He stepped outside, pulled a metal coat hanger from his car, twisted it open, formed a loop. Before she could ask what he was doing, he'd inserted the homemade rod between her car window and its rubber molding. Twisting, he pulled up the door lock.

"You're an expert at breaking and entering?"

He laughed, a good, clear laugh. "Working with troubled youth teaches you all kinds of things."

"Is that what you do? Work with troubled youth?"

"Some of what I do, like my father before me." His head tilted slightly, as if observing her.

"Your father, Mr. Skipwith. I remember him. He was my family's lawyer—for a long time."

"Until he passed away. Now it's just me."

"I'm sorry. My sympathies. He was a fine man."

"Thank you. It's been a long time. You don't remember me, do you?"

Ginny frowned. "Should I? I mean, I was young when I left home, so I don't think . . ."

"I remember you. Ginny Pickering. New Scrivelsby High. Debate Club. Gardening Club. FFA. FHA. 4H. I was a year ahead. We shared a semester in French II."

Ginny didn't recall, and she didn't know what to say. She'd never imagined anyone remembered her, let alone her high school clubs from fifty years ago. Had he investigated her to see if she was really who she said she was? Was he setting her up for some legal harangue? Not likely. Flirting? Least likely. Ginny nervously tucked a stray curl behind her ear. "Your letter said you wanted to talk with me. I don't know how I can help you. I don't know anything about Harold's will."

Will Skipwith sobered. "It's not Harold's will I need to clarify; it's your mother's."

"Mama's been dead for decades. All that must have been dealt with ages ago. Harold would have seen to it."

"Your mother left the farm to you and your brother together with the stipulation that it not be divided or sold unless you both agreed. If one died, it was to go in full to the remaining sibling. Unless you made some arrangement I don't know about . . ."

"What?" Ginny's head spun. "That's not possible. Mama disinherited me. Harold made sure I understood that. Everything went to Harold, lock, stock, and barrel."

Willoughby Skipwith spoke slowly. "No. That's not accurate."

"It is. You must be talking about an old will . . . written before . . . before I left."

"Before you married." He spoke quietly, as if making an accusation.

Ginny felt heat rise up her neck. She eyed him sharply. "Since you know that, why are you asking me these things? Mama changed her will after I left, after Curtis and I married."

"She didn't. If you were led to believe that, you were misinformed. The farm belongs to you in full now. Half of it always did."

Ginny felt the colors around her swirl. Will reached out to steady her but she pulled away. "He said—he said Mama—" Ginny couldn't take in the implications of it all, of the lie . . . if it was a lie.

"Perhaps you'd best sit down, Mrs. Boyden." He led her to the porch step. "Have you eaten anything this morning?"

"Not since I locked my car—yesterday."

"Not good. How about I take you into town and we get some breakfast?"

Ginny started to shake her head, but that made her dizzy. Her temples ached like crazy. "Coffee would be good. But I'm a mess. The electric isn't on. No lights or hot water . . ."

"The electric company's not come?" He seemed more than perturbed. "I'll make sure they're out here today. Let me drive you to the diner."

She wasn't in a position to object, and she needed to understand about Harold and her mother—whatever that meant. She nodded, stood, and returned to her car. "Give me five minutes. I need to change clothes."

He hefted her case from the trunk, insisted on carrying it into the house, and smiled. "Take ten."

A second cup of black coffee cleared the fog from Ginny's brain. A full country breakfast took care of the rumbles in her stomach. "I can't believe Harold did this. Why?" But even as she spoke, she knew why. *Jealousy. He was always jealous of Curtis and me, always afraid that Curtis would somehow usurp his place as son. He was angry with me—believed I'd stolen his best friend, his brother. Did he fear we'd take the farm?* "How could he possibly get away with such a lie?"

"I can't answer the first question, but I'm afraid I have an idea about the second. At the time your mother passed, my father was your family's attorney. It was near the end of the war—the year my older brother was killed in the Pacific. I'm not making excuses for shoddy work, but I can only say that Dad was not himself, not for quite some time. I didn't enter the practice until some years later. By then, Harold had been working the land alone for several years, you were not here, and no one was the wiser. No one questioned or knew to question it.

"Dad died in 1970. I don't believe he knowingly did anything illegal. That was not his way, and he always held your parents in the highest regard. Whatever happened, the details of your mother's will were not carried out. I'm sorry."

Ginny listened, but the words sounded like something out of an old movie.

"I wouldn't have questioned it if Harold hadn't said something that gave me pause during our last visit, which started me digging through Dad's and the courthouse's files." He sat back. "I will say you were not the only one misled. Both of Harold's sons assumed the farm belonged to their father and expected to inherit in full. I'm afraid you might find them ready to contest.

"The question came up the day Harold called, said he wanted to confess something about the land, but when I visited it wasn't clear what. By then his dementia was fairly pronounced. He spoke your name again and again."

Dementia. Delirium. I know too much about that. "Two sons? I didn't even know until I saw his wife's headstone in the cemetery yesterday that he'd married—except that your letter implied it."

Will frowned. "Elaine, his wife, died in childbirth with Mark, their second. Luke and Mark are the two sons. Luke is married and still living at Promised Land, the home Harold and Elaine built."

Ginny winced. *Promised Land. Promised Land was land promised to me! Daddy and Mama promised that acreage to me and Curtis . . . if we'd wait to marry. But we didn't.*

"He's the one most likely to contest. Luke and his wife, Bethany, lived with Harold and worked the farm. These last few years as Harold failed, they took care of him until he passed—mostly Bethany, that is. The other son, Mark, has been hard to track down. I hope my letter informing him of his father's demise catches up with him."

"I really cannot afford to go to court, Mr. Skipwith—Will."

"I promise I will help you and the family sort this. I feel partly responsible."

"You weren't even a lawyer when my mother passed."

"No, but my father was her lawyer and she expected—rightly so—that her wishes and the details of her will would be carried out by my family's firm. I need to see this put right."

Ginny nodded, her head still in a daze. "His brother doesn't know where he is?"

Will sighed, pushing back from the table. "Mark had a hard time in Vietnam. Came back pretty messed up. PTSD, anger issues. Alcohol and drugs . . . his wife, too, from what I remember. The last I knew he couldn't hold a job, never stays in one place for more than a few months to a year. They had a couple of kids. It was through the foster-care system that I was able to track their firstborn down, and then Mark. I don't know what became of the wife, where she is. I sent a letter three weeks ago to Mark's last known address but have yet to receive a response."

What a mess—a mess I understand better than you'd know, Will Skipwith. "Do you think the older one—"

"Luke."

"Luke. Do you know, does he drive a red pickup with the outline of an evergreen tree on the side?"

Will nodded. "You've met him?"

"I think he came to the house in the night. Whoever it was, he pounded on the door, I think intending to frighten me."

"You didn't open the door?"

"No, I was scared out of my wits!"

Will nodded. "Luke's a good man. His father treated him unfairly and it's no surprise he's bitter. But he can be hotheaded, especially if he's had a few drinks."

"That sounds like Harold."

"Some friendly advice, Mrs. Boyden." His palm covered her hand.

"Be careful. Lock your doors at night. I wouldn't expect Luke to do anything stupid, but people have surprised me before."

Ginny looked up, unnerved by the warmth of his hand on hers. She sat back, pulling away, nursing her coffee cup. "Does he have any legal right to the farm? I mean, he's worked it all these years with his father. Is there some kind of squatter's rights, or, you know, like a common law marriage because someone's been there working the land all this time?"

"Technically, no. He may well feel there's an ethical link. They've worked the land and paid most of the taxes, but they've also benefitted from the land and what it's produced. Even so, you were scammed out of your inheritance. The farm was not Harold's to will to anyone, and he never actually made a will, although he told Luke he'd taken care of things.

"There's more I should explain. The farm's in trouble. Harold made a number of poor business decisions in his last few years . . . overextended himself with the bank, ordered too many new trees trying to cultivate more acreage than was possible for any two people.

"He couldn't perform the labor he once did, couldn't clear the needed land for all those trees, and he couldn't—or wouldn't—pay for the extra help Luke needed to do it. From what he told Luke, I think he imagined he could put the farm back the way it was when your father passed, but that was impossible. Too much had gone wild over the years. Part of that was a matter of not allowing anyone else on the farm."

He sat back. "There's no way to say this without sounding . . ." He hesitated. "Harold became paranoid in the last few years. He didn't trust anyone—not even his son."

Ginny nodded. She could imagine that of Harold. *Besides that, what must it have been like to keep up such deception all these years, especially where his son and daughter-in-law were concerned?* "Harold must have feared someone would find out the truth—must have known it would eventually come out."

Will didn't answer that. "Try as he might, Luke couldn't keep it all going alone. Until it became clear that Harold had sunk the farm in serious debt, Luke didn't know the extent of their troubles."

"What does that mean? How much debt?"

"The last two years' taxes weren't paid—so there's a tax lien, which means the property can't transfer or a new title be recorded until they are paid."

"How much?"

"I have the figures in my office. I can get those to you next week." Will drew a deep breath, as if he hated bearing bad news. "The worst may be that Harold drew a substantial loan from the bank, using the farm as collateral."

"Why? The land has long been paid for—even before my parents' day."

"Those thousands of trees he ordered and who knows what all—imagining he'd expand the farm clear up the mountain before he'd even talked to Luke about clearing the land."

"All those trees—"

"Everything Luke couldn't plant died. It nearly destroyed him. Harold hid the books, but Luke knew the bill would have to be paid. He didn't know about the loan until too late. When Harold spent money freely, Luke figured it meant they were doing better than he imagined. By the time he realized the truth, there was nothing he could do. I don't know yet what this past Christmas season netted, but it couldn't have been nearly enough."

Ginny shook her head. She couldn't believe it, not after all the years her parents had scrimped and saved and finagled every which way to keep the farm going.

Will shrugged. "It will be a major decision, whether to pay that off and give the farm a go or sell it and have the taxes paid from the sale. If you decide to sell, it will need some fixing up."

"Fix it up to sell—how much needs to be done?"

"You've seen the house. At the very least—besides a good cleaning and painting the inside and updating fixtures and appliances—you're looking at a new roof, sanding and painting the partial frame outside, tuck-pointing around the stone chimney, maybe a new furnace. I don't know about the plumbing and electric. That needs to be assessed. Then there's the option of adding air-conditioning. People want that these days."

"I can't possibly afford all that. What about Luke? Do you think he wants to buy it?"

"I'm sure he'd love to, but there's no way he can afford it. He'll be lucky to clear this year's taxes, let alone the back taxes. But those taxes and the loan are up to you now—unless you sell."

Ginny closed her eyes, completely overwhelmed.

"I know this is a lot to take in."

"No kidding."

"Take the rest of the weekend, think about it, pray about it if you will. Come see me in my office next week. I can show you your mother's will, and all the paperwork and account books. I'm still working through Harold's old records, spotty as they are—that's where I found your letter with your address."

"My letter?"

"One you wrote to your mother, back during the war years. I don't know if she ever received it."

Ginny thought she might choke, might stop breathing. *Not only did you steal my land, Harold, you stole Mama from me.*

"I'll make sure the electric is turned back on, and I can get someone out to give the inside a good cleaning."

Ginny did her best to swallow the lump in her throat. She needed to think everything through, but not now, not with Will sitting across the table from her. "Just the electric, please, and a phone put in. I can clean . . . and I want to. As long as I need to be here, I'll spend some time with everything . . . alone. But I need that telephone right away. I need to know I can call for help. I don't want another scare like last night."

Will nodded. "Understood."

CHAPTER FOUR

BY THE TIME WILL RETURNED GINNY to the farm, the electric-company man had come and gone. Ginny knew getting the telephone in working order would take a few days more. Still, the lights worked, and for that she was grateful. Once she found the fuse box and figured out what she needed to do, the hot water heater began making noises that sounded alternately worrying and hopeful.

Two hours later, after a tepid shower and hair wash, Ginny felt human. As long as she was going to stay a few days, the first things she needed to do were clean the kitchen, get the refrigerator going, if it still worked, and make a grocery list. Enough people had stared at her and Will in the diner that she wasn't eager to return, and she'd seen no other restaurants in town. Anyway, saving money was at the top of her list. She had her own dreams to fulfill.

At least the kitchen was tidy. All traces of food—cans and boxed goods—had been removed from the cupboards. The dark layer was dust and cobwebs, not grime. She had no idea if Harold and his wife had lived there for any length of time after her mother had passed or if they'd built their house on Promised Land before. Things looked just as Ginny remembered, as if her mother had finished washing and drying dishes after supper, hung her apron on the hook behind the pantry door, and walked from this life into the next.

I hope it was that easy for you, Mama, that you didn't suffer, that you went with your boots on like Daddy did, like you always said you wanted to. Ginny couldn't bear to think of her mother lying in bed for months, waiting to die. She couldn't think about not being with her, not being there to care for her to the end of her days if she'd needed that kind of care.

Ginny closed her eyes against that pain and swiped tears puddling in their corners. *This won't do. Hating Harold won't help. I've got to pull myself together, take care of whatever I must. Blast you, Harold, for making such a mess! For causing so much heartache!*

Ginny grabbed her purse from the counter and her jacket from the row of hooks on the wall behind the front door—the row of hooks Curtis had nailed there for her mother the day she'd said that she wished she had someplace to hang more coats in this old house. *How pleased you were by that little kindness, Mama. You hugged Curtis. He warmed like you'd given him the moon.*

Ginny sighed. Everywhere she looked she saw—remembered—Curtis or her mama or daddy as they were then. Even Harold, although most memories of him were not so pleasant.

A war raged inside her heart. She wanted to remember those days, that Curtis, the boy she fell in love with, the one whose heart she knew before the war worked its horror in him. She wanted to fall in love with her husband again, at least with the memory of him, wanted to remember him as he was and not what time and misery and a long road to death had made him. She wanted to erase the distance and anger that he'd expressed and even more that she'd felt toward him in those later years. Could she do that by staying in the house? Or would the memories kill her?

Ginny couldn't say. She needed to put her demons to rest and move on. She'd stay only as long as required to get things settled about the farm. Maybe in that time she'd find the answers she needed. She couldn't stay longer. She wouldn't get sucked into anger and regret like she imagined Harold had.

For now, she'd get those groceries. *One foot in front of the other.*

She'd just locked the front door and started down the steps when a man appeared from around the side of the house. He looked nearly as surprised to see her as she was to see him. He stopped, stared, then walked more slowly toward her, blocking the walkway to her car.

"So"—he pushed back the bill of his hat—"the prodigal returns."

Ginny drew back her shoulders. "I beg your pardon?"

"You're Ginny Dee Pickering?"

"Ginny Pickering Boyden. And you are?" Though she knew. He looked enough like Harold that there was no doubt.

"Luke. Luke Pickering, firstborn son of Harold Pickering, owner of Wetherill Pickering's Christmas Tree Farm. Dad always said you'd come back one day, do your best to take our farm."

"Apparently it's my farm."

He shook his head and stepped closer. "We threw our whole life into this ground. Every tree, every bush, every acre turned. He said it would be ours—mine and Mark's."

"You need to talk with Mr. Skipwith."

"It's not right—not fair. If I have to go to court to prove it, I'll—"

"You're right, it's not fair. Your father withheld the truth from me, and he apparently withheld the truth from you, but—"

He stepped closer yet. "I'm telling you—"

"You need to go now." Ginny crossed her arms over her stomach to hide her trembling hands. "If you have anything further you want to say, please say it to Mr. Skipwith. Please leave."

He stopped, his jaw set firm. "I needed to see what the woman looks like set to ruin her family, her own blood, set to sell off five generations of Pickering family legacy."

"I've not decided anything. And it's five generations of Dymoke legacy—your grandmother's land. My father, your grandfather, was the Pickering. Mama let him change the name of the farm. I don't suppose you knew that either."

Ginny imagined smoke might pour from his ears. Luke, his mouth in a grim line, shoved his hat farther back on his head, turned, and disappeared around the house without another word.

Ginny didn't ask or follow to see where he was going. She fell into her car and drove, too fast, up the lane to the main road.

CHAPTER FIVE

GINNY'S HANDS DIDN'T STOP SHAKING, not even when she gripped the grocery cart. She hated confrontation and she didn't know, despite Will's assurance that Luke was a good man, if he could be dangerous, what he might do to prevent Ginny from committing what he perceived as a terrible injustice.

Milk, eggs, bread, oatmeal, bananas, coffee, flashlight, batteries. Concentrate, Ginny, concentrate. She pushed the cart into the dairy aisle.

"Ginny Dee?"

Ginny turned. She hadn't gone by Ginny Dee since she'd left home. The words sounded different than they had coming from Luke.

"Ginny Dee Pickering, is that you?" The woman speaking didn't look familiar, and yet something about the way her smile turned up one side of her face more than the other struck a chord in Ginny's mind. "I'm Louise. Louise Shellhorn."

"Louise?" It was like raising the dead, but then, everything and everyone in New Scrivelsby seemed that way.

"Class of '42."

Ginny tried to smile in return.

"Oh, my goodness—you must be the mystery lady!"

"Mystery lady?"

"I'm sorry." Louise shook her head and threw her arms around Ginny for a quick hug. "It's so good to see you . . . and such a surprise after all these years. What are you doing here?"

Ginny knew she should have thought before coming to the closest local market. She was bound to run into people she knew, or people who remembered her. Somehow she'd imagined a few wrinkles and gray hair disguised her. "My brother died." It was true and all Ginny could think to say.

Louise nodded. "Of course. Harold. I'm sorry." She shifted her purse to her other shoulder, her stance a little less comfortable. "Are you here to sell the farm? Wetherill Pickering's Christmas Tree Farm has been an institution here—since before I can remember."

"I just arrived yesterday. I didn't even know I owned it until this morning." Ginny hadn't meant to say that, hadn't meant to say anything about the farm to anyone. There was so much she didn't know.

"Of course. Harold . . . that man! That's why you were with Will Skipwith this morning."

"Excuse me?"

"At the diner. You know how fast word travels in New Scrivelsby. Half the women in church have been trying to set Will up or garner his attention for years, but he's never given one of them the time of day. His wife died not a year after they were married—car accident, you know. Oh, well, of course you wouldn't. And then to see him with an attractive woman at breakfast on a Saturday morning . . . Let's just say you've been dubbed 'the mystery lady.'"

Ginny sighed. Small-town gossip was the last thing she needed.

"I'm sorry. Sometimes I say such stupid things. It's really good to see you, Ginny Dee. So many from our class have moved—or passed. We could use some fresh blood here. Is your husband with you?"

Ginny couldn't tell if Louise was genuinely concerned or if she was gathering fodder for gossip, but she knew she'd best set the record straight. "He passed some years ago."

"I'm so sorry. Maybe you'll stay, then?"

"I don't think so."

"It would mean a lot to Bethany if you did."

"Bethany?"

"Luke's wife, Bethany."

Ginny bristled. "I haven't met her."

"Oh. You'll love her. She's the sweetest thing. She took real good care of Harold his last few years, and you can imagine that was no easy task. He was—oh, I'm sorry. There I go again. He was your brother."

Ginny shook her head. "Harold wasn't easy, I know that. What were you about to say?"

"Just that he was a hard man. Hard to work with, hard to live with. Luke could have made a go of that farm if Harold would have let him, or if Luke had taken the bull by the horns with his father. Harold was hard on Bethany, too, even though she did everything for him. I've seen what these years have done to both of them. It's a shame. Well, hard as it will be for them to leave, maybe it's best they start over somewhere while they're young."

Ginny's head felt it might split.

"I've said too much. I didn't mean to. I hope you'll join us at church tomorrow. Come sit with me if you do."

"Thank you, Louise. It's good to see you."

"You too." Louise hugged her again. "Don't be a stranger."

By the time Ginny drove back to the farm and stashed her groceries, she was wiped out. Still, she couldn't make herself climb the stairs to lie down and had no will to explore the rest of the house. Too many ghosts at every turn. Between breakfast with Will and all he'd shared, the confrontation with Luke, and Louise in the grocery store, there were too many issues alive and well.

The only thing that helped in times of stress was getting her hands in the dirt, spreading the roots of plants, pulling weeds, deadheading, pruning—whatever needed doing out of doors.

Ginny donned the work jeans and boots she kept in the trunk of her car and headed for the cemetery. She needed to make certain yesterday's torrential rain hadn't snapped the flowers she'd transplanted. And she needed a good long talk with her mama and daddy. Ginny knew they weren't there, but it was the last place their earthly forms had been, and she needed to touch that, to feel that, to be there.

She pulled open the black iron gate and headed straight for their graves. She might even give Harold a good talking-to for what a jerk he'd been all these years. From what Louise had said, he'd not just ruined her and Curtis's lives but he'd ruined his own son and daughter-in-law's prospects. She knew what it was to be deceived, to have your hopes and dreams smashed, and then to be betrayed. And what did it mean that his other son, Mark, was out of touch and hadn't come to his funeral? Was it true that he couldn't be found, or was there estrangement as well as whatever the younger man was dealing with from the war? What had Harold done to him, said to him?

Ginny knew firsthand about living with a veteran with PTSD, what it could do to a man and to that man's family. She shook her head as she thrust her shovel beneath a stubborn root on her daddy's grave. *What an unholy mess!*

Ginny pulled the weeds she could. She dug the tougher ones, hoping to get the roots. She clipped what she couldn't dig. For some of the bigger tree roots that had grown into the cemetery she'd need a pruner, maybe an axe.

A half-dead cherry tree in the corner might need a stump grinder. She'd leave the crab apple that had grown up in the middle of the cemetery—a tree beautiful in every season, food and a haven for songbirds. She liked thinking they kept watch.

Whatever the outcome of the land, Ginny determined to see the family cemetery cleaned and restored. She brushed soft crab apple petals from her mother's headstone.

"Mama, I wish you were here. I wish I understood what you wanted, what you'd have me do now . . . how you felt toward me then." Soon her talk with her mother became prayer. "Dear God,

I need help. I've no idea what to do here. I can't afford those back taxes, let alone that bank loan—it would take so much of the money I've saved to start my new life, the life I believe You've led me to. The young man I met today was angry, sure he was entitled. But the man Louise described is broken—broken by his father, the same brother that lied to me.

"I don't want to treat Luke like Harold treated me, but what else can I do but sell this place? I can't stay here, can't run it. Luke can't run it alone. Near as I can tell he's probably sinking lower and lower into debt trying to keep it going now . . . and it's all a disaster. They'd be better off starting over somewhere new. The peach orchard is gone; the blueberry bushes are overgrown and don't look like they've been tended in forever. They must be the original ones—over fifty years old. I don't think they can be recovered. It's too much. But what would Mama and Daddy think if I sold their farm? What would they say if I sold off the land in the town Mama's family founded two centuries ago?"

"So, it's true. You're going to sell."

Ginny jumped. She hadn't realized she'd been speaking aloud or that anyone else had entered the cemetery. She swiped a stray lock of hair from her eyes and stood up.

The woman she faced might be mid- to late thirties, dark-brown hair, brown eyes that looked more than sad—defeated. Taller than Ginny's five feet six by a couple of inches but with shoulders slumped as if she'd long carried too great a weight. Ginny swallowed. "You must be Bethany."

The woman nodded. "You must be Ginny Dee. Aunt Ginny Dee."

Ginny drew in a sharp breath. No one had ever called her *Aunt*. But she nodded, accepting the moniker, not displeased by it but uncertain. Praying to God and thinking things through theoretically, wondering how the long-ago dead might feel about a thing, was far different from destroying someone's living, breathing dream.

"Luke told me."

"I don't know what I'm going to do. I didn't even know that the farm belonged to me until this morning. But I don't see how I can keep it, how I can run it."

"Luke could run it—if you let us stay."

Ginny grimaced. "He hasn't been able to turn a profit, at least that's what I hear. And there's major debt, and a tax lien."

Bethany seemed to stand straighter, strength infusing her spine, squaring her shoulders. "That was because of Harold. Harold and his big ideas, borrowing all that money with no way to pay it back. He drove Luke like a field hand—a slave, not a son."

"This farm is hard work. I remember that."

"Neither of us flinch at hard work. But Harold wouldn't listen. He strangled the purse strings, made every decision—not good ones."

"Luke didn't stand up to him?"

Bethany looked at Ginny as if she pitied her. "You really didn't know your brother, did you? I don't know what he was like growing up, but to Luke—and me—he was a tyrant. He ruled the roost. Sometimes it seemed as if he made decisions just to spite Luke, just to push him, test him, see if we'd leave, even punish us."

"But you took care of him until the end. I heard that too."

Bethany sighed. "That's what families do. We don't get to choose our blood and we don't abandon them." She said it as if Ginny didn't understand that basic truth, a dig underlining Luke's calling her *prodigal.*

Ginny looked away.

"I'm sorry." Bethany reached out her hand toward Ginny. "I didn't mean that how it came out."

"No? Luke clearly thinks that."

"I know how you must have wanted to get away from here. If your parents were anything like Harold—"

"They weren't. Nothing like him. At least not the Harold you've described. He wasn't always like that."

"I never knew different, and I don't think Luke did, at least not since his mama died."

"He must have been very young when she passed."

"When Mark, his brother, was born. He said his dad turned mean after that—like some imposter father."

"A stranger?"

"Yes."

It was the first thing anyone had said about Harold that Ginny could fully grasp. She'd felt such hurt and anger when Curtis came back damaged from the war. It was as if he'd died and an imposter, a stranger, had come home in his broken body. Ginny loved him, or she'd told herself she did, but sometimes she felt she'd loved the man who went away and not the one who came home. She'd tried to, but he was uncommunicative, broken inside and out, and while some of his body had mended, the healing inside his head had never come, so her healing inside had not come either.

"Please don't make us leave."

Ginny shook her head, trying to focus on the moment, trying to understand. "Why would you want to stay? Luke grew up here, but you? After all you've been through, all Harold promised, and it wasn't true . . . after all this farm's done to you both and the state it's in now, why would you stay, even if you could?"

"Because it's Luke's home, our home—the only home—" Bethany stopped. Her eyes darted toward the far side of the cemetery, to the three tiny lambs nestled amid ivy vines and forget-me-nots, and back to Ginny. "Because it's where . . ." But she didn't finish, couldn't finish. She turned, her eyes wells of unshed tears, and walked swiftly from the cemetery. Ginny understood at last.

CHAPTER SIX

GINNY SPENT THE WEEKEND cleaning the house with a vengeance, as if somehow that could atone for years of neglect and push away regret. But with every sweep of the broom, every swish of the mop, while polishing furniture with beeswax she found under the sink, amid muscular scrubbing of windowpanes, and even during the outdoor beating of carpets, memory after memory assailed her. She fought them and nursed them and fought them again.

She washed the sheets for every room in the house, then figured out how to run them through her mama's wringer machine and hung them in the sun on makeshift lines she ran from cording found in the kitchen whatnot drawer. Quilts and curtains must wait for another day.

Exhausted, Saturday night she dreamed of her mother and father, glimpses of moments when firelight danced in their eyes across the room, of how they'd cared for one another in big and small ways, of how hard they'd worked to keep them all going—snapshots of her family's life together. She woke reliving the day when her father had fallen in the field—his heart giving way a final time—and she and Curtis had not been there, when they should have been.

There was no means of turning back time, no means of telling her parents how sorry she was, no way to reclaim their lives. That was the thing. She couldn't change or fix the past, but was she responsible? Should she have been? Hadn't they lived the lives they chose? And now, didn't she deserve a chance to live her dreams? Ginny didn't know.

If the weather held and she couldn't settle things on Monday, she'd tackle Mama's rose garden. She'd explored it that afternoon in between wash loads. That garden was the place Ginny'd loved most growing up, the refuge she and her mother had shared. It was the one place on the whole farm their spirits forged together. They'd even carved their initials on the back of the bench Daddy'd built for them—Mama's initials on the left, like a beginning, and Ginny's initials on the right, a promise for the future.

Ginny had found the bench—still standing in the midst of the garden, weathered and with one arm missing though it was. *Mama wouldn't have left it there if it hurt her too much to think about me.* That was a comfort she wanted to believe, a thought she indulged.

Of all the things on the farm, Ginny would most love to restore her mother's rose garden, threaded with pots of mint, to lure again the rainbow of butterflies. *Wings of hope, Mama called them. It will require a phenomenal amount of labor, but it could be my love gift—my penance and love gift to Mama. Even if the farm is sold—especially if it is sold.*

Her mother had offered herself and her time to Ginny in other ways, teaching her all the ways of homemaking, but once Ginny'd turned twelve, she was not so inclined to the kitchen or needlework. She'd lived to regret that as an adult, wished she'd heeded her mama's heartfelt call to share more of those skills and knowledge. Ginny surely could have used such knowledge in the years she needed to make one meal stretch for three.

Mama did that every single day. How she ever fed and clothed us all on what Daddy brought in, even with the bounty of the garden, is a mystery to me.

Sunday morning, she heard the same truck she'd heard before, only this time she saw it through the trees, driving up another lane to the main road. Luke and Bethany, surely on their way to church.

She knew without looking where the truck had come from. *Promised Land*. She knew from Will that Harold had built on the land promised to her and Curtis . . . land with the clearest view of the mountains, the perfect place for a small orchard, and a fairly flat yard for family days of croquet and softball, red rover and tag. Most of all, land to create the gardens Ginny had dreamed of, the gardens she and her mama had imagined for all the years of Ginny's young life, gardens that no one could afford to cultivate during Depression years.

Better days will come. That's what Mama always said, what she promised. That Harold had deliberately stolen that land was a knife too sharp in Ginny's heart, a pill too bitter. He knew how much she'd loved that land, how she'd dreamed of it, talked of it. She wouldn't go there. She wouldn't look.

Too much. Too much. Too much. Sunday night Ginny wrestled in her sleep, tossing, turning, punching her pillow. Sounds that she couldn't identify came in the night, but she wouldn't get up to investigate. *I don't care what Will Skipwith does with this place; I can't stay. He'll have to deal with it . . . sell it.* She'd made her decision, but that, too, felt like a knife in her heart.

By five o'clock in the morning Ginny was wide awake. Her meeting with Will wasn't until ten, but there was no point in staying in bed. For the first time since arriving she didn't dress but pulled an old sweater over her pajamas and headed down the stairs.

Opening the back door, she breathed in the Virginia mountain air—clean, cool, refreshing. It was a gift, a fragrance from days gone by.

Ginny blinked. She needed to stay focused on the present.

Coffee calling. She missed the ease of her automatic drip coffee maker, but she was used to her mama's old percolator now. It made coffee as good as she remembered—better than any she'd made in years . . . Smooth and creamy and full flavored, the aroma unbeatable—a sweet fragrance.

She'd poured her first cup and nested at the table when the back door opened. Ginny's heart jumped to her throat. But it wasn't Luke. It was a slip of a girl, maybe ten or eleven at most, skin and bones, stringy brown hair, enormous eyes.

"S'cuse me, ma'am. That coffee?"

Ginny nodded, speechless.

"Any to spare?"

"Where did you come from?"

"Front porch."

"My front porch?"

"Yes'm."

At that moment a frightful, high-pitched caterwauling came from somewhere outside the house, raising the hair on Ginny's arms. "What in the world?"

"That'll be Marley. Or Cooper."

Ginny stood up, knocking over her coffee, spilling the scalding liquid across her hand.

"Where's your front porch door?"

Ginny shook her burned hand, nursing it against her stomach, and pointed vaguely toward the hallway, thinking she must surely be dreaming. But coffee didn't burn your hand in dreams.

The girl bounded down the hallway and threw open the front door. Ginny followed, cautiously.

Two snot-nosed children, just as dirty and with hair just as stringy as the older girl's, curled into one another against the front porch railing. Ginny looked left and right, wondering if there were more, looking for the children's mother or father, but no one was in sight. "Where did you all come from?"

"Tennessee . . . last." The older girl spoke as she plopped down on the porch and drew the two younger ones into her arms—a girl of four or five and what might be a boy, although his hair was so scraggly and over his eyes it was hard to tell, of perhaps two or three. At least the caterwauling stopped. "West before that."

"We thought you left us," the little girl whined, mournful eyes on the older one.

"I told you I'll never leave you, never let them take you from me again. You're not to worry that way."

Ginny knew there must be a story behind all this, but first things first. "Where are your parents?"

The little girl shrugged, looking more afraid than anything else.

"Pa's gone to fetch milk," the older one said, matter of fact. "From the dairy up the road. Said there used to be one and he hoped there still is. Didn't want to come in hungry and empty handed." She lifted her chin, as if proud of that fact.

Ginny tried to shake the fog from her brain. "What about your mother?"

"What about her?" the girl challenged. "She's gone."

"Gone?" *What does that mean?* "Who are you? What are you doing here?"

"Arlo. Arlo Sage Pickering, age nine, soon to be ten—double digits." She set her hand on the smaller girl's head. "My sister, Marley Saffron Pickering, age four, and our brother, Cooper Dylan Pickering, age three." With each name she emphasized *Pickering*.

"Mark's children." Ginny remembered what Will had said.

"Yes, ma'am." Arlo brightened. "Who are you?"

"Ginny Pickering—Ginny Pickering Boyden."

Arlo's brows shot up. "Aunt Ginny Dee?"

There it is again. Aunt. Ginny nodded. "I guess I am."

"Don't you know?" Marley asked, red-rimmed eyes wider yet. Cooper sucked his three middle fingers.

"Yes, I do. What are you doing here?"

"Granddaddy Pickering died so Pa figured maybe he could come on home now. Us too."

Ginny looked up the lane. There was no sign of another living soul. *Did he drop the children off and run? Why didn't he take them to Luke's house? Luke's his brother. And where is their mother?* Ginny sighed. There was no use asking those questions now. "How long have you been out here?"

"We got in about three."

"Three o'clock in the morning? Alone? Out here in the cold all this time?"

"It's not too cold. Pa said we'd best not wake anybody. Best wait."

"I'm cold." Marley took up the thread, burrowing deeper into Arlo's thin side. Cooper shivered, nearly gray with cold.

"Come in, come in. We need to get you all warmed up and fed."

"Hungry," Cooper pleaded.

Ginny's heart melted at those blue eyes the size of saucers, even while she inwardly blasted the man who'd left them on her porch. *Is he really coming back? When?*

She ushered the children into the kitchen, the warmest room in the house. "Wait here." She ran upstairs and pulled quilts from her bed. She regretted that she hadn't had time to wash them, though the children wouldn't notice. There were only two but the children were so small and thin that they could huddle together.

In the kitchen the two little ones crouched by the stove. Arlo had pulled open the refrigerator door, but red traveled up her neck when Ginny entered the room.

"I was just seeing if maybe there's something we could eat. The little guys—" She stopped, worried eyes on Ginny.

"Come here," Ginny ordered. "Wrap up together under these blankets. I'll see to something to eat."

Arlo complied, eyes cast down on her siblings, snuggled together.

Ginny was sorry for the gruffness in her voice, but she was not used to having anyone show up unexpected on her doorstep or rummage through her refrigerator. She'd lived alone, though with her landlady, a long time. She felt as if her moorings had been torn loose.

"Oatmeal," Ginny mumbled, pulling the Quaker Oats box from the pantry. She glanced at the children from the corner of her eye. "Raisins, honey, milk, orange juice." *You need some fattening up. When on earth did you eat last?* But she wouldn't ask that either, not yet.

It only took a few minutes for the oatmeal to bubble and for Ginny to add a pinch of salt, a cup of raisins, and sprinkle some cinnamon over the pot. She wished she'd bought sugar but was glad she'd bought whole milk and honey. The children watched her every move but stayed where they were until Ginny brought the jug of orange juice from the refrigerator. Then they stood as one, their eyes suddenly alight.

She'd barely set three glasses on the table before they were at her elbow, the blankets a forgotten puddle on the floor. Arlo and Marley gulped theirs without stopping for air. Cooper nearly dropped his glass on the floor, but Ginny caught it just in time, then held it for him while he drank.

Once the glasses were emptied, the girls heaved a collective sigh, as though orange juice had been the thing they most craved in life.

"Sit down, girls, sit down. Cooper, here, let me help you up." Ginny lifted Cooper onto the chair. He seemed too weak to climb up on his own. "We've plenty, so there's no rush. If you want more I can make more." She ladled out six bowls, just in case the children's parents really did come back. What she'd do if they didn't, Ginny had no idea.

"What's this?" Marley stared at the mixture in her bowl.

"Oatmeal."

"What's oatmeal?"

Ginny couldn't imagine not knowing what oatmeal was. "It's good, warm food, that's what. Now, eat up."

Arlo dug in. Marley took a tentative taste and frowned. Cooper waited to see what Marley did.

"I don't like this," Marley said, pushing the bowl away.

"I thought you were hungry." *What I really thought was that you were starving. Now you're a picky eater?*

"It's not sweet."

They've probably lived on sugar diets. But Ginny remembered how she hadn't wanted to eat her oatmeal as a child—until her mama introduced honey. She picked up her honey bear and drizzled a good amount of honey over Marley's oatmeal. "Stir that in and taste it."

Marley eyed her with suspicion.

"Just try."

Marley stirred and took another tentative taste. Her thin brows rose. She tasted again and smiled, wide. "This is good. This is good! Cooper, try it!"

Ginny drizzled honey over Cooper's bowl, stirred it for him, then stood back. "Arlo? Do you want some?"

Arlo nodded. Once she tasted the sweet mixture, she closed her eyes and said, "Thank You, Jesus."

Marley looked up. "We forgot."

Cooper reached his small hand toward Marley. Arlo dropped her spoon in her bowl and reached for her brother's and sister's hands. "Thank You, Lord, for this food. Please help Pa find the milk and come back quick. Amen."

"Amen," the two smaller ones echoed, and dug in once more.

Ginny wondered if she was in some kind of time warp, like they talked about on *Star Trek*. *Three nearly frozen, dirty, half-starved children appear out of nowhere then pray on their own? Where are you, Mark? Please come back. What will I do with them if you don't?*

Arlo scraped her bowl clean. Marley finished most of hers, and Cooper made a dent but gave up after a few minutes, as if the lifting of the spoon to his mouth was work too hard. His eyelids drooped.

"Maybe you'd all like to lie down for a while . . . until your father gets back." Ginny stood, as if that would help move the process along. "There's a sofa and comfy chair in the living room." She nodded vaguely toward the hallway they'd all come through and took Cooper's hand to lead him. But Arlo grabbed the little boy's hand from Ginny, her eyes shooting panicked daggers Ginny's way.

"I'll take him."

Taken aback, Ginny picked up the fallen blankets and followed the children into the living room. *I'm not going to steal him, for goodness' sake. That girl's a child herself.* She pressed her fingers to her temple, willing away her building headache. "I'll do up the dishes and maybe your father will be back by then." Saying the words out loud made her feel better, hopeful, as if the wish might come true. She might have tucked them in, but Arlo took over, as if she were their mother, as if Ginny weren't there.

Back in the kitchen, Ginny realized she hadn't eaten her own oatmeal. She sat down, but her appetite was gone, and her worries were up. She shook her head in disbelief, scraped the bowls, and washed the dishes. What she needed more than food was another cup of coffee. Strong, black coffee.

Halfway through her cup there was a loud pounding on the front door. Ginny stood, wondering if she'd have to get used to strangers pounding on her door. *Only through today. After today, I don't have to stay.*

Before she reached the living room Arlo had thrown the front door open. "You came back!" she announced, relief flooding every syllable.

"'Course I did. I wondered where you all went. You didn't bother anybody, did you?" A man's voice held nearly as much trepidation as Arlo's had.

"Your children were hungry, and thirsty, and tired," Ginny accused, relieved he'd returned but determined not to let the children's father off the hook.

The man nodded, removed his cap, and held forth a mason jar of milk. "Sorry. We didn't mean to disturb you. We got in late. I went to get milk."

Ginny didn't take it, didn't say a word, still waiting for an explanation. The room felt too close, as if proverbial camels had entered and she might not be able to get them out.

Arlo took the milk. "We'll need this. Best keep it."

"Are you Ginny Dee?"

No "Aunt" this time. "Ginny Boyden—Ginny Pickering Boyden. And you are?"

"Mark Pickering." He held out his hand.

Ginny hesitated but took it. At least his hands were clean, cleaner than the rest of him, cleaner than the children.

"I guess you're wondering why we're here."

"Indeed."

Mark moistened his lips, shifted the cap in his hands. "I got a letter from Mr. Skipwith. He said Pa died . . . my pa."

Ginny nodded.

"The funeral must be passed."

"Yes." Ginny softened. After all, whatever his past history, whatever his current circumstances, Harold had been this young man's father, and his father was dead. "Before I came. Your brother can tell you more. He and Bethany were here then. They don't live in this house, if that's what you were thinking."

Mark's color rose. "No, ma'am. I know where Luke lives. It's just—I didn't think anybody was living here, at least not till we got in last night and I saw a car parked out front." He seemed to be groping for words. "So, you live here now?"

"No." Ginny didn't know how much to say. *Will the truth undo him, set him off? Will said Mark had anger issues . . . PTSD. Did he mention alcohol, or am I assuming that?* Ginny knew about PTSD, that it came out in so many different ways. She smelled body odor but no alcohol; he seemed dead sober. "I'm here for now, until things get settled with the farm."

"They're not settled?" Mark's brow creased.

"No. Did you expect they would be?" Ginny wanted to know how much Mark knew, what he knew.

"I thought—Pa always said that the farm would be divided between Luke and me."

"You came back to claim your share?"

"To see if Luke wants to buy my half. He's always wanted the farm. I never thought you'd be here. I thought you—" He stopped.

She sighed. Everyone was in for disappointment if what Will Skipwith had told her was true. "I think you need to see Mr. Skipwith, hear what he has to say."

Mark studied her, looked at his children, then at his feet, and nodded. "I'll see him today."

Ginny considered, uncertain whether she'd regret her next words. "You all look done in. Why don't you come in, have something to eat. You can all get baths. I'm going in to see Will later this morning. Maybe he can explain everything to both of us."

Mark looked up, breathed, and smiled a smile that cut Ginny's heart, momentarily reminding her of her father. "I'd surely appreciate that, ma'am. We're a little worse for wear."

Understatement. "Well, come in, then. You can bring your clean clothes. I'll run some bath water for the little ones first."

Arlo stood in front of the little ones. "This is all we've got. Clothes, I mean."

"What you're wearing?" Besides being dirty, everything looked severely worn, right down to their holey sneakers.

"Sorry to say she's right. We left in kind of a hurry . . ." Mark fumbled.

"We couldn't go back to the foster homes for our stuff. They might not of let us leave. You can't trust them." Arlo stood, defiant, daring Ginny to challenge her word.

Ginny wouldn't ask, wouldn't open that kettle of fish. Knowing wouldn't change their current circumstances. She knew what it was to have nothing, though it was a long time ago for her. "I'll run the bathwater. Let me check the drawers upstairs. There might be something there." She didn't wait for an answer, but her wheels spun. *Soap, shampoo, towels.* She set the toiletries on the side of the tub, then ran upstairs and threw on some clothes, running a brush through her hair. Uncertain what she'd find and unwilling to think it through, she checked the drawers in her parents' downstairs bedroom. Her mother had been petite, not like Ginny. Maybe there was something she could belt up for Arlo. If her mother hadn't gotten rid of her father's clothes, or if something of Harold's was still there, maybe Mark could use it.

Ginny corralled what little she'd found in her arms and headed for the bathroom. She'd scrub the children's hair and check for lice. *You just never know.*

But before she could get back to the bathroom, Arlo had locked all three inside. Ginny rattled the knob. "Arlo. Open this door."

"When we're done."

"I can help Marley and Cooper while you get your bath."

"That's my job. We'll manage."

End of discussion.

There was no way she'd be able to wash the children's clothes in time for the appointment with Will, and Ginny had no intention of showing up in town with three little ragamuffins. She grabbed her purse, huffed through the parlor, and headed for the door.

"I'm sorry about Arlo." Mark spoke from the corner of the living room. "She's got a mind of her own."

"No kidding."

"It's because she's afraid somebody will take the little ones away."

"Does she have reason?"

"Not now." Mark stood straighter.

She wouldn't ask more, *not now.* "I have to run an errand. I'll be back soon. Tell the children not to put those dirty clothes back on. I'll bring something clean."

"You don't need to—"

But Ginny didn't wait to hear. She was out the door and down the steps, driving away in her car before she ever looked in the rearview mirror. There wasn't much she could do about much in life, but she could do this simple thing. An outfit for each of the children. She didn't know their sizes, but she could guess. It looked like they'd all outgrown what they were wearing anyway.

If that's foster care, I'll eat my hat. Surely social workers wouldn't let kids be dressed like that. Surely they'd see to it they have decent shoes. There's got to be more to their story—something Mark's not saying and Arlo's not telling. She couldn't help but smile at the thought of Arlo. She was just as stubborn as Ginny had been as a youngster but a lot less trusting. *Something horrible must have happened to make a girl that young so jaded.* Ginny didn't want to imagine what that might be.

An hour later she was on her way home again, thankful that at least the next town had a Walmart. She hoped the children would agree to wear what she'd bought, hoped they'd like what she'd picked. Surely their father would insist.

Without a telephone she couldn't warn Will Skipwith or his secretary that they'd soon be deluged with Pickerings, including three short ones who she hoped would sit patiently and quietly in the waiting room while Will went over things with her and Mark. *Maybe Luke should be there too. It would save time and fuss if we just got this all out in the open and over with.* She didn't relish the idea of seeing Luke again, not unless Bethany was there to keep him in check.

At the last possible moment, she stopped by the attorney's office. It wasn't open yet and no lights shone from the inside. Ginny scribbled a note and slid it through the door's mail slot, hoping Will would see it and decide if grouping everyone together was a good idea, hoping he'd agree to sharing her mother's will with them all. At least she'd bring Mark. Without a telephone at the farm, she had no other choice. Any longer delay would complicate life further. They might never leave. Then what would she do?

CHAPTER SEVEN

ARLO HAD HAD ENOUGH of grown-ups telling her what to do, promising and arranging things then not following through. You couldn't count on them, couldn't trust them. She wouldn't fall for Aunt Ginny Dee's smooth talk and lure of new clothes and fancy hair. Arlo hadn't had her hair braided by another soul since she was five years old and wasn't about to start now.

She couldn't do anything about Marley. Marley loved having her hair brushed and parted and braided. She loved her new pink dress and strappy sandals. That was okay for her, but Arlo wouldn't be caught dead or alive in pink. It was a good thing the woman had brought her a blue skirt and white top—plain, at least not frilly.

Cooper loved anything blue or red, so the blue and red dinosaur shirt and navy pants Aunt Ginny Dee'd brought him shot him over the moon with happiness.

Traitors. We're all being bribed, even Pa in that old shirt that belonged to his grandpa. There'll be payback. There always is. Arlo just didn't know what.

Aunt Ginny Dee handed Arlo a hairbrush and nodded to her tangled head of hair. "Take care of it yourself if you'd rather. Just take care of it."

Arlo set her jaw but took the brush and worked away, wincing with every pull through her rat's nest. Her hair had been knotted and tangled for so long, how was she supposed to do anything with it? "Got any scissors?"

"Scissors?"

"I can cut the knots out."

"That's not necessary." Aunt Ginny Dee looked as if she wanted to say something more but bit her tongue. "In the kitchen drawer, next to the sink."

Arlo would take care of it herself, even if she looked like a homeless leper when she was through. Aunt Ginny Dee said no more, and her pa said nothing, appeared to notice nothing, but then, he never did. By the time she was done cutting, Arlo figured that the job must not be too bad. Even so, she'd no interest in checking it out in the mirror. *Leave well enough alone.*

"It's time we were on our way," Aunt Ginny Dee said. "Mark, you know Mr. Skipwith's office?"

"Sure, I remember. We'll meet you there."

"Can I ride with Aunt Ginny Dee?" Marley begged.

"Me too!" Cooper echoed.

"No!" Arlo wasn't about to let them out of her sight. "We'll ride with Pa."

"You're not the boss of me, Arlo Pickering! Can we, Pa, please?" the little ones whined.

"You need to stay with your father," Aunt Ginny Dee said. "I'll see you there."

That shut them up, and for the first time, Arlo felt a smidgen of gratitude toward the woman.

On the way to the lawyer's office, all four Pickerings packed into their rattletrap pickup, Arlo asked the thing that had been eating at her. "What's she doing here, Pa? If the house is yours and Uncle Luke's, what's she doing here at all?"

"I can't answer that. I don't know."

"Do you think she's trying to steal the farm out from under you?"

Her pa shook his head. "I hope not. I can't fight anybody in court." He swerved to miss a pothole in the road. "She seems a decent woman . . . not like Dad described."

"Maybe it's a show. Maybe she's acting all kissy-kissy so you let your guard down."

Her pa drove in silence for a time. He pulled into a parking space near the center of town. "Mr. Skipwith was always good to me, straight with me." He looked at Arlo. "He'll set things right."

Whatever that means. Arlo nodded, but her insides didn't agree.

Aunt Ginny Dee was waiting for them just inside Mr. Skipwith's office. A woman rose from behind a desk piled high with papers and smiled at Arlo's pa, a big, bright smile that made Arlo nervous but lit Pa's face. "Mr. Pickering?"

"Mark Pickering." Her pa nodded, pulling off his cap.

"Mr. Skipwith will be with you in a moment. Would you and Mrs. Boyden come into the conference room?"

"My kids too?"

"The children can sit out here with me. I can find some drawing paper—maybe even some crayons." She smiled at Marley and Cooper while Arlo scowled at her.

"Okay, thanks, ma'am. You guys, sit. Do what she tells you. Arlo?"

Arlo didn't answer but ushered Marley and Cooper toward chairs lining the wall and a little kids' table with a stack of magazines.

Cooper made a beeline for the first *Ranger Rick.* "Brown bears!" His little-boy squeal lifted the corners of Arlo's mouth. It wasn't often they found a room fit for kids.

The woman ushered Pa and Aunt Ginny Dee into a side room. Arlo could hear her offer them coffee before she came back to the waiting area with a stack of paper and a tub of crayons.

"Mr. Skipwith must get a lot of kids in here." Arlo wondered why so many kids had to come see a lawyer. That didn't sound good.

The woman laughed, a giggly kind of laugh. "Well, he sees a lot of grown-ups with kids. He knows how hard it is to get a babysitter, so I guess I'm it. My name's Sheila Baxter—Miss Baxter."

Arlo scowled again. She didn't need a babysitter.

The front door opened, discharging a buzzer that Arlo hadn't heard when they'd walked in. A tall, broad-shouldered man with a square jaw stepped in and pulled off his hat, ignoring Arlo and the little kids. A pretty but worried-looking woman with dark hair trailed him. She smiled at Arlo, but her eyes brightened when she looked at Marley and Cooper. Arlo was used to that and looked away.

"Mr. Pickering. Mrs. Pickering." The secretary stood again. "The others are in the conference room. You can go right in. Mr. Skipwith will be here shortly."

Arlo sucked in her breath, her eyes wide. *Uncle Luke.* She looked away again, but not fast enough.

"Arlo?" the woman asked in wonder.

Arlo crossed her arms over her chest but nodded. The woman smiled again. "It's been so long since we've seen you. You were a toddler when we saw you last—a baby. You've grown."

Arlo had no memory of them. "That's what babies do."

The man smirked, but the woman ignored Arlo's sarcasm.

Marley and Cooper looked up. "Are you Aunt Bethy?" Marley asked, as innocent as you please.

"I think I must be." The woman knelt, and Marley ran into her arms before Arlo could pull her back.

"Beth, don't," Uncle Luke warned, but she ignored him.

"What's your name?"

"Marley . . . and that's Cooper." Marley pointed to her brother. "Arlo's our big sister."

"I had no idea Mark had more children . . ."

The man set his hand on the woman's shoulder, and she stood, reluctantly releasing Marley, then gently pushing her away, which Marley clearly didn't understand.

"Let's get this over with." Uncle Luke drew his wife toward the conference room.

Arlo pulled Marley onto her lap. She gripped her sister tighter than she meant to, enough to make Marley squirm.

Arlo swallowed back the bile that rose in her throat. Lawyers' offices and grown-ups talking behind closed doors had proven nothing but trouble in her life, and this looked no different.

CHAPTER EIGHT

BETHANY NODDED TOWARD GINNY DEE but couldn't take her eyes off Mark. He wasn't as tall as her husband, not as muscular, but then it was likely he hadn't been working outside for the past ten years, given the pastiness of his face. Was he still drinking himself into stupors? It didn't look like it, didn't seem like he would be given those three beautiful children in the lobby if he had been, but how could a person tell? How could she—or Luke—know? She nodded toward her brother-in-law and took the chair Luke pulled out for her.

And what about "Aunt Ginny Dee"? The woman who sat across the table and beside Mark looked about as strung out as a cat on a clothesline. *What does she want out of all this—just to sell the farm, take the money, and run? Or something more?* She'd been clearing the family cemetery first thing, something Bethany hadn't had time to do. And if they were all moving—being forced to move—what was the point, except for tending her own babies' graves?

The door opened and Will Skipwith walked in, half smiling, nodding to everyone collectively. "Sorry I'm running a bit late this morning. I trust Sheila made you all comfortable." He set a thick folder down at the head of the table. "Can I get anyone coffee?"

"Or a strong drink?" Luke nearly sneered at his younger brother.

Bethany pressed her husband's knee beneath the table. That was no way to start things off.

Mark's eyes swept between Bethany and Luke. They changed in that moment from blue gray to steel, but he didn't speak.

Mr. Skipwith cleared his throat. "Well, then, let's get down to things. Mark, welcome back. Thank you, Ginny—Mrs. Boyden—for letting me know Mark was in town. It helps to have everyone here together." He opened the thick file. "I've made copies for each of you of Helen Dymoke Pickering's last will and testament, as Mrs. Boyden requested this morning. You can each read that at your own convenience. If you have any questions, you know my door is always open to you. The gist of the matter is that—"

"What about Dad's will?" Mark broke in.

Mr. Skipwith removed his reading glasses and set them on the table before him. "He didn't make one."

"That can't be," Luke spoke up. "He said he willed everything to us—to me and Mark."

Will Skipwith spoke slowly. "He might have said that. I have no doubt he wanted that to be true, but I'm afraid your father knew that the farm and everything on it belonged equally to him and his sister, Mrs. Boyden, and that when he passed, if Mrs. Boyden was still alive, it would all belong to her."

"That's not what he said," Luke insisted.

"I understand that." Mr. Skipwith leveled his gaze.

"Hold on. He knew the land wasn't his to give—all along?" Mark frowned.

"Yes, I believe he did. He knew that from the time of his mother's death he was to share all of the farm equally with his sister."

"That's not what he told me either." Aunt Ginny Dee looked only at her folded hands.

"No, he misrepresented the situation to Mrs. Boyden as well."

"Dad said you left because you didn't want anything to do with the family or the farm, that you gave it up."

"That was never true. He told me—" Aunt Ginny Dee's color rose, but she stopped.

Bethany saw it all too clearly. *She's afraid of what she'll say, as if she thinks we didn't know who Daddy Harold was, what he was like, what he was capable of. So, he tricked her too. Dear God, please help us! What a mess this family is, what a rotten mess.*

"He said our house—Promised Land—was Bethany's and mine. Are you telling me that's not true either?"

Mr. Skipwith returned his glasses to his nose.

Luke pushed suddenly back from the table, ran his hand through his sandy-brown hair, ready, Bethany knew, to pull it out by its roots. Bethany closed her eyes. *Our house. Everything. This can't be happening.*

"It will be up to Mrs. Boyden what she does with the farm in its entirety. As you know, Luke, but perhaps, Mark, you don't know, there are two years of back taxes due, and a loan in arrears."

"You came here to sell, didn't you?" Luke glared at Aunt Ginny Dee.

"Luke, you're pushing," Bethany whispered. *Don't push. Don't make an enemy out of her. She might change her mind. She might—*

"I didn't come here to do anything. I came because Mr. Skipwith asked me to. I didn't know any more about this than you did. But what can I do but sell? I can't pay taxes or a loan on a farm that isn't paying for itself."

"But it could. Given half a chance, it could." Luke's voice rose.

"But it hasn't, has it?" Aunt Ginny Dee spoke softly, refusing to pick up the gauntlet Luke had thrown down.

Bethany didn't have to look at Luke to know his jaw was set like marble, ready to break.

"I haven't seen the figures yet, and I haven't looked over the farm, just the house—my parents' house and the barn. But it doesn't seem to be a going concern. There used to be you-pick blueberries, but I understand what's left of them has grown wild. There was a good-sized peach orchard, but it's gone entirely. I only saw the sign for Christmas trees. I haven't even walked those fields. I've no idea what shape they're in."

Bethany answered, knowing Luke wouldn't say. "Daddy Harold plowed most of the blueberries under before Luke and I ever married. He said there was no way he and Luke could keep up with them. The peach trees got out of control—too tall to pick without equipment, so Harold had them cut down."

"Why?" Mark asked.

"Why?" Luke all but shouted. He stood, pointing a finger at Mark. "Because you weren't here—nobody was here but me to do everything. You know he'd never let anyone else work the farm— couldn't trust a living soul. You have no idea what it was like to buck Dad once he got an idea in his head. I had to take him to court to get him declared incompetent before I ever even saw the books. But you didn't know that, did you? By that time it was too late."

"Luke, let's settle down here and talk civilly. We won't get anywhere by—"

"By what? Telling the truth?" He ignored Will. His eyes stayed on Mark. "You ran off to Nam and then hippie land, turned into a pothead, and left me trying to keep it all going while Dad dove into dementia full throttle and ruined the farm." He leaned over the table. "We haven't seen you in, what—eight years? And now you waltz in, three kids in tow, wanting your half? Well, it turns out that it didn't matter you were never here to lift a finger because big surprise, little brother, we get nothing! Not the one who ran and not the one who stayed!"

"Sit down, Luke." Mr. Skipwith stood, both hands on the table, reminding Bethany of her high school principal, who brooked no back talk. "Every person at this table is struggling to deal with the truth, with the past and with the present and with what to do about the future. Every person at this table deserves a modicum of respect, including you."

Aunt Ginny Dee looked up. Bethany held her breath, glad someone older and wiser had the nerve to speak to her husband like that. *Please, Luke, listen.*

Luke breathed heavily but sat down.

"I'm here to interpret these documents, to tell you what the law says about the details of Mrs. Pickering's will, not to tell you what decisions you all should make going forward. But I will say that I've looked over the records for the farm.

"Forgive me, Mrs. Boyden, if I'm speaking out of turn, but I realize that you have a great deal at stake here financially and that you all have a great deal of emotion and family pride invested in Wetherill Pickering's Christmas Tree Farm. It's been an institution in this town for generations."

Every eye was glued to Mr. Skipwith. He sat down and continued. "There is a tax lien on the property. It cannot be transferred or a new title recorded until those taxes are paid. Now it's possible for Mrs. Boyden to sell outright, and to pay the back taxes from the proceeds of the sale. It might be possible to sell most or, if necessary, all of the land to pay back the loan, depending on what the land might sell for. It's also possible to let the bank foreclose. That might be what Mrs. Boyden needs or intends to do. That's entirely up to her." He held up his hand when Luke started to object. "But what I will say is that if areas of the farm could be improved—the houses, the barns and landscaping—then the place could sell for a great deal more, more than enough to cover the taxes and the loan. Even then, all the land might not have to be sold."

Luke set his elbows on the table and put his head in his hands. Bethany dared to lay a hand on his back.

"But that would take work and time and money." Mr. Skipwith spoke quietly.

"Truly, Mr. Skipwith, I can't pay for all that."

"I understand, Mrs. Boyden. But if certain parties were willing to do the labor in exchange for remaining on the land until the farm was either sold or brought back to a profitable condition, then—"

"You mean us," Mark broke in. "You mean Luke and me work the land, make the repairs, do the labor in exchange for staying on while—"

"You?" Luke laughed. "You stay on? You work with me? That'll be the day. Watch out, Miss Ginny Dee, he'll be freeloading—"

"Free labor isn't freeloading, Luke." Mark's dander was up now. "I came back because I heard Dad died. It's true enough that I hoped to cash in my share of the farm. I wanted to sell it to you because you've always loved this place and you and Bethany belong here. I get that, and I need to get back on my feet. But even if I got nothing, I meant to come back and see if I could work here, make a home for my kids."

Bethany's chest tightened.

"You mean dump them here."

"I mean make a home. This used to be my home, too, in case you forgot. I didn't expect it to be again in that way, but I thought maybe I could work here, earn my way, and give my kids some stability. And in case you forgot, I didn't run off to Nam; I was drafted."

Luke looked away, but Aunt Ginny Dee's eyes took the measure of both men. Bethany was sure of it.

"I need to see those figures . . . but do you really think we could pull the farm together and obtain a reasonable price?" Aunt Ginny Dee spoke cautiously.

"I do. As I said, it would take the payment of back taxes and some investment, but I think it would be worth it even if you decide to sell. If it is a matter of reasonable time—all things being equal—the bank might renegotiate the details of the loan payments. I can speak on your behalf with the bank manager. I know they don't want to foreclose."

Mark leaned toward her. "What if we work together to make the improvements—if you let us stay?"

Aunt Ginny Dee shook her head. "I don't know. I hadn't planned to—"

"Say we work through one more Christmas season, see if we can turn a profit. It might even make it worth keeping the farm—keeping Luke and me on to work it?" He looked at Luke. "If you want to, I mean."

Bethany could feel Luke processing every word, his struggle to trust his brother, his anger toward Aunt Ginny Dee for showing up, his shame and hurt and humiliation at having been duped yet again by his father, and his fear to hope, to trust. "One season isn't long to turn it around."

"But it's something," Mark pushed. "Would it be enough to hold off the bank, to wait and see—to try?"

Aunt Ginny Dee said nothing, looked at no one, and the seconds ticked by, turned to minutes. Everyone waited.

Finally, Luke relented. "Maybe, if she agrees. If you work like the devil."

"As long as that devil's you, I can do it." Mark almost grinned.

"What do you say, Mrs. Boyden? Is it worth thinking about?" Mr. Skipwith pressed.

Aunt Ginny Dee looked as if she were being drawn into a wind machine backward and didn't want to go. "I need to think about it. As I said, I need to see those figures."

"We can do that right now, after the boys leave."

Aunt Ginny Dee nodded. "I need strong coffee now."

"Yes, ma'am." Mr. Skipwith smiled and stood to pour her a cup. Tension crackled through the room, but nobody said a word. Another minute passed while Aunt Ginny Dee sipped her coffee.

"I guess we're done here for now, right?" Mark stood up, reaching for Mr. Skipwith's hand.

Mr. Skipwith gave a solid handshake in return. "Yes, I'd say so. It's good to see you, son. I look forward to seeing more of you and those fine-looking children you brought with you."

Mark nodded, then reached his hand across the table to Luke. "It's good to see you, too, Luke. Bethany. I'll see you at the farm. I hope we can work together."

Luke didn't respond, so Bethany reached out and took Mark's hand. "Welcome back, Mark."

"Aunt Ginny Dee—"

"I've only said I'll think about it." She wouldn't look up.

Mark nodded and picked up his cap.

Before Mark was out the door, Luke warned Aunt Ginny Dee, "Watch out. He's a freeloader. He'll dump those kids and leave you high and dry."

"Luke!" Bethany knew that wasn't fair. Mark might not be reliable, but he'd never dumped his kids with them. If he had, Bethany wouldn't have let them go.

As Bethany and Luke reached their truck, Bethany took one long look at the children now headed toward the other end of the street in Mark's wake.

"Don't even think about it, Beth. They'll break your heart, just like Mark broke Dad's. Just like Ginny Dee broke Granny's. Don't get attached."

But Bethany made no such promise.

CHAPTER NINE

BY THE TIME GINNY STOPPED at the grocery market and headed to the farm late that afternoon, her head ached from the mountain of papers Will had shown her.

Figures upon figures in account books, tax documents, notices of payments overdue, and more recently, Luke's cancellations of Harold's impossible orders for even more trees and shrubs, all with penalties for cancellation.

The farm should be operating at a twenty-five to thirty percent profit. It was a miracle, given all she'd learned, that a profit margin was shown at all on Harold's incomplete and unfiled tax records. She realized, however, that any "profit" shown may be because her brother had not included missed payments for the outstanding loan.

Even though the working acreage had been severely cut back since her father's death, Ginny feared that a second or even third year of loss was in sight—dangerous for any farmer. If the taxes were recalculated and amended to their advantage and they didn't turn things around this year, the farm could be redesignated as a hobby rather than a business, in which case no deductions could be claimed and the taxes would become astronomical—prohibitive for turning a good profit. The bottom line was plain—and ultimately blared loud and clear in red ink.

She understood from Will that Harold had fallen into a bitter depression after his wife's death, that although Will would never say it to Mark, Harold blamed his son for Elaine's death in childbirth. He'd never treated Mark like the son he was, though he worked both boys hard on the farm from the time they were big enough to help.

The bank loan, Will assured her, had been taken out unbeknownst to Luke or Bethany—a loan for $125,000. With that Harold had bought a new, first-rate tractor and ordered twenty thousand seedlings, intending to cultivate the abandoned peach orchard, as well as land beyond that had long lain fallow, and land farther up the mountain that had never been cultivated, when what they'd needed was regular supplies of mulch, fertilizer, herbicides, deer repellent, and most of all more hands to work the fields.

During the years Harold was able to work, he and Luke had been able to plant new seedlings over the prescribed one eighth of their working fields—about three acres per year, roughly three to five thousand trees, depending on the species. Twenty thousand seedlings delivered at once was simply out of the realm of human possibility for one man to plant.

When Luke realized what his father had done, he tried his best to stop the delivery, but it was too late. They'd arrived at the farm when he was out of town. Luke planted what he could, but thousands of seedlings died.

It wasn't until Harold nearly set the barn on fire that Luke forcibly took his father to the doctor and the diagnosis for dementia was documented. Even then, it took a while for Luke to gain guardianship and power of attorney to legally control the accounts.

That's when Luke discovered even more orders for shrubs and trees, that the last two years in taxes hadn't been paid, and that his father had taken out a loan against the farm. Before that, Luke knew they had to have been operating at a loss, even though his father had claimed they were doing great. With the way Harold had spent money, Luke hadn't known what to think. The discovery of the loan nearly broke him.

Just how big the current loss was, Will and his accountant were still trying to figure out. In any case, there were the tax lien and the bank loan to be repaid. All the farm's paperwork had come to Will as the executor of Harold's estate.

As near as Ginny could tell, Harold had lived in a fantasy world that grew with time, imagining he could do the impossible, very much like their father had, only he'd gone further down that rabbit hole to the detriment of the farm, to the ruin of his son and daughter-in-law. He hadn't the resources or the manpower to pull together whatever it was he envisioned. Though he never should have taken out that loan, he'd have been better off using it to hire help, but his paranoia wouldn't allow it. It was a wonder his son and daughter-in-law didn't hate him. Ginny figured that said a great deal about the two of them. And that gave her pause.

Was it like that for Mama the last year of Daddy's life—when he ordered those blue spruce trees and blueberry bushes even after she'd warned him there was no way he could plant them all, even with our help, let alone care for everything we already had in the ground? And no way we could pay back that loan?

Harold and I were still in school, but Daddy ignored that. If it hadn't been for Curtis coming—if old Mr. Skipwith hadn't brought him out to help—we never could have held it together. And then Daddy died, and Curtis and I left. Mama must have felt betrayed, abandoned.

But Will's father had brought Curtis, and Curtis had worked like two men, all day while Harold and Ginny were in school, until late in the day, and every Saturday. He didn't graduate from high school but earned his GED in the Army. *If it hadn't been for Curtis . . .* The words played over and over in her head.

For years she'd felt betrayed by Curtis for getting wounded in mind and body in the Pacific, for coming home so different, so changed. It had felt like abandonment.

And now here we are, history repeating itself. Mark, damaged from the war, if all Luke and Will say is true. The farm overcommitted and the finances in ruin. It's a wonder with Harold's dementia that he held it together as long as he did. But in the end, he made it so much worse.

Ginny pulled to the side of the road and set the car in park. "Dear God, I don't want to hurt Luke or Mark or Bethany or the children. They're my blood, my only blood kin left on the planet. But they need—the farm needs—more help than I can give them. There's some crazy brokenness in this family, cycles that keep repeating themselves in ways I don't understand.

"Even if I give all my money, give up all my dreams of going to England, everything I've worked for to start fresh, I can't rescue this, not on my own. But is that what You want me to do? Give up everything? Again?

"I can't do that. I just can't, Lord. I gave up everything—my entire life—for Curtis. He was my husband and I know that was right, but isn't this at last the time for me? It's what I've been saving for all these years. This mess feels like some kind of cruel trick."

There, she'd dared to say the words aloud. Curtis was no longer there to blame, to be angry with, but what about God? Was she angry with God? Could she ignore Him?

I can't change this. I can't take on this farm or this family or all their troubles. They've got to figure their own lives out, just as I did.

Ginny set the car in motion and drove the rest of the way to the farm with her jaw set but tears puddling in her eyes. She'd do what she had to do.

In the drive she hefted her grocery bags and slammed the car door behind her. She fully expected to find Mark and the children inside, taking over the run of the house. Well, she'd have to set them straight.

But the lights were off, and all was quiet. "Mark?" she called from the hallway. "Arlo?" she called up the stairs. There was no answer, and come to think of it, she'd not seen Mark's ramshackle truck in the drive.

"Well, that's that." Ginny set her groceries down on the kitchen counter, stopping short. *I know I left the breakfast dishes in the sink. Where are they?* The idea that Mark or Arlo had come back, cleaned the kitchen, and left took the heat from Ginny's fire. She sat down at the table.

I should feel relieved. But what she felt was empty.

An unbidden image of her mother, fifty years ago, came to mind. *The day I left, you'd have sat at this very table, and this emptiness is what you'd have felt—only more so. I just met them. I didn't even want them here, and yet . . . But you lost your only daughter.* Ginny swallowed. *I'm sorry, Mama. I'm so sorry. I missed Daddy so much, and I couldn't lose Curtis—not then. I could only think of myself—and Curtis. I never considered how hard it would be for you. I'm so sorry.*

Ginny laid her head on the table, over her arms, as if the table still held something of her mama, as if she could lay her head once more on her mama's breast and sob her sorries.

If Ginny fell asleep, she didn't know it. At length there came through her dreams a pounding, an ongoing, relentless pounding.

Ginny raised her head. Dusk had settled in, what she'd read they called the gloaming in Scotland. *Scotland. England. I'll be there soon.* Ginny stood and stretched. The pounding came from outside, but nearby. She stepped through the back porch door. The pounding came louder, and there was a light in the barn. *Luke? What's he doing in there?*

She'd peeked in the barn her second day, but it looked a disaster, as if it hadn't been used for more than storage in ages. Ginny didn't want to confront her nephew but needed to know what he was up to. Perhaps she could see without alerting him. Pulling on her sweater against the evening chill and flicking on her flashlight, she made her way across the yard and through the small orchard. The pounding never stopped.

Gingerly, Ginny pulled open the barn door. But it wasn't Luke.

"Aunt Ginny Dee!" Marley squealed and ran, arms wide open, to Ginny. Ginny braced herself, not ready, overwhelmed by the child's enthusiastic welcome and her thin arms wrapped tight around Ginny's knees.

The pounding stopped. Mark turned, taking nails from his mouth, still holding his hammer. "Aunt Ginny Dee."

"Mark. When I didn't see your truck, I thought you'd all gone." She looked around the barn. It was half cleared out, swept nearly clean.

"I—I hope you don't mind. I thought—if it's all right with you—that I could help around here, clean things up."

"I can't pay you, Mark. There's no way—"

"I'm not asking for money. We need a place to stay—for a while. Until you sell or decide what you're going to do." He set the hammer down and placed his hand on Cooper's head. At the sight of Ginny, the little boy had jumped from his barrel perch and run to Mark's side, three middle fingers in his mouth. "We won't be trouble. I promise. I just need to get on my feet." His eyes swept his children. "I need a place I can work and see after them. And I'll work hard. I can help turn this around."

Ginny hesitated. She looked down to think but found Marley's big brown eyes looking up at her. "Please let us stay," the little girl begged. Ginny looked up. Arlo stood several feet away, in the half light, arms crossed, staring at Ginny, the expectation of denial in her eyes.

Breathe. Breathe. Everything's happening so fast, Lord. What do I do?

They all waited, staring at her. Marley's eyes. Mark's eyes. Desperation. Need. Longing for yes.

An image came to Ginny's mind. *I was barely sixteen, married, pregnant. Curtis had gone to boot camp. I wrote home, begging Mama to let me come home for the duration of the war. I needed help, needed hope, needed home, needed Mama. And no answer came. I wrote again, more desperate. Harold finally wrote that Mama had said no. I tried not to blame Mama and Harold for the loss of our baby, but there were dark days . . .*

"Please, Aunt Ginny Dee." Marley brought Ginny back to the moment. "I'll be good."

Ginny's heart melted. It was all she could do to keep standing. She couldn't say yes. She couldn't say no. "Until I sell. That's all. That's all I can promise."

Marley squeezed her thanks harder. Mark visibly breathed and nodded, finality in his stance. Ginny took that as a criticism.

"Because I don't know what else I can do. I can't—"

"I understand. Just until you sell. Thank you."

Ginny nodded. "The girls can have my room. You and Cooper can take Harold's old room just across the hall. I'll sleep downstairs in Mama and—"

"No." Mark stopped her. "We'll sleep out here. This used to be seasonal workers' quarters—I guess you know that. We'll be fine out here. I'm fixing the bunks up, just a little rickety."

"You can't sleep out here. There's no heat or electricity."

"We have battery lights, and I found a couple of old lanterns that still work. The nights aren't that cold and getting warmer, and we have bedding in the truck. We'll be fine."

Ginny wasn't expecting that. She'd argue, but it was all so unexpected that she couldn't think. She'd think about it tomorrow. "Well, come in for breakfast and for the bathroom, anyway."

"There's facilities out here and a pump. I'll send the kids in for the bathroom tonight, but I can get everything up and running by tomorrow night. We won't be trouble. I promise."

"You said that." Ginny knew she needed to be careful. "Breakfast, then."

"We can go to the diner in town."

"And use up every penny you own and waste the food I've already bought?" She could be firm too. "Bacon, eggs, and toast. Be there." Ginny turned to leave but Marley tugged on her skirt.

"With jelly?"

Ginny smiled. She couldn't help it. She walked out of the barn so they wouldn't see her cry. "And orange juice," she whispered.

CHAPTER TEN

ARLO COULD HAVE KICKED HERSELF. *Overslept again.* She pulled her pa's T-shirt over her pajama top and slid her feet into well-worn flip-flops. There was no time to dress or think about hair or teeth brushing. Marley was missing—again.

She had a pretty good idea where her sister had gone. No matter how many times Arlo had scolded over the last month, insisting Marley wait for her in the morning, she was out of bed first thing, before anyone else was awake, out the barn door, and making a bee-line for Aunt Ginny Dee's kitchen.

Arlo didn't like that her sister was drawn to Aunt Ginny Dee like a magnet. She didn't like that Aunt Ginny Dee had taken such a shine to her sister. Marley was in for disappointment, for real heart-ache when their grandaunt found a buyer for the farm. They'd all be sent packing and never see the woman with the runaway reputation again. Leopards never changed their spots and neither did people. That's one thing Arlo knew. The other thing she knew was that she was responsible for the little ones. She was the one to hold the family together. That meant keeping an eye on them and keeping their pa on the straight and narrow.

She'd seen what a loosening of the reins could do, and she wasn't about to let that happen again. She'd just check on Cooper before she left, make sure he was still sleeping. The lump in the little bed beside Marley's looked too small. Arlo pulled back the covers to find rolled-up burlap sacks. "Marley!" Arlo knew the deception was her sister's doing. Cooper wouldn't have thought of it on his own.

By the time she reached the back door to the screened porch, she heard Marley's giggles and Cooper's high, sweet voice singing, "Oh, ye'll take the high road and I'll take the low road, and I'll be in Scotland afore ye!" a song Aunt Ginny Dee sang as often as she sang "Danny Boy" and "My Wild Irish Rose." Arlo's eyes flipped to the heavens. *Those two copy everything she says and does. She's turning them both into Celts.* Arlo had heard about Celts in school—back when she got to go. Aunt Ginny Dee was obsessed with Scotland, England, and Ireland . . . something to do with Dymoke ancestry, which she said they all carried in their blood.

Arlo didn't know anything about her pa's grandmother. She was a Pickering, through and through, and so were Marley and Cooper. Whatever came from her own mother's side, Arlo didn't know, didn't care, and wouldn't claim. Any mother who'd run off and leave her kids—especially a baby as little as Cooper was then—didn't deserve to have her ancestry owned.

Arlo pulled open the back kitchen door. Cooper stood in high form on a wooden chair by the kitchen sink, his hands in sudsy water, singing away.

". . . on the bunny, bunny banks of Loch Lomond!"

"It's not 'bunny, bunny,' it's 'bonnie, bonnie'!" Marley insisted.

Cooper looked crestfallen; his worried face turned up to Aunt Ginny Dee.

"'Bunny, bunny' is just fine." Aunt Ginny Dee spoke softly, drying dishes beside Cooper. "I'm sure there are lots of bunnies in Scotland."

Arlo shook her head. *He'll never learn anything if she lets him get away with that stuff.*

"Arlo!" Marley exclaimed. "Want breakfast?"

"You were supposed to wait for me."

"I forgot. You were sleeping and I was hungry."

"Good morning, Arlo. We have pancakes and sausage this morning. I'll dish you up a plate." Aunt Ginny Dee turned to the stove but didn't look at Arlo, so she missed the scowl Arlo served her.

"Look, Arlo! See my ponytails Aunt Ginny Dee made me? She calls them pigtails—isn't that funny?" Marley danced around the table, singing, "Oink! Oink!" flipping her two ponytails, as pleased as Arlo had ever seen her.

"I can't have pigtails," announced Cooper, "'cause I'm a boy."

"You could," Marley corrected, "if you let your hair grow long as mine."

Cooper shook his head. "Pa wouldn't like it."

"No," Arlo agreed, "he wouldn't. He didn't like it when those foster people didn't cut it."

Aunt Ginny Dee set a plate loaded with steaming pancakes and sausage in front of Arlo, along with a pitcher of warmed maple syrup. Arlo didn't want to be grateful, but she was. Saying so was harder.

"There's more if you want them."

Arlo grunted.

"You're welcome." Aunt Ginny Dee went back to drying dishes.

Arlo prayed a prayer just long enough to let the little kids know she'd done it, then drowned her pancakes in maple syrup. They nearly melted in her mouth. Arlo couldn't remember eating so good as they'd eaten in Aunt Ginny Dee's kitchen this last month. She knew it must be costing her a fortune. All she could figure was that the woman was rich, no matter that she said she wasn't. Well, she'd be getting money from the sale of the farm, so she ought to feed them well. After all, their pa was working his tail off to fix up the place and, in the end, he wouldn't get a red cent from it. They all knew that.

"Arlo, I wondered if you'd like to help me with a garden this morning? I thought, as long as we're going to be here through the summer, we might as well plant some vegetables."

"Me too! I want to help make a garden!" Marley jumped up and down, a pogo stick on two legs.

"What do you want me to do?" Arlo wasn't eager to commit, though she knew her pa would say she should.

"Your father is bringing the rototiller over. He'll turn the old garden, but we'll still need to chop clumps with our hoes. Once we get the soil fine enough, we can plant seeds. I'm thinking we could go into town to the farm store and pick out some seeds soon as we're all dressed and ready. Would you like that?"

"I want to go to town!" Cooper flipped suds out to the floor in his excitement.

"We can all go—as long as it's okay with your father." Aunt Ginny Dee was careful to always say that, but whatever she wanted to do was always okay with Pa. Arlo figured he was relieved to be rid of them for a time. But too much free time for Pa worried Arlo. It made it too easy for trouble to find him.

Arlo shrugged. "I guess." That was as much as she was willing to give. She needed to be careful not to act too happy, careful not to care, careful not to trust her aunt. Any one of those things set you up for hurt, and Arlo didn't need any more hurt, or disappointment—not for herself and not for Marley or Cooper.

By the time they'd gotten Pa's okay and Arlo was dressed and combed to suit Aunt Ginny Dee, Cooper had disappeared.

"He's gone over to Uncle Luke's," Marley announced. "Pa said Uncle Luke's gonna work on lining up water hoses and Cooper wants to help."

"I told him not to go over there. He's too little to do that!" Arlo all but shouted.

"He likes Uncle Luke," Marley defended. "Likes to do stuff with him."

"Uncle Luke doesn't like him, and he won't watch out for him." Arlo felt her temperature rising.

"Laying hosing is safe enough," Aunt Ginny Dee said. "He won't get hurt. You need to let him—"

"He's my brother, not yours!" Arlo retorted. "He's my responsibility."

"No," Aunt Ginny Dee said quietly. "He's your father's responsibility, and he gave permission."

"Forget town. I'm not going—and neither are you, Marley!" Arlo let the screen door slam behind her. She'd find Cooper and they'd stay in the barn, despite Marley's howling that she wanted to go to town. *Aunt Ginny Dee started this. She should have made Cooper stay in the kitchen. She should have watched out for him. I can't let my guard down like that. No telling what might happen.*

"Arlo!" Aunt Ginny Dee called. "Stop—now!"

Arlo stopped, her heart beating fast. Aunt Ginny Dee never yelled like that. Arlo wanted to ignore her but knew she'd be in trouble with Pa if she did. Still, she wouldn't turn around. *They don't understand. Even Pa doesn't get it. We've got to stick together, not get sucked in with—*

A hand rested on Arlo's shoulder, making her flinch. "You've got to let go, just a little. I know you feel responsible, but there's others to help carry that burden now."

"For how long?" Arlo's jaw set so hard her teeth hurt.

"For as long as it takes. For as long as we're all together."

Arlo turned on her. "And just how long will you stick around? You, or Uncle Luke or Aunt Bethany? Cooper deserves better. Marley deserves better. You can't—"

"You all deserve better."

Arlo pulled away.

"Some things you have to take one day at a time, Arlo. Take the good there is without fearing the bad that may never come. And you have to let your brother and sister have that good too."

"I don't want them hurt."

"I know that. But I'm not going to hurt Marley, and Luke is not going to hurt Cooper. No one wants to hurt you."

Arlo might want to believe that, but she knew it was a lie. *It's always a lie.*

"Now we need to get on to town. We need to pick up those seeds and seedlings and I want to take you and Marley for some sturdy sneakers and garden gloves. We'll even see if we can find some little ones for Cooper. You'll all need them for gardening. There's a sale at the Farm and Feed. We can do all our shopping there. Maybe we'll have time to stop for an ice cream."

Ice cream and shoes. New shoes. Arlo hadn't had new shoes since she'd outgrown her old pair, the ones before the last foster family, except for the summer sandals Aunt Ginny Dee had bought them their first day.

"Let's go. We can get back in time to fix lunch and maybe we'll be able to plant before supper."

Arlo knew she was being sucked in and she shouldn't allow it, shouldn't weaken, shouldn't go, but the lure of new shoes was strong. *Maybe this once. Just this once.*

❧

Arlo had never helped to plant a garden. She'd never planted a seed or a seedling on her own, no matter that her parents had called themselves "flower children." She remembered them talking about living off the land, growing their own food and herbs, returning to nature, but it was just that—talk. They never did anything about it and never showed Arlo how it could be done.

So Arlo had no idea, not until her pa tilled an old garden space and Aunt Ginny Dee made them crumble clumps of dirt and collect stones in bushel baskets, then showed them how to dig small holes, gently spread the roots of seedlings, and plant and water them. She showed them how to plant onion sets, and potatoes spaced in deeper trenches, cut-side down and eyes pointing up. After that they planted seeds by running a shallow trench using an old stick, spaced out the seeds, then gently covered them with a fine layer of dirt. Some seeds they buried deeper than others. Arlo wondered how Aunt Ginny knew which was which or what was what but wouldn't ask.

When the watering can was full, Aunt Ginny Dee gave it to Arlo, trusting her to ration the water between the seedlings. Marley begged to sprinkle the seeds with the watering can when it became half empty, but sometimes she poured too much, and the seeds washed out of their trench. Aunt Ginny Dee was patient with her and showed her how to replant.

Cooper wasn't much help at all in the garden, more of a *let's dig this up and see if it's growing* sort. "Maybe it's not so bad he helps Uncle Luke a little," Marley suggested after Cooper dug up three tomato plants before anybody caught him.

It took six days to see the winter squash seeds sprout, ten days for the spinach, ten days for pumpkins and about the same to see cucumbers and beans show points of green through the black mountain dirt.

Arlo figured there was some kind of satisfaction in that—plant a seed, water, then wait for something to peek out of the ground. Some sign of hope to show for your work. It wasn't like fixing a meal from a can or washing dishes or even clothes. Those things got eaten up or dirty again in no time. But a plant was a living, growing thing, sort of like a person. It didn't disappear unless you ripped it out or forgot to water or feed it through neglect—also sort of like a person, in Arlo's mind.

She'd just begun to think that maybe all this would work out when Aunt Ginny Dee announced she'd be leaving.

CHAPTER ELEVEN

"I'LL BE GONE LESS THAN A WEEK. Your father's going to use my kitchen for your meals, and your Aunt Bethany has promised to look in on you if you need anything." Ginny explained the plan to the children over breakfast for what felt like the umpteenth time. But it didn't help. Marley still cried and Cooper sat in the corner, refusing to eat, sucking his three fingers, a habit he'd all but given up in the last couple of weeks.

"I need to go back to New Jersey and get my things. I'll be back, and I'll bring some flowers we can plant. I promise. You like flowers, don't you?"

Marley howled louder. "Don't go, Aunt Ginny Dee! Please don't go!"

Arlo crossed her arms and glared, as if to say, *I knew it. I told you so.*

"Arlo, I need you to help Marley understand."

"Oh, we understand all right." Her voice dripped with sarcasm. "We've heard that line plenty of times."

"I don't know what you've heard, or what you believe, but I will be back."

Arlo snorted and pulled Marley by the arm. "C'mon, Marley. Get up, Cooper. I told you guys not to get—"

"I love you, Aunt Ginny Dee! I don't want you to go!" Marley howled as Arlo dragged her siblings out the door.

A crying fest. How has it come to this? When has anyone ever begged me to stay? Who last said they loved me? It was so long ago Ginny couldn't remember. She should leave right away. Alternately, she wanted to run after them, wrap her arms around the little ones and Arlo, if she'd let her, and vow she'd not go. But that would be silly—ridiculous. She was just going for a week—less than a week—to close her affairs in New Jersey. She really was coming back . . . for now.

But it's true, I won't stay. This is just until we fix things up, through another Christmas season, like Mark asked. We'll put the farm on the market by next spring. Then what? Then I'll go to England—already so much later than I intended. I need to go. And they'll need to go somewhere to start a new life. Somewhere. Where, dear God, will they go? Where will they find a home?

Arlo, with her deep need to belong, to be wanted, her stubborn pride and protective shield—protective of her younger siblings and her own heart, though she'd not admit it. Marley, with her huge brown eyes and desperate need to be loved and cuddled, the one who loved to work with you whatever you were doing in the kitchen or the garden or just walking to the mailbox. Cooper, with his little-boy smile, eager to join anything and anyone, especially to follow Luke from pillar to post whether Luke wanted him to or not. *What about them, Lord? I can't supply all their needs. I can't be their savior. Only You. Only You know what they need. Only You can supply their lives. Do You see them? Are You listening?*

Ginny stowed her overnight bag in the back of her car and left before she could reconsider. She'd close her room in New Jersey. Her landlady needed a new boarder to take over the lawn, and it was silly to keep paying rent when she had a place to live and needed to be on the farm to help bring it up to snuff. She'd toss what she didn't need and bring everything else back. She hadn't planned on keeping her few pieces of furniture. If her landlady didn't want them for her next boarder, Ginny would donate them to Goodwill or one of the local thrift shops.

The thing she intended to make room for in her car was a hefty number of cuttings and roots from the garden she'd created for her landlady, especially the unique ones she'd bred over the years. She couldn't lose those. She'd visit the garden center where she'd worked for decades and purchase flats of annuals and a few perennials she especially loved from their supply. She knew exactly which companion plants she wanted to add to her mother's old rose garden and to the cemetery.

She hadn't even set foot in the space behind Promised Land where she and her mother had dreamed over her future garden—a garden that Ginny and Curtis had planned before he went to war, on land that now belonged more to Bethany and Luke than to her. But maybe, if the relationship between her and Bethany continued to grow, she could plant something there—a secret promise, or a memory, the seed of a dream, however unfulfilled. No one need ever know what it meant to Ginny, but she would know. It would be for her and Curtis and for all the dreams they'd once shared, the garden dreams that her mother had known and encouraged. And then the farm would go to someone else, someone new, someone who held no appreciation of what every plant and bush and tree meant.

Ginny's smile was bittersweet as she drove. She'd been able to prune and salvage a number of the old roses in her mother's garden, to plant wide pots of mint—contained but fragrant and already alluring to butterflies. It would take a couple of years for the roses to come back fully after her severe pruning. She wouldn't be there to see that, but she could imagine. Perhaps she could convince whoever bought the farm to take photographs and send them to her in England.

A lump formed in Ginny's throat. Photographs were not the same as the real thing, not the same as the brilliant color, the haunting fragrance, the soft petals, lush green foliage, and sharp thorns of a well-bred, well-tended rose. But that dream now and the hope of a photograph in the future were all she had, all she dared claim.

Once she was in England, she'd create it all again. She could take cuttings from the farm's garden and plant them in England—if customs and the gardener there would allow it. And why wouldn't he? They were cuttings from the farm originally settled by Dymokes from England.

How ironic. The Dymokes in England were her family by ancestry. The Pickerings in Virginia were her family now. Both places held traces of her blood kin but neither felt truly hers, and the farm, the home where she was born and raised, would likely sell before another year was out.

There's no place like home. There's no place like home. That's what Dorothy kept saying in The Wizard of Oz, and it's true . . . for those able to claim a home of their own. For those who are part of a family, with a place to belong.

CHAPTER TWELVE

BETHANY CAREFULLY DOTTED the centers of pineapple rings with bright red maraschino cherries, then spread thick yellow cake batter over the buttered and brown-sugared arrangement—in two pans. She was preparing two of everything this week. With Aunt Ginny Dee gone, Bethany was determined to make hay while the sun shone.

For the last month she'd kept her distance from Mark and the children, as well as Aunt Ginny Dee, even though Aunt Ginny Dee had hinted, Bethany was sure, at wanting more—something Bethany could imagine wanting too. Luke had warned her repeatedly to stay away, all but forbidding her to "get sucked in with those kids." He knew her heart. She knew he was trying to protect her, and she'd unwillingly obeyed.

But with Aunt Ginny Dee away and Mark working just as hard as Luke to pull the farm together, there was no way the man could cook for his family. Arlo insisted she could take over, but Bethany had seen what that meant—the cheapest sugary cereal on the store shelf for breakfast, grilled cheese or bologna sandwiches for lunch, spaghetti from a can or mac and cheese from a box for supper, with the rare addition of fish sticks. How could a grown man work on that? How could children grow and thrive with no nutrients to speak of?

Not on her watch. Without Daddy Harold to care for, Bethany

had more time on her hands than she wanted, and Luke had some strange notion that a woman should not work in the fields, no matter that she was fit and able and he could use every hand available. Those children—those three lovely, motherless children—needed her. At least, they needed someone. Bethany knew she needed them.

Roast beef, mashed potatoes, carrots, peas, and pineapple upside-down cake should do the trick. Mark and the children could eat for a couple of days off of that, as could she and Luke. How much simpler it would be to invite them all for dinner, to gather round her own table. But Luke wasn't ready for that . . . not yet. She'd introduce him to the idea, slow and steady. Yes, slow and steady would win the race.

The needy muffler from Luke's truck roared down the lane toward the house. Bethany stiffened as she slipped her Tupperware container of meat and vegetables into her basket. She'd hoped to get the meal over to Aunt Ginny Dee's kitchen before Luke returned for the day.

The back door opened. "Mmm. Something smells good." Luke whipped off his hat and gave her a peck on the cheek.

"Pineapple upside-down cake, harbinger of spring!" Bethany smiled but looked away.

"It's June."

"Never too late for something good."

He eyed the basket of food on the table and crossed his arms, leaning his back against the counter. "Wouldn't have anything to do with me, though, would it?"

"You like pineapple upside-down cake, don't you?" Bethany teased.

But the light had gone from Luke's eyes. "You've got to leave them alone. Forget about them. They're no good for—"

"They're your family. That makes them my family, too." Bethany had had enough. "I took care of your father until the day he died, and I did it as willingly as I could, as kindly as I was able without so much as a thank-you from him."

Luke softened. "I know you did, Beth. And I'm sorry—sorrier than I can say that he was like that—that I didn't stand up to him for the way he treated you. I never should have let things go as far as they did like that, or with the farm, with him. I'm amazed you were able to do all you did."

"So don't deprive me of what is pure joy while I have it—while we have it."

"I just don't want you to get hurt."

"You mean you don't want to bend!"

"Maybe I don't." She heard the conflict and the hardness enter his voice.

"You're like that elder brother in the Prodigal Son story. You won't forgive Mark. You won't welcome him or his children home. Like it or not, Luke, this is his home as much as yours." Silence stretched between them. Bethany placed her hand on his arm. "What are you afraid of? That he's going to take the farm away from you? That's already done, and it has nothing to do with Mark."

Luke turned away but Bethany reached for his back. She spoke quietly. "You say you don't want me to get hurt. I'm hurting now. I've been hurting a long time. I'm lonely, Luke. I'm childless—we're childless—and it means everything to me when those children are glad to see me—Marley and Cooper, at least. That little boy idolizes you. He follows you everywhere he can get away with, or haven't you noticed?"

"I can't do this, Bethany. He's not my son, and Mark—"

"You can. You can do so much more than you realize, just not in your own strength." She pulled him to her. "The thing I learned in taking care of your father is that you can't keep a hard heart when you touch someone, help someone, physically care for someone. It melts the hard feelings inside and that's a good thing."

"For you."

"For anyone. But we can't do all those things alone, and that's okay; we don't have to. You know that saying—that Scripture on the picture in your grandparents' kitchen? *I can do all things through Christ which strengtheneth me.*"

Bethany felt her husband stiffen beneath her hands, as if refusing to allow the escape of whatever emotion he felt. She wasn't sure what that emotion was and knew she wasn't likely to learn after he walked out, letting the screen door slam behind him.

CHAPTER THIRTEEN

ARLO'D TAKEN ALL SHE COULD from Marley and Cooper that morning. Her pa had left early, saying he wouldn't be back till late. He'd taken the truck to pick up a load of lumber from Leesburg and see about selling the last of the blueberries to a couple of local grocers, then had some errands to run. Arlo just hoped those errands wouldn't take him through some bar. He'd vowed not to drink, and she knew he hadn't yet, but stress had always been the precursor to binges, and he surely had enough stress now.

He'd left Arlo in charge. Things were going fine until Arlo ordered Marley to wash the pile of breakfast and lunch dishes and set Cooper to dry. She'd just carried their load of laundry to the barn—one of Aunt Ginny Dee's rules never to let things pile up—and was nearly up the back porch steps when she heard a crash from the kitchen and Cooper shouting, "You better get down—I'm gonna tell Arlo!"

"What now?" Arlo raced through the door.

"Shut up, Cooper! You're not the boss of me," Marley shouted back, "You're just a little kid who wears diapers!"

"I don't wear diapers anymore!" Cooper pushed Marley's chair from the counter side.

Marley sat on top of the refrigerator, glaring down at Cooper.

"What are you doing up there?" Now Arlo shouted.

"She's stealin' cookies!"

"Not stealin'—allowed! Aunt Ginny Dee said we could have some if we're good."

"Well, you're not being good. Get down from there, now!"

"I can't get down. Cooper stole my chair."

Arlo reached for her sister and Marley, fearless as ever, jumped into her arms. Marley's chin quivered. Arlo didn't know if it was from guilt, shame, remorse, or frustration, and she wasn't about to ask. Marley could manipulate the socks off of grown-ups, but Arlo wasn't falling for it.

"All right, you two. Outside. Go play, and don't come back till supper."

"What about the dishes?" Marley looked too innocent.

"I'll do them. I'd rather do them. Out!"

They were gone in a flash.

Peace reigned for the space of half an hour. Arlo turned on the radio and sang along to the station that belted out bluegrass music, the kind her pa liked best. Arlo's favorite was "Gold Watch and Chain," one she and her pa sang in harmony. She was just to the part about "only say that you'll love me again" when Aunt Bethany appeared, making Arlo jump.

"That's lovely, Arlo. I didn't know you could sing like that."

"Yeah, well, Pa and me, we like to sing."

"That's good. That's really good." Aunt Bethany set a basket on the table.

Arlo's mouth watered, despite herself. She didn't know what to make of Aunt Bethany. She kept bringing food over even when Arlo told her not to, even when Pa told her not to. Arlo figured she should be insulted, like Aunt Bethany was saying she didn't know how to cook, but the truth was Arlo didn't, not much.

The day before she'd even brought a bag of clothes from the church rummage sale that she thought might fit "you girls" and a new outfit for Cooper because they didn't have any little-boy things at the rummage sale.

Arlo would have liked to send it all back, but there were things they needed—summer shirts and shorts, a dress for church, a couple of men's shirts for Pa. Aunt Bethany had even bought each of them fresh underwear from the Walmart. She had a good eye for sizes and colors they liked. Arlo didn't much like the training bra she'd brought her but figured maybe it was a good idea . . . maybe.

Everything fit except the hem needed taking up in Marley's dress and a button was missing on one of the shirts for Pa. Arlo could handle a needle and thread, if she had one, but she wouldn't ask.

"Mr. Skipwith and some men from church are coming out tomorrow to begin sanding down the clapboard, getting the outside of the frame side of the house ready to paint. I'll be cooking for everybody, and I sure could use some help. Would you and Marley come see what you can do? Cooper too?"

Arlo had never been to Aunt Bethany and Uncle Luke's house; they'd never been invited. But to seem too eager, to say she wanted to come, well, that didn't seem right either. "Pa might need me."

"Your dad's going to be working with the men. Mr. Skipwith's organizing it—sort of a workday surprise for Aunt Ginny Dee—good faith."

Arlo didn't say anything.

"Well, if you want, just come on over. I'll be fixing a big breakfast for everyone—pancakes, sausage, eggs, grits, stewed apples—and a big lunch later." Aunt Bethany didn't wait for an answer but unpacked her basket of food on the table, then walked out the back door.

Arlo knew she should have said thank you, or something, but it was all too much. And why were they helping Aunt Ginny Dee get the house ready to sell? If they sold it, they'd all have to move. What did Aunt Bethany mean by *good faith*? What about bad faith? Arlo didn't know.

She'd feed herself and the kids a little later and set aside a plate for Pa. She'd just set Aunt Bethany's cake back on the counter when Marley ran through the back kitchen door, letting the screen door slam.

"Arlo, help! Cooper's down by the creek and he can't get out—his foot's stuck."

"What do you mean, his foot's stuck?"

"We were making mud pies on the edge, and he fell in, but now his foot's stuck and the water's comin' up!" Tears streamed down Marley's face.

"Show me where!" Arlo was out the door and halfway down the steps.

"Wait for me!" Marley's shorter legs pounded the ground, but she was several yards behind Arlo.

Arlo reached the creek bank but saw nothing of Cooper. "Cooper! Cooper!" she cried. "Where, Marley? Where is he?"

"Keep going, keep going." Marley pointed downstream, huffing and breathless.

Arlo ran, yelling at the top of her lungs. "Cooper! Cooper, where are you? Answer me!" She finally stopped, sweat pouring, heaving, bent from a stitch in her side, and Marley far behind. But there was no sign of Cooper. "Please, God," she begged, "help me find him. Help me find Cooper before it's too late."

Marley caught up with her. "He's on the other side." She pointed to the far side of the creek.

"You crossed the creek?" Arlo gasped in disbelief. "You know you're never supposed to go in that creek!"

"Save him!" Marley cried harder.

"Stay here!" Arlo ignored her new sneakers, sprang into the creek, slipped on slimy rocks, sank to her knees, struggled to stand, then waded across. "Cooper! Cooper, can you hear me?" She called and prayed and called again.

On the far side she thrashed through underbrush. Why she couldn't see him farther down the creek she couldn't understand, unless . . . but she couldn't go there, not even in her greatest fear. "Cooper! Cooper!" she called, crying out, "Please, God! Please!" She had one purpose, to watch over Marley and Cooper, and she'd failed.

She'd failed her little brother. She'd failed her pa and Marley. *Where are you?*

From somewhere down the creek and beyond the bend, a dog barked. Not a growl but an insistent *bark, bark, bark!* Arlo's heart constricted. She'd had little good experience with dogs—her foster family had kept a fierce and terrifying chained Doberman—but she wasn't about to let a dog, no matter how sharp its teeth, keep her from finding her brother. She pushed forward. "Cooper! Cooper!"

Round the bend and twenty feet farther she saw him near the center of the creek, water nearly to his shoulders, his face red from crying and arms wrapped tight around the neck of a sopping wet and bedraggled black mutt—a mutt that barked nonstop but stood still as a statue as the current rushed past.

"Cooper!" Arlo reached her brother and the dog. Her knees gave way in relief. The dog stopped barking.

"Stuck," Cooper cried. "Stuck!"

Arlo reached for Cooper's knee below the fast-running current, ran her hand down his leg, could barely keep her own face above water as she felt his sneaker caught in the tree root.

"The water's gettin' high on me, Arlo. I'm scared—and cold!" the little boy sputtered, words barely beyond his blue lips.

"I know, little buddy. I know. I'm gonna get you out of here. Don't you worry." But Arlo was worried. His shoe was stuck but good. "If I can just get your shoe untied, you can slip your foot out." She couldn't see beneath the churned water of the free-flowing stream and Cooper was right: the water was getting higher or the hole he was standing in was getting deeper as his other foot sank into the mud of the streambed.

"I don't wanna lose my new shoe—it's red!"

Arlo cursed the shoe but worked feverishly trying to untie the double-knotted laces, her fingers numbing in the cold water. *I've gotta get him out of here. Please, God, help us!*

The dog shifted and Cooper slipped, his shoulders under the

water, his mouth catching a passing leaf and gulp of stream water. Choking, he coughed and gagged.

"Cooper! Stand up! Hold onto me!"

The little boy cried harder, gasping, fear flaming from his eyes. "I can't. I can't get up!"

Arlo tugged on the root that strapped his foot, but it held fast. She pulled Cooper to a half-standing position, bracing him against her knee. The dog stood still, allowing Cooper to maintain his grip on its neck.

Arlo took a deep breath and pushed her head beneath the water, grasped her brother's ankle with two hands, and pulled. Unbalanced, Cooper fell backward but his foot wrenched loose. Sputtering, spitting clumps of leaves and whatever she'd swallowed, Arlo caught Cooper round the waist and lifted him, coughing and choking, above the water. The dog swam out in slow motion. Hitting solid ground, he shook, flinging a torrent in every direction, then disappeared into the woods.

Arlo grabbed Cooper beneath his armpits, tugging him through the water and up onto the bank where they both fell into the brush. She covered his shivering body with her own, thankful, relieved, but still shaking, then rubbed his icy arms and legs and feet.

His limp arms reached for her. "You saved me. I love you, Arlo."

Arlo lost it. She lifted him onto her lap, hugging him fiercely. "I love you too. Don't you ever scare me like that again. Don't you ever go near this creek again. Do you hear?" She kissed his muddied golden head and held him tight against her. *If you'd died, I would die. I love you more than my life, Cooper Dylan Pickering. More than my life.*

From a distance she heard Marley calling, crying.

"C'mon." Arlo pulled Cooper to his feet. "We've gotta go get Marley."

"My shoe—my red shoe is gone. I can't walk without my shoe," Cooper whined.

"Dead right it's gone. Climb on my back, I'll carry you."

By the time Arlo got all three of them cleaned up, they were too tired to clean the mess they'd made in Aunt Ginny Dee's bathroom, too tired to eat, Aunt Bethany's basket of food forgotten.

Arlo had just gotten Cooper and Marley tucked in and fallen onto her bunk when she glimpsed the barn door crack open and a familiar black mutt with a long white patch on its chest, reeking of wet dog, amble in and make a beeline for Cooper. The dog circled twice and plopped on the floor by Cooper's bunk.

Arlo breathed, closing her eyes. Their grown-ups might object, but she didn't care. She was just thankful for another pair of eyes to watch over her brother.

Arlo never woke until Marley climbed in beside her, beneath the covers. Less than a minute later Cooper snuggled in too. It was still dark, but slivers of daylight crept through cracks between the door and flooring of the bunkhouse. Their pa still snored, home at last, but oblivious to the terror that had taken place the day before. Arlo shushed the two tucked in beside her. It was Arlo's favorite time of day, this opening of the morning when they were all tucked in together, safe, at least for now.

"Doggie's gone," Cooper whispered.

Arlo sat up. "Where? When? When Pa came in last night? We were probably out cold. That's the only time the door could have been opened."

"It's okay," Cooper assured her. "He'll come back. He's a good dog."

"But we can't keep him," Marley stated, matter of fact.

"Why not?" Cooper sat up. "He's our dog. He came to live with us. He saved me—him and Arlo."

"You know Pa will say no. He'll cost too much money to feed and there's no room in the truck when we leave."

When we leave. Arlo hated Marley's words in a way that surprised her. Wasn't leaving what she wanted, at least what she expected? What she knew would happen because it always did? They'd have to go, and it was better to get on with it, not get too attached, not get disappointed. Nothing could change that, could it? Even Aunt Ginny Dee, with all her hugs and fussing over them, had gone off. She said she'd be back soon but wasn't yet, and Arlo wasn't holding her breath. Grown-ups said one thing and did another. Arlo pushed the covers away. "Get dressed, guys. Don't wake Pa."

"Let's stay here," Marley begged. "It's cozy."

"Not today. We've got things to do."

"What things?" Marley sat up, as eager for an adventure as she was for snuggling.

"I'll tell you outside. Now go."

For the first time without being told, Arlo took a brush to Marley's hair, worked it into a ponytail looped with a rubber band. She did the same to her own, though with no mirror she wondered if she'd done a decent job. She even ran the brush over Cooper's short hair—shorter than it had ever been, thanks to Aunt Ginny Dee's regular haircuts. "Brush your teeth."

"Brush teeth?" both kids echoed.

"We haven't even had breakfast! I'm hungry!"

"Do it." The good thing about her sister and brother, Arlo figured, was that they usually listened to her. She was the oldest, the one responsible. Everything about them, and sometimes Pa, was up to her. She drew a shaky breath. *But I can't be responsible for everything, not all the time. We need more eyes, more ears.* "Come on," she whispered when their pa turned over, still asleep but no longer snoring.

Arlo took each of their hands and forged ahead, which delighted Marley and Cooper. Marley skipped along and Cooper walked two steps, ran three, walked two steps, ran three to keep up. They bypassed Aunt Ginny Dee's kitchen door.

"Breakfast?" Cooper asked.

"We'll eat, but not there today."

"Where? Where are we going?" Marley tried to pull Arlo to a stop, but Arlo wasn't stopping. She knew if she slowed down, she might rethink what she was about to do. She couldn't risk that.

She marched them through the back garden and the small orchard, across the first Christmas tree field, and down the lane to Promised Land.

"Aunt Bethy's house?" Marley danced. "Cooper, we're going to Aunt Bethy's house!"

"Uncle Luke!" Cooper cheered.

"This once." It might still be too early, Arlo didn't know, but she dared not stop, dared not lose her resolve. She knocked on the back door, stepped down, and picked up her brother and sister's hands, holding them tight. Nobody came. Arlo knocked again, stepped back again.

At last the door opened and a bleary-eyed Uncle Luke towered above them. He frowned, as if trying to focus, to understand what the three at the foot of the steps were doing there. He pushed the mop of sandy-brown hair from his eyes, then raised his brows. "Everything okay?"

"We came to help."

"Help?"

"Aunt Bethany. She said she needed our help fixing breakfast for everybody."

"Luke? Who is it?" Aunt Bethany called from inside the house.

"Mark's kids." He didn't sound too happy.

A moment later Aunt Bethany pulled the door wide. She was still in her bathrobe. "Come in! Come in!"

Arlo hedged. "You said you needed help."

Aunt Bethany looked puzzled, slightly taken off guard, then as if she remembered. "Yes! I do, I do! I'm so glad you're here." She pushed past Uncle Luke and ushered them into the house. "I'm late getting started, so we need to get going."

"I'll help you." Cooper beamed at their uncle. Uncle Luke looked at Aunt Bethany. Arlo couldn't tell what message he sent, but she didn't think he welcomed Cooper's help.

"You best stay with me, Cooper." Arlo placed her hand on Cooper's shoulder. "Aunt Bethany needs us."

Cooper's face fell.

"Let's get you something to eat first." Aunt Bethany pulled chairs from the kitchen table. "We can't work on empty stomachs."

"Beth," Uncle Luke cautioned.

"You get dressed while I find something for us all to nibble on. We'll have real breakfast when everyone gets here."

"Everyone?"

"Luke, we talked about this. There's a work group from the church coming with Mr. Skipwith to scrape and sand Aunt Ginny Dee's clapboard and see if some of the stonework needs repointing. You'll be able to help with either."

"I have work in the west field."

She ignored him. "We're all helping and I'm preparing breakfast and lunch for the work crew. The children are here to help me. Now go."

He looked ready to object, but she ignored him. Cooper and Marley climbed up to share a chair. Aunt Bethany beamed. "Arlo, look in the fridge for the orange juice. Marley, there are cups in the sideboard. Cooper, napkins are in the drawer there. Can you fold them for me? We'll have a muffin to get us started."

It felt good to Arlo to be told what to do, to see that the little kids were put to work, and to know that Aunt Bethany had a plan for the day. It was a relief for somebody bigger, older, to take charge.

Arlo had never worked a waffle iron, but Aunt Bethany was patient with her, and she soon caught on. By the second batch Arlo lifted waffles golden brown and fluffy from the iron while Aunt Bethany browned sausages in two giant cast-iron skillets. Cooper folded every paper napkin Aunt Bethany owned. Marley climbed onto the counter to collect plates from the cupboard.

By eight o'clock Arlo could hear the distant rumble of car and truck motors through the orchard. By eight fifteen, men walked through the trees and down the lane to the benches and planks Uncle Luke had slammed together across sawhorses in the yard.

"Pa!" Cooper squealed, running straight into his arms.

Mr. Skipwith clapped Pa's shoulder. "Fine-looking children, Mark, every one."

Pa scooped Cooper up and held him close.

"They're worth whatever sacrifices it takes on your part to keep them."

Pa's neck reddened, right up through his face. Arlo edged closer.

"I saw you watching me in town, last night, when we came out of the bar, but I swear," her pa whispered to Mr. Skipwith, "I didn't drink, just caught up with some old friends. We just shot some pool, passed the time—that's all."

Mr. Skipwith leveled his gaze with her pa's but didn't hesitate. "I believe you, Mark. I'm more concerned with the company you're keeping to do that. Trouble follows Rob."

Pa bristled. Arlo knew he didn't like being told what to do, but if he'd take criticism off anybody, it was Mr. Skipwith. Pa trusted him, looked up to him. Still, Arlo held her breath until she saw the fight go out of her pa.

She glanced nervously at her Uncle Luke as he walked closer, watching the exchange, his jaw set.

Mr. Skipwith turned then, acting like that conversation had never taken place. "Luke, Bethany, this is mighty good of you to host us. We'll work hard in appreciation for this fine meal. I know it will mean a lot to your Aunt Ginny."

"Helping her move the sale closer." Luke looked away from Mr. Skipwith, but it didn't seem to deter either man. Arlo's ears perked again.

"That may be, but I wouldn't count the farm out yet," Mr. Skipwith cautioned. "You still think you can make a go of it?"

Uncle Luke looked him in the eye. "I know I can. I just need some help."

"Looks to me like you've got it. Right here. Right now."

Luke looked less certain.

"Anyway, it's a start. This breakfast looks fit for kings. You want to pray?"

"Not sure I'm the one to do that."

"It's your home. You're the spiritual leader of your home, son."

Uncle Luke looked at Mr. Skipwith, blinked, then looked at the group. Arlo held her breath. Everybody was waiting for him, even her pa.

Finally, Uncle Luke bowed his head. Everybody else did the same.

"Lord, we thank You for this food, for the hands that prepared it, and for the men here to help today. Give us the strength to do what You will." There was a long pause. "Help us *be* what You will. In Jesus' name, amen."

When Arlo lifted her head, she caught a cautious flicker of hope in her pa's eyes.

CHAPTER FOURTEEN

LATE SATURDAY MORNING Ginny said goodbye to her landlady and lowered the back seat of her car to create more open space. She loaded her last sets of botanical presses, straps, driers, and ventilators, then spread a clean tarp over the remaining trunk space before hefting the seven large clay pots she'd filled to the brim with soil, perennial roots, bulbs, and cuttings, as well as Graham Thomas and Abraham Darby roses. She set in the four long flats of Vinca minor ground cover and the tray of annuals that she'd bought from the garden center. There was just room on the front seat and floor to stack her suitcases and two boxes of books.

It was all more than she'd be able to keep when moving to England, but since she expected to be in Virginia for the next several months, she might as well enjoy all she owned. She could always donate later what she couldn't carry. Most of all, through her favorite plants she could leave a little of herself in New Scrivelsby.

She hadn't planned to keep the botanical presses and related artistic equipment. She'd only ever used it all as a hobby, creating gifts for friends and local auction events to raise money for good causes. It wasn't practical to cart all that to England.

She'd meant to donate the lot to the community college arts

department, but it occurred to her that Marley and Cooper might like to learn to press flowers and leaves, might have fun collecting them and making pictures. She'd bet Arlo would, too, if she'd allow herself the freedom to enjoy the craft, and if she'd allow Ginny to teach her. If the children enjoyed the hobby, she could give her supplies to them. If not, she could donate them somewhere in New Scrivelsby.

Ginny had intended to return to the farm Sunday or Monday, but she'd finished all she needed to do in Cape May County and, truth be told, she missed the farm. She missed the children. Both of those things sent red flags to her heart.

With no one living in her house to answer the phone, calling ahead with her change in plans would mean contacting Bethany or Luke. She didn't especially want to do that, and long distance was a charge she didn't want to place on her landlady's bill. They'd have their meal plans in place, and after the long drive back, Ginny wouldn't be ready to pick up her kitchen apron that evening anyway.

If she wasn't too tired, she might go to church the next day. She'd come to like attending the New Scrivelsby Community Church. She liked the older pastor, appreciated when he tried to bring in the times and culture in which the Bible was written, enjoyed those insights that she'd not seen on her own and hadn't heard before.

She'd like it even better if Mark and the children would go with her or if it didn't feel strange that Luke and Bethany sat close to the front on the other side of the church, never acknowledging her or inviting her to sit with them. Maybe they didn't see her; maybe no one told them she was there.

She knew that was a fantasy on her part, but she wouldn't make it awkward for them. After all, it was their church and she was just a visitor, a transient. But she needed to go, needed to worship with other people, to sing the hymns, hear the sermon. She was careful to sit near the back, going in at the last minute and slipping out right after the benediction, when everyone stood to sing the final hymn. *No attachments. I won't be there long.*

Ginny sighed as she pulled onto Route 95 South. Maybe one day, once she was in England, she'd find a church she could really take part in, become part of a church family. She'd be a foreigner there, a transplant, hopefully one day an immigrant. Would she be accepted? She didn't know. *One day at a time, Lord Jesus. One day at a time.*

Pulling onto Christmas Lane late that afternoon, Ginny was surprised at the number of cars and even pickup trucks pulling out of the long drive from the farm. A couple of drivers smiled and waved; one blew his horn, stuck his thumb out the window in a thumbs-up gesture, and grinned broadly. Puzzled, Ginny waved back.

By the time she reached the house the only vehicle she saw was the familiar green Chevy station wagon belonging to Will Skipwith, but he was nowhere in sight.

Something was different about the house. At first glance she couldn't tell exactly what it was. It took a full thirty seconds before she stepped out of the car, stared, and whispered, "The paint's gone." *Sanded to the bone.*

Marley and Cooper ran, laughing, from the side of the house. A black dog with a long white patch on its chest—its head nearly as tall as Marley—loped beside them, panting, its bright eyes glued to a big stick that Cooper held high.

"Throw it, Cooper! You've got to throw it!" Marley ordered.

Cooper threw it wild. It whacked Ginny's car. Ginny jumped. The children stopped dead in their tracks. They caught sight of Ginny; their eyes filled with joy and then sudden trepidation. Ginny was thankful the stick hadn't hit her, thankful it hadn't cracked her windshield or left more than the tiny scratch it did on the driver's door of her car.

"Uh-oh," Marley whispered.

"Aunt Ginny Dee!" Cooper's chin wobbled.

"He didn't mean to." Marley took Cooper's arm, ready to shield him. "It was an accident."

Tears filled Cooper's eyes.

"Yes, I see that, but you shouldn't be throwing sticks—ever."

"He just wanted Bailey to fetch it."

"Bailey?"

"Our new dog. Isn't he beautiful?" Marley wrapped her arm around the panting black dog beside her, its one ear cocked up and the other flopped down. "Arlo named him Bailey because he's our Christmas dog!"

"Christmas dog?"

"Yeah, you know, like George Bailey in our movie."

"Movie?

"*It's a Wonderful Life*!" Marley sounded as if she shouldn't need to explain. "That's Pa's favorite movie, so we named him Bailey because he saved Cooper's life."

"Saved Cooper's life?" Ginny's head spun and she didn't know what to say. *Is Bailey part of the proverbial camel moving into my tent?* "Where did he come from?"

"He saved Cooper's life!" Marely repeated. "Yesterday! Cooper fell in the creek and near drowned, and I ran to get Arlo and Arlo couldn't get him out at first and Bailey kept his head up till Arlo could come but she couldn't get his red sneaker. It's at the bottom of the creek somewhere. That's why he's got no shoes, but Aunt Bethany says she'll get him some more."

It was a long and confusing speech—Marley in full storytelling mode—but Ginny's takeaway was focused on the fact that Cooper was still alive, not drowned, and the sudden realization that while she'd not been here disaster had struck, or very nearly. "Where was your father when all this happened?"

"Gone to Leesburg with Uncle Luke."

"Where is he now?"

"Behind the house. They're all back there. Nearly done."

"Nearly done what?"

Marley shrugged. Cooper had stopped crying and spoke up. "Big doings!"

"They scraped off all the paint," Marley explained. "Pa said they'll paint next, but not today."

"Who did all this?"

"A bunch of men. Mr. Skippy started it."

At that moment Will walked from the back of the house to the front, Luke on one side and Mark on the other. Whatever joke was being told must have been a good one. All three smiled as they walked. One look at Ginny and they stopped short.

"What's going on?"

Will sheepishly tipped his painter's cap. "Ginny. We didn't think you'd be back for another day or two. We'd hoped to surprise you. Welcome home."

Arlo and Bethany walked from the other side of the house, deep in conversation—the first time Ginny'd seen the two together without Arlo's arms crossed over her chest.

"Surprise me?" *Surprise is an understatement.*

"You came back!" Arlo sounded stunned.

"Of course I came back—early." She stressed the *early* part.

Marley hugged Ginny's legs and looked up into her face. "We scraped your house. Us and all those other guys."

"I see that."

"Next time we'll paint. Pa says I can paint too."

"Me too! I can paint too!" Cooper asserted.

"I don't know what to say." All Ginny could think of was that there was no way she could pay all those men. "What will this cost me?"

Mark's face clouded. Luke stiffened.

"Nothing but a smile." Will spoke softly, doing his best to ease the tension. "It's a gift from Acts."

"Axe?"

"Acts—like in the book of Acts, where everyone lived and worked together. The men from the church join forces once a month and help someone in the community—acts of kindness—Acts. Today was your turn—all the Pickerings' turn."

"So, we're a charity case now?" Her words accused, a pail of ice water thrown over the group.

"Nobody receives the care of Acts because they're a charity case." Will spoke gently but stood firm. "We help because we're the church—families helping families. Wetherill Pickering's Christmas Tree Farm has been an institution in New Scrivelsby for decades. Every local family gets their Christmas tree here—has done for three generations. We just wanted to help."

Ginny looked at all the faces—the faces that had just moments before been smiling and easy together. And now, with her few words, no one was smiling. Each looked tense or defensive, just as they had when she'd left for New Jersey.

They came together while I was away. What have I done to them now? Ginny put her hand to her mouth, failing to cover the quiver there. "I—I'm sorry. I didn't mean to sound ungrateful."

But Luke had already retreated into his hard shell. Ginny saw him lock eyes with Bethany and motion her toward home. Arlo crossed her arms over her chest. Marley looked up, confused. Mark called the children to follow him to the barn.

"Thank you—all of you!" Ginny called, knowing it was too little too late.

"I'll see you all at church tomorrow, Mark." Will sent Cooper after his dad. Mark didn't turn but lifted his hand in acknowledgment.

Will didn't move.

"I was rude."

"Suspicious."

"I'm sorry, I'm just not used to . . ."

"Not used to anyone helping? Doing something special just because?"

"No." Ginny removed her hand from her mouth. "But I didn't mean to—"

He smiled. "Mess up?"

She nodded, no longer offended but sorry to offend.

"We all mess up, Ginny. No shame in that."

"But they looked so—" Ginny couldn't finish.

"They're tired now. You'd have been proud of them today. They worked hard, did a good job. Really pulled together with the rest of the crew. I believe they enjoyed it, surprised themselves they can work so well together."

"A miracle."

"Miracles happen." Will held her gaze.

"Do they?" She wasn't certain.

He stepped closer. "More often than you know."

Stepping apart felt unnatural, until she broke eye contact.

"Looks like you have quite a load there. Can I help you with it?" He replaced his cap.

"Oh, no. Thank you. It's mostly plants for the farm, the garden."

Will smiled again. "That sounds promising."

She didn't want to give the wrong impression. "I just wanted to . . . leave something of myself here, for when I'm gone."

His smile fell. "Sounds ominous. You've got a long life ahead."

"That's not what I meant." *You know that.*

"Well, you won't want to leave them in your car. Let me help." She hesitated.

"Learn to say yes, and thank you, Ginny," he scolded gently.

She stepped aside. *He's the dearest and the most aggravating man. How did he get them to all pull together like this? Why couldn't I?*

By the time they'd unloaded Ginny's car and set all the plants on the porch and into the shade, the sun had lowered in the western sky. Will hefted her two suitcases and set them inside the front door. Ginny hauled her botanical presses, hugging them to her chest.

"What are those?"

"Botanical presses—for flowers and leaves and such. I thought I'd show Marley and Cooper how to press flowers. Arlo, too, if she's interested."

"That's a fine idea. The children need hobbies—fun things to do. They like to help and they're smart."

Ginny stared at him. "For someone without children, you

certainly know how to work with them—the young ones and the grown-up ones."

Will shrugged. "Dad taught me well." He headed for the steps. "I'll see you in church tomorrow."

Ginny blushed, sure she couldn't face the congregation after all they'd done. "Oh, I don't know if—"

Will didn't speak until he reached his car. "Luke and Bethany go every week. I've seen you there."

"Yes, but—"

"Mark and the children are coming tomorrow for the first time. They need you with them."

"Do they?" After her recent performance, she couldn't imagine anything further from the truth.

"More than you know." And he was gone.

CHAPTER FIFTEEN

AS GINNY DRESSED FOR CHURCH the next morning, she wondered if the children and Mark would come over for breakfast or if her poor and ungrateful performance yesterday had frightened them away. She couldn't blame them if they avoided her.

From what she saw they were on growing terms with Luke and Bethany. Ginny knew she should be glad for that—the brothers working together, the little ones with their newfound dog, Bethany and Arlo walking together. She was glad. *It's just that . . . I don't want to be forgotten.* There. She'd thought it through, confessed it in her mind.

Ginny gave herself a little shake. She needed to be bigger than this, better than this. *What matters is that the brothers reconcile, help each other.*

Bethany can be a wonderful aunt, a mothering figure for the children, if the men work out their differences. It would be an answer for Bethany and her yearning heart. Ginny believed it, wanted that for all of them. *I'll be leaving soon. It shouldn't matter for me. But what about the farm? When I leave, when I sell, what then for them? They'll all have to move and that will break up the family again. They'll have to move because of me. And where will they go? What will they do? Will Mark even be able to keep his children?*

The downstairs kitchen door opened, bringing Ginny back to her senses and quickening the beat of her heart. She hurried down the stairs, pasting on her best smile.

But the only one in the kitchen was Mark, opening the refrigerator. He looked up, but there was no smile. "Just replacing the milk we borrowed while you were gone."

"Thank you." Her smile faded. "Are the children coming in? I can fix breakfast—won't take but a few minutes."

"No, thanks. I picked up some pastries when I went for the milk. We'll eat in the barn."

"That's not necessary, Mark. I really don't mind—"

"Probably for the best." His hand was on the door to go before Ginny could get her words out.

"I'm sorry for the way I behaved yesterday, Mark. It was just . . . all so unexpected. I never imagined you'd all work so hard to help me like that. I'm not used to anyone doing things for me."

He hesitated but didn't turn to face her. "It was Will's idea."

"I can't think why. Such a generous thing to do—from all of you. I didn't know how to respond. I'm sorry."

He turned to face her.

"Thank you. Thank you, Mark."

"Letting us live here, it's a lot for us. I wanted to help you . . . help the family. It seemed a good way, and Will . . . Well, it's hard to say no to Will."

Family. Does he mean Luke and Bethany? Does he mean me? She knotted her hands, hoping to find words, the right thing to say, but nothing came. He turned again to leave. "Coffee. I'm going to make coffee. Would you like some to go with your pastries?"

He didn't answer right away.

"I bought fresh cream yesterday . . . With sugar? I brought some chocolate milk from the dairy for the children."

Seconds ticked by. "Okay. Yeah, sure. Coffee sounds good."

Ginny breathed. "I'll put the pot on right away. Tell the children there's chocolate milk—if you want, I mean."

He nodded, opened the door, walked through, but said quietly over his shoulder, "They like chocolate milk."

A half hour later Ginny poured liberal glasses of chocolate milk, made certain Mark's coffee cup stayed filled and warm, and did her best not to reach out and touch the children while they ate and drank. Cooper didn't want all his pastry and offered to share with Ginny what he hadn't slipped to Bailey, who, ears cocked one up and one down, waited patiently for crumbs beneath the table. It was squished, and the sweetest, stickiest gift Ginny could imagine, but she wouldn't have cared if Bailey had taken the first bite. She was that glad to sit beside Cooper. Even Arlo seemed to loosen up a little.

Ten o'clock came and Mark herded the children toward the barn to get dressed.

At the back door, Ginny gathered her courage and said, "Will said you're planning to go to church this morning."

"Yeah, well, we thought we'd give it a try."

Arlo shot back defensively, "We always used to go."

"Oh? I didn't know."

They were gone before she garnered enough courage to invite them to sit with her, the thing she most wanted to say.

Almost an hour later Ginny drove to church alone. Mark's truck was still parked behind the barn—at least, Ginny hadn't heard it rumble up the drive. She didn't wait for the service to start this time but found her usual empty pew near the back.

The congregation stood for the opening prayer. The first hymn was well underway when the church door opened behind Ginny. She imagined it was the last usher stepping in for start of service, so she didn't turn to look, resistant to making eye contact. The thundering of little feet pounding the wooden floor behind her came as a surprise, though not as great as the surprise of Marley zooming into the pew, headed straight for her side, Cooper on her heels, and Arlo trying to shush them. Mark followed. They all took up hymnbooks, Arlo craning over the other two to see the number on Ginny's page.

Ginny thought her heart might burst. She held her hymnbook lower when Marley tugged her hand, so Marley and Cooper could see the page even though they couldn't read the words. She couldn't read them either, though it had nothing to do with the print and everything to do with the sudden grateful wells in her eyes.

Family. Family in church. It was the first time Ginny could say that since Curtis went to war in 1943. *Nearly fifty years. Thank You, God. Thank You.*

Pastor Edwards welcomed everyone. There were announcements and prayer concerns read, followed by a Scripture reading from Luke 15: the story of the prodigal son and his father who ran to welcome him home on his return. Ginny had a hard time concentrating. She was more taken with the wonder of Marley's arm resting on her thigh and the fact that Cooper had crept to her other side and leaned his head against her rib cage. She didn't want to move, didn't want to breathe for fear they'd disappear or change their position. She wrapped an arm around each one, the words *thank You, thank You, thank You* flowing from her heart in an unbroken rhythm.

Arlo eyed her tentatively but did not pull the little ones away.

Pastor Edwards's voice rose as he neared the end of the Scripture reading.

The relevance of the Scripture, of the story and the pastor's joy broke through Ginny's prayer of thanksgiving. *It's us. We're a family of prodigals. Me. Mark. What about Luke—the older son, never the prodigal . . . but is that true? Is that possible? Aren't we all runaways from God in one way or another, at some time or another? Haven't we all deserted Him, broken His heart, demanded our inheritance—bent on grabbing our wants?*

It was a new thought but held great familiarity. Ginny swallowed, remembering the day less than a month after they'd buried her father when Harold returned home angry, resentful. He'd tried to enlist but was rejected, declared 4-F on account of his flat feet. It was the same day Curtis received his draft notice, and the day she began to break her mother's heart.

It was hot that spring, Ginny's last year of high school. She was slated for graduation, her crowning achievement—and neither her father nor Curtis would be there.

Curtis had taken the bus for some kind of orientation meeting. He'd be back by Monday but had a mere twenty-one days to "settle personal affairs" before reporting for boot camp. Boot camp, and then the war, wherever it took him.

Ginny was frantic. She couldn't lose Curtis too. "Please, Mama, sign for me. You know Curtis is a good man. I love him and you know he loves me."

Ginny still remembered how her mama had laid her work-worn hand gently on her cheek and tucked a loose lock of hair behind her ear. "Precious daughter. I know you love him. I know Curtis is a good man, but he's going to war, and you're young."

Ginny had pulled away.

"I know you don't want to hear this, but listen to me. Waiting won't rip a strong cord of love; it won't break. I want you to be sure once he comes home. War can change people." At least she never said *if he comes back*. For that, Ginny was grateful.

"Then let us have what happiness we can have before he goes."

Wearily, Mama shook her head. "When he comes back, if you still want to marry, I will bless your marriage with all my heart. You know I love Curtis. I'll welcome him as your husband and as my son. I'll give you your grandmother's ring. It's meant for you. And Promised Land—it will belong to the two of you. But your daddy said to wait, and I agree. I can't change his last wish, and I need you here now. I've just lost your father. I can't lose you too."

"You can't change it because Daddy's not here, but because he's not here everything *is* changed. I can't lose Curtis. I don't want him to forget me. I can't wait, Mama. We can't wait. I want to go be near where he's stationed."

"You have no idea where he'll end up and you haven't even

finished school. You won't be able to get a decent job. I need your help here and—"

"Curtis will get pay from the Army."

"That won't be right away and won't be enough once he's deployed."

"Then give us whatever you and Daddy plan to give us someday. Help us get started now. That can get us going. Now is when it matters."

She remembered her mother's face. It was as if Ginny had slapped her, but Ginny's need to go was too great to back down.

Curtis returned from his orientation the next day.

Ginny poured her heart out to him as he sorted his belongings, packing away everything he'd not take to boot camp. "It's not fair. We shouldn't have to wait. Mama and Daddy were barely older than me when they got married and nobody stopped them."

"They're afraid of what the war might do to me, and what that might do to you." Curtis boxed his set of books.

"I love you. Nothing's gonna change that." She'd pulled him toward her, wrapped his arms around her. He'd buried his face in her hair. "Let's go—now. Let's not wait. Please."

"You're a temptress, Ginny Dee. There's nothing in this world I want more."

"Then let's do it. Let's go. Tonight." She'd pulled him closer yet. She knew what she was doing to him, hoped he'd not regret it, but she didn't care. She couldn't stay on the farm with Harold lording it over her and her mama treating her like a baby and all the time waiting and wondering if Curtis would return alive.

He shook his head. "Ginny. Ginny Dee. Your mom. We can't—"

"Once it's done what's she going to do? She'll get used to the idea. I'll come back here after . . . after you go. I'll work like a dog on the farm if that's what she and Harold want. When you come back, we can both work here. This is our home. Daddy promised us Promised Land, remember? It's ours—Mama even said. It will always be ours, but getting married now we'll have had our time together before you go—what no one can ever take away from us. You'll be able to take our memories with you. I'll be able to hold on, knowing I'm your wife."

"What she said, about no money until I get Army pay . . . It's true. I don't have enough for more than bus tickets."

"I'll get some."

"Where?"

"Let me worry about that."

"Ginny Dee. Pastor Raymond won't marry us without your mama signing for you."

Ginny had pulled away from him then. She hadn't wanted to hear it, but what he'd said was true.

"Maybe—"

"Maybe what?" Ginny was ready for any straw.

"I heard some guys talking about going up to Elkton, Maryland, to get married. There's some wedding chapel there. They call Elkton the Marriage Capital of the East Coast. Used to be you could get married there without any waiting period."

"Used to be?"

"Now only if you're in the military or being drafted for the war."

"Like you." She looked up into his eyes, hoping, pleading.

He looked down at her, and she knew his power to choose was gone. She saw him swallow, moisten his lips, felt his chest heave up and down. "Like me." He pulled her mouth to his and sank his lips into hers.

Ginny'd waited until her mama was fixing supper. She snuck into her mother's room and lifted her grandmother's ring from her jewelry box. She found fifty dollars stuck in the bottom of a sock in her daddy's old sock drawer and tucked both into her skirt pocket. It wasn't right. She knew it at the time but convinced herself she had to do it. The ring would one day be hers anyway. She wouldn't sell it unless she had to. She'd tell Curtis later. Together they could pay back the money from his Army pay.

She'd been so convinced her mama would yield, would understand when all was said and done, would let her come home once Curtis was deployed. But Mama never answered Ginny's letters, not even when Ginny found herself pregnant and alone, not even when she lost the baby. The only letter she'd ever received came from Harold. Ginny'd memorized it.

You thought only of yourself when Mama needed you most, when we should have stuck together as a family. You broke her heart. So now she has no husband and no daughter. As far as I'm concerned, my sister's dead. You stole Grandma's ring from Mama. Well, enjoy it. You've got your inheritance and that's all you'll ever get. Forget coming home. You and Curtis made your bed, now you've got to lie in it. Mama can't take any more heartache, and I won't.

 Leave us alone.

Harold

Pastor Edwards left his pulpit and walked to the center aisle, still speaking, drawing Ginny's attention back to the moment.

"From a long way off the father spotted his son. He could only have done that because he'd been looking, hoping, praying for the return of his boy—the one who'd gone his own way, the son who'd demanded his inheritance, no matter that his father still lived.

"Picture it: He sees his wayward son in the distance. Surely by this time the young man's bedraggled, dirty—no longer the cocky young man that left. He's more alone than he's ever been.

"But the father doesn't care about any of that. He's been looking for his son, longing for his son. No matter that that son had broken this father's heart, the man wastes no time, not a single moment. He lifts his robes and runs—runs! A thing no dignified patriarch would dare do in that time and place—straight down that long road, past all the village people and naysayers ready to cast the young man out for the disgrace and financial loss he'd brought the family and community by squandering his portion of the inheritance. With great, unbounded joy that father embraces his son, welcoming him home. Can you see it? Can you picture it?"

Ginny could. She stroked Cooper's hair. She squeezed Marley's arm, and she looked at Mark, whose eyes found hers. *Prodigals. We're both prodigals. Why, after all these years, do I still feel like a prodigal waiting on the doorstep? Does that ever change?*

Once we come home, who do we become? Who do I become?

"Surely that young man was overwhelmed," the pastor continued. "He began his confession—*I have sinned against heaven, and in thy sight, and am no more worthy to be called thy son.* He wanted to work for his father. He never expected to be reinstated as a son. But that father ignored his son's limited vision. He said to his servants, *Bring forth the best robe*—that would have been his own robe—*and put it on him; and put a ring on his hand*—that would have been his own family signet ring, a sign of authority—*and shoes on his feet.* Servants did not wear shoes. Sons wore shoes. He called for the fatted calf and a party to make merry for *this my son was dead, and is alive again; he was lost, and is found.* Can you hear it? What a party! Music, dancing, celebration!"

Heads nodded. Hands went to throats, including Ginny's.

"When the older son came in from the fields, he asked what all the hoopla was about. He was told that his brother had come home, that his father had killed the fatted calf, because he'd received him safe and sound. The party was not so much for the son himself but because the father was rejoicing, celebrating.

"But the older son refused to rejoice with his father—his father, who he knew had been heartbroken and longing for his younger son a long time. The older son became so angry he wouldn't even go inside to the party, not to his father and not to his brother, not even to save face for the family in the community.

"So that father humiliated himself a second time that day. He left his party and went out to his older son, entreating him to come in. Entreating—beseeching, begging his son.

"But this son was jealous, furious that he'd stayed home and worked for his father and the family all these years and yet his father had not given him a fatted calf to celebrate with his friends. This older son said, *But as soon as this thy son was come*—notice he didn't say 'my brother'—*which hath devoured thy living with harlots*—how did he know what his brother had done with the money? He'd not even spoken to him. But he said to his father, *Thou hast killed for him the fatted calf.*

"By this time the father could well have lost his temper, but he didn't. He still loved this angry, ungrateful, jealous, self-righteous son. He said, *Son, thou art ever with me, and all that I have is thine. It was meet that we should make merry, and be glad: for this thy brother was dead, and is alive again; and was lost, and is found.*

"The message is this: Come home. Come home. No matter where you've been, no matter what you've done, you can always come home to our Father in heaven who loves you. He's waiting for you. He's not waiting with a hickory switch or a branding iron. He's not even standing off to the side, arms crossed over His chest, ready to read you the riot act. He's been looking for you, waiting, longing, and He's running to meet you, to embrace you, to welcome you home.

"Are you ready? Are you willing?"

Ginny couldn't swallow the lump in her throat. She glanced at Mark, tears streaming down his face.

"Let us pray."

Ginny didn't slip out the back door during the last hymn this time. She waited with the children. From the corner of her eye, she saw Mark wiping his eyes on his sleeve, saw Arlo lay her hand on her father's arm.

Ginny's heart swelled. There'd been no one to welcome her home, no one longing for her return as far as she knew, but could she be that person for Mark and his children? She wanted to become that person, that Running Father. She wasn't sure how to do that and still hold on to her own dreams, still protect her heart in case—*when* they left again. *Show me, Lord. Make me in Your image. Make me like You.*

After the last amen and before Mark and the children and Ginny made their way from the pew, a man stopped to speak to Mark, delaying their leaving a bit more. By the time the man shook Mark's hand and turned, people, including Bethany and Luke, were filing down the center aisle to exit.

Ginny was glad she was at the far end of the pew. She wondered if Luke and Bethany knew Mark had planned to come to church. She watched. For a few brief seconds Luke's eyes met Mark's. Ginny couldn't see Mark's face, but Luke looked as if he'd been caught in a train wreck. He nodded once, at least Ginny thought he did, toward Mark, some sort of acknowledgment. But what did it mean?

The moment passed and the tide of people swept by, hesitating only for those ahead to shake the pastor's hand at the door. Ginny had never actually met Pastor Edwards. Her palms sweated. She needed to thank him, thank someone, for the work the men of the church had performed at the farm yesterday.

She didn't hear what passed between Mark and the pastor. The children, between them, distracted her, as Arlo did her best to explain to her younger sister why she wasn't allowed to take money out of the collection plate even though the man had passed it down the pew in front of them all, and telling Cooper he wasn't allowed to take home the pencil and paper he'd discovered in the pew's holder.

By the time Ginny reached the pastor she had a little thank-you speech planned, hoping it would somehow reach the ears of the Acts group. But she wasn't prepared for the man's enthusiastic smile or taking her hand in both of his warm ones. "Miss Pickering, I'd heard you're back. I'm so sorry I haven't been out to the farm to meet you yet."

"Mrs. Boyden," Ginny said automatically.

"Mrs. Boyden, my apologies. We're all glad you and Mark and the children have come. I hope you'll come again."

"I will. Thank you for your sermon, Pastor Edwards." Ginny meant it, wanted to say more, had intended to say more, but couldn't in that moment remember what it was.

"Welcome home, Mrs. Boyden." He smiled, releasing her hand.

Welcome home. Welcome home. Welcome home. If there were more precious, needed words in the world, Ginny didn't know them.

Halfway down the steps Marley ran up to meet her. "Can I ride with you, Aunt Ginny Dee?"

"Me too," Cooper urged. "I want to ride with you."

She looked at Mark, sure he would say no. But it was Arlo who grabbed the children's hands. "You stay with us."

But Ginny didn't want it to end. *Family. We can be family.* "I was thinking of going to the diner for lunch. Will you all join me?" She looked at Mark.

Embarrassed, taken off guard, he looked away for a moment, clearly searching for words.

"My treat. I've missed you all." The words surprised Ginny as much as they surprised Mark and Arlo. "Please."

"Go to the diner for lunch! Yay!" Marley jumped for joy. "Can we ride with Aunt Ginny Dee, Pa? Can we?"

For the first time Arlo seemed speechless, but Mark nodded, looking as if he wasn't quite sure where this whirlwind was taking him. "I guess, if it's okay with Aunt Ginny Dee."

Ginny wasn't used to having children in her car. Would they sit still? Wear their seatbelts? But her heart warmed as an image came to mind. *Sweet rain in the heat of summer.*

CHAPTER SIXTEEN

ARLO MEANT TO FOLLOW HER PA to the field after breakfast at Aunt Ginny Dee's that Monday. She was just half a minute behind, long enough to bend down and tie her sneakers on the back porch, when she heard Aunt Bethany in the yard.

"Mark—can I speak with you a moment?"

"Bethany. What's up?"

"This isn't really my business, but I'm just wondering—what about school? I know Marley and Cooper are little, but shouldn't Arlo be in school?"

Before he could answer, Arlo bounded off the back porch. "That's right. It's none of your business."

Aunt Bethany's eyebrows nearly reached her hairline.

Pa set his hand on Arlo's shoulder. "We'll start that up in the fall." He pulled the bill of his cap lower but didn't look at Aunt Bethany or Arlo. "When we're settled."

Aunt Bethany didn't look satisfied. "What grade are you in, Arlo?"

Arlo shifted from one foot to the other. She should have seen this coming down the pike. But her pa came to the rescue.

"We've had to move quite a bit and the kids haven't been with me all the time."

"I understand that. I'm just asking what grade Arlo's in." Aunt Bethany was no longer talking to Arlo. It wasn't a good sign.

"I'll catch up, soon as we get settled somewhere."

"Going to school isn't optional, Mark. It's the law. If social services realizes Arlo's not been attending school—"

"You keep them out of here!" Arlo all but shouted.

"Arlo, calm down." Pa tightened his hand on Arlo's shoulder.

"She'll turn like the rest of them, Pa. Don't let her—"

"Arlo, go inside."

"But, Pa."

"Now. I need to talk to Aunt Bethany. Alone."

Arlo jutted her chin.

"Inside, I said. Now."

Arlo glared at her aunt, eyes pleading with her pa, but finally turned and stomped toward the house. She let the screen door slam but crouched behind the rocker on the porch to listen.

"I'm not trying to cause trouble, Mark. I've no intention of contacting social services, but someone else might if Arlo's not registered in school."

Arlo heard her pa draw a deep breath and let out a long sigh. "We've had to move so much. It's not been easy."

"I understand that." Aunt Bethany's voice softened. "Can Arlo read? Can she do math?"

Blood boiling, Arlo clenched her fists but dared not let on she was listening.

"She can read, but I guess she's a mite behind. She adds our grocery bills, keeps track of our cash. If we're still here in the fall, guess I'll get her started at the school."

There was a long pause.

"They'll want to know what grade she's finished. They'll test her reading and math at the very least. If she's too far behind . . . it will be hard for Arlo to be set back."

"You mean with little kids. I guess so."

Arlo peeked over the railing in time to see Aunt Bethany nod.

"I can help her . . . if you'll agree . . . if she'll let me, work with me. I've volunteered one day a week at the elementary school the last few years, helping children with vocabulary and reading. Arlo's bright. I believe I could catch her up to her grade level if we work through the summer."

Arlo couldn't take it anymore. "I'm not workin' on math all summer! And I'm not stupid! I can read."

Her pa didn't even turn. "Get out here, Arlo. Now."

She'd given herself away, but she'd needed to defend herself. *Aunt Bethany's not even my blood aunt. What right does she have? She's got no say over me!* Arlo stomped down the stairs, jaw set, arms crossed over her chest.

"What she says is right. You're not gonna want to be set back with the little kids." It wasn't a question. Pa didn't even look at Arlo.

"She's not the boss of us, Pa. We might not even stay—you said so."

"I hope you do stay, Arlo . . . all of you—with all my heart." Aunt Bethany tried to make eye contact with Arlo. Arlo felt it but refused to meet her halfway.

"How do you see this working, Bethany?"

"Arlo could come to my house for lessons—not like school, but that we'd work together."

"Luke's okay with this? You talked it over?" Pa wrapped his arm around Arlo's shoulders. This time she knew that meant he had her back, even if she didn't like where this was going.

Aunt Bethany looked away then. "It's only right. I want to help. I want to see Arlo succeed." She pinched her lips, moistened them. "I'd rather meet at my house. I want the children to feel at home there."

"But that's not our home." Arlo wouldn't let Aunt Bethany take over, no matter how much she thought she knew best.

"Arlo—enough."

"That's true, Arlo. Maybe it's better we meet in the barn or maybe at Aunt Ginny Dee's. I don't think she'd mind. Just until you feel caught up. We'll make it fun."

"I feel plenty caught up." Arlo wasn't buying *fun*.

"You work with her until your Aunt Bethany says you're caught up. We straight, Arlo?"

Arlo dug the toe of her sneaker in the dirt.

"Are we straight?"

Arlo knew Pa didn't like repeating himself.

"Yes, sir."

"Appreciate this, Bethany."

"It's my pleasure. I know we'll get along fine."

Arlo knew no such thing.

By the second week in June the county's school year was officially over but Aunt Bethany was just warming up. Everybody helped in fields or gardens in the morning. Every afternoon, just after lunch, Aunt Bethany spread workbooks and piled readers by Aunt Ginny Dee's front porch swing—the swing Arlo had helped sand and give a fresh coat of paint so she could loll away summer hours. Not so she could sweat her brains out doing multiplication tables and fractions and whatever Aunt Bethany dreamed up next.

The decent thing about Aunt Bethany was that she often ended math lessons with a cooking or baking lesson using whatever she'd taught that day—like multiplying cups of flour or adding fractions with different denominators to come up with the right amount of sugar or decreasing fractions to find the right amount of vanilla extract to include in the recipe, or figuring how to increase all the ingredients to double or triple the batch of chocolate chip cookies or cupcakes or to make one regular pie and one small one.

Arlo'd never known much about cooking, and though she wasn't about to admit it to Aunt Bethany, she liked this kind of learning best. Marley begged to help but she had to stand on a chair to reach a bowl over the counter. Cooper stood on chairs tiptoe, ready to lick every spoon that dripped chocolate or cookie dough or cake batter.

Arlo worked hard not to show how pleased she was when something turned out and the family gleefully gobbled it up.

Aunt Ginny Dee didn't seem to mind the mess they made in her kitchen so long as they cleaned up and she got the first taste of Arlo's experiments. Arlo even caught proud glances between Aunt Ginny Dee and Aunt Bethany. Maybe all the fuss wasn't so bad, and maybe it would be good not to have to sit with the little kids in school come fall . . . if they stayed and if she couldn't talk her pa into letting her stay home.

Reading came later in the afternoon. First, Aunt Bethany or sometimes Aunt Ginny Dee read to all three of them from *The Secret Garden,* and that was pure magic. Arlo could imagine sneaking off to her own private garden with a rusted key and could just see those curtains and fountains of roses in her mind's eye.

But when it came time for Arlo to read out loud, it didn't go so well. It wasn't that Arlo didn't want to read; she'd just never done much of it, and the books Aunt Bethany figured she should be able to handle had words that were hard to sound out. Sometimes Aunt Bethany's mouth turned grim, and she tapped her fingernails, waiting for Arlo to hurry up. Those days Arlo was tempted to throw the book in the hedges and run off to the creek to catch tadpoles. But Aunt Bethany kept a direct line to Pa's ear, and Arlo was charged with setting a good example for the littles.

One such miserable session ended in a confrontation between them so bad that Aunt Bethany gathered up the books she'd brought and marched home to fix supper without a word.

Arlo pushed off hard with her bare feet, so hard the back of the swing hit the porch rail behind her.

Aunt Ginny Dee didn't even look up, just sat in the rocker nearby, shelling peas. "How'd you like that book?"

"It's stupid."

Aunt Ginny Dee nodded. "Maybe there's a better one, a more interesting one."

"They're all baby books. She wants me to read baby books."

"I don't think that's what she wants for you."

"Okay, so I'm the one that's stupid. I said it. Happy?"

"You're not stupid and I'm not happy." Aunt Ginny Dee looked up, considering. "I've never much liked people telling me what books to read. I like to pick my own. You need to pick your own, something that interests you."

"Like that's gonna happen."

"Have you ever been to a library?"

Arlo slowed down, letting the swing creak without pushing it to fly off its hooks. "We stopped at one outside Memphis to go to the bathroom."

"What was it like?"

"Tons of books—all on shelves. Near lost Marley when she saw this room they had for little kids, full of toys and books and short chairs."

"She liked that, did she?"

"Screamed bloody murder when we pulled her out."

"Did you check out a book?"

"What?"

"Did you take a book with you?"

"That woulda been stealing."

"Not if you had a library card."

Arlo let the swing go still. "I don't know what you're talking about."

"A library card lets you check out books. I've learned lots about gardening and cooking from library books."

"You mean if you have some card, they let you take books for free—legit?"

"Borrow. You can borrow books for free. Then when you're finished with those, you take them back and borrow others. Best of all you get to pick which ones you want."

Arlo was certain there was a catch. "You do that?"

"In New Jersey, where I lived. As long as I'm living here, I might as well get a library card and borrow some books. I can learn just about anything I want to know through books. Reading helps pass the time in the evenings." Aunt Ginny Dee kept shelling peas. "Maybe I'll go tomorrow."

Arlo was intrigued.

"Want to come?"

Arlo toed the floor, letting the swing move gently.

"If you found some books you like, you could read those instead of the ones Aunt Bethany brings. I don't think she'd mind what, as long as you're reading."

"They'd let me—take some, I mean?"

"Borrow. Yes, if we get you a card of your own. Marley and Cooper too. They might even have a special children's section they'd like."

It seemed impossible that anybody'd be giving books—or anything—out for free. "Horses. I want a book about horses."

"Horses." Aunt Ginny Dee nodded again.

Arlo could hardly believe her pa said yes. The next afternoon, instead of math or reading, Arlo, Marley, and Cooper piled into Aunt Ginny Dee's car and drove into New Scrivelsby. The ten-minute drive shot Arlo over the moon, doubt and anticipation fueling each step up the outside stairs to the old library. It must have been somebody's giant house once upon a time. Aunt Ginny Dee said that for the last sixty years it had housed the town's historical society on the upper floors and the public library on the main floor and basement.

It wasn't near as fancy or open or modern as the one they'd set foot in for ten minutes near Memphis, where they'd been shooed out for coming in barefoot. Not that Aunt Ginny Dee let them come barefoot or dirty. Even their hair was washed, combed, and braided. Their clothes were washed and ironed, and summer sandals—not flip-flops—shod all three pairs of feet. Arlo had been inclined to fuss over all that, but now, walking into the library, she held her head up and it felt good.

"Ginny Dee—Mrs. Boyden." The lady behind the front desk looked up, surprised. A girl about Arlo's age sat beside her, gluing book slips into the backs of books.

"Good afternoon, Louise." Aunt Ginny Dee smiled.

"Well, now, who all do we have here?"

"This is Arlo, Marley, and Cooper, my family."

"Yours?" The woman's eyes went wide.

"My grandnieces and grandnephew."

"Pickerings. We're all Pickerings," Arlo interjected, nodding more to the girl than to the woman.

The girl's eyes brightened in return. "Wetherill Pickering's Christmas Tree Farm?"

"That's right." Aunt Ginny Dee nodded.

"This is Emily, my granddaughter." The woman named Louise looked smug, as if having a granddaughter upped her in the food chain.

"We go there every year for our Christmas tree. I always wondered what it would be like to live on a Christmas tree farm," Emily enthused.

Arlo grinned, ready to launch into all the dramatics she could summon.

"Mark's children." The woman's mouth grimaced as if she were sucking lemons. "I heard he'd come back with . . . children."

"Yes." Aunt Ginny Dee kept smiling. "We're here to register for library cards and find some good books."

"Well, you have to be a county resident to get a card, you know."

Aunt Ginny Dee nodded. "Yes. Is there a problem?"

The woman leaned over the desk and whispered loud enough to be heard in the back room, "Not for you, I suppose, if you're staying. But can you actually vouch for them? I mean, will they bring the books back? I don't believe Mark ever stays anywhere long—transients, and I've heard he's . . . not always responsible. Done a bit of time, I understand."

Arlo felt heat climb her neck. She was about to give the woman what for when Aunt Ginny Dee pressed a hand on her arm. "Our address is Wetherill Pickering's Christmas Tree Farm. I believe a card for Arlo and one for me will be adequate. I can check the little ones' books out on my card. Now, do you need anything more to issue us the cards?"

Emily's eyes widened at the interchange.

Louise sat back, lifting her chin, but looked down her nose at Marley and at Cooper, who stood digging a booger out of his nose. Instinctively, Arlo slapped his hand away.

Marley grabbed Cooper's hand and whispered, "Stop it, Chicken Snot."

Arlo wanted to sink into the floorboards. She felt her jaw tighten. Itching built behind her eyes. This wasn't how she wanted to start out in a new town with the first girl her age that she'd met. But she was used to her siblings, used to bad things said about her pa, and she was used to snotty looks from grown-ups who didn't even know them. Well, she didn't have to take it. Marley and Cooper shouldn't have to take it. No book was worth that. Arlo grabbed Marley's and Cooper's hands and headed for the door. "Let's go."

"Arlo—" Aunt Ginny Dee spoke after her, but Arlo didn't turn.

Just as she reached the door, it swung inward. "Arlo Pickering!"

"Mr. Skippy!" Marley all but jumped into his arms.

"I'm glad to see you all!" Mr. Skipwith leaned down, smiled with his eyes, and looked like he meant it. "Come to get some books?"

"Horses!" Marley sang.

"Horses? Books about horses? Is that right?"

Arlo shifted Cooper's hand. "We were gonna find some, but not now. We gotta go."

Aunt Ginny Dee's hand reached for Arlo, making her pause. "Hello, Mr. Skipwith. It's good to see you."

"And you, Mrs. Boyden." Mr. Skipwith nodded, his smile stretching bigger still. "I saw your car parked out front."

That seemed to fluster and please Aunt Ginny Dee. "We just stopped in to get library cards and find some books, but . . ."

"About horses, I understand." His eyes flashed to Louise, whose mouth formed a rigid line.

"Arlo loves horses!" Marley danced, nearly on Mr. Skipwith's toes.

"I can understand why. Horses are magnificent animals. Did you have a particular book in mind, Arlo?"

Arlo felt the librarian's eyes following her, felt Emily's eyes on her. She shook her head. She didn't know any books to say. She just wanted to leave.

"One of my favorite horse books has always been *Black Beauty*. There're some sad parts to it, but it's a wonderful story. I think you'd like it too. Maybe you'd like to give that a try. See what you think."

Arlo considered, reluctantly.

"Mrs. Shellhorn"—Mr. Skipwith crossed to the desk—"do you think you could find us a copy of *Black Beauty*, and maybe some other books about horses while you're at it?"

Mrs. Shellhorn's whole face changed to a different person when she stood to answer Mr. Skipwith. "Certainly, Mr. Skipwith."

"And what books are you interested in, Marley?"

"Ballerina—I want to be a ballerina!"

"I can see you'll make a fine ballerina. And Cooper, what do you like?"

"Cooper likes trucks—big trucks—and puppies." Marley took charge for her brother.

"Excellent choices. Could you kindly add books about ballerinas, trucks, and puppies to that list, Mrs. Shellhorn?"

Now the librarian bristled. Arlo guessed she was none too pleased to be given a laundry list of books for "transients." But she still smiled at Mr. Skipwith. "I can see what we have. It will take quite a bit of time." She looked impatiently at her watch.

"No doubt, and it's much appreciated." He nodded sympathetically, then turned to Aunt Ginny Dee, who was doing her best to keep a straight face. "Mrs. Boyden, could I interest you and the children in some ice cream? That would give Mrs. Shellhorn time and freedom to find your books."

"Ice cream! Chocolate!" They were the first words Cooper had uttered since they'd walked into the library. His face lit like sunshine.

"That's really not necessary, Mr. Skipwith." Aunt Ginny Dee seemed about to decline, but Arlo caught her eye, sending her plea to get away.

"It would give me great pleasure, and I think I know three young folks who might like to try the diner's new twirling counter stools," Mr. Skipwith tempted, a twinkle in his blue eyes.

"Please, Aunt Ginny Dee?" Arlo pleaded in unison with Marley and Cooper.

"Well, I suppose we do need to wait," Aunt Ginny Dee conceded.

"Perhaps Emily would like to join us?" Mr. Skipwith's smile stayed in place.

Emily popped up from her seat, eyes lit like twin Christmas trees, but her grandmother set a firm hand on her head. "Thank you, Mr. Skipwith. Emily will remain with me. She's my helper for the day."

Without looking back, Aunt Ginny Dee ushered the three young Pickerings through the door, saying, "We'll be back for the books and cards in a little while, Louise. Thank you."

Arlo couldn't look at Emily's disappointed face but stole a backward glance at her grandmother. *Ice Queen.*

CHAPTER SEVENTEEN

THE DINER WASN'T BUSY MIDAFTERNOON, and for that Ginny was grateful. Not so many tongues to wag, although she was certain Louise would spread the word that Will Skipwith had taken her and her three charges for ice cream.

She just didn't know which spin Louise would put on that— eliciting pity for herself for being railroaded into catering to Ginny Boyden and delinquent Mark's children, making Will out to be the Good Samaritan who took pity on New Scrivelsby's most recent charity-case prodigals, or attributing it to a budding romance between Will and Ginny. Ginny didn't like any of those options, but there was not much she could do about it.

"Far away?" Will asked once they'd placed their order and the children were happily twirling on the counter stools.

"What? Oh, sorry. I was just thinking of Louise . . ."

"Wondering what she'll have to say about our outing?" Will smiled.

"Yes," Ginny admitted. "It shouldn't matter, but—"

"You rescued us, Mr. Skipwith," Arlo declared. "Fair and square."

Ginny turned. She hadn't realized Arlo was listening.

"You did. I had to get out of there. That Mrs. Shellhorn is a dragon—"

"Arlo," Ginny warned.

"You do me great honor, Arlo. A gentleman longs to rescue beautiful damsels in distress from dragons and all manner of dangers."

"What's *damsels*?" Marley stopped twirling.

"You, young lady." Will grinned. "You're a lovely little damsel."

Marley laughed, throwing her arms up in the air and twirling again. "Hey, Cooper, we're damsels!"

"Just girls," Arlo chided.

"Can't Chicken Snot be a damsel too?" Marley's face fell.

"Chicken Snot?" Will laughed.

"I'm Hot Shot." Marley puffed out her chest.

Ginny needed to stop this.

"Hot Shot and Chicken Snot? How did you get those names?" Will asked.

"Ask Arlo." Marley and Cooper went back to seeing who could twirl the fastest.

Arlo heaved a sigh. "Not me. Some mean kids down Texas way. We were at a playground—after school, when anybody can go. Some big guys came and told us we had to leave. I said no, so they got rough, tied me to the ladder of the slide. Cooper's forever picking his nose, and he was that day."

"He keeps feathers from his pillow in his pocket," Marley broke in, "so he twirls them in his snot. They're little friends. We were just playing with them."

"Anyway," Arlo pushed on, "they shoved him down in the gutter and called him Chicken Snot. I couldn't get loose, so Marley stood up for him and fought till they beat her, so they called her Hot Shot."

"That's terrible!" Ginny couldn't grasp all the children had been through in their short lives. Playing with snot, beat up by ruffians, tied to a slide.

"It's not terrible!" Marley piped up. "Now Arlo tells us stories. Hot Shot and Chicken Snot—we're always the heroes!"

Ginny groaned, wishing she could sink beneath the counter stool once she realized the waitress was listening with raised eyebrows.

"Very creative, Arlo. I'll wager you're a good storyteller." Will ignored Ginny's groan.

"She makes up stories every night before we go to sleep." Marley beamed at her big sister. "They're the best!"

"You've turned something meant as an unkindness into something grand, Arlo. Not everyone can do that. Not everyone would try. Maybe you should write your stories down." Will looked directly into Arlo's eyes until the girl blushed and looked away.

Ginny closed her eyes. She wanted to grab the ears of whoever called the children those names. But that wouldn't help them now. *How is it that Will took on a whole different view—found the way Arlo turned it into something positive, something healing?* Ginny dipped the long-handled spoon into her ice cream sundae, wondering at the kind of man Will Skipwith was and what made him so, wondering if she could look at life in such a way, find a way to be that positive.

As they walked back to the library, Will and Ginny lagged a few steps behind.

"You've got a brave and resourceful girl there, Ginny."

"It sounds like she's had to be brave . . . and resourceful, even more than I knew. Mark and their mother led them a merry chase, that's for sure, by his own confession. Children should never have to go through all they have." Moments passed before Ginny turned to Will. "You're so good with children. It's a shame you never had a family of your own. You'd have made a wonderful father."

He looked closely at Ginny. "I met Marion in college. We married as soon as I passed my bar exam and settled here in New Scrivelsby. We'd always hoped—planned for children. But that didn't happen."

Ginny remembered what Louise had told her but didn't know whether to say. She waited for him.

He hesitated. "Marion was killed in a car accident before—well, before our lives together had barely started."

"I'm so sorry, Will." She reached for his arm. "And you've never remarried."

He shook his head, but his eyes held Ginny's. "No. A soulmate's not easy to come by."

"No," she agreed but looked away. She understood the pain of a loss so great, and how hard it was to give your heart away a second time.

He cleared his throat. "I saw the work my father did with kids in trouble, kids like Mark—even—" He didn't finish, but Ginny knew who he meant. "The change a little bit of encouragement and a helping hand made in those boys' lives—what a difference. That made me want to do the same, at least be on the lookout to do the same."

"You could have done that on a bigger scale somewhere else."

"I never wanted to go anywhere else. We came back to New Scrivelsby directly after law school. This is home—always has been. There are plenty of people in need of a helping hand right here."

"You see good even where others see trouble."

"It's not about seeing the good right off. It's about looking for the good, for the image of God in every person."

"That's hard to see in some people." Ginny thought of Louise. She thought of Mark and Luke, despite how hard they were working. Their anger showed through in so many ways, especially Luke's. It had shown through Curtis from the moment he returned from the Pacific. It had shown through her as she'd hardened her heart toward him.

"Maybe that means they're hurting, more than we know. Hurt, fear, grief—all make people do and say things that can come out rough. Being trapped in their hurts and fears keeps folks from seeing the good around them, the good in others."

Hurt, fear, grief . . . hallmarks of my life. Too focused on my own hurts and fears—is that why I don't see the good in people right off? Why I didn't see the good in Curtis when he . . . But Ginny couldn't go there.

When they reached the library steps, Will stopped.

"Aren't you coming in?" Ginny wasn't looking forward to facing Louise alone. She felt so much braver with Will beside her.

"You'll take it from here. Louise's bark is worse than her bite. I'd best get back to the office. But this was a pleasure, ladies, and gentleman. I thank you." He winked at Cooper.

"Thank you, Mr. Skipwith." Arlo stood on a step high enough to look Will in the eye. "For the ice cream, for everything."

"You're more than welcome, Miss Arlo. You enjoy those good books. I'd like to talk them over with you. I'm mighty fond of horses myself."

Arlo smiled, shyly, Ginny thought. Marley hopped from one foot to the other, plucking flowers from the urn overflowing with magenta begonias. Cooper grinned and picked his nose for good measure.

"Ginny." Will nodded, smiling, locking his blue eyes with hers an extra moment, then turned and walked away.

"Will." Ginny smiled at his back. Marley handed up a small bouquet. They were lovely and bright, probably forbidden to pick, but perfect for the moment.

CHAPTER EIGHTEEN

BETHANY KNEW THE NEW BOOKS were good for Arlo; they were also beyond the girl's reading capability. Had Louise known that when she picked them out or did she simply assume Arlo was reading at that level? They were a little beyond average even if Arlo had been caught up to her grade. But they still had July and August. If there was any way possible, Bethany would have Arlo reading rings around the girls in her grade . . . whatever grade that was.

The early July days ran hot, afternoons worst of all. By one o'clock Bethany knew Arlo had lost all interest. The little ones no longer wanted to help with baking, and all eyes drooped sleepy. But afternoons were the only time allotted to Bethany with the children and she was not one to give up, at least not until Arlo threw down her math workbook.

"I can't do this math, Aunt Bethany. It's too hot. Baking makes it hotter still."

Bethany couldn't argue with any of that. Neither of their houses owned air conditioners, and the electric fan, good as it was, could not keep up.

Bethany was about to throw in the towel when Aunt Ginny Dee came to the rescue. "What would you think about changing up our schedule now the weather's so hot? I don't believe there's much of anything the children can do in the fields to help Luke or Mark now that they're sculpting trees, and our vegetable garden's in. Just a little weeding, mostly picking berries and early vegetables, and pulling Japanese beetles from the roses. What if we planned the first hour in the gardens and you spent the rest of the morning with Arlo—while it's cooler? The children could take the afternoons free. Any further garden chores we need doing could be left until after supper, when the heat of the day wears off."

Bethany fidgeted, as if by relinquishing her schedule she might fail. She saw Aunt Ginny Dee's wisdom but didn't like giving in or doing the easy thing.

"Please?" Cooper begged. Cooper, who didn't have to be in lessons at all. "I wanna be with Pa and Uncle Luke. They need me!" Bigger, bluer eyes were never seen.

"You can't be out in the fields while they're sculpting trees—it's too dangerous." Bethany was firm. "But," she sighed, "I suppose it won't hurt to change the way we do things."

"Hooray!" shouted Arlo.

"We'll give it a try—if you work really hard in the mornings. But any slacking off and we're back to the old schedule."

"I'll work like a drudge all morning, I promise!" Arlo crossed her heart and spit into her palm.

It was all Bethany could do not to laugh, though she knew she should be appalled, or at least pretend to be appalled. She shortened the lesson that day—a mercy for all.

CHAPTER NINETEEN

GINNY WAS RELIEVED to have her house back to peace and quiet in the afternoons. Whatever garden work she wanted to do among the roses or the vegetables she did before breakfast, before hungry tummies trooped through her back door. Early morning was her favorite time of day—watching the sun rise over the mountain, streaking the sky in apricot, lavender, and gold; feeling the garden dirt beneath her bare feet and through her fingers; watching dew-kissed roses unfurl their petals and collecting bouquets of mint for tea amid the butterflies.

She wasn't much for carrying a tune, but she hummed as she worked—hymns she'd learned in childhood. "I come to the garden alone, while the dew is still on the roses" and "O Lord my God! When I in awesome wonder consider all the worlds Thy hands have made." In those moments she felt a swelling in her heart and a special kinship with the writers of those hymns, praise and thankfulness to a Father who loved her and forgave.

Now that she'd worked her mother's rose garden into shape, it was all she could do not to spend her savings on new plants for the gardens, digging new beds. She could see how it could all expand, where she'd add a trellis here, an archway there, a swing in the orchard for the children and a pergola over a picnic table area. She'd like to create a maze of flowers and shrubs for the children to wander through—a real secret garden—and a wildflower garden in the meadow. Those ideas kept her awake at night. She dreamed of all she imagined and woke with hope in her heart, only to grasp reality. *There's no sense in doing any of that. I'm going to sell. Who else would keep it all up? I'll need that money when I move, might even need it here until the farm sells.*

The thing she could do without making a huge investment, the thing that meant she could take some of her mother's rose garden with her, was to press the flowers. Even if she didn't frame them or create crafts, she could press them and mail them to England when she went. *Memories. Sweet memories.*

She fingered the petals of her mother's favorite—a blushing pearl. Ginny didn't remember the name of that rose—or any of the ones her mother had planted. But she could look them up, figure them out, at least for the most part. She'd no idea how old the roses in her mother's garden were, or where each one had come from—the store, catalog orders, the "old country," friends swapping cuttings or bare roots? Her mother had done all of that. If she'd kept a catalog of her plantings, Ginny hadn't found it. There were so many things Ginny wished she'd asked her mother.

If she was going to press the flowers, she'd best get to it once the dew dried, before they drooped.

She didn't realize how long she'd spent in the gardens that morning or that Marley and Bailey were perched on her back porch step, watching her, until the sun rose warm enough to make her pull off her sweater. "Marley! I didn't see you there. You must be hungry."

Marley smiled, slinging her arm around Bailey, who licked her cheek. "It's okay. I like that song. I like when you sing."

"I didn't know I was—singing."

"That's funny."

Ginny smiled—*a girl and her dog. What a picture.* There was something about that little girl. *A child after my heart.* The thought surprised Ginny, but she realized it might be true. Arlo was bright and creative, outgoing, the oldest and the protector of her siblings. Cooper was precious, willing to cuddle, smart as a whip—an engineer and builder in miniature, and a charmer. But Marley, who loved to garden and bake and discover all manner of things—mischief or not—just because she could, for the delight of it all, was more like Ginny than any of the children.

Ginny crossed the lawn and set her gardening basket by the step. She sat down beside Marley and took the little girl's hand. "Did you know that flowers all have names? Botanical names and common names—the names we know them best by."

"I know flowers have names."

Ginny smiled. "Did you know that long ago people gave each flower its own special meaning?"

Marley shook her head.

"Red roses, for instance, can mean love or romance, even courage. Pink roses mean appreciation or sometimes admiration."

"What about yellow roses? I like that yellow rose over there."

"Yellow—let's see, I think yellow roses mean friendship, new beginnings, and joy."

"Like sunshine!"

Bailey barked approval.

"That's exactly what it's like! I think you're full of new beginnings and joy, so that's the perfect rose for you."

"Can that rosebush be mine?"

"I don't see why not. In fact, I think that's a very good idea. Everyone needs their own special rose."

Marley's smile outshone the sun.

"What shall we make for breakfast this morning?"

"Pancakes!"

"Pancakes?"

"With raisins. I like raisins in my pancakes, and cimmanon. And sausage. And orange juice."

"Cinnamon," Ginny automatically corrected. "Pancakes, sausage, orange juice. Now, that sounds good. With butter and maple syrup on top?"

"Yay!"

Ginny smiled. "How about you help me? We'll get everything ready before the others come over."

Marley hopped up, a pogo stick in motion, Bailey prancing beside her. "Can I wear your apron?"

Ginny laughed. "It's a little big for you, but we'll work something out." Her heart swelled again. This is what she'd longed for all her life—children, family—and now it had come late in life in the most unexpected way and for the briefest of times. *Best not get attached.* Bethany had said that Luke warned her of that very thing, cautioning her to guard her heart. Ginny knew she should heed that warning too. Still . . .

Once Arlo and Bethany were settled on the front porch with lessons and Marley and Cooper were intent on mixing mud pies beneath the porch, Ginny returned to her rose garden, clippers and a vase of water in hand. She'd start small, choosing the most open flowers, roses in their prime, ones with approximately the same shape and thickness to keep the presses even, making certain that all traces of moisture were eliminated. She didn't want to waste one to too much hydration. They'd turn brown or at least lose their vibrant color, and color was what Ginny loved most in pressed flowers. They brought the joy of spring and the loveliness of early summer into winter—forever reminders that life was not done, simply waiting to bloom again.

She'd clipped two dozen nearly perfect specimens when Bailey began barking, pawing at the latticework by the back steps, and Cooper sent up a howl from beneath the porch. Ginny dropped her basket and ran toward him. "What is it? What's wrong?"

Bailey barked frantically, nonstop. Cooper screamed louder. Marley dragged him from beneath the porch.

"What happened?"

"There's a snake!"

"A snake! Did it bite you? What did it look like?"

Cooper howled louder, throwing muddy arms around Ginny's knees. Marley's lower lip trembled. Bethany and Arlo appeared through the back porch door as Bailey lunged in and out beneath the porch.

"Get Bailey away from the porch—there's a snake underneath!"

But it was too late. The black, four-foot-long snake struck out at Bailey. Bailey swiped it hard with his paw, sending it into the yard.

"Bailey!" Marley screamed. "It's gonna bite Bailey! It'll kill Bailey!"

Ginny couldn't think about the dog now. Frantic, she pulled the children away from the snake battle and stood Cooper at arm's length, searching for bite marks impossible to find on his mud-streaked limbs. "Where did it bite you, Cooper? Show me!" Cooper screamed louder still.

Before she could get a word out of him, Arlo grabbed a garden rake and swiped the snake farther into the yard. "Get Bailey in the house—now!"

Bethany grabbed Bailey by the collar and pulled him up the stairs and through the screen door. All the while he barked, lunging back toward the snake.

"Cooper, it's okay!" Arlo pressed the snake's head to the ground with the rake, no matter that its long body twisted and curled. "It's just a rat snake. They're not poisonous," she pronounced, as if the world had not just come to an end.

"Arlo! What are you doing?" Ginny's heart raced at the sight of the girl and the snake. She couldn't be in two places at once.

"It's okay—I've done this before. It won't bite me."

"Did it bite you, Cooper? Answer me!" Ginny's heart still raced. "Marley, did you see—did it bite him?"

Tears streamed down Marley's face. She shook her head, but uncertainly. "I don't think so. I'm not sure."

Ginny wanted to hold her, comfort her. It wasn't her fault, but Marley looked as if she took the blame for Cooper's woe. "Let's get you hosed off, Cooper, and see what we can see."

Cooper gulped big sobs but gradually stopped screaming.

From the corner of her eye Ginny saw Arlo reach down and grab the snake behind its head, pick it up, and waltz off toward the creek.

"Arlo!" Bethany gasped, running down the steps now that Bailey was secured inside. "Wait!" But Arlo wasn't waiting.

Ginny turned the nozzle to shower and gently washed Cooper's limbs. "Marley, help me get his clothes off while I hose him off."

Marley pulled her brother's muddied, wet shirt and pants off until he stood naked and shivering. Ginny searched from head to toe but found no bite marks. She sat on the ground and drew him into her arms. "It scared you, didn't it? That snake."

Cooper bumped his head up and down, pressing it tight against Ginny's heart. She held him closer. "Marley, go grab a towel from the bathroom—a big one."

Marley ran, eager to help her brother. Ginny saw this, saw the love between the children in Marley's concern and equal willingness to accept blame or to help. She saw it in Arlo's quick thinking to take control of the situation and remove the snake, or whatever might threaten her siblings. For all they'd been through, for all the ways Mark and his wife had failed their children, these little ones were growing into resourceful and caring people, just as Will had said, and they couldn't be doing that alone.

Marley wrapped Cooper's back with the towel. Ginny drew it round him until he looked swaddled, like a baby. Cooper giggled, his lashes wet with tears.

"Let's get you some dry clothes, little man. You too, Marley." For the first time Ginny realized Marley was still caked in mud, likely tracked through her house by now, and at Ginny's behest, no less. Well, it didn't matter. Nothing mattered but that these little ones were safe. And Arlo too. Where was she? Had she and Bethany deposited the snake in some safe and faraway place? Not that that would deter a snake intent on claiming its territory. *One thing at a time.* "Marley, wait. Let's hose you off first."

Before lunchtime all were clean, dry, and dressed, none the worse for wear.

"That was a big snake." Cooper's eyes stood like saucers in his small face.

"Yes, it was." Ginny soothed all three children as well as Bethany and herself with chocolate chip cookies and milk, not caring that it would spoil their lunch. She was just so grateful they were all well and safe. It had been a long time since she could do anything for those she loved, anything that truly comforted or helped them.

Curtis. I couldn't help you, not so you noticed. What was it in the war, so horrid, that you could never say, never get it out of your mind, your very DNA? If there had ever been a way to open that door, it was long past now. Closed.

And yet sometimes she saw that same haunted, hunted glaze in Mark's eyes, if only for brief moments. It worried her. Curtis had drowned that glaze in the drink, the same demon that she knew nipped at Mark's heels. She hadn't smelled liquor or seen any sign he was drinking, but she recognized the strain, the pull, and wondered if he was as sober as he appeared, or if he was just so much better at hiding it. *Can Mark help me understand? Help me forgive? Forgive Curtis? Forgive myself for not being what he needed? Can I help Mark? Is it too late?* Ginny didn't know.

CHAPTER TWENTY

THAT FIRST AFTERNOON Arlo was drunk with the freedom of hours to herself, hours she wasn't about to share babysitting Marley and Cooper. After all, she'd rescued them all from the giant rat snake. *Scaredy-cats!* Arlo had learned early how to handle snakes when they'd lived in Texas. She knew the difference between poisonous and non-poisonous snakes from lessons her pa gave her on the fly—better than book learning, Arlo figured, and something not everybody knew, apparently.

After a good long wade in the creek with Bailey, keeping watch for snakes, she picked blackberries in the shade of the woods—plenty to eat on the go and enough to make a cobbler for supper, just like Aunt Bethany had taught her. Maybe, if Aunt Ginny Dee had enough cream and whole milk left over, and some rock salt, she could convince her to let them make vanilla ice cream to go with it. Arlo's arm always got tired turning that crank. She'd need to beg Pa to help, but it would be worth it.

By the time she and Bailey returned to Aunt Ginny Dee's kitchen, Arlo saw a new project in the works, one that had nothing to do with supper plans.

Vases of stems and leaves, their flower tops all cut off, stood on the counter. Stacks of wood, like latticeworks cut down, each the size of nearly a quarter of the tabletop, and stacks of cardboard and thick white paper cut the same size were piled along the floor. Thick black straps with metal clasps hung over the backs of chairs.

Aunt Ginny Dee, her brow puckered, leaned over the table, worrying rose petals, pressing them face down against long sheets of the thick paper. Marley's and Cooper's fingers were employed in holding down roses whose petals had already been spread.

"What ya'll doing?" Arlo spoke softly, sensing the concentration before her.

Marley didn't even look up, but kept her fingers poised over the petals. "We're pressing flowers. We're gonna make pictures."

"Me too." Cooper nodded, slipping the rose half an inch sideways.

"Hold it still, Cooper," Aunt Ginny Dee warned. "Don't let it get away."

Arlo set her bucket of berries in the sink. "But you're squashing them."

"Pressing, preserving them," Aunt Ginny Dee corrected. "Have you seen the picture over the piano in the front room? The one with flowers and a Scripture?"

"*In Thy Presence Is Fullness of Joy.*" Arlo had studied it, could picture the needle-worked lettering through punched paper and the wreath of pressed flowers framing it, then the green leaves that created a kind of laurel wreath around that—a description Arlo had just read in one of the books she'd taken from the library.

"That's the one. That's the kind of thing we can make."

"We're gonna make a beautiful flower picture!" Marley bubbled. "What for?"

"What for?" Aunt Ginny Dee looked up. "Just because—because we can, because we want to. I used to make these for gifts sometimes. I brought some leftover frames with me from New Jersey. You might like to make some too." She glanced at Arlo.

"Did you make the one over the piano?"

Aunt Ginny Dee straightened. "No. My mama made that. I helped her press the flowers. We didn't have presses like these then, just laid the big flowers and leaves between sheets of plywood. The smaller ones we pressed in the pages of our family Bible." She smiled, and Arlo knew she was remembering.

I hardly have any memories of my ma, and none like that. But Arlo pushed the thought away. She wouldn't give her mother the time of day in the light of day, not even to grant her own memories.

Arlo picked up a manila envelope that lay on the table, one with photograph corners peeking from the edges. She pulled out the slim packet—pictures of flowers, full and alive, and photographs of flowers pressed, then some with those same flowers in frames, some with words written and some without, just flowers and leaves. "Did you make all these?"

"Yes. I took photos of the ones I gave as gifts, so I could remember, so I could make something similar again if I wanted. But each time they come out a little different."

"Different flowers." Cooper nodded, sage-like.

Aunt Ginny Dee laughed. "That's right, Cooper. Every flower is different—unique—like people. One of a kind . . . like you." Aunt Ginny Dee slipped a skinny straight pin into one of the flowers, pushing it tighter against the paper, then picked up a second sheet of the heavy white paper. "Now, Cooper, Marley, carefully lift your fingers and step away. I'm going to press this sheet on top, just like we did the other layers." Marley and Cooper solemnly stepped away. "Arlo, can you hand me that sheet of cardboard behind you?"

Arlo grabbed a couple.

"Set it on top of this sheet, no moving or adjusting. We want it pressed straight. Please."

Arlo followed her instructions to a T. Aunt Ginny Dee set one of the wooden lattice pieces on top, lining it squarely with the layers of paper and cardboard and flowers beneath.

"Okay, now the straps. We need two. Arlo, open those clasps and pull the straps through, please, then lay two straps across the table." Aunt Ginny Dee lifted the stack of flowers and sheets and wooden latticeworks. Once Arlo laid the straps straight, Aunt Ginny Dee set the bundle on top, adjusting the straps so they lay even and parallel to the length of the wooden presses, looping them around the top. "These straps will keep the presses tight. See how I brace them with one hand and pull the strap tight with the other? Then they're locked. We do that on both sides."

"Are they done now? Can we take them out?" Marley clasped her hands in anticipation.

"Oh, no, we've only just started. In a couple of days we'll open up the presses, replace the papers with new ones to be sure the moisture is being absorbed, then buckle them up again."

"So, how long does it take to get the flowers to look like the ones in the pictures?" Arlo was fascinated that something so pretty and permanent could come out of something as short-lived as a rose, thanks to paper and cardboard and wood.

"A couple of weeks, sometimes three, then we can work on making pictures."

"Are you going to fill all these presses?" Arlo counted five more stacked on the floor.

"Probably. If the roses keep blooming. They don't much like hot weather, so we'll see."

"Are they just for roses?" Arlo didn't see why they needed to be.

"No, you can press any kind of flowers, or leaves, even stems. I just wanted to preserve some of my mother's roses to remember."

"For when you're gone from here?" Arlo accused. "When you leave?"

Aunt Ginny Dee straightened. "Yes, I suppose so . . . so I can take the roses with me. So I can remember."

Arlo turned on her heel, knowing that she'd want only to forget this time and place when they were shoved out, hightailing it in midnight runs from town to town, looking for bathrooms and showers, sleeping in the truck bed until they landed in some other place. "Come on, Marley, Cooper. Let's go back to the barn."

CHAPTER TWENTY-ONE

BETHANY PULLED THE PIE CRUSTS from the oven, wincing as the side screen door slammed behind Luke, a sure sign that he was in a temper.

"Bethany!" Luke called, even though he was just around the corner, pulling off his work boots, kicking them onto the mat.

"In the kitchen." She'd wait. No sense running toward trouble. He only used her full first name when he was cross.

While the par-baked crusts cooled, she mixed sugar, flour, lemon juice, and ginger together, then folded in the blackberries. The crumble topping sat at the ready. Blackberry pie for dessert, thanks to Arlo's largesse, would hit the spot for everyone.

"You've got to do something about Cooper and Bailey. They're underfoot everywhere I go, every time I turn around."

She almost smiled. "What've they done now?"

"Cooper's out there begging me to put up a tire swing and he just keeps following me around, asking can I do it now, when can I do it, and on and on."

"So do it. You have a dozen old tires behind the barn. You won't miss one—or three, one for each of the kids."

"I don't have time to mess with that and I'm not about to encourage them. You've got to do something."

"What has it got to do with me? He didn't ask me."

Luke stood in his stocking feet in the middle of the kitchen floor, hands on hips. "Because you're the one who's encouraged those kids to hang around. They should be with their pa."

"You sent Mark over to Maryland. He's gone to pick up that load of fertilizer in Brunswick, or did you forget? Cooper's too little to be left alone. He's got to be with one of us, and you're his favorite."

"No."

"He adores you." She turned away. "Seems like you'd be grateful somebody does."

"What? What does that mean?"

"Nothing." She knew better than to fight with Luke. It never ended in her favor. She hesitated, considering, then stopped, a spoonful of blackberries stretched before her. "No, that's not right. I did say something, and I'm going to say it again. You should be glad somebody wants to hang around you, glad that little boy looks up to you. We're never going to have children of our own—you know that as well as I do. Cooper's the closest you're ever going to have to a son, at least by me. You're his uncle. We're his family. Family!"

"I never—"

"That's right." She slammed the berry bowl onto the counter. "You never—you never reached out to one of those children who need you. You shut yourself off from them, from your aunt and your brother and from me half the time, all the people who are working their tails off trying to make this farm survive. You forget that Aunt Ginny Dee could have turned this place over to the bank or sold it for the loan and back taxes the moment she walked into town, that we could be forced from here with nothing if not for her generosity and your brother's hard work—and if I don't miss my guess, not for those children who need each and every one of us."

"That's not fair, Beth. My dad—"

"Harold lied to us—lied to you and lied to me, all the while letting us cater to him till his dying day, those lies still on his lips. He used us, Luke. He used us and he kicked out his own son and kept his sister from her mother."

Luke's jaw clenched. He turned his back and heaved a sigh that sent his shoulders up and down. By the time he turned back, he'd lost the set jaw and his color had paled. "I know this is not what you signed on for. It's not fair. None of this is."

Bethany breathed. "You're what I signed on for, Luke. You and me. But not like this, not us fighting and barely speaking except to argue. I'm sick and tired of tiptoeing around you. Ever since Aunt Ginny Dee and Mark came, you've been grumpy and irritable and sometimes downright grouchy to Mark and those children. They're not the ones that lied to you. They're not the ones that cheated you. They're here to help and they don't deserve your attitude. None of us do." She pulled off her apron and threw it to the counter, heading for the back door.

Luke reached for her. "Beth. I'm sorry."

She pulled away. "When you're sorry enough to be the husband I married, let me know. But don't just say it. Don't you dare just say it, because I won't put up with your temper tantrums anymore. I won't."

Bethany let the screen door slam behind her, something she'd never done, not once in her memory.

CHAPTER TWENTY-TWO

GINNY SAT AT THE KITCHEN TABLE too late at night, eyes squinting from the dim overhead light as she ran her fingers down the long columns of last month's figures. *July income—too little. July expenditures— far too great.* Even now, with having done little to improve the house beyond the scraping and painting, the labor generously contributed by the Acts committee from church, she was dipping too far into her savings. Luke and Bethany were supporting themselves from their small nest egg. How long that might last, she didn't know.

Ginny's grocery bill for her and Mark and the children more than shot her budget, even with everything the garden brought in, a garden she shared with Bethany. That didn't count electricity for the house, gas for the tractor, and all that the farm needed—expenses she'd assumed from Luke—her car's upkeep, and the clothes she'd bought the children. They would soon need more as the weather changed and school began. How she'd make it until the end of the year without more hefty withdrawals from her bank account she wasn't sure. Thank heaven for her monthly Social Security checks. They weren't huge, but they definitely helped.

Ginny cupped her head in her hands. "Lord, I don't know what to do here. I told them I'd wait until the end of the year—until after another Christmas tree season. If I don't sell soon or surely by the end of the year, I'll lose so much of my savings, and then what? It could mean giving up my trip to Scotland and Ireland, going directly to Scrivelsby Manor, and I'd still not be able to help any of them long term. What would You have me do, Father?"

The back screen door creaked. Ginny looked up to see Arlo standing barefoot in the doorway in her pajamas, Bailey by her side, long black tail waving like a flag. "What's wrong?"

"Nothing." Ginny swiped tears from her face and forced a half smile. She hadn't even realized she'd been crying.

Arlo plopped down in the chair opposite Ginny. "Doesn't look like nothing." She fingered the ledger pages before Ginny could pull them back. "Money trouble?"

Ginny didn't want to worry Arlo. It was not her concern, and she was a child. "It's nothing. You should be in bed . . . asleep." Bailey crept over and nuzzled Ginny's knee. Gratefully, she reached down to scratch behind his cockeyed ears.

Arlo grunted. "I'm not stupid, Aunt Ginny Dee. I know we're costing you a bundle. Pa worries about it too."

"Well, he shouldn't, and neither should you. We'll manage." She closed the book. *Out of sight, out of mind.* At least she hoped it would be out of Arlo's mind. *She's had worries enough and too much for a girl her age—things she should not even know about yet.*

"Maybe we can help—Marley and Cooper and me."

Ginny's heart thumped. "You help all you can now. I know that, and I appreciate it."

"No, not dishes and garden and stuff. Something to make money."

Ginny sighed. "Even the grown-ups are having a hard time figuring that one out."

"But you have all the stuff."

Ginny tilted her head. "All the stuff? What stuff?"

Arlo pushed back her chair and left the room. When she returned, she held one of Ginny's botanical presses. She slapped it on the table—a little too hard for Ginny's head or the good of the table. "Those pictures you have—of the presents you made with the flowers. I'll bet people would buy them if we made some. I bet people would pay lots of money for them, especially with all the roses you've been pressing. And Marley and Cooper and me can get more—tons more wildflowers. They're blooming everywhere now—Queen Anne's Lace, goldenrod, purple and pink wild sweet peas, blue cornflowers. We even saw some wild pink roses along that old wagon trail leading to the high meadow."

"When were you in the high meadow?" Ginny didn't like to think of the children wandering so far afield all alone.

Arlo shrugged. "We go all over. Our treks are for fun, but we could be picking flowers to press, and when they're pressed, we could glue them into pictures."

It was late. Ginny was bone-weary and ready to send Arlo back to bed once she gave her a glass of milk and a cookie to help her sleep. "It's a nice idea, but I don't think so. We can't take on any more now, Arlo."

Arlo jutted her hip and spread her hands before her. "We can do it. You don't have to do anything but show us how. I'm a quick learner."

"I know you are." Too tired to argue, Ginny relented. "I'll think about it."

"What's there to think about?"

Ginny sighed, getting up to pour two glasses of milk. Maybe milk and cookies would help her sleep too. "Tomorrow. Let's discuss it tomorrow."

Arlo visibly bit her lip. At least the cookie helped slow the turning of wheels and rush of ideas Ginny saw behind the girl's eyes.

Ginny overslept, something she hadn't done since Mark and the children started coming over for breakfast. If she'd tried, the stomping of feet would have brought her to her senses. But even with the sun high in the sky she'd heard no such thing, just a click downstairs, a click that sounded like the phone being placed in its cradle. Ginny pulled her watch from the bedside table. Nine thirty. *What? I can't believe it. Where is everybody? Surely they didn't sleep this long too.*

Ginny was up, dressed, and down the stairs by nine forty-five, but there was not a child in sight and not a dish out of place. Even so, the back door stood ajar. Ginny checked the back and side yards but there was no one there, and no one out front of the barn.

Maybe they went into town for breakfast—or over to Bethany's. Either was a stretch in Ginny's mind, but she didn't know what else to think.

Ginny had just downed her second cup of coffee and the last of her carrot muffin when she heard the crunch of tires on stone out front and went to take a look.

"Will, good morning! This is a surprise." Ginny pushed a wayward curl behind her ear, wishing she'd washed and set her hair last night.

"Is it? Arlo didn't tell you I was coming?"

"Arlo? No, I haven't seen her this morning."

"Ah, out and about on business, I'll wager."

"Business?"

"You do know you have an entrepreneur on your hands, a very insistent one at that."

"I've no idea what you're talking about."

Will grinned. "I believe our girl is setting the groundwork to convince you."

Our girl. Confused, Ginny still liked the sound of that.

He strode up the porch steps, stopping so close to Ginny that she thought she ought to step back, but didn't. "You look lovely this fine morning, Ginny Dee."

Ginny didn't know what to do with that. It was not something she'd heard in ages, years. He'd not called her Ginny Dee before. She hadn't minded that the others did, but it sounded more personal coming from Will. She pressed her hands down her skirt, willing them to be still. "You're turning into something of a flirt, Will Skipwith. Would you like a cup of coffee? There's still some in the pot . . . and a muffin? We made them fresh yesterday."

He smiled. "Just what I was hoping."

Heart flutters were new to Ginny, or at least resurrected from so long ago that she didn't know how to interpret them. She couldn't think about that now. *Pour the coffee, Ginny, just pour the coffee and don't make a ninny of yourself.*

"Mmm," Will moaned after biting into the muffin. "There's nothing like this at the diner. What's in this?"

"Carrots, pineapple, raisins, nuts, a little coconut, and all the usual things that make up muffins. I call them carrot muffins but Arlo calls them The Best Day Ever Muffins."

"Ha! I told you that girl's an entrepreneur, and a natural one. Smart as a whip."

"So you said. Now, tell me what this is all about."

"When Arlo telephoned this morning, we—"

"Arlo telephoned you? This morning?"

"Yes, you didn't know?"

"No idea." Ginny felt herself blush. "I confess, I overslept. As far as I know they've not even been in for breakfast."

"They're probably scouring the hillsides, seeking treasure."

"Will, you're talking in circles. Tell me what's going on."

The back door slammed open. "Aunt Ginny Dee! Look what we found!" Marley tore into the kitchen, Bailey at her heels. "Mr. Skippy! You came!" Marley threw her arms around Will. He sloshed his coffee onto the table but hugged her warmly in return.

Arlo trooped in next, the light of triumph in her eyes and a long newspaper cone of wildflowers over her arm.

Cooper trailed, dragging a wilted bouquet of daisies that looked as he did, a little bedraggled and worse for wear. "I'm thirsty," he whined.

"Where have you all been?" Ginny poured a glass of water, helping a weary Cooper climb onto the chair.

"Exploring. Investigating. Researching. Discovering." Arlo reeled off her list with the import of a journalist hot on a story. "Look, just look what we found." She opened the newspaper cone and spread her largesse of wildflowers across the table—blue cornflowers, brown-eyed Susans, Queen Anne's lace, pink and lavender sweet peas, pink shrub roses, and white floribunda roses. Dozens and dozens. "We need to get these in the presses. Now."

Ginny was stunned.

"Marley," Arlo ordered, "get a vase and fill it with water. We don't want them to wilt before we can press them."

"Arlo, where—"

"Aunt Ginny Dee, where are those extra presses you said you have? We're gonna need them, probably all of them."

"Tell me what to do, Arlo. I'm here to help." Will set his cup and plate into the sink.

Ginny felt like a tornado had swept through her kitchen. "Arlo, Will—tell me what you're doing." She saw but needed to stall for time to think, to figure how to capture this runaway train.

Arlo glanced between Ginny and Will, her eyes a question.

Will took up the mantle. "Arlo phoned me this morning with a brilliant idea. She told me about the botanical pictures you've made for gifts and that you've taught the children how to press flowers too."

Ginny feared she knew where this was going and began to shake her head.

"Hear us out, Ginny. This could work."

She was being ganged up on. Arlo looked so hopeful; Will looked so sincere; Marley looked up at Will as if he were the grandfather she'd always wanted. Ginny was outnumbered, outgunned, and though she needed to put her foot down, intended to fuss, she wasn't at all certain she wanted to.

Ginny taught Will how to tease open wild roses, how to disengage the petals of sweet peas so each petal could be dried flat, how to press Queen Anne's lace and spread the intricate petals of cornflowers.

Before long she was working with Marley and Cooper on one press while Will and Arlo worked on another. Within two hours they'd removed all the flowers Ginny had set to press two weeks before and had all Ginny's presses full and strapped with the bundle of fresh beauties that the children had scavenged across the hills and through the woods. There were even some flowers and leaves that Ginny didn't recognize, ones she either didn't know or couldn't remember the names of. Excited, intrigued, Ginny felt her curiosity rising, as if at a mystery to be solved.

Working in close quarters, from time to time her arm brushed Will's. Did he feel the electric current she did? She refused to look in his face but was fairly certain he inched closer.

When the presses were full, Arlo carried them to the front room. Marley and Cooper swept leftover petals and stems from the tabletop and Will found a broom and dustpan to sweep the leavings from the floor.

Ginny put the kettle on, no matter that it was too hot for tea.

Arlo stood in the doorway to the hall, feet spread, fists on her hips, a smile of satisfaction on her face. "Now we wait."

"Wait for them to dry flat?" Will emptied the trash into the basket.

"But we don't just wait," Arlo ordered. "Aunt Ginny Dee says we have to change the papers every two or three days, and we'll have to figure out what the pictures will look like."

"Design," said Will, as if he and Arlo were managing the project together, which took Ginny aback a little.

"Where are your pictures, Aunt Ginny Dee? We can look at those to get us started."

All eyes turned toward Ginny. "Exactly what are you imagining we'll do with all these flowers?"

"Sell the pictures, of course." Marley looked as if even Cooper knew that.

"That sounds like a good idea, but we don't have a market, a place to sell them."

"Ginny," Will enthused, "I've seen the picture your mom created. Just think."

"I appreciate that, but—"

"Did you see the movie *Field of Dreams*? *If you build it, they will come.*"

"This isn't baseball! I understand what you're saying, but how will we—"

"Mr. Skippy said he'd help, and see, he is!" Marley jumped and spread her arms wide, as if that settled everything.

"Let's get some samples together. I'll hang a couple in my law office. I'm sure Rosemary will let us hang two or three in the diner. I have no doubt that once people see them, they'll want to buy—especially as Christmas approaches. Wetherill Pickering's Christmas Tree Farm is a local tradition. Use that name and people will buy. Let them see the pictures and they will buy."

"It can help save the farm," Arlo pleaded. "Even if you don't want it, we can help Pa and Uncle Luke and maybe they can buy it."

Ginny's heart caught.

"We can even do pictures for special events," Arlo pushed again. "Birthdays, weddings, anniversaries, graduations, stuff like that. Maybe write some sayings underneath the flowers."

"Scriptures, phrases, quotes." Will caught Arlo's fever. "Let me see the pictures, Ginny. Arlo says you're an amazing artist."

Ginny felt heat flush her neck, both from Will's attention and the wonder that Arlo had told him about it and commended her, that she was so alight with a surefire plan. "They're just pressed flowers."

Will laughed. "Better yet. God's the artist and you're the gardener."

"Just like Adam and Eve in the garden of Eden!" Marley celebrated some more.

Ginny felt her breath hitch. *Can this be, Lord? Is this the path You've opened?*

A knock came at the back screen door. "Aunt Ginny Dee? It's Bethany. May I come in?"

Cooper ran to the door and flung it wide, just missing Bethany's nose. "Hi, Aunt Bethy! We're making pictures!"

"So I heard." Bethany smiled, stepping in with a heavy basket over her arm.

"You heard?" Ginny couldn't grasp it.

"This morning. Arlo told me all about it. What a great idea! That's why I wasn't over for morning lessons, but I did bring lunch. I figured none of you would have had time to think about it. Fried chicken for a special day."

"Yay!" Marley trilled. "I'm hungry.'

"Me too!" Cooper echoed. "I'm hungry too! Fried chicken! I love fried chicken!"

Before Ginny could say a word, Arlo was setting out plates, Will pulled another chair from the front room, Marley grabbed flatware from the drawer, and Cooper climbed up in his chair, ready to dig in. Bethany spread a feast before them.

Will stood close to Ginny as the children rattled on in high-pitched voices to their Aunt Bethy about all the flowers they'd found and pressed that morning. "A little overwhelming, is it?"

Ginny nodded.

"They love you. They love the farm. They don't want things to change—just want to stay and are ready to do whatever they can to help make that happen."

Ginny's heart filled and her eyes pooled. *Stay? I never meant to stay. But, this, this family, Lord* . . . "Arlo shouldn't have drawn you away from work, Will. You have no obligation here. She shouldn't have—"

"The children aren't the only ones hoping you'll find a way to stay . . . if you want to. I think Arlo knows that . . . She's a very bright young lady."

The room had gone quiet. All eyes rested on Will and Ginny. Bethany smiled, just a little. Will gallantly pulled out a chair for Ginny beside Arlo. They all sat down. Ginny looked at Will across the table, not at all sure what the settling tornado meant, but she nodded and smiled. Will clasped Marley's and Cooper's hands on either side of him, bowed his head, and offered grace.

CHAPTER TWENTY-THREE

DESPITE AUNT BETHANY'S reading and math lessons, which she'd grown not to mind so very much, the summer passed too quickly for Arlo. Treks across the creek, over the mountain, and through the woods to collect wildflowers and leaves for pressing occupied every free afternoon.

Sometimes she took Marley and Cooper along, if she wasn't going too far, but sometimes she stole away on her own, craving the beauty, the adventure and solitude of walking the hills alone. Sometimes she packed a thermos, a snack, a book, and was gone until supper.

She'd have slept alone on the mountain if Pa had allowed it. Every moment fed her soul, healed some deep part of her that she hadn't even known was hurting. If time could stand still, Arlo would have been content.

But hushed conversations between Aunt Ginny Dee, Aunt Bethany, and her pa niggled at the back of Arlo's worrier. Words like *school*, *registration*, *testing* unsettled her perfect world.

One bright Tuesday in late August, Aunt Bethany took her shopping—just the two of them—and let her pick out two new dresses, three pairs of slacks and blouses, a sweater, new socks, and shoes with the toes closed in, along with all manner of underthings, a flannel nightgown, slippers, a robe, and a set of pjs. Arlo had never tried on so many clothes, let alone owned them. Aunt Bethany even took her to a hairdresser—a place Arlo had never set foot in and had no intention of going. The hairdresser cut a foot off Arlo's braids and bobbed her hair. When the chair whirled around so she could face the mirror, Arlo hardly recognized the girl staring back at her except for her freckles.

They met Mr. Skipwith for lunch, where he oohed and ahhed over Arlo's new do. After ice cream, which Arlo could hardly eat she was so full of hot dog and newness, he accompanied them both to the Walmart in the next town so Arlo could pick out her own backpack and school supplies as his gift. He said he often did that for boys and girls in the community—he'd done it for her pa when he was young, and it was his pleasure. Arlo's head swam and ached from the bounty. She'd no idea what her pa would say to such charity, for surely it was. Aunt Bethany vowed it was just what families did for one another, and besides, she declared she'd already gotten her pa's permission. *Family.* That, too, was bounty.

By the time the first day of school rolled around, Arlo felt ready. She could read any book Aunt Bethany gave her and cipher enough to keep track of all their botanicals, those pressed and mounted and those still drying in the presses. She could calculate fractions for cooking and baking nearly as quick as Aunt Ginny Dee. She could even estimate the number of evergreen trees needed to cover an acre with six feet in between each one and eight feet between each row. She couldn't imagine what else she might ever need to know but was willing to give the new school and teacher a try. She even tolerated shoes for a full day beforehand, just to practice.

What she didn't expect was to be asked the first day of school to write an essay for homework and create a presentation in class about her summer vacation. "What vacation?" she asked her pa. "I never went on a vacation in my life. We worked all summer."

"But it was work you loved, right?" Pa asked. "Write about that. Talk about helping in the garden and collecting all those plants and those pictures you're making with Aunt Ginny Dee."

Arlo nodded, remembering her early morning and late afternoon treks over the mountain as the sun rose or dipped, the silver-sweet songs of birds and the colorful flash of butterfly wings that accompanied her. Bailey had been there too. As glued as he was to Cooper and Marley, he trotted every step by her side or led the way as they trekked over the mountain.

Arlo had never written an essay before, but all the reading she'd done over the summer helped. Once she'd begun, it was as though the words poured out of her like water from a high mountain fall.

She tucked one of the smaller framed botanicals—one she'd created by herself—in her book bag the morning of her presentation. An oval-framed wreath of laurel leaves, intertwined with pink and lavender sweet peas, an open darker pink rose in the middle. It was a piece Arlo was proud of, one that Aunt Bethany and Aunt Ginny Dee had declared good enough to sell, but Arlo hadn't wanted to sell this one. It was her keeper, a reminder of mornings good and fresh on the mountain in summer.

Kids that had already presented their essays carted in souvenirs from trips to Florida or shells from trips to the ocean to show and tell. One girl brought a keychain with an image of Niagara Falls. It seemed like everybody had been somewhere exciting—everybody but Arlo, and that made her nervous. But Arlo hadn't wanted to go anywhere else. She wanted to stay—to stay on the farm and the mountain forever. So that's what she said.

Arlo stood, turned to face the class, and swallowed the dry cardboard in her throat. The paper rattled in her hand and two boys in the back of the class snickered.

"Greg, Turner, pay attention. It will be your turns next." Miss Norris called the boys out, but she was clearly bored with the presentations. Arlo's confidence wilted. "Tell us where you went this summer, Arlo."

Arlo licked her lips, forcing her eyes from Greg and Turner and the cross-eyed expressions they both made behind Miss Norris's back. "I didn't really go anywhere, not anywhere away. My family came from out west in the spring, and we stayed here on the mountain. I live with my pa and my sister and brother and Aunt Ginny Dee and Aunt Bethany and Uncle Luke at Wetherill Pickering's Christmas Tree Farm, and I love it. There's no other place like it."

"That old Christmas tree farm? Just a bunch of fields of cut-down trees," Jake Stillcoat, a good-looking boy half a head taller than Arlo, snickered. Half of the class, especially the girls, followed suit.

"Jake, that's enough." Miss Norris spoke firmly but hardly anybody paid her any mind.

"It's more than that. I don't mean the Christmas trees. Until I moved here, I never saw the sun rise over the mountain in so many colors or set in a flame of fire before dusk. I never saw trees stand dark against a sky studded with stars—so many you'd think they were fireflies alive in the heavens."

The room went quiet. Miss Norris looked up, tilted her head. "Go on, Arlo."

"Before I moved here, I never knew the names of flowers, or what they mean—that there even was a language of flowers. Aunt Ginny Dee taught me that every flower has a name—a botanical name and a common name, and every flower, every plant has a meaning. You can send a whole message to another person in a bouquet of flowers and it's secret unless the person you're sending them to can understand that language too."

You could hear a pin drop.

Arlo pulled the frame from her backpack and held it close to her stomach. "My brother and sister and I collect flowers and leaves. Sometimes we find them in Aunt Ginny Dee's gardens, or we go hunting wild ones together. Sometimes I trek the mountain alone, searching out new and higher places. I find new haunts all the time and new flowers and leaves—some I know the names of and more I don't—and bring them back home where Aunt Ginny Dee helps me press them. We have to change the papers every couple of days to get the moisture out, so they don't mold or go brown, so they keep their color. But once they're dried, we use a special glue, Aunt Bethany does the lettering because her printing's the best, and we make pictures out of them, like this."

Arlo turned her picture around and held it up. She dared to look at the class, surprised she held their attention, especially the girls. But the boy who'd made fun of her crossed his arms over his chest and glared.

"That's beautiful!" Emily, Mrs. Shellhorn's granddaughter, gasped. "You made that yourself?"

Arlo nodded. "It's not hard once you know how. Just takes patience, and you have to be careful not to tear the flowers. We make all sorts of pictures and sell them."

"You said all the flowers mean something. What do those mean?" Ann Prescott asked.

Arlo warmed. "That's a really fun part, learning the meanings. The dark green laurel leaves symbolize growth, good health, and renewal. That fits, because I think that's what moving to New Scrivelsby and the mountain has done for me and my family. Some folks say laurel leaves mean fame—like the laurel wreaths Roman and Greek emperors used to wear—but I like renewal. That's a good word.

"Sweet peas mean thank you—gratitude and friendship—and that's fitting, too, because friendship's what my family found here, and we're grateful. Dark pink roses can mean gratitude, too, but also love and joy. All of these together say what I feel about the farm, about staying here. I just hope we can—stay, I mean." Arlo sat down, shoved her picture back into her book bag, and kept her eyes on her desk. Heat traveled up her neck. She'd never talked so much to strangers in her life.

Miss Norris walked from the back of the room. As she passed, she placed her hand on Arlo's shoulder and gave it a little squeeze. "I hope you can too. That was lovely, Arlo, and your picture is lovely too."

"I want to learn how to make those," Emily whispered. "Will you show me?"

Arlo hadn't expected that. As soon as Emily spoke, two other girls sitting nearby whose names Arlo didn't remember whispered, "Me too. Show us?"

Arlo smiled shyly and nodded. "Sure. Come out to the farm. It's not hard." *Can making friends be that easy?* Arlo'd never had friends before, not more than Marley and Cooper.

"Tomorrow? After school?"

"Sure, we can take the bus home. Aunt Ginny Dee will help."

"Sit with us at lunch."

"Girls, no talking," Miss Norris reprimanded, but not too seriously.

Emily smiled at Arlo and Arlo smiled back. Maybe the school year wouldn't be so bad after all.

When the bell rang for lunch, Miss Norris had the class line up by the door. Arlo took time to stow her book bag on a shelf in the back of the classroom so found herself at the end of the line. Miss Norris led the class through the hallway and into the cafeteria. Arlo was almost through the cafeteria door when Jake, the boy in front of her, the one who'd made fun of the farm, turned and slammed her against the wall.

"You and your brats stay off the mountain, you hear me? Stick to your flower garden and Christmas trees. I won't say it again."

The breath flew from Arlo. Still, she wasn't one to back down from a fight. "What do you care? What's it to you?"

Jake blinked, clearly not used to anyone standing up to him. "You heard me." He gave her an extra shove, hard enough to leave a bruise on her upper arm, and walked through the cafeteria door.

❦

The encounter shook Arlo. She didn't know what was up with Jake Stillcoat, why he cared what she did on her family's farm, or why he sidled up to Emily at lunch, taking the last seat at her table—a seat she was sure Emily had saved for her. But Jake was good-looking, especially when he smiled, and Emily and the other girls at the table ate his attention up like candy.

Arlo tried not to watch, but she had a perfect view from what she realized was the reject table—the table where a few leftover kids sat, together only because they were not included, not invited to join cliques of well-established friends.

What did I expect? There are bullies everywhere, and I'm new here. More disconcerting was when Emily cast worried glances Arlo's way.

Arlo dared not think about that, dared not care. Emily, and the two girls whose names Arlo didn't know yet, had all said they'd ask their moms if they could come out to the farm after school the next day so Aunt Ginny Dee could teach them how to press flowers. Arlo would think on that, plan for that, look forward to that. She wouldn't let Jake's meanness spoil her anticipation.

❦

After school Arlo flew from the bus and down the long lane to the house. She slammed open the back kitchen door to find Marley and Cooper standing on kitchen chairs—Marley shaping cookie balls and Cooper cleaning the bowl with one finger.

"Arlo!" Aunt Ginny Dee sang. "You're home! How was your day? How did your presentation go?"

"We're making cookies to celebrate you!" Marley chirped.

"Miss Norris really liked it and I think the other kids did too, mostly. Emily and two other girls are all coming over tomorrow. They want to learn how to press flowers. That's okay, isn't it? Please say yes. I told them you would."

Aunt Ginny Dee's brows raised. "You invited them all here?"

Arlo nodded, plucking a cookie from the cooling rack. "They can ride the bus home with me, and their moms will pick them up before supper. Please?"

"Well, that's unexpected, but I don't see why not," Aunt Ginny Dee mused, tapping her finger to her chin. "Perhaps we should save some of these cookies for tomorrow so we can have an after-school tea party at the same time. What do you think?"

"That would be great!" Arlo hugged her aunt, something so rare that Aunt Ginny Dee stiffened in surprise, but then she wrapped her arms around Arlo and squeezed tight.

CHAPTER TWENTY-FOUR

BETHANY HELPED AUNT GINNY DEE prepare for the tea party. They spread Grandmother Pickering's best damask cloth, the wedding present from England that she'd preserved in a drawer laden with lavender and, as far as Aunt Ginny Dee remembered, had used only for weddings or birthdays.

Marley and Cooper found the prettiest pink and yellow roses blooming in the rose garden. Bethany cut long stems of purple salvia and mint to round out the bouquet and arranged a low centerpiece for the table. She brought over some rosebud china she saved for special occasions, as delighted as Aunt Ginny Dee and Marley to be part of creating a girls' tea party.

Of course, Cooper and Marley needed to sample every type of little sandwich—cucumber with watercress and cream cheese on white bread, paper-thin sliced ham with a smattering of mustard and butter on rye, pimento cheese on wheat, and egg salad with dill on white.

Aunt Ginny Dee made lavender and orange scones—the recipe her mother had said came from the Dymoke family in England. Bethany looked up a recipe for mock Devonshire cream. They filled cut-glass bowls with jam made from Bethany's own strawberries. The kitchen smelled heavenly.

"Are we overdoing it?" Bethany asked as they stood back late afternoon, awaiting the arrival of the girls.

"Probably," Aunt Ginny Dee mused, "but why not? If the girls think this is special, they might want to come again. That would be good for Arlo. She needs friends. Anything we can do to help."

"Yes," Bethany agreed wholeheartedly, stroking Marley's hair. "Anything."

The women smiled at each other. Bethany's heart warmed. *Children. Family. Companionship. Friendship—for Arlo and for me. Thank You, Lord, for Aunt Ginny Dee. I don't know what the future holds for any of us, but the present is good, a bounteous gift.*

At three o'clock the women set the kettle to boil and Marley and Cooper, cross-legged, posted watch on the front porch. By three fifteen Bethany began to fidget, checking the front door or parlor window. By three forty-five both women were worried.

"Where could they be?" Bethany set the kettle off the boil. "Unless their bus broke down? Maybe I should drive toward the school and see?"

"But you don't know exactly what route the bus takes. What county roads."

"No, I don't."

"Maybe we should call Mark, see what he thinks, see if he wants to go by the school—or phone."

But just then Mark and Luke drove down the lane with a pickup load of mulch. Bethany ran out the back door. "Mark! Luke! Stop!" She ran after the truck, tried to wave them down, but it was too late; the fruit trees had blocked their rear view of the lane and they'd driven on toward the fields. Bethany stopped, almost to the barn and out of breath, when she noticed that the barn door stood open and Bailey, who usually stood watch, waiting for Arlo, was nowhere in sight.

The rule was for everyone to make certain the barn door remained closed at all times lest skunks or other critters made their way in. With Mark and the children living there, everyone was careful. She was about to close and latch the door when she heard Bailey whimpering and a bit of snuffling that could only be human.

"Bailey?" Bethany called, stepping inside. "You okay, boy? Where are you?" Bailey came right away, took Bethany's skirt in his mouth, and tugged her forward. "What is it? What is it, boy?"

More snuffling came from the loft above. "Hello? Who's up there?" No one should be. Bailey raised up on hind feet, paws clinging to the ladder, as if he wanted to climb. That's when Bethany glimpsed Arlo's book bag thrown across the bunk. "Arlo? Honey, is that you?"

No response.

Bethany gave Bailey a grateful scratch behind the ears and climbed the ladder, peeking over the top into the loft. She couldn't see into the dark, but the snuffling stopped. "Arlo?" She crawled onto the flooring and peered into the space packed with boxes and old trunks, bales of hay and all manner of things Bethany had never explored. She listened carefully and finally heard breathing and sniffles off to her left. She crawled forward until she'd cleared a beam, hoping she wouldn't place a hand on rats or mice or squirrels or bats or whatever made their homes in old barns.

Finally, her eyes adjusted to the dim light, and she recognized a huddled form against an old trunk, swiping at eyes with a sleeve. Bethany didn't speak but crawled close to Arlo and wrapped her in her arms. Arlo shuddered, her still-thin shoulders evident through her top.

"Whatever it is," Bethany whispered, "I'm so sorry for this hurt. Whatever caused it, you don't deserve this hurt. You're a good girl, Arlo Pickering, a sweet girl, a brave girl."

That opened a floodgate, one that Bethany believed had long been dammed. She didn't ask, didn't try to calm Arlo, but let her cry.

Minutes passed before Arlo lifted her head from Bethany's shoulder. Bethany passed her the tissue she always kept in her pocket and Arlo wiped her face, blew her nose, and handed it back.

"The girls couldn't come?" It was the only thing that made sense to Bethany.

Arlo shook her head. "They wouldn't come."

"Maybe later."

"Never. Nobody will ever come here."

"I thought they were all so eager."

"Yesterday they were. Before Jake Stillcoat—a boy at school—told them about Pa."

"Your dad?"

Arlo swallowed loud enough that Bethany heard. "He said Pa's a druggie and a drunk, that he's been in and out of jail more times than he can count—like a dog going back to eat its vomit."

"That's a vile thing to say!"

"It's not true! Pa did some time once—*once*. That was all and it was a long time ago, before I was even born."

Bethany pulled Arlo even closer. "Ages ago. Your pa is a good man. Look how hard he's working to make a go of things here, to help Aunt Ginny Dee, to make a home for you and Marley and Cooper. Not many men are so brave and strong as that, especially not when—"

Arlo pulled back. "Not when what?"

Bethany could have bitten her tongue. She hadn't meant to say it, even though she'd thought it a dozen times over the last several months. She sighed. Arlo was old enough to hear the truth, old enough to need the truth. "Not when he's doing it alone, without your mom. It's hard for a man alone to know what children need the way a mother does, but your pa is doing all those things the best he can. And he brought you here where you have Aunt Ginny Dee and me to help. We all love you, you know—you and Marley and Cooper—and we're so glad, so lucky to have you here. The farm is a good place for all of you, for all of us together."

"Emily doesn't think so. She was all excited about coming yesterday, but not anymore. She said if her mom had known about my pa and the people Jake said he hangs out with, she wouldn't have said yes."

"Why would she say that? Why would this boy Jake say such a thing?"

"He said his uncle shoots pool with Pa at the bar in town, that he knows all about him and that he's still the same piece of trouble he ever was."

"His uncle?" But then Bethany remembered. *Jake's mother has a twin brother . . . the one that Luke said started Mark drinking back in high school. What in the world is he doing here? I thought he'd moved away.*

"I don't know anything about that, Aunt Bethany, I swear." Arlo frowned. "Sometimes Pa goes out at night when he thinks we're all asleep, but I don't know where."

"Let's not jump to conclusions. You know your pa's not drinking. You'd have smelled it on him."

"He's not. I know what he's like when he drinks, and he's not done it for a long time. He promised me he never would again."

"He wouldn't be able to work like he does if he was, so don't you worry about that. It sounds as if Jake is looking to cause a rift between you and the girls . . . but why, I can't imagine."

"Emily believes everything Jake says because she likes him, because he acts like he likes her, but I don't believe it. I think some of the kids are a little bit afraid of him."

"I don't understand that kind of meanness. But I'm sorry, Arlo. I know what this day meant to you and I'm just so sorry."

"I thought those girls wanted to be my friends. Some friends."

"Don't count them out yet. Things have a way of coming right side up, but it might take time."

Arlo's shoulders sagged.

"In the meantime, they're missing out on an incredible tea party—sandwiches, scones, petit fours—"

"Petty what?"

Bethany smiled and hugged Arlo. "Petit fours—little cakes with amazing frosting and tiny icing flowers piped on top." She stood, pulling Arlo to her feet. "Come on—we're not letting that tea party go to waste. Let's go! Marley and Cooper can hardly wait to dig in!"

"I'm not sure I wanna eat anything, Aunt Bethany."

"Maybe not now, but just you wait and see what's there. Take a look, and if you don't want to eat, you don't have to. But just take a peek. Aunt Ginny Dee's outdone herself, and Marley and Cooper are so excited."

"But all that work and the girls didn't come."

"Doesn't matter. We didn't do it for them. We did it for you because we love you. We'd do it a million times over for you, Arlo Pickering."

Down the ladder, Arlo's feet dragged toward the house. But when the back door opened, Marley and Cooper flung themselves into Arlo's arms.

"We didn't know what happened to you!" Marley cried.

"You came back!" Cooper wrapped his arms around her leg.

"'Course I did. I'd never leave you." Arlo reached down for her brother.

"Or me." Marley's eyes asked more than said.

"Or you—ever!" Arlo's grip on her siblings left them breathless.

Aunt Ginny Dee watched, off to the side, and set the teakettle back on the burner. Her brows rose in question, but Bethany simply shook her head—*No, the girls aren't coming.*

"Look what we made you, Arlo!" Marley grabbed her sister's arm and pulled her to the table.

Arlo's eyes grew three times their size. "Wow! You guys made all of this?"

"Aunt Ginny Dee and Aunt Bethany helped, but we picked all the flowers!"

"Time for a feast!" Aunt Ginny Dee declared, setting a three-tiered tower of finger sandwiches, scones, and petit fours in the middle of the table.

A smile hovered around Arlo's lips.

That was praise, joy, and relief enough for Bethany.

CHAPTER TWENTY-FIVE

SEPTEMBER STOLE THE INTENSE HEAT from the mountain, yielding the last great bounty from the garden before frost. October brought cold nights and mornings, brilliant blue skies that made Arlo's chest ache for the beauty of it all, and lots of autumn bonfires and get-togethers that Arlo wasn't invited to.

The girls at school hadn't warmed up so there were no sleepovers or birthday party invitations, even though there were lots of whispers and giggles and note passing going on before every weekend.

Once Jake had firmly twisted Emily around his little finger regarding Arlo, he dropped her. Arlo figured it served Emily right, being such a ninny for a boy, but somehow Emily blamed Arlo for their breakup, as if there was anything to break.

That little bit of satisfaction didn't make lunchtime any less lonely. Even when Jake stopped eating with Emily just before Halloween, she'd pushed her tray between the two seats, making sure everybody knew there was no room beside her. Arlo tried not to care. She'd long begun taking a book to lunch and reading while she ate. The other kids at her table had little to say.

By November hard frost had taken the last of the flowers and there was nothing in the vegetable garden but a few rotting pumpkins, gleanings left for wildlife.

The botanical business was booming—at least in Arlo's mind. Mr. Skipwith had sold five pictures from his office, and Rosemary, over at the diner, had sold twelve, five to locals and seven to folks passing through, all for a better price than even Aunt Ginny Dee had expected.

Aunt Ginny Dee, Arlo, and even Marley had been working with the presses and arrangements every spare minute, preparing more botanical pictures to sell at the church Christmas bazaar, hoping folks would find them irresistible Christmas gifts.

Arlo figured the best thing she could do on Saturday mornings was to fuel a steady supply of leaves and holly—anything they could press through the winter to add to the houseplants and African violets Aunt Ginny Dee grew inside. She'd already gleaned leaves through the fall before hard frost—reds so brilliant they raced Arlo's blood, yellows so bright they rivaled the sun.

There might not be another Saturday Arlo could search. Extra outdoor work for the Christmas tree season had already begun for Pa and Uncle Luke, which meant picking up their home chores. Aunt Ginny Dee and Aunt Bethany talked about making and decorating wreaths to sell alongside the Christmas trees, something the farm had not offered for years. Arlo would help with those evenings and weekends, but before that she determined to make one more collecting trek over the mountain.

In the half dark, Arlo slid from her bunk before Marley or Cooper opened their eyes. Dressed in layers and with Bailey on her heels, she slipped into Aunt Ginny Dee's kitchen and pocketed one of last night's baked potatoes, a biscuit, and a slice of Virginia ham wrapped in wax paper. She poured a thermos of milk and mixed in some chocolate syrup. She'd be back by lunch, but a girl needed something to keep her going. Over her shoulder she slung the satchel; tucked inside was a pair of sharp scissors and the pen and notebook that Aunt Ginny Dee had made her for the collecting and recording of plants.

Climbing the mountain with Bailey was one of the greatest joys of Arlo's life. Collecting botanicals for the presses had become her quest, a great purpose to be shared with Bailey, her best friend after Marley and Cooper.

The great thing about dogs, Arlo thought as she trooped, *is that they never ask questions, never talk back, never nag, never want you to be anything but you. They don't mind who you are or what your pa did or where you came from.* For Arlo, sick and tired of watching her p's and q's at school five days a week, Bailey's joy and faithfulness were a reprieve and a gift. He didn't care where she went or what she did; he was just happy to go along, and he didn't need watching every minute like the little kids.

Arlo reached the first ridge in time to see the sun spread its rose and golden fingers over the mountain. Clouds of frosty air puffed from her mouth. She stopped, huffed bigger clouds into the dawn, threw up her arms, and raced up the mountainside until a stich grabbed her side. Laughing, she grabbed Bailey, who happily rolled with her across the heavily frost-crusted grass.

She'd never climbed this high or explored this far away from home. With no Christmas trees or fields of anything she recognized, she didn't even know if she was still on Pickering land—but how could it matter? Nobody lived up here, so far off the road or beaten path. Once she settled, she realized she'd best take note of her surroundings, to be sure she'd find her way back.

Arlo ducked into a small copse of trees that led down into a hidden valley. Soft green fern, reminding her of maidenhair fern, spread across the ground, not yet taken by hard frost. *A wonder. How did you escape frost? Aunt Ginny Dee won't believe this!* Arlo dropped her satchel onto the forest floor, took out her sharp scissors, and snipped stems from as close to the ground as she could. Pressing each one carefully between the pages of her notebook took time, but even that was part of the joy. Aunt Ginny Dee would be so pleased. She loved ferns and none grew close to the farm. *What happens to you when the snows come, little fern? Way up here all alone.*

Bailey's insistent bark drew Arlo to her feet, thinking of bears and deer. It wasn't deer-hunting season, but Arlo knew not everybody on the mountain kept to the hunting dates. And bears had no sense of territory, especially if they were hungry. Those were the two reasons her pa had warned her not to stray too far up the mountain, especially not alone.

"Bailey! Bailey! Come back!"

He didn't come back, but kept barking, barking. Arlo's blood ran cold, but she tore through the trees, following Bailey's bark through the valley and up a steep hill, out into the open in a high, sunlit field on the edge of a lake.

A skunk.

"Bailey! Get away—now!"

But it was too late. The little critter had sprayed Bailey with a good dose of everything it had, and Bailey responded by yelping, barking, running in half-blind circles, rolling on the ground, and pawing at his nose and face.

"Oh, man! Bailey! Are you okay? Settle down, boy. We'll get you home. Oh, wow. You stink! Aunt Ginny Dee's gonna kill me. She's never gonna let you in the house! Crazy dog."

Bailey whimpered, heading for sympathy and Arlo.

"No you don't—you stay away. I'm not petting you now. We're gonna have to clean you up. We're gonna be in such trouble." *At least we're coming back with fern. Maybe that'll help offset the trouble.*

She was about to turn back when she noticed the leavings of plants she'd never seen. A whole field of mostly harvested something. She snipped one. Green, with leaves beginning to yellow just a little on their fringes, and prickly centers—like flowers, but not. Arlo'd never seen a plant like that, and there were rows of them—a couple acres or more—mostly harvested, but not all. It was an odd-looking plant, but Aunt Ginny Dee pressed all kinds of things and combined them into beautiful pictures. She liked including "unusual specimens" as she called them, "leaves that give texture to an arrangement." *Well, these sure have "texture."*

Arlo clipped a bouquet. The plants were too prickly and thick to press in her notebook as she'd done with the ferns. She'd need to wait until she could work with Aunt Ginny Dee and the straight pins when they opened the real presses back home.

Arlo sighed. *I can't think about that now. I've got to get Bailey home. Pa'll know what to do, but I don't know how I'll ever get him and his stink by Aunt Ginny Dee.*

By the time Arlo and Bailey reached the farm, the sun was high in the sky. Halfway across the field they met Pa. "Arlo, where've you been? I been looking all over for you and that fool dog. Whew! I can smell you two a mile off."

"Skunked, Pa. Bailey got skunked. I couldn't get him to come back in time."

"No kidding. Did you get sprayed too?"

"No, sir. It's just he smells so strong."

"Tomato juice. We'll have to soak him in tomato juice behind the barn. Aunt Ginny Dee will never let him near her kitchen."

"One good thing: I found some new botanicals. Maybe that'll soften her up."

Pa gave Arlo an "in your dreams" look, enough that Arlo stopped talking.

By the time they reached the backyard, Aunt Ginny Dee stood with fists on her hips outside the back kitchen door, Marley and Cooper at her side, holding their noses. Aunt Bethany's screen door slammed. Everybody and their brother knew they were coming.

"Bailey!" Pa whistled. "Come here, boy. That's it—follow me. We've got to get you cleaned up. Arlo, ask Aunt Ginny Dee for all the tomato juice she can spare. Tell her what happened."

"I can smell what happened. You stay outside, Arlo, and I'll hand you the juice. It's a good thing we juiced that abundance of tomatoes, but I wasn't planning on washing this dog with it!"

"Sorry, Aunt Ginny Dee. I couldn't stop him." Arlo pulled her satchel off her shoulder. "But I did find some good leaves—ferns and something new, I think. Some weird plant full of texture." She smiled big, hoping Aunt Ginny Dee would be thrilled.

"I suppose there's redemption in most things. I'll trade you jars of my juice for your satchel. You go on and help your pa."

Arlo figured she'd gotten off easy. Nobody'd even asked how far afield she'd gone.

CHAPTER TWENTY-SIX

GINNY SHOOK HER HEAD over the foolishness of dogs and girls. It had taken three days to put up all the tomatoes and juice from the bounty of the garden. It would take nearly half that juice to get the stink off Bailey. Still, as annoying as it was, Ginny couldn't help but smile. It reminded her of the time Harold and Curtis had gone hunting raccoon in the dead of night. Well, they'd found coon, but got good and skunked in the process.

Three days Mama kept them home and made them sleep in the barn, even after they both soaked in tomato juice. Well, Bailey's not coming in that back door anytime soon. I just hope Arlo didn't get it too. She'd never live that down at school.

Ginny sighed as she pulled open Arlo's satchel. *That girl does beat all. At least the satchel didn't get it.* She lifted Arlo's notebook first and found the fern stems—delicate and as carefully pressed as anyone could do in the field.

What a wonder. I'm proud of you, Arlo Pickering. You're turning into a real botanist—or at least a floraphile!

The back door opened. Bethany walked in. "Whew! Who got skunked? I smelled it from my house."

"Bailey—at least I hope it's only Bailey. He and Arlo were out exploring and collecting again. I guess he ran into a bit of trouble."

191

"Trouble! I'll say . . . Oh, look, fern! Where did you get those?"

"I didn't. Arlo found them on her trek this morning. That girl does find the prettiest things."

"Those should press out beautifully."

"I can't imagine where she found them that they hadn't browned in the frost. Our miracle girl." Ginny dug deeper in the satchel, surprised by the prickly, sticky feel of what lay in the bottom. She pulled out the half-crushed bouquet of leaves and turned them over, not sure what she was seeing.

Bethany gasped. The women looked at each other and Ginny frowned.

"Is that—is that what I think it is?" Bethany touched the spiky leaves.

"It sure looks like it to me. Where on earth?"

"Where did she find it? Does she know what it is?"

"I can't imagine she does. She was so excited about finding something new and different."

"This is not good."

Ginny sighed. "We should find out where it is and call the police."

"Oh, wow. Luke will have a conniption."

"We can't just let it go. We have to report it."

"But the police?"

"Will. I can call Will. He'll know what we should do."

"You don't think . . . Wait." Bethany placed her hand on Ginny's arm. "Just wait. Don't call, not yet. Let me talk to Luke."

Ginny wasn't sure she felt comfortable with that. The sooner it was reported, the sooner it would be out of their hands. *Unless . . . does Bethany think . . . No, I won't go there. I don't believe it.*

CHAPTER TWENTY-SEVEN

"MONDAY." Bethany laid the two stems on her kitchen table before Luke. "That's all the time Aunt Ginny Dee would agree to wait before calling Will. She said he'd know what to do. And she's right. If we don't tell the authorities, we'll be considered involved in some way."

Luke pushed work-roughened fingers through his hair, drew his hand down the side of his face. "I should have known. I should have guessed there was a reason he came back."

"There was a reason Mark came back—three, and they're good children. He's worked his tail off helping turn things around here. I can't believe he'd risk—anyway, where would he even have found the time?"

"Maybe he was in the area before he ever showed up here. Maybe he's just been using us, using the land, stringing us along."

"That's a lot of maybes. Just ask him."

Luke huffed. "You think he'd say?"

"You won't know unless you ask. He deserves that. He's blood. He's your brother. You can't jump to those conclusions."

"Don't tell me you didn't." Luke's eyes penetrated Bethany's.

Bethany looked away. *It can't be true. It can't.*

"Aunt Bethany?" Arlo called from the back door. "Aunt Bethany?"

Bethany pressed Luke's arm and went to open the door. "What is it, sweetie?"

"Aunt Ginny Dee said to ask you if we could borrow a couple more jars of tomato juice. We've used all hers to scrub Bailey and he still smells—not so bad, but not too good either."

"Sure, come on in. I'll get them from the pantry for you."

"Hi, Uncle Luke." Arlo stopped. "I didn't mean to get Bailey skunked. I'll work the cost of the tomato juice off. Just tell me what you want me to do."

"There's no need, Arlo. Bailey's getting skunked was not your fault." Bethany would have no recriminations dealt.

Luke picked up one of the stems. "Where'd you find this?"

Arlo's eyes brightened, then went wary. "Up the mountain."

"Where?"

Arlo looked away.

"I said, where? Tell me now."

"Luke, you're scaring her." Bethany turned to Arlo. "You're not in trouble, Arlo. We just want to know where you found it; we need to know."

Arlo looked as if she didn't believe that. She drew a breath so deep her shoulders rose and fell. "Up the mountain. Higher than I've ever been. I know I shouldn't have gone so far, but it was a great morning—it just felt so good, especially after I found the fern. I knew Aunt Ginny Dee would love those. And then Bailey started barking and at first I couldn't find him, but then I kept following his bark and he was at a standoff with that skunk and there it was."

"This plant?" Bethany encouraged.

"A whole field of them! Up by a lake. I don't know whose land it is or what that plant is. I'm gonna look it up in my book, but there must be a full acre of it growing."

"The high meadow," Luke said. "Mark's meadow. The one Pop promised him."

Bethany and Luke shared a look. Bethany held her breath, determined not to cry.

"Pa's meadow?" Arlo asked. "I didn't know he had his own meadow." She looked from Bethany to Luke. "What's wrong? Shouldn't I have picked it? I won't do it again. I promise. I didn't know."

"No." Bethany drew Arlo into a hug. "It's not your fault. None of this is your fault."

Luke threw the stems to the table, his face grim. He pulled his work boots and flannel jacket from the mudroom and headed for the door.

"Where are you going?"

"To see for myself."

"Luke!" But he was gone.

"Am I in trouble?" Arlo looked up into Bethany's eyes, worried as a child could be.

"No, sweetie. You're not. I promise you're not." But that was all Bethany could promise.

CHAPTER TWENTY-EIGHT

ARLO DIDN'T KNOW WHAT TO THINK. Uncle Luke, Aunt Bethany, even Aunt Ginny Dee all seemed vexed about the plants she'd brought back, though they wouldn't tell her why. Aunt Ginny Dee liked the fern but that didn't make things okay.

Pa grumbled over the time it took from his work to clean Bailey and over the tomato juice wasted in bathing him to get rid of the stink.

Marley and Cooper pouted because Arlo had taken off that morning without them. All in all, it was a lousy Saturday that had started out so perfect. Even Bailey looked at her like she'd betrayed him with that tomato juice bath.

Arlo decided laying low was her best option, so she grabbed her latest read, *A Christmas Carol*, from Aunt Ginny Dee's bookshelf, bundled up in an old quilt, and took up residence on the front porch swing. She was just to the part where Scrooge was meeting the Ghost of Christmas Past when Uncle Luke's truck barreled down the lane and past the house, screeching to a stop outside the barn. She heard the cab door slam and the barn door thrown open against its hinges.

Arlo crept around the house in time to see Uncle Luke grab her pa by the shirt collar and throw him up against the barn. He shoved something green and yellow in Pa's face—surely the same plant Arlo had picked that morning. She couldn't hear what Uncle Luke said, but she heard her pa swear.

"What are you talking about? It's not mine. It's not me! I've got nothing to do with that. I didn't even know about it!"

"Liar! I should've known. Snake in the grass—that's what Pop called you. Snakes don't change their shape."

"Luke! When would I even have done that? I've been here, working every minute with you."

"Not every minute, apparently. Don't deny it. You were seen in town chatting it up with Rob and his buddies, and we both know where that leads."

"What's that supposed to mean?"

Uncle Luke shook his head. "Expecting the truth out of you is like wishing for snow in August. This isn't a new field. It's been harvested. Who's your buyer?" He gripped Pa's collar harder, looking like he might choke him.

That's when Pa pushed him off, shoved him backward so hard Uncle Luke nearly fell in the dirt. Arlo's throat caught. Uncle Luke scrambled to get his footing and picked up a two-by-four, ready to tear into Pa.

Arlo could see nothing but blood coming and headed for the fray. But Aunt Ginny Dee caught her and shoved her back. "Stay out of this, Arlo. I mean it. Go back in the house with Marley and Cooper. Keep them busy."

Arlo wanted to protest, but Aunt Ginny Dee was halfway to the barn. "Stop it! Stop it, you two, or get off my land. I mean it! Brothers will not fight on Pickering land!"

"He's going to bring this whole thing down on all our heads. I told you not to trust him! Well, I'm not going to jail because you and Bethany went all soft on those kids. You hear me? I'm not!" Uncle Luke seemed to realize what he was about to do and threw the two-by-four to the ground.

"I swear, Aunt Ginny Dee, I had nothing to do with that. I didn't even know about it."

Uncle Luke stepped closer to Pa. "You were arrested for using and selling."

"That was more than ten years ago! I did my time, and you know it. I haven't even smoked since. And I've been sober for two years."

"So why were your kids taken away?"

Pa looked as if somebody had gut punched him. "Not for weed."

"Stop!" Then Aunt Ginny Dee said something more Arlo couldn't hear.

"Crystal couldn't stop using," Pa pled. "She tried coming back, even tried rehab—but after Cooper was born, she . . . and they took her away."

Arlo couldn't hear everything he'd said or what came next. She crept closer. Phrases and snippets came.

". . . drunk driving. I did my penance for that too. I haven't had a drink since. I swear. If I had I'd never of gotten my kids back."

"Right." Uncle Luke smirked. "Right. You always could spin a yarn." He swore, looking like he might explode, but glancing at Aunt Ginny Dee, he turned and walked away.

Aunt Ginny Dee stared a long time at Pa, but Arlo couldn't tell what she said. Finally, she turned on her heel and walked back toward the kitchen. Arlo stepped behind the camellia bush, not wanting to be caught eavesdropping.

Sunday was miserable. Everybody went to church. Nobody in the family sang the hymns except Aunt Bethany and Arlo, who only mouthed the words. Nobody spoke or looked at one another or met the preacher's eye. Pa's shoulders rounded and he spent the day gazing off into the distance, as if to some faraway land, as far removed as when Ma took off. And that scared Arlo.

Ma's leaving had been the beginning of all their worst troubles. Things had been bad enough before with Ma flitting in and out of reality, drinking, doing drugs, staying out all hours, and forgetting to feed the little ones or to change Cooper's diaper. But when she'd disappeared for good and Pa was on his own with the kids, it was like he teetered on the edge of some cliff Arlo couldn't pull him back from.

That's when he'd started drinking more than one or two shots a night. He lost job after job. What money he'd made went to more drink. There were days and nights Arlo had nothing to feed Marley or Cooper. She'd stopped going to school at six and a half years old just to make sure they stayed safe. She'd even stolen food—shoplifting baby formula, an apple here, a box of mac and cheese there, until she was caught.

That's when the foster-care people stepped in and split them up. She didn't know all that had happened to Marley and Cooper during that time, but she knew from her own experience things happened that never should—like not knowing if her pa was dead or alive or knocked out drunk someplace or if she'd ever see him or Cooper or Marley again; like having older kids push her around or touch her in ways she knew they shouldn't. And things didn't happen that should've—like being given enough food to eat or decent shoes to wear or a coat when it was cold, or even medicine when she was sick. She couldn't let them be separated again—not ever. She'd promised Marley . . . never ever again.

All she knew was that this trouble had something to do with those plants she'd brought back, but she didn't know why, or how picking a bunch of leaves could be so terrible. Was it like shoplifting? If it was, why weren't they all mad at her? Why were they mad at Pa?

Arlo didn't know, but she knew someone who might. Someone she could trust to have her back, and Pa's.

Monday, after school, Arlo didn't ride the bus home but took off on foot for Main Street in New Scrivelsby. Half a mile later the buzzer sounded as she opened the door to Skipwith and Son, Attorneys-at-Law. There was a man sitting, slouched, in the waiting room, reading a newspaper, one muddied boot propped over his opposite knee as if he had all the time in the world for everything.

Miss Baxter looked up from her typing. "Arlo! What a nice surprise. Are you here with your dad?" She looked over Arlo's shoulder, hopeful. Arlo's mouth tightened. She knew Miss Baxter was sweet on her pa from the way she eyed him at church—a thing Arlo didn't much like, but she needed Miss Baxter's help now and she knew that honey drew bees better than vinegar.

"Not today, just me. I need to see Mr. Skipwith. Please, ma'am."

"Well . . ." Miss Baxter glanced at the closed door to Mr. Skipwith's office. "He's with a client now. You'll have to wait. Do you have an appointment?"

Arlo looked at her like she was short on marbles. "I'm a kid. I don't make appointments."

Miss Baxter smiled indulgently, as if Arlo was a very little kid. "No, but Mr. Skipwith does and I'm afraid he's booked for the afternoon."

Arlo leaned over the desk and stage-whispered, "I need to see him real bad. Now. He said to come anytime."

Arlo must have conveyed urgency. Miss Baxter leaned over the desk to whisper back, "Have a seat. When he comes out of his meeting, I'll ask him."

Arlo nodded. She knew she couldn't—shouldn't—expect more, but she was so revved up that sitting in the waiting room, across from the guy who looked somehow familiar but as much like a thug as anybody she'd ever seen, didn't appeal. She took a seat as far away from him as possible in the small waiting room. Her leg jiggled in time to her heart's racing.

The man across from her looked up, eyed her up and down, smirked, and went back to reading his newspaper.

Arlo looked away, anywhere but at him. She didn't know how she was going to get home except to walk, unless Mr. Skipwith or Miss Baxter gave her a ride, which she knew she shouldn't ask. Bursting in on Mr. Skipwith was impulsive, but she was desperate. He'd surely know what to do.

She'd do anything to stop the anger and tensions at home, anything in the world to make sure she and her pa, Marley, and Cooper weren't sent from the farm, weren't divided up into foster care again. She knew if Uncle Luke had anything to say about it they'd already be gone.

A half hour passed before Mr. Skipwith's office door opened and he ushered out a middle-aged man in a three-piece suit. "Thank you for taking my son under your wing, Mr. Skipwith. I know this is his best chance to make things right. I don't want him to start life with a record."

"Community service can be a good path forward, Mr. Trumo. We'll see if the judge agrees. I don't think there's anything further we can do until the hearing."

The man nodded and shook Mr. Skipwith's hand. "We'll talk then?"

"Yes, of course. Try not to worry. Have a good day."

Arlo couldn't wait another minute. The second the man turned toward the door, she jumped in front of Will Skipwith so that he nearly tripped. "Mr. Skipwith!"

"Arlo! This is a surprise. Are you here with your aunt?"

"No, sir. Just me. I've got to see you. Please. It's an emergency!"

Miss Baxter stood. "Your four o'clock appointment is here, Mr. Skipwith." She nodded toward the arrogant man still seated, staring at them.

"Please," Arlo begged. "It will only take a minute and it's a matter of life and death."

"I told Arlo she'd need to wait until after—"

"I'm sure we can take a minute for life and death matters, Miss Baxter." Mr. Skipwith smiled. "Mr. Warner, I'm sorry to keep you waiting. I'll be with you shortly."

The man grimaced, grunted, and picked up his paper again.

Mr. Skipwith held out his hand toward his office door. But Arlo couldn't wait. "It's all about some plants I picked high on the mountain. I just wanted to give them to Aunt Ginny Dee to press for our pictures—"

Mr. Skipwith closed the office door. "Slow down, Arlo. Take a seat and tell me what's happened."

"I found some plants on the mountain—up high—me and Bailey. I know we shouldn't have gone so far alone but that's not even what they're mad about," Arlo nearly shouted.

"Calm now. Lower your voice. Who's mad?"

"Aunt Ginny Dee, Aunt Bethany, Pa, but mostly Uncle Luke. He's accusing Pa of planting them, but Pa says he didn't, and I don't know why they care. Aunt Ginny Dee believes him but she's talking about calling the police anyway and Uncle Luke wants to send Pa away and that means all of us. This is the best home we've ever had, Mr. Skipwith."

"Let's just take this thing apart and look at it piece by piece. What does your pa say?"

"Nothing. That's just it. He's saying nothing and he just sits and stares. I'm afraid he'll . . ." But Arlo couldn't finish.

"What is it? What are you afraid about your pa?" Mr. Skipwith sat with his hand on her shoulder. His compassion nearly undid Arlo.

"I'm afraid he'll start drinking again. He hasn't for a really long time, but this is the way he looked when Ma up and left us. And it was after that, when he started drinking and lost his job and was staying away all hours, that they took Marley and Cooper away, and me. I promised Marley that I'd never let that happen again—I promised!"

"No one is talking about taking any of you away. I'm sure of that. Now, you believe this trouble has to do with plants you found?"

"I don't know what else. They're all mad. I never meant to steal anything. They were just sticky green leaves. Uncle Luke almost strangled Pa." Arlo couldn't hold it in any longer. Her shoulders shuddered and the tears began to fall until there was a torrent of sobs.

Mr. Skipwith brought a box of Kleenex and handed her two. He tipped her face to look into his. "Your aunt has already told me some of this, Arlo, and I can assure you that you are not in trouble and not to blame in any way. I believe your pa. He's a good man. We'll get it straightened out. I'm sure there has to be an explanation that will satisfy everyone."

Arlo shook her head. "I don't think that's gonna happen."

"Well, we'll see, won't we? Now, if you didn't come to town with your aunt, how did you get here? Who brought you?"

"I skipped the bus and ran from school. I didn't know where else to go, and you said I could come see you if I ever needed—"

"I'm glad you came. You come to me anytime; my door is always open for you, Arlo, but now we need to get you home. Your pa and aunt will be worried when that bus shows up and you're not on it. I need to talk to that man in the waiting room for a few minutes. I don't think it will take long. You dry your eyes and take this bottle of water and wait for me with Miss Baxter. I'll have her call your home and I'll drive you when I'm finished here. We'll get this thing settled. Whatever it is, we'll figure it out. I don't want you to worry, understand?"

Arlo nodded, but inside she wasn't sure that even Mr. Skipwith could fix this trouble. Still, it was good he was on her side, on Pa's side. She closed her eyes and wrapped her arms around his waist. If she could have a grandfather, Mr. Skipwith would be the one she'd choose.

Mr. Skipwith opened his office door. "Miss Baxter, Arlo is going to sit with you for a few—" He stopped. "Where is Mr. Warner?"

Miss Baxter shrugged. "He left, not long after you and Arlo went in. I guess he didn't want to wait."

"Sorry." Arlo looked up at Mr. Skipwith. She'd messed up again. He nodded absently but didn't look pleased.

CHAPTER TWENTY-NINE

AFTER THE CHILDREN HAD GONE TO BED, Ginny called a family meeting in the kitchen with Bethany, Luke, and Mark.

"I had a visit from Will Skipwith today when he brought Arlo home."

"Arlo? When did she—"

"She went to see Will because she was upset—because all of us are upset and acting like angry children. She's terrified that you two brothers—I almost said *knuckleheads*—are going after each other tooth and nail. She's afraid that she and Marley and Cooper will be taken away and sent into foster care again."

Mark glared at Luke but appeared to lose energy and looked away.

"Now, I told Will everything."

"You what?" Luke's voice rose. "You agreed to wait."

"Only until today. Be quiet, Luke, and listen." Apart from stopping the fight outside the barn it was the first time Ginny had ever bossed Luke. *High time and overdue.* "You should be thankful I did because he gave me good advice. He doesn't believe for a minute that Mark planted that field."

Mark looked up, a modicum of relief in his eyes.

"He can't know that." Luke crossed his arms over his chest and pushed back from the table.

"Yes, he can. He had the devil of a time tracking Mark down to tell him of your father's death because Mark was busy having the devil of a time getting his children out of three foster-care homes. With all that he was doing in Tennessee there's no way he could have been in this area before he showed up on my doorstep."

"That doesn't mean he didn't have some deal going on with—"

"I didn't. I wouldn't. I swear I'd never risk my kids for something so stupid."

"The children. Above all"—Ginny took her time looking each one in the eye—"the children are the biggest reason we have got to stop fighting and pull together and take care of this. If you can't get past your own pettiness and animosities for yourselves or for the sake of saving this farm, do it for these children. They deserve better. They deserve the best from each of us. They're Pickerings."

Bethany placed a hand on Luke's forearm and squeezed. It seemed to settle him, enough that he breathed a huge sigh, his arms still crossed.

"Will said that we need to check all our land, anywhere a field could be planted, anywhere we haven't physically walked in the last few months. Arlo found one field but that doesn't mean there aren't more."

Luke and Bethany exchanged worried glances.

"That could mean clear the other side of the mountain. All of that is Pickering land." Mark's brow creased.

Ginny wanted to say "Dymoke land" but kept to the point.

"We hardly have time for this." Luke shook his head. "We've got to begin cutting trees to ship this week."

"I'll do it," said Bethany. "I can do it."

"No!" Luke, Mark, and Ginny said at once.

"It's too dangerous," Luke went on. "We don't know who's behind this, how big the operation is. If they've taken over a whole field already, that means there's money involved—probably big money."

"But you just said you don't have time."

Luke pushed back from the table in frustration. "We have to get those trees cut and baled by next weekend or we'll miss our ship date."

"I'll do it," Mark said. "I'll cover the fields before dawn and get back by eight to cut and bale."

"You can't cover all that ground on foot in that time. And besides, I—"

"You want to see for yourself. You don't believe I'll tell you the truth," Mark challenged. "Even though I'm the one with everything at stake here."

"You're not the only one with everything at stake. If we get closed down for selling marijuana, we'll lose this farm."

Ginny clasped the hands of both her nephews. "We're not being closed down and we're not losing the farm. Luke, I think you should go with Mark so you can see everything for yourself."

Mark looked up, hurt in his eyes.

"It's not that I don't believe you, Mark. I do believe you, but Luke is the one who has to be convinced. If you two can't make peace and work together, I vow I will sell this farm and I'll do it now, before the Christmas rush."

Bethany gasped. "You wouldn't. After all our work?"

"It's not what I want but I will not tolerate this bickering. It wasn't just poor business decisions that endangered the farm. This kind of thing, this high-handed posturing between siblings—lies, recrimination, betrayal, refusal to help one another, refusal to forgive—brought us low. We can do better. We can all do better than this and we will, or we won't do it at all." She let go of the men's hands and sat back, waiting.

Only heavy breathing could be heard in the kitchen, and the ticking of the clock in the hallway.

Finally, Mark looked across the table to Luke. "What do you say? Will you go with me? We can get an early start."

Luke's jaw looked like granite. Bethany looked as if she were holding her breath.

"Luke?" Ginny had taken about all she was willing to from him.

He nodded. "Six. I'll be ready at six. We can take the truck on that back wagon trail as high as it will go."

Mark nodded and stood. "I'll meet you at the truck. Bring head-lamps and floodlights. We'll have to go on foot part of the way."

"I don't see how anybody'd get to those high fields with machinery to work them, anyway," Bethany said.

"I don't either," Ginny sighed. "But we have to know. We have to be certain before we notify the police."

"Leave the police out of this," Luke warned. "We'll take care of it."

But Ginny did not agree.

CHAPTER THIRTY

BETHANY'S FINGERS AND BACK ACHED from three hours of clipping and twining evergreen boughs into wreaths. She and Aunt Ginny Dee had been working all morning in the cold barn, wrapped in layers and sporting fingerless gloves. Bethany had to hand it to Aunt Ginny Dee: the woman worked nonstop for the sake of her family.

"I'm so glad you convinced Mark to let the children sleep inside now. It's far too cold for them out here."

Aunt Ginny Dee sighed. "I just wish Mark would come inside too. He doesn't seem to feel he belongs or that he has a right, but that's not true. He could share Harold's old room with Cooper. Half the time Cooper slips into the girls' room to be with them, anyway."

"He's so little." Bethany smiled. "He just doesn't want to be alone."

"Mark doesn't need to be alone either. I wish he understood that. Pickering men are so stubborn. My daddy was stubborn; I guess it runs down the line."

"Luke's to blame. He hasn't made Mark feel welcome . . . or trusted."

"Well, I hope investigating these fields together will help that. I trust Mark."

"I do, too, but Luke says he acts suspicious."

"Luke's the older brother—he doesn't trust the younger son who's returned to the family."

"Like in that parable Pastor Edwards spoke about, you mean."

"I do . . . and I understand that. I'm that younger sibling too. Harold was my older brother, only I didn't have the nerve to come back home. I just trusted what Harold wrote me. I've wondered, ever since I came back, if Mama even knew I wrote or if Harold kept my letter from her. I wonder, would she have welcomed me after all . . . like that running father?"

"Like you did Mark."

Aunt Ginny Dee set down her clippers and stretched her back, looking up. "We all have the chance to be any one of those characters—the runaway, prodigal son who finally wants to come home; the older, selfish, self-righteous brother who doesn't want to forgive or share what there is; or the running father, the one who doesn't hold the past against either son but welcomes each of them home once they come. I've been both of those brothers in my life, Bethany. I want to be the running father now."

"I can't imagine you were ever the older brother in that story, Aunt Ginny Dee—just the opposite."

Aunt Ginny Dee shook her head. "Oh, I was. I was self-righteous and selfish and angry, and all of that with the one who deserved far better from me."

"You mean Curtis?"

Aunt Ginny Dee looked as if Bethany had struck her in the face.

"I'm sorry. It's none of my business." Bethany hesitated. "It's just that you hardly ever mention him, and yet, from what I've heard—from folks who've lived around here a long time—you two had a great love story."

Aunt Ginny Dee sighed and sat down. "And you wonder."

"Curious."

Aunt Ginny Dee set her sights on something far away, something not in the barn but, Bethany knew, in memory.

"I loved Curtis with all my heart."

"Like the running father."

Aunt Ginny Dee gave a ladylike snort. "Not exactly . . . If anyone treated him like that it was Mama and Daddy. He'd been in trouble with the law when he was young—nothing terrible, but he needed a fresh start. He'd stolen food for his younger brother and himself. They were near to starving.

"Mr. Skipwith—Will's father—brought him out to the farm. Curtis needed a home, at least temporarily, and Daddy needed the help. Mama and Daddy welcomed him with open arms, even though he wasn't their blood son. And Curtis was good to them, a hard worker, and a good and faithful son in so many ways. He was the handsomest thing on two feet that I'd ever seen, and I loved him with all my teenage heart. And he loved me."

Aunt Ginny Dee bit her lip. Bethany wasn't certain she'd go on, but she waited until the older woman took up her story.

"Daddy had a sudden heart attack in the field one day. Curtis and I were supposed to be nearby, helping, but we'd run off to go swimming—and smooching—together. It was summer and hot . . . so hot the roses had stopped blooming. Even the butterflies had flown . . . or seemed to."

Aunt Ginny Dee shook her head, as if trying to push the memory away. "Daddy died a few days later. Harold blamed me—me and Curtis—and rightly so."

"His heart attack couldn't have been your fault." Bethany set her clippers on the worktable, sat down across from Aunt Ginny Dee, poured a cup of hot cider from their thermos, and passed it across the table. Aunt Ginny Dee cradled the warm cup in her hands.

"That's what Mama said. But I didn't believe her. I always thought she must blame me, no matter what she said, especially after I got that letter from Harold telling me I was dead to them."

"That was wicked, and surely a lie. She wouldn't have left your room just the same, waiting for you, if that were true." Bethany had endured more than she'd ever shared from her father-in-law and knew not to trust him.

"Maybe. But I didn't know about that then, or about our rose garden, that she'd kept the bench Daddy made us with our initials carved in the back. We used to sit there together, just sit . . . and watch the butterflies. Wings of hope—that's what Mama called them." Aunt Ginny Dee looked at Bethany. "The moment I saw that bench I wanted to take it as a sign. I don't know if I'm grasping."

"You're not." Bethany felt sure. If she'd had a daughter, she would love her with all her heart and nothing that daughter could do would make her love her any less. She had to believe Grandmother Pickering felt the same.

"But she's not the one I wronged most, and I can never make that right, not this side of eternity." Aunt Ginny Dee's gaze returned to the past.

"Tell me."

"I've never told anyone."

Bethany waited and the silence stretched between them. She didn't want to push, didn't mean to pry, but Aunt Ginny Dee was giving so much to all of them and somehow Bethany felt that if she could just breach the hurt that she saw in Aunt Ginny Dee's eyes in unguarded moments, it could be a release and a gift to her, maybe even a bond. Someday, Bethany needed to talk about her own losses, her own hurts. There wasn't a woman she felt she could confide in that way, not unless—maybe—it was Aunt Ginny Dee.

Minutes passed before Aunt Ginny Dee broke the silence.

"When Curtis came home from the war, he was changed. He'd lost both his legs. Nothing he'd done before the war was open to him—not farming, not working on farm machinery. Our ability to have children was gone. He felt like pieces of a man, but not a man. Worse, he was angry, broken. Shattered inside."

"Like Mark after Vietnam?"

Aunt Ginny Dee shrugged. "I can't say how it was for Mark, but I can guess. Curtis was depressed, terrified of the smallest sound, and he wouldn't speak. Sometimes he physically shook—he was restless, then reacted violently when something startled him, like the backfire of a car or if one of the orderlies in the hospital dropped a tray. Anything that reminded him of gunfire.

"They called it combat fatigue—on top of all his physical losses. I never knew what he'd seen, what he'd done in the war. He needed rest, they said, but it was never enough. He couldn't rest. The nightmares, the flashbacks never stopped, whether he was awake or asleep.

"I think Mark still has some of those. I've heard him in the night, even out here in the barn. And little things Marley and Cooper say about their father make me think that. I think that's why Mark insists on staying in the barn by himself. It's better for the children if they're in the house, not hearing his nightmares." Ginny sighed. Bethany saw her caught between the past and the present.

"Doctors tried all kinds of treatments on Curtis for months—morphine at first, for the pain, and tranquilizers for his nerves. None of that helped the nightmares. So they tried hypnosis, then shock treatments, thinking they could wipe the horrid memories from his brain. Well, they wiped lots of things from his brain, including anything he'd ever felt for me, but not what he'd heard, what he'd seen, what he'd done."

"He didn't know you?"

Aunt Ginny Dee smiled sadly. "I don't mean that. He knew who I was, I think, most of the time. But he was no longer in love with me. I didn't matter to him. The Curtis I fell in love with loved me with all that wonderful passion of youth." She shook the memory away, as if it was too painful. "He was a gentle man when we married—a boy, really, now that I look back. He'd sooner tend the broken leg of a deer than shoot it for meat. Curtis wasn't meant for war. Who is?"

She stood and pulled off her gloves, calling it a morning. "After the war, when he couldn't rest in the day and couldn't sleep at night, couldn't work the land—couldn't seem to adapt to the prostheses they offered him—he turned so angry. Angry at himself, angry at God, angry at the world, angry at me."

Bethany tried to imagine. *What if Luke hadn't been declared 4-F for his flat feet like his father? What if what happened to Curtis and to Mark had happened to him? Could he have survived that? Could we?* "What did you do? How did you cope?"

"Not well. I was hurt that he didn't love me like he once had, and angry too. It wasn't what I'd signed up for. I'd scrimped and saved and worked two jobs through the war, so eager to have him come home, and . . . I'd lost our baby." Aunt Ginny Dee's voice broke.

"Aunt Ginny Dee." Bethany reached for her, the pain of knowing that terrible loss in her core, but Aunt Ginny Dee held her at arm's length.

"I was pregnant and wrote home, begging to come home. Mama never answered. Only Harold."

"She couldn't have gotten the letter."

"I don't know—not for sure."

"She would never have turned you away. You have to believe that."

"I want to believe it." Aunt Ginny Dee looked up, tears in her eyes. "Wanted to believe she still loved me."

Bethany ignored any hesitation and crossed the space, drawing the older woman into her arms and rocking her back and forth, as she would have rocked her own children, had she been able to bear them.

"After the war, even if Curtis had wanted me, we couldn't—he couldn't—"

"I know. I understand," Bethany whispered, tears streaming down her face.

Aunt Ginny Dee pulled away, but gently. "I might as well tell you everything. I've never told a living soul."

Bethany passed her the tissue in her pocket and waited, not sure how there could be more.

Ginny wiped her face, knotting the square between her fingers. "When they sent him home . . . they said there was nothing more they could do, and he could be home . . . I still had to work. He could be alone during the day, but I know he was miserable. We had a little house by then—just a shoebox really, but it was ours. I'd been so proud of it, so eager to share it with him before . . ."

"Of course you were. That was a tremendous accomplishment for you to—"

"He hated it. He hated being cooped up all day while I worked, hated that I was the breadwinner. He could have done something, adapted in some way to do some kind of work . . . at least I thought so at the time. Other men who'd lost limbs found ways to work. I think deep down I resented that he wouldn't try. But he couldn't. I know now that he couldn't . . . at least not then.

"I don't know who supplied him, and he wouldn't say, but somebody did, maybe an Army buddy. But he found a way to get liquor, a steady supply. Staying drunk dulled everything for him. But it made him mean, and surly. One night I'd had enough. I found all the liquor in the house and poured it down the drain. I told him not to have one more bottle brought into the house, or he'd have to go."

"You were at the end of your rope. I'd have done the same."

Aunt Ginny Dee looked at Bethany, grateful, sad, as if she knew she meant well and yet couldn't understand. "I came home the next day and found him. He'd cut his wrist, nearly bled out."

"Oh, Aunt Ginny Dee."

"He was still alive." Aunt Ginny Dee stopped and looked Bethany full in the face. "I just wanted the pain to stop—for both of us. The truth is, when I saw him like that, I didn't want to call for help. I didn't want to save him. The man I'd loved with all my heart. The man I'd left my mama to marry in a whirlwind before he went overseas."

Bethany held her breath. "He wasn't that man."

"I did call for the ambulance." She looked away. "And he survived . . . barely. But he could never come home after that. He ended up in a facility with round-the-clock care.

"I never told anyone that he'd tried to kill himself. Oh, the doctors knew. The hospital knew, but I needed to protect his reputation . . . and mine . . . At least that's what I thought then. I thought, if only I'd been enough for him, he'd never have done that. I know now that's not true, but it seemed true then."

Bethany wanted to interrupt, to insist she couldn't have healed his mind, transformed his heart, but she didn't want to stop the needed flow of words.

"I sold our house. I worked two jobs to make certain he had the care he needed, but I didn't visit, not often. Days my landlady and coworkers believed I went to spend with him, I'd drive to another beach or visit a garden or go to a movie and sit in the darkened theater alone. It was my escape . . . my own little secret. My dirty secret. I told myself that I had a right to my own life, my own sanity."

"You did."

"But I stopped loving him, you see. I'd vowed to love him forever and I didn't."

"How could you?"

"How could I not? He'd given his life for this country as surely as if he'd died on the battlefield. It didn't matter that we hated war, feared war, that he hadn't wanted to go. The point is I deserted him. Emotionally, I deserted him. A few years later, he died. I think he lost the will to live."

What could Bethany say? Would she have done the same if Luke came back that way? Wouldn't she? Was that why Crystal turned to drugs and drink and finally left Mark and the children? Or was she too far down that path before he ever came back from Vietnam to make a U-turn? "This is why you won't let Mark fail, isn't it? A second chance—for both of you."

"Mark came back. He was messed up, and from what I gather he messed up his family, but he's trying now. He stands so much better chance than Curtis ever did . . . if we love him, if we believe in him, help him, welcome him home."

Bethany understood. "And there's the children."

"Arlo. Marley. Cooper. Precious children."

"Children we never had."

"The children neither of us ever had, the children we can help now, give a home and a family."

"Does that mean you'll stay—you'll help them? You won't sell the farm?"

"I can't make that decision based on emotion. It won't pay the bills."

"I know—I know. We have to make the farm solvent." Bethany pulled her gloves off. "So much easier said than done."

"In any case, I won't be here. I'm going to England. But if we can clear the tax debt and repay the loan, make it profitable enough to keep the farm, create an ongoing concern, you will be solvent. You and Luke and Mark and the children. If those brothers can work together and turn this farm around, it could be a home for all of you. That would make it worth it to me not to sell, even when I go to England, even when I'm gone. But that's a big *if*."

"Don't go, Aunt Ginny Dee. Stay. This place wouldn't be the same without you—not now, not ever again. You've made—"

But Aunt Ginny Dee shook her head. "I've waited too many years to fulfill my dream."

"I understand that. But are you sure England still holds your dream? Is that the dream you want now?"

CHAPTER THIRTY-ONE

ARLO BELIEVED MR. SKIPWITH MEANT WELL, believed he would try to make sense of everything that had gone wrong, but she wasn't convinced he could bring peace between Uncle Luke and her pa. They seemed like two big old bears from different dens, each protecting their own, neither allowing that territory could be shared.

She hadn't seen either of them before going to school on Tuesday or Wednesday. Aunt Ginny Dee said they'd gone off before daylight both mornings, searching fallow Pickering acres up and down the mountain. She wouldn't say if they found anything, but late Tuesday night Arlo had leaned over the upstairs banister and heard her pa say, "It looks like the only field. It's mostly harvested. A few rows have been covered against frost so it looks like they're not finished. Luke doesn't want to bring the cops in."

"If we don't tell the authorities, it will look like—"

"I know. I know. He's afraid they'll shut the whole farm down. He wants to take care of it himself—ourselves. I'll help. We'll get it done. As soon as we're able we'll go back and plow it under, make sure every trace, every plant is gone. But we've got to get that first load of trees shipped out or we'll miss our slot."

"Is there any way to tell who's done this?" Aunt Ginny Dee had asked.

"Not now. But I swear, while we were there it felt like there were eyes on us. We both felt it."

"You saw someone?"

"No. Just felt like it. That's all. Keep your doors locked at night—for you and the kids."

Arlo had tiptoed back to her room. She heard her pa's boots in the hallway and the back kitchen door lock clicked behind him, and then the front door lock clicked. She wasn't sure if that made her feel safe or more afraid.

At night the men worked till dark and then by battery lights cutting and baling trees, getting them ready for shipment. Arlo knew they had to be exhausted, but Aunt Ginny Dee said this was what could turn the farm around—shipped trees. Uncle Luke hadn't been able to pull together a big-enough harvest on his own the last five years to do that. Now, the combination of shipped trees and cut-your-own trees they'd sell beginning the day after Thanksgiving could make or break the farm. A good harvest and sale could go a long way toward paying the back taxes and catching up payments on the bank loan.

Wreaths and garlands Aunt Ginny Dee and Aunt Bethany and Arlo were piling up, as well as the botanical pictures, would surely help, but trees, Aunt Ginny Dee had said, were the backbone of the farm.

Arlo prayed for her pa and uncle, prayed they'd get along and that they'd have the strength to do the work needed, prayed they'd all be able to stay on the farm long after Christmas.

That second week in November the school buzzed with anticipation for the Thanksgiving holiday and school break. Teachers had a fit trying to get kids to settle down to work. Lower grades spent an hour each afternoon working on a Thanksgiving play about Pilgrims and Indians and the first Thanksgiving feast. Arlo was chosen to narrate. She was relieved she didn't have to dress up as anything more than a regular person, although she did think Emily looked really good in her Indian costume with fake braids.

The Tuesday end-of-school bell rang, followed by a rush to the buses. Arlo was nearly to the outside school door when someone grabbed her from behind and shoved her into the stairwell. With the breath knocked out of her, and her face pushed against the wall, she couldn't even scream.

The voice behind her was Jake's. He jerked her arm up behind her, so fast and hard she thought it might break. "So, you ran crying to old man Skipwith. Let me make this clear to you, Little Miss Plant Girl. You stay off that mountain—you and your family—and mind your own business. Find a way to keep your crew home, and keep your mouth shut. It'd be a shame for that little kid sister and snot-nosed brother of yours to come to a bad end before Thanksgiving, now wouldn't it?" He gave her arm a hard twist. "We're not playing with you. Don't forget it." He threw her books down the stairs, gave her one last shove against the wall, and was gone.

Arlo crumpled to the floor, her arm twisted but good, her head in a spin.

By the time she pulled herself together, collected her books, and made it to the outside curb, the bus was gone. It was a long walk home—two miles—but she didn't dare go for help, not to her teacher and not to Mr. Skipwith. *If Jake's watching me, who else is? And who's watching Marley and Cooper?* Terrified, Arlo set out for home as fast as she could.

Arlo's bad dreams had stopped months before. That night they came back with a vengeance.

"Ma. Ma! Wake up, please wake up. Cooper needs you. He's choking on something, and I can't get it out of his throat. Wake up, Ma! Please—wake up!"

But Ma flipped her hand at Arlo, like swatting away flies. She was out of it again—in la-la land—the remnants of colorful pills and an

*empty gin bottle spread across the bed. And then the fire came. "Pa! Help!"
But Pa was gone.*

*Smoke crept up the stairs and beneath the door. It wound slim fingers
around wooden bed legs and up the scrolled posts. "Stop! Stop!" Balls of
fire burst into flame, raging, plowing their way through bed covers and
pillows toward Marley and Cooper as they slept on and on. Arlo swatted
the flames, tried to stomp them out but there were too many and they
came on too fast. "Stop! Stop! Please, God, I can't stop it!"*

"Arlo! Arlo, wake up! You're dreaming. Wake up!" Aunt Ginny
Dee bent over Arlo's bed, stroking her arm, holding her hand. She
pushed damp hair from Arlo's forehead. "It's a nightmare, a bad
dream, sweetie. It's not real."

But Arlo's heart pounded. It pounded so loud Arlo thought it
might burst through her ears.

"Your nightclothes are soaked. You need to change. You'll catch
chill."

Arlo shivered. She'd sweated right through her pjs and now she
was cold.

"Come, I'll help you." Aunt Ginny Dee pulled a fresh nightgown
from Arlo's drawer and helped her change, careful of her wrenched
arm.

This was the first time Arlo had owned more than one set of
nightclothes, the first time she'd owned a nightgown. It had felt like
abundance, even a waste, when Aunt Bethany had bought it for
her. Now she was glad, thankful, for how easy it was to pull over her
head.

"This is the second night in a row you've had bad dreams, Arlo.
Is it your arm? Are you certain no one hurt you?"

"No, I fell down the stairs—tripped on my shoelace, that's all."

"All right. If you say so. Is something else troubling you?"

"No." Arlo knew she spoke too quickly. She could see in the half-
light from the hallway that Aunt Ginny Dee's eyebrows rose in question. She turned her face away, hoping Aunt Ginny Dee wouldn't
ask more questions. She didn't want to lie, but she dared not tell

the truth. Everything, everyone she cared about lay at stake. *Marley. Cooper. God, please help me save them.*

"Is there anything you'd like to talk about, anything at all that you'd like to ask me?"

"No." It was all Arlo dared say. If she opened her mouth, it might all spill out, and then no one would be safe. No one.

CHAPTER THIRTY-TWO

GINNY WAS CERTAIN something tormented Arlo. The girl was jumpy as a cat with its paw shoved in a light socket. Twice in three nights she'd suffered terrible nightmares.

The countdown to Thanksgiving and the big push through Christmas Eve were underway. Although they'd only glean wholesale prices from shipped trees as opposed to getting full price for cut-your-own, it was important this year to sell everything they could. Luke and Mark worked from dawn till dark and then some, cutting, baling trees, and getting them ready to ship.

She couldn't put more of a burden on either of them, and she knew if Arlo would not tell her what was wrong, she was unlikely to tell her father, who insisted on staying in the barn, cold as it was.

At least the children were tucked in warm and snug in the upstairs bedrooms. Once Arlo, Marley, and Cooper had moved into the house, Ginny had taken to using her parents' downstairs room. She'd felt funny about that at first but had grown accustomed to it, and finally realized what a joy it must have been for her mother to open the curtains each morning and look out upon her rose garden before breakfast, even in cold weather when nothing featured but rose hips. With Arlo's nightmares, Ginny'd taken to sleeping with her door open, just in case Arlo called out.

Once Arlo was off to school that Friday, Ginny phoned Bethany and shared that the girl had experienced yet another nightmare. "Poor thing wears purple bags under her eyes. I think she's afraid to go to sleep now, afraid the nightmares will come. She had bad dreams when she first came, Marley told me, but I don't know what's started them up now."

"Unless it has something to do with all this marijuana mess," Bethany mused.

"But how could it? We've never even told her what the plant was or the problem. No, I think it's something more than that."

"Well, she knows that we're all worried and she knows it has to do with the plants she found. I don't know what Mark's told her. Will said she's worried that she'll be taken away, that she and the littles will be separated. That's got to terrify her. The idea terrifies me."

"I thought between us we'd put those fears to rest. I just don't know what to do, but I think she needs a distraction. You've been helping a lot already with the wreaths, Bethany, but I'm wondering if you might want to join us for some cookie baking today after school and tomorrow. I was even thinking we could get some things to decorate a couple of the trees near the house—make it more festive for when people come to pick out trees. I think Arlo might like that, might really get into helping if we make it interesting, though she'll have to be careful of her arm."

"That's a fantastic idea! Luke told me there are garlands stored in the barn. I don't think they've been used for ages—never that I've known. Maybe they're still good."

"Let's take a look. Marley and Cooper will be up for the excitement."

"I've always thought we should make the selling of our trees more of an event. Maybe even sell hot cocoa with cookies. The kids could help with that too—Arlo especially."

"That would make a good distraction for her," Ginny agreed.

"Exactly. I can haul those boxes of garlands from the barn. I think they're in the loft. When do you want to begin?"

"How about this afternoon? We'll settle on our recipes, and I'll take Marley and Cooper shopping for ingredients. I think they need to get out of the house. They're going stir crazy."

"Let's all go together and stop at the diner for lunch—make it extra fun. With Luke and Mark gone for the weekend to deliver trees, I'm totally free."

"Perfect!

⸙

By midafternoon Ginny, Bethany, Marley, and Cooper had shopped, loaded the kitchen counters with cookie-baking staples, and dragged boxes and bags of cherry-red and silver garlands to the lane.

By the time Arlo stepped off the bus, they had wrapped the four trees nearest the house in garlands and were threading hooks through large outdoor ornaments. Marley and Cooper danced up and down the lane, wrapping one another in garlands and waving red and blue balls meant for the trees.

"Arlo!" Bethany called. "Doesn't this look great? Come help us!"

Arlo stopped in the middle of the lane. She looked at the trees, at Marley and Cooper dancing, decorated to the hilt like little Christmas trees themselves. A smile tipped the corners of her mouth.

"Come see what's in the box! Pick what color ornaments you want!" Marley and Cooper giggled, dragging their sister by her good arm.

Feeling her age, Ginny arched and stretched her back. She'd developed an ache deep within from all the bending and lugging. But when she glanced at Bethany and the women exchanged smiles for the joy of the children before them, Ginny knew it was worth it. *Please, Lord, help Arlo's nightmares stop. Replace whatever fear lurks in her mind with new thoughts, new goals and aspirations.*

"Where did all this stuff come from?" Arlo, wearing a garland around her neck in the spirit of a lei, pulled tinsel from her hair.

"The barn," Bethany said, pulling open another bag bursting with garlands. "Luke said they used to decorate the trees in the lane when they were first planted years ago, until—" She stopped.

"Until what?" Ginny asked.

Bethany looked at Arlo, then away, and shrugged. "Until they just didn't anymore. These have been in the barn for ages, ever since Luke was a little boy. It's actually the first time I've seen them."

Until Elaine died, when Mark was born. That's what she means. I wish I'd known Elaine. Ginny wouldn't pursue that, but she would pursue change and joy now for the sake of the children—her family.

"How much garland is there?" Arlo asked. "Enough for all the trees?"

"No idea," Bethany admitted. "Let's see."

"Keep going!" Cooper whooped, charging up and down the lane, shedding tinsel, arms spread wide like a Christmas superhero.

They worked until dusk set in, until their fingers and toes were nearly frozen, until they'd decorated ten trees, and still tinsel remained.

"I wonder if this is going to be like the oil that never ran out in the temple?" Bethany mused. "I'm beginning to think there might be enough here to decorate all the trees, right up to the road."

"Six more," Arlo counted. "Looks like there'll be enough."

Ginny shook her head. "Maybe, but my oil has run out. We need to call it a day and get these children warmed and fed."

"Cocoa!" Marley begged. "Can we have cocoa, please, Aunt Ginny Dee, please?"

"That sounds really good." Arlo packed up the last of the garlands spread on the ground.

Bethany and Ginny exchanged smiles. "What do you say, Bethany? Cocoa and pizza?"

"Count me in! Let's make it a pajama party!"

"Yay!" Cooper whooped some more.

"What's a pajama party?" Marley stopped dancing.

Bethany laughed and Ginny grinned. "It's a party where everybody wears pajamas and you all sleep together—overnight."

"Will you sleep at our house too?"

Bethany looked at Ginny.

"You're welcome to stay, Bethany, but don't feel you have—"

"I'd love to. With Luke away the house feels way too quiet."

"Yay!" Marley squealed. "You can sleep with me, Aunt Bethy!"

"No," Cooper begged. "You have Arlo. Sleep with me, Aunt Bethy. I have a big bed!"

Bethany laughed, Arlo smiled, and the children hopped up and down all the way to the back kitchen door. *Perfect*, Ginny thought. *Absolutely perfect.*

By Saturday night all the trees in the lane were festooned and five dozen Surprise Cookies, three dozen snickerdoodles, and two pans of creamy nut-and-cherry fudge were bagged and stowed in the freezer, awaiting the day after Thanksgiving, when they'd open the farm for Christmas tree sales and set up for wreath and cookie sales. They'd begin rolling sugar cookie and ginger cookie cutouts after church on Sunday.

Bethany went home Saturday evening, saying she'd love to stay but was in desperate need of a good night's sleep. She'd spent Friday night nestled beside Cooper, who'd tossed and turned and needed to get up twice to use the bathroom.

Sunday morning Ginny was tired but happy and most of all relieved. Arlo had slept two nights straight through—no bad dreams. The purple bags beneath her eyes had faded.

Ginny was happy to let Bethany drive them all to church in her van. Besides, driving together meant they would sit together. The men wouldn't be back until that evening and the women were making family headway in their absence. Ginny just hoped the forward momentum would continue once Luke and Mark returned.

She didn't raise her hand when Pastor Edwards asked for prayer concerns, but she prayed for Mark and for Luke, that they would bond on this trip, that they would pull together for the common goal that meant everything to both of them—all of them. That they would not only settle their differences but cement their relationship. *No more prodigal son, no more judgmental elder brother, but family— real family.*

Ginny's heart swelled through the second hymn. She glanced along the pew, packed beside her: *Cooper, Marley, Bethany, Arlo— family.* It was what she'd always, desperately wanted. Now here it was, within her reach, and yet she was still planning to leave it all behind. *England. Scrivelsby. Gardens.* Somehow, faraway places and new beginnings didn't hold quite the urgent draw they had a few short months ago.

Ginny closed her eyes. She couldn't afford to think this way. She'd given up her dreams long ago and had lived to regret it . . . or had she? Would she ever really have left Curtis? *A number of wives left their husbands after the war, even during the war. Dear John letters—that's what they called those goodbye letters. I had no intention of doing that. I couldn't wait for you to come home, Curtis. I loved you, needed you . . . but the man who came back . . . Why?*

She opened her eyes. *Because you couldn't, that's all. That's all there is to say . . . except I'm sorry. I'm sorry I couldn't—didn't—stand by you until the end. I'm sorry I closed my heart to you. Would it have made a difference if I had . . . if I'd only . . .* But Ginny didn't know.

Weary after their busy weekend, Ginny offered to treat Bethany and the children to Sunday lunch at the diner. "Let's get a good sit-down meal. I'll make applejack for supper—a yummy apple and cinnamon upside-down dish covered in milk that Mama used to make—but a good hot meal now would not come amiss."

"Fried chicken?" Arlo asked.

"Oh, that sounds good," Ginny agreed.

"Mashed potatoes!" Marley chimed in.

"With gravy!" Cooper shouted.

"I'm getting hungry now!" Bethany laughed.

They even topped the meal with chocolate cake and ice cream. Happy and stuffed, they headed home, eager to see the sun shining on their decorated trees and ready to roll out cookie dough for cutouts.

Bethany slipped a cassette in her car's tape player as she drove. Instantly Christmas carols blared, and they all sang at the top of their lungs. Turning into the lane of Wetherill Pickering's Christmas Tree Farm, Bethany stopped the car dead.

The top of each and every evergreen all the way to the house had been savagely cut—decapitated. Garlands, broken Christmas balls, and broken-off evergreen boughs lay strewn down the middle and across both sides of the lane.

"What happened to our Christmas trees?" Marley cried.

"They're broke," Cooper whined. "They're all broke."

"No . . . No. Who could do such a thing?" Ginny whispered. "Why?"

Arlo was the first out of the car. The little ones followed. Bethany left the engine running and stepped into the lane, but Ginny sat, frozen in disbelief, watching her family search the carnage. All the while Bailey barked madly from the barn.

Arlo was the first to find the sign nailed to the tree nearest the house. She held up the huge, dripping, bloodred letters for Ginny and Bethany to see: *WARNED*.

CHAPTER THIRTY-THREE

BETHANY STAYED WITH AUNT GINNY DEE and the children until bed-time, nursing hurts and bewilderment, doing her best to calm fears and disappointment. She helped ready the children for bed and tuck them in, in full agreement with Aunt Ginny Dee when she allowed Bailey to sleep at the foot of Cooper's bed for moral support and protection.

Afterward, the women brewed tea and nearly collapsed in chairs by the fire, their feet up and covered with afghans. Bethany worried, nearly sick, especially about Arlo. "Did you see, when Arlo picked up that sign? She looked stricken, frightened to her core. She hasn't said more than two words since."

"And she hasn't left Marley or Cooper's side. She's afraid and pro-tecting them—too much for a girl her age. Something's not right; something more than we can see is going on with her, but I don't know what or how to fix it."

Upstairs a door opened. Feet padded across the hallway. Bethany and Aunt Ginny Dee looked at each other, listening, waiting.

A minute later they heard a loud thump. Cooper giggled and Bailey barked, followed by a dragging of something heavy across the floor.

"What now?" Aunt Ginny Dee asked, looking too weary to get up.

"I'll see. You stay put." Bethany tiptoed up the stairs to find Arlo and Marley dragging Cooper's mattress through his doorway and across the hall to their room, Cooper and Bailey riding on top. "What are you doing, Arlo?"

"He's staying in with us." Arlo spoke as if it was final.

"It's another pajama party!" Marley exclaimed and Cooper clapped.

"School comes early tomorrow," Bethany warned.

"It's not a party." Arlo was firm, clearly not in party mode. "But he's coming."

"Okay." Bethany knew better than to challenge Arlo. It might not be wise, and they might not get the sleep they needed, but community brought comfort and Arlo had already spent most of her life protecting her siblings. She wasn't likely to stop now.

"She's terrified," Aunt Ginny Dee said when Bethany returned to the parlor and told her. "I don't know what to do, how to help her."

"Neither do I. And those trees—whoever did that—"

"We should call the police, or at least Will. This is out of hand."

"Just wait. Please. Until Luke gets home. I want to ask him. He's worked this farm all his life, Aunt Ginny Dee. Don't take this decision out of his hands. Please."

Aunt Ginny Dee nodded once, but Bethany knew it was unwillingly, knew she trusted Will and looked to him for help and guidance and maybe more, even though she wouldn't admit it or wasn't ready to see it.

It had been a long and wearying day. By nine thirty Bethany saw that Aunt Ginny Dee was done in. "Why don't you go on to bed? I'll wait here, if you don't mind, for the men. I don't really want to go home alone, and they'll need to hear what happened."

"I hate leaving you up alone, but truth be told I can't keep my eyes open. Morning and getting Arlo off to school will come early."

"Go on, then. Get some rest."

"Rest, but I don't know if I'll sleep. It all feels . . . I don't know . . . violated. The farm doesn't feel the same safe place it did before. People who would do that—what else might they do?"

Bethany felt the same, but she saw Aunt Ginny Dee as older and fragile in ways she hadn't considered before. Bethany needed to remain strong—they all needed to remain strong. "We can't allow ourselves to think that way. Surely that's what the perpetrators want. They're trying to scare us."

"At one time I would have said that Pickerings don't scare easily. I'm not sure I feel that way now, not with the children upstairs."

"Luke and Mark will be back soon. They'll know what to do, and we won't be alone."

Aunt Ginny Dee hesitated, nodded, and turned to go to her room. Without turning back, but with a tremble in her voice, she spoke softly. "Thank you for being here, Bethany. Thank you for . . . for everything you've done here for so long. I wish . . ." But she didn't finish. She tried again, but Bethany could tell her tears were too near the surface.

"I'm where I want to be, Aunt Ginny Dee."

Aunt Ginny Dee didn't turn but raised her hand in grateful acknowledgment as she disappeared down the hallway.

The grandfather clock bonged a quarter to ten before Bethany heard the truck on the lane. She breathed a sigh of relief even as she braced herself, grabbed her coat and a flashlight, and headed outside to meet the men.

"What the—" Luke was cut off as he stepped from the truck.

"What's happened here? Are the kids all right?" It was Mark's first fear.

"They're fine. We're all fine." Bethany slid into Luke's arms. "But when we came home from church, this is what we found. This mess, and this sign." She picked up the bloodred threat to show them.

"I don't believe this."

"It was all done before we got here."

Luke pulled Bethany closer, and she melted into the warmth, the security of her husband.

"This has to be about that field." Mark pushed his hands through his hair. "I knew there was somebody watching us. I felt it."

"We both felt it. But this. I don't believe this. It's—"

"We've got to do something."

"Aunt Ginny Dee wanted to call the police, or Will, but I convinced her to wait until you got home. I'm afraid, Luke. I didn't tell her that, but I'm afraid, and I know she is too. Especially for the children. We all kept inside—just not sure if whoever did this might come back. We'd decorated all the trees as a surprise, and we hoped it might help Christmas tree sales. It looked so good before—"

Luke pulled away from Bethany but kept her hand tucked firmly in his and turned to Mark. "You're absolutely sure you don't know who these people are? You have no connection—"

"How can you ask me that? You know I don't. You know I wouldn't risk my kids or the farm or—"

"We believe you, Mark. You believe him, don't you, Luke?" As frightened as Bethany was, she knew they needed to pull together, not apart.

Luke took too long to answer, but finally . . . "Sure."

Mark exhaled, frustration in his stance, but apparently willing to take Luke's half-hearted concession. "We need to call the police. This has gone too far. If we don't stop it now—"

"No."

"What do you mean, no?" Mark's voice rose.

"If we call them now, they're going to want to know why somebody'd do this, what the warning means."

"So we tell them! We should have told them about the field the minute we found it."

"Use your head. If we tell them, they'll want to see the field. It's mostly harvested. Who's to say we didn't plant and harvest and sell it and the threat is for us to stop? Everybody and their brother knows the farm's in financial trouble, that we're close to losing it. It's been on the prayer list at church since before Pop died."

"Will would believe us—he already knows about the field."

"The police don't. And now, between the shipments and the coming Christmas tree sales and those botanical pictures and if

Aunt Ginny Dee kicks in, maybe we'll save it . . . maybe. But who's gonna understand that? Who will believe that once it comes out that there's a weed field harvested on our farm? Who'll buy their tree here?"

"You mean who's gonna believe it because the field is mine and I'm the local boy gone bad. That's what you mean, isn't it?" Mark challenged.

Luke didn't deny it.

Bethany felt the tension rising. "We know you didn't do it, Mark."

"But Luke thought it."

"And if I did . . ." Luke didn't finish.

"The police would, for sure." Mark shook his head, turned away, gripping the back of his neck.

"There's only one thing we can do." Luke let go of Bethany's hand. "Plow the field. Tonight. Now, before anybody else sees this. Get rid of every sign of it."

"That will only make it worse when the police see it. It will look like we sold the crop and tried to cover it up!" Mark all but shouted.

"How do we know that even now whoever did it won't tell the police about it and blame us anyway? I say we plow the field and then tell the police—or maybe Will. He'll believe us and he can go to the police with us."

"I don't know, Luke. I think Mark's right. We should at least tell Will first, before you touch that field. And we need to tell him about these trees. We can't pretend this didn't happen—I mean it's so visible. And I'm afraid—if they did this now, what will they do next?" Bethany felt the situation spiraling out of control.

Luke rubbed his hands down his face. He looked as if he hadn't slept in the two nights they'd been gone.

"We told the kids it must have been some mean prank."

"That's a pretty vindictive prank. Who would believe that—and the warning?"

"We don't tell anybody about the warning." Luke spoke as if it was final.

Mark shook his head. "We need to tell the police. You don't know what people like this will—"

"It's too late and too dark to do anything tonight," Bethany urged. "Even if you plowed now, you couldn't be sure to get all of it in the dark. Sleep on it, both of you. Let's talk in the morning when our heads are clearer. You're both exhausted. Please." She pulled Luke toward the truck and the promise of home.

"She's right. Listen to your wife for once. I need some shut-eye." Mark grabbed his backpack from the cab. "How's Arlo?"

"Too quiet. Scared. We haven't told her about the connection to the field. She didn't believe me about the prank. She's too smart for that. I didn't know what else to say—I just didn't want to scare her more than she already is."

"Thanks for that, for looking after her." Mark sounded as weary as he looked. "I'll see you guys in the morning."

Luke walked Bethany to the cab door. As she climbed in, Bethany heard a soft click on the cold night air. She turned, searching the dark, but didn't see anyone.

CHAPTER THIRTY-FOUR

ARLO DIDN'T WAIT for Aunt Ginny Dee to call her Monday morning. She'd been awake since she'd heard Aunt Bethany run out the door the night before, when she'd snuck outside in the cold to listen to every word her pa and aunt and uncle had said.

Arlo didn't know what was so bad about that crop in the high meadow, only that somebody else had planted it and it must be valuable and wrong and a secret to them. Jake had warned her to keep her family away from the mountain. He knew that her pa and uncle had been to the high meadow, that Mr. Skipwith knew about it, and now their Christmas trees in the lane were ruined.

Somehow, she had to stop her pa and Uncle Luke from going there, from plowing that field under. No telling what would happen if they did. All she could think of was Jake's threat to Marley and Cooper. No, Arlo couldn't leave them—not for a minute.

Arlo mussed her hair and rebuttoned her pajama top so it set askew. She shuffled into the kitchen and conjured the most pitiable voice she could. "Aunt Ginny Dee." She waited until her aunt turned toward her.

"Arlo—you're up early." She stopped. "Are you all right, dear?"

Arlo shook her head. "I don't feel so good."

"Didn't you sleep? Is your arm still bothering you? Does your head hurt?" Aunt Ginny Dee set down her tea towel and crossed the room. She laid a hand on Arlo's forehead. "No fever. Can you tell me what's the matter?"

"I just feel sick. I don't think I can go to school today. I want Pa."

Aunt Ginny Dee wrapped an arm around Arlo. "Come, sit here. I'm making a pot of chamomile mint tea. Let me pour you a cup. It helps everything."

"Not this. I probably need to see a doctor. I really need Pa." Arlo gripped her stomach with both arms as if it ached.

"Does your stomach hurt?"

"I just feel awful."

"Arlo, does this have to do with the trees yesterday?"

Arlo couldn't look Aunt Ginny Dee in the eye and lie. "I just feel sick. I want Pa."

"Your pa's gone out already. You know he and your uncle have their hands full this week."

"Where? Where did he go?" Arlo's panic shot through the ceiling. Was she too late to stop them?

"Luke got a phone call early this morning that the buyer would take another fifty trees, so they're out cutting, getting them ready to bale and deliver."

"Oh. Will that take them all day?"

"When they're loaded, they'll still have a two-hour drive, so I expect it will. They'll be lucky to make it before the nursery closes."

Then they're not plowing the field, not today. Arlo didn't know if she'd ever felt so relieved.

"Now here, drink this. Chamomile mint tea with honey does wonders for nerves and tummy troubles." Aunt Ginny Dee smoothed disheveled hair back from Arlo's forehead. "I'll fix some breakfast and we'll see if you don't feel better. If you're really sick, I can take you to the doctor. Okay?"

Arlo didn't answer but sipped the tea. "Too hot."

"Let it cool just a little; the warmth will do you good."

Arlo knew she needed to improve. If they weren't plowing the field today, Marley and Cooper would be safe with Aunt Ginny Dee. She should go to school. She might need to fake an illness another day, and she couldn't risk Aunt Ginny Dee taking her to the doctor for no good reason.

Arlo wished she could have seen her pa before leaving for school. Walking to the bus stop, up the lane of decapitated trees, gave her the willies. It was as if ghosts stood sentinel, no longer the kindly trees they'd lovingly decorated to surprise her pa and Uncle Luke. *I guess they were surprised all right.*

Standing at the end of the lane, waiting for the school bus, she felt exposed, as if somebody might be watching, waiting. She knew that was crazy, but that's what she'd heard her pa and Uncle Luke say—*we felt somebody watching us.*

If it was true then, it might be true now. They might be waiting to see what we'll do, what I'll do.

They must have been watching to know we'd be at church when they cut those trees. They know where we are, what we're doing. Please, God, keep Pa and Uncle Luke safe. Watch over Marley and Cooper and Aunt Ginny Dee and Aunt Bethany while they're away . . . while I'm away. I'm the one they want, anyway. I'm the one Jake warned.

The bloodred letters of warning loomed large in Arlo's mind, bigger than life. It was a relief to climb onto the bus.

It wasn't Arlo's imagination that Jake's eyes followed her throughout the day, or that he shadowed her, even to the pencil sharpener. She knew he was trying to rattle her, and though she pretended she didn't notice or care, it worked. The minute she got up from the lunch table to stow her tray, he followed on her heels. She dared not walk back to the classroom alone but waited by the door, in full view of the cafeteria, to trail Emily and her clique. Even then, he followed her and only stopped short when she ducked into the girls' bathroom, nearly bumping into Emily, who turned and looked at her like there was something wrong with her.

Arlo couldn't afford to care, and she dared not miss the school bus. She didn't wait to claim her coat from the back of the room but took her books and ran straight for the bus and plunked herself down behind the driver, even though it wasn't her normal seat. She'd just have to fight Janice Pelt for it, if it came to that.

One day down. Arlo drew a deep breath. *But what about tomorrow?*

CHAPTER THIRTY-FIVE

GINNY WAITED UNTIL ARLO had gone for the bus and Bethany had taken Marley and Cooper outside to begin cleaning up the lane before dialing Will's number.

"Will? It's Ginny. Good morning. No, not so fine today. I'm worried."

Ginny poured out all that had happened—Arlo's nightmares, the attempts she and Bethany had made to raise Arlo's spirits and distract her, the decorated trees, the decapitated trees, and the fact that Mark and Luke were arguing about whether to plow under the field of marijuana before or after going to the police.

"I thought they were going to report it after we talked."

"They're afraid if they do that, the police will shut the farm down pending an investigation. Then they won't be able to sell the trees, and if we can't sell the trees . . . well, you know what that means. We could lose everything."

"They should have reported it right away. The longer they let it go, the worse it looks."

"I know. I know, but it's their decision."

"It's your land, Ginny. Clearly somebody's behind this, pressuring, someone willing to do injury to keep that field a secret."

"I know that too. I just don't want the boys to lose everything they've worked for, and this is our only chance to clear that tax debt."

"Breaking the law is not the solution. Beyond that, these people have threatened you."

"We haven't broken any laws; we just haven't reported it yet. But I'm afraid, Will. The trees—you should see them—they're ruined. Who will want to buy Christmas trees from a farm that looks like this?"

"I'm more concerned for you and the children than I am for the farm."

"I'm afraid, too, but what more can they possibly do?"

"That's what you don't know. There's big money in marijuana now, and big money can make big enemies. How large is that field?"

"I'm not sure—three acres, maybe, Mark guessed."

"A gold mine for somebody, but a field that size also means that this operation involves more than one or two people."

"I can't imagine who around here could pull all that together."

"The buyers are probably not from around here. Still, there's got to be a local connection."

"But who?"

"I need to check some facts, but I have a hunch—at least a possibility, and I can share that with the police."

"Please wait. Mark and Luke are cutting and delivering trees today. They'll be back late tonight. They won't even be able to plow until tomorrow or to talk to the police themselves."

"The marijuana harvesters could be back and clear that field before then—then what?"

Ginny sighed, feeling trapped between Will and her nephews, between saving and losing the family she'd come to love. "Maybe if they do, they'll leave us alone."

"That's not how these people work, Ginny."

"I can't lose the farm, Will, not now."

His voice softened. "Are you thinking to stay, then?"

"No. I don't know. I—" Ginny wasn't sure she knew what she

wanted, what she was thinking, but after seeing how upset Arlo was over the trees, how each of the children needed this makeshift family, and even the way Mark and Luke finally seemed to be pulling together—at least a little—she'd made a decision. "I know I said I'd only wait through the Christmas season to sell, but I've decided to stay until the school year is finished. I hope I can pay off the tax debt by then and renegotiate with the bank—if we do well this Christmas season—and I want Arlo to finish her grade in one school.

"If we can't make a go of the farm, enough to pay the taxes and catch up the bank loan and get along, I'll need to pay what I can and sell at least part of the land sooner. After that, if the boys want to buy the remaining land or part of it over time at a reduced price, I'll do that. If they don't, I'll sell and share the proceeds with Luke and Mark so they can start over somewhere else, so the children can have a home, though I won't tell them that yet. I want to see how they do between now and then, if they can really continue to pull together. I won't generate more division among them. Keeping the farm in the family is not worth that."

"And if you can make a go of it, make it a going concern?"

"In that case, I want to keep it, let them work it and make their homes here, earn their livings here—as long as they want."

"Does that mean you'll stay too?" She heard the hope in his voice.

"Six months ago, I would have said no—unequivocally."

"And now?"

"I don't know. I never expected to find family here, Will. I never had children of my own and now it's almost like I have grandchildren. I never had a real home or a chance to open my home to family." She gave a nervous chuckle. "I never expected to be any more than the prodigal daughter who'd disappointed or the judgmental person I had no right to be. And now, with Mark and the children here, and with Luke and Bethany . . ." She hesitated, fearful of being misunderstood and yet not understanding her own heart. "And I never expected you."

"Ginny Dee." His voice came through the line, gentle, clear, warming old wounds and battle scars in Ginny's heart. "I never expected you either. You've been a long time coming home, dear lady. I hope you'll stay. I hope you know that."

Ginny did know it, and her heart, so weary when she'd picked up the phone, sang.

Ginny spent the rest of the day helping Bethany clear the rubble from the lane—useless garlands and shattered Christmas balls. Worst of all were the tops of the trees—like so many three-foot Christmas trees, a village worth in miniature. There was no way they could shape the remaining three-quarter stumps to look like anything. They'd have to be cut down, but when would Luke or Mark find the time? Surely not before Friday when the farm was set to open its cut-your-own fields.

By the time Arlo stepped off the school bus the lane was cleared and Ginny and Bethany, accompanied by Marley, Cooper, and Bailey, had dragged the last of the miniature trees to the side of the barn.

"I guess we can sell tabletop trees." Bethany's enthusiasm had waned long before Marley and Cooper's energy gave way.

"We can try, though I don't know who will buy them or for how much," Ginny admitted with no conviction. "I'm more concerned with how the lane looks with all the treetops sawed off."

"Creepy," Arlo said.

"Super creepy," Marley echoed.

"One day at a time," Ginny said. *Sufficient unto the day is the evil thereof.*

The men returned late Monday night, too late to talk and too late to plow. Ginny was already in bed when she heard the truck pull past the house. She didn't know whether to be relieved or frightened.

Will's warnings about how things might appear to the police

had played over and over in her mind throughout the day, and now, on top of the risk to her family, she'd unfairly put his integrity and reputation at risk. Will knew about the marijuana field, and he'd not reported it either. What might that mean for him—her family's lawyer? What would it mean for Mark, who already had a record involving drug and alcohol use? And if Mark was arrested, convicted, what would that mean for Arlo, Marley, and Cooper? She didn't know, couldn't think, dared not ask Will, but desperately wanted all of this to be over.

Before she closed her eyes, Ginny determined to tell Luke and Mark that she was going to call the police and report the field first thing Tuesday morning. She'd get this settled, once and for all, before anyone—her family or Will—took the blame. She'd tell Mark at breakfast.

But when morning came, Mark did not. A trip to the barn revealed an empty bunk. A phone call to Bethany informed Ginny that Luke and Mark had left before dawn with the tractor and plow. They'd determined to plow under the high meadow before another day passed.

CHAPTER THIRTY-SIX

THE FIRST THANKSGIVING PLAY was set for Wednesday afternoon—the last event before early release from school for the long Thanksgiving weekend. Arlo could hardly wait. It was the one thing that had distracted her from the decapitation of the trees.

She was nervous about narrating, but excited too. Since she'd learned to read well, she loved reading aloud with expression and dramatic flair. The thrill of reciting was much the same. She'd discovered she had a talent for memorization. She'd recognized in rehearsals how she could captivate her classmates with words, eyes, and gestures. She couldn't wait to do the same for Aunt Ginny Dee, Aunt Bethany, Marley, and Cooper and to show those girls in her class that she was a force to reckon with. Her pa had said he'd try to come. She knew he and Uncle Luke were working hard, but if the whole family could just be there it would make it the best ever.

She hadn't reckoned on the venom of Jake Stillcoat, who, being the tallest boy in the class, played the role of Massasoit, chief of the Wampanoag tribe. Miss Norris had said that Massasoit was a generous, magnanimous host who'd taken pity on the Pilgrim strangers and helped them through the winter. Arlo didn't think Jake fit that bill, especially when he loomed over her before the play and hissed, "Stupid girl. Should've listened."

Arlo knew Jake had somehow been connected to the cutting of trees in their lane, though he couldn't have done that alone. But there was nothing she could do now to repair or replace the trees whether she kowtowed to Jake or not. Her pa had said they'd have to be cut down, the stumps pulled, and new trees planted early spring . . . if they were still there. Arlo had every intention of still being there, Jake or no Jake, threats or no threats.

"I'm not the stupid one." Arlo had never stood up to Jake, but there, with her family about to watch her perform, and knowing she'd go directly home with them after the play with four wonderful days free of school and Jake, she could afford a little bravado.

"What's that supposed to mean?" Jake glared but waited.

"Have you looked in the mirror lately?" She smirked and, lifting her chin, turned away. Being afraid of Jake hadn't helped her. She knew she needed to stand up to bullies, but she needed to do it when she was safe.

The play went off without a hitch, at least as far as Arlo was concerned. She delivered her lines spot on, and when she finished the final narration, the teachers and students and family members in the audience erupted in applause. Arlo linked hands with all her Pilgrim and Indian classmates and took a bow, and then another.

Ten minutes later she was surrounded by Aunt Ginny Dee, Aunt Bethany, and Marley and Cooper. "Where's Pa? Where's Uncle Luke?"

"I'm sorry, honey, but they couldn't come. They're working hard to get that final quarter field cut and baled. The buyer wants shipment by tonight."

Arlo knew the farm came first—the farm always came first. It was a hard truth, but if it meant they could stay in New Scrivelsby, it was worth it. Staying was worth everything, whatever it took.

She was surprised when Mr. Skipwith walked up the center aisle.

"Arlo, that was a fine job. I do believe you'll make a great orator one day—maybe even an attorney." He winked at Arlo, then at Aunt Ginny Dee, who glowed like somebody had just plugged in the lights on a Christmas tree.

"Thanks, Mr. Skipwith. I didn't know you were coming."

"Wouldn't miss it. The perfect beginning to Thanksgiving."

"No," Marley piped up. "Turkey tomorrow—that's the best part!"

"And pie!" Cooper shouted. "Aunt Ginny Dee made pumpkin pie and apple pie."

"I wouldn't miss that either." He placed a hand on Marley's head.

"We'll sit down for dinner about two, but come early, Will. I'll put you to work." Aunt Ginny Dee's cheeks pinked.

"I'll be there bright and early." He smiled. Marley and Arlo both slipped their hands into Mr. Skipwith's. With everyone there, except Pa and Uncle Luke, Arlo thought her world might be nearly perfect, until she caught Jake staring at her. Her bravado gone, Arlo tightened her grip on Mr. Skipwith's hand, which made him look up. She witnessed the smile leave Mr. Skipwith's face when he saw the hardened glare in Jake's eyes before he turned away.

🌹

Pa and Uncle Luke were baling and loading the last of the Christmas trees bound for local stands when they all returned to the farm. Arlo wanted to tell her pa about the play, about how well she'd done, but she knew there was no time.

Arlo appreciated Aunt Bethany and Aunt Ginny Dee, and she was glad that Marley and Cooper had been there, but she'd wanted her pa to see. She wanted him to be proud of her. She wanted to make up for the trouble she knew she'd caused about the plants and the field and the cutoff trees.

"When this rush is past, he'll want to hear all about it," Aunt Bethany whispered, her arm around Arlo. "I know he will. And I took pictures, so he'll get to see. You looked just beautiful on stage, Arlo—a natural."

"For now," Aunt Ginny Dee declared, "we need all hands on deck for cookie decorating. We have all those sugar and ginger cookie cutouts but not one decorated. Opening day is day after tomorrow, and we're serving cookies and hot cider, remember?"

"Wait till you see, Arlo! Aunt Ginny Dee and Aunt Bethy made all colors of icing and lots of sugar sprinkles."

"Lots and lots!" Cooper whooshed his arms as wide as he could.

"Let's get to it. We'll need to get them finished and bagged. The Thanksgiving service for church is tonight, and I promised we'd bring three dozen pumpkin muffins for the reception afterward, so I'll bake while you all decorate."

"Can we have pizza for supper?" Cooper wanted to know.

"That sounds like a fine idea," Aunt Ginny Dee said. "I have a pizza crust in the freezer. You and Marley can help Arlo make it."

❦

By the time the cookies were bagged and stored and the pizza made, dusk was falling. It was nearly time to leave for church. Uncle Luke had driven off with the last load of trees bound for Pennsylvania. Pa was chainsawing the remaining decapitated trees on the lane.

"Pa, aren't you coming in to eat? It's nearly time for church." Arlo had so much to tell him about the play, the cookies, and everything. Maybe she could ride with him to church.

"I'm almost finished here. Better to see no trees when folks drive in on Friday than to see these."

Arlo understood, but with the felling of every trunk she felt the weight of guilt. "I'll help. I can help drag them off."

"No, you go on, eat, and get to church. I just want to finish cutting. I can drag them off in the morning."

"Are you coming to church?"

"Not tonight. I'm beat. I'm heading for bed the minute I'm done. You go on now."

"I'd rather stay here and help you."

"You heard me. Go on now. You can help me drag the trees in the morning."

Inside, she pouted. "Pa's not coming in. He's not coming to church either. Said he wants to finish those trees and that he's beat.

I told him I want to stay and help him, but he said I should go with you."

Aunt Ginny Dee cupped Arlo's cheek with her palm. "Your pa's bone-tired, sweetie. Let him finish and get some rest. We'll go on to church. It's Thanksgiving and we all have so much to be thankful for. If he's that done in, he won't come up to the house when he's finished. Let's wrap up some pizza for him and send cookies and muffins out to the barn. He'll see them when he's ready to go in."

"I'll heat some cider for a thermos," Aunt Bethany offered.

"Perfect. Arlo, go on and get changed for church, then you can take this basket out and set it on the table for him. It will be a nice surprise. I know he'll be hungry."

But when Arlo took the basket to the barn, she was the one surprised. There was a present for her pa already on the table, wrapped in colorful tissue paper with a ribbon and bow at the neck, and a note that read, *Time to celebrate, brother.* She'd never known Uncle Luke to give her pa a gift. She didn't like the shape of that gift. It rang too many fire bells in her head. Still, it was a gift. *Things must be better between them, lots better.*

"Arlo! Time to go!" Aunt Bethany's voice called from the lane.

Arlo stole one last glance at Uncle Luke's gift. She just wished she could feel completely glad.

CHAPTER THIRTY-SEVEN

NO ONE WAS MORE PLEASED than Ginny when Will met their troop in the parking lot and helped carry the boxes of muffins into the hospitality area. No one was more surprised when he accompanied them to Ginny and the children's standard pew near the back of the church.

Geography did not keep heads from turning or eyebrows from being raised in question. Ginny tried hard to ignore the silent inquiries. She wasn't sure she understood herself and, uncomfortable with the scrutiny, shifted in her seat. But the moment Will laid a warm and comforting hand on hers, she settled, as if sitting next to Will Skipwith in church was something she'd done all her life. As if smiling up at him, sharing a hymnbook with him—for there were not enough in the pew for everyone to hold their own—were the most natural things in the world.

The last time she'd shared a hymnbook with a man in church had been with Curtis in Cape May County, the day before he left for boot camp. Ginny swallowed, remembering standing next to her new husband, believing that it was the beginning of everything bright and beautiful, never dreaming they stood on the threshold of disaster. They both knew then that statistically there was a chance he would not come home alive or that he might be injured. But surely he could beat the odds. They'd both suffered enough in life, and they were young and golden, with all of life and all the world ahead of them. Standing tall and strong in church that Sunday felt like a promise—a hope and a promise and a vow.

That strength, that surety had been one of life's hardest things for Ginny to lose. She could have lived with Curtis in the wheelchair. Hard as it was, she could have accepted never having children. But she couldn't stem the tide of his cursing, of his anger, of his perpetual disappointment in life and in her.

Even now, she wasn't sure what she could have done that would have made a difference for him, but she knew she'd given up too easily.

Ginny glanced at the children beside her, at Bethany flanking them on the far end of the pew, then up at Will again, glad to stand so close while he belted out the opening lines of "We Gather Together" in a strong baritone.

> *"We gather together to ask the Lord's blessing;*
> *He chastens and hastens His will to make known;*
> *The wicked oppressing now cease from distressing.*
> *Sing praises to His name: He forgets not His own."*

Ginny sang the words, knowing they were meant for her, for them, for all her little family. They'd all been through so much in the last several years. She'd long felt insignificant, as if the Lord had forgotten her, and yet now, here they were together, stronger. Perhaps He'd not forgotten her after all—not forgotten any of them.

> *"Beside us to guide us, our God with us joining,*
> *Ordaining, maintaining His kingdom divine;*
> *So from the beginning the fight we were winning:*
> *Thou, Lord, was at our side, all glory be Thine!"*

Mark and Luke and Bethany—perhaps all this time, all these years they'd fought so hard to hang on were not losses but achievements of milestones, preparation for now, for the fight they were at last winning. That could only have happened with the Lord at their side.

> *"We all do extol Thee, Thou Leader triumphant,*
> *And pray that Thou still our Defender wilt be.*
> *Let Thy congregation escape tribulation:*
> *Thy name be ever praised! O Lord, make us free!"*

Yes, Lord. Make us free from our pasts—each of us. Free Luke from his bitterness. Free Bethany from her heartbreak over the loss of her children. Free Mark from his trauma in the war and all the shame of his past. Free Arlo and Marley and Cooper from their fears of separation. Free Will from the losses of his life—his years spent alone, with no wife and no children. And free me, Lord, I pray, from guilt and regret. Open our eyes to all that You've set before us, our Defender, our Leader triumphant! O Lord, make us free!

Will leaned closer as he took back the hymnbook and set it in the pew holder before him and whispered, "You all right, Ginny?"

Ginny squeezed his arm and nodded, smiling through pooling eyes. "Never better. Never in all this world."

Ginny couldn't focus on the pastor's message. She knew he spoke of giving thanks, but her own heart was so full, so overflowing in praise, in worship, in thanksgiving for all that the Lord had opened in her mind, in her life and in the lives of her family.

The hospitality time after the service stretched longer than anyone expected. Every woman there, Ginny was certain, needed to get home to make stuffing for a turkey, boil cranberry sauce, bake a pie or two, or any of a dozen other preparations for her family's Thanksgiving feast the next day. But it was such a happy, joyful time that no one seemed anxious to leave, to go out into the cold November night, even when the cookies and muffins were gone.

Ginny and Bethany had just emptied the second coffee urn when the first strains of sirens rose above the din of friendly chatter. Never a welcome sound, the sirens wailed closer. The two women exchanged concerned glances but kept at their task. Arlo packed up the few remains of the spread. Marley and Cooper helped collect emptied paper cups and plates for the trash bag Will held for them.

The door leading to the parking lot flew open and a breathless Fennimore Harding burst into the room. "Fire out at Pickering's! Lovettsville and Brunswick are sending trucks, but we need every able-bodied man!"

Just that quick, life turned. Ginny's head spun so that she stumbled, and Bethany grabbed the coffee urn.

"Pickering's!" Arlo went deathly pale. "That's us."

"Ginny." Will shook her gently. "You and the children stay here. I'll come back for you."

I'll come back for you—that's what Curtis said, before he went to war. "No, Will! No!"

"You'll all be safer here. Pray it's not much. But keep the children here." Just that quick, he was gone.

"Aunt Ginny Dee!" Arlo begged, tugging Ginny's arm. "Pa's out there. We've gotta go back!"

"Mr. Skippy said stay here!" Marley's eyes widened. Cooper looked like a baby deer caught in headlights. Bethany wrapped her arms around them.

"I'm not staying here while Pa's out there." Arlo grabbed her coat from the hook.

Louise Shellhorn placed a hand on Ginny's arm. "I can keep the children if you and Bethany want to go."

"No," Bethany spoke up. "We're going together."

"But the fire! You don't know what you'll find," Louise objected, as if she had right.

"We won't get in the way of the firemen, but our family's there. We're going back." Bethany brooked no dissention and that shook Ginny from her stupor.

"Clean up for us, Louise. Please. That's what we need you to do. We've got to go now." Ginny pulled coats from the long row of hooks and with trembling hands pushed little arms inside. Bethany grabbed both their purses and coats and headed for the door, Arlo ahead of her.

"Seat belts," Bethany ordered, not waiting for the children to comply before thrusting the car into gear.

Ginny couldn't breathe. Her chest, so tight, felt it might rupture. *Please, God, not Mark. Not Will. Please. Please. Please. Take the house, the barn, but not them. Please.*

By the time they reached the farm so had a dozen locals in addition to fire trucks from Brunswick and Lovettsville. Fifteen minutes later an even bigger truck from Leesburg tore down the lane. But it wasn't the house on fire, and it wasn't the barn. It was the Christmas tree fields. Fields and fields of white pine, Virginia pine, Norway spruce, Fraser fir.

Arlo was the first out of the car, tearing toward the barn. "Pa! Pa!"

"Arlo! Arlo, come back!" Ginny left the little ones with Bethany and tore after the girl, but Arlo didn't stop.

Before either of them reached the barn, Ginny heard Bailey, frantically barking, lunging against the door. Arlo jerked it open, and Bailey was free, still barking madly.

By the time Ginny reached the inside she found Arlo standing over her father, shaking him for all she was worth, trying to wake him. But he was out cold, a near-empty bottle of Jack Daniel's on the floor at his side.

CHAPTER THIRTY-EIGHT

"PA! PA!" Arlo cried, shaking her father. Frightened for him, desperate to cover the reek of alcohol, angry that he'd betrayed her trust. "Wake up, Pa! There's fire! You've got to help!"

"Leave him, Arlo. He can't help us. He can't help himself. Not now." Aunt Ginny Dee tried to pull Arlo away, but Arlo jerked from her grasp, tears of futility and shame streaming down her face.

Suddenly blasts of water hit the outside of the barn, making Arlo jump. "Is the barn on fire? We've got to get Pa out!"

"No, leave him for now. They're dousing the barn and house in water so they won't burn. It's a precaution. The fire is still far away. If it looks like it's coming nearer, we'll get help to get him out. For now, it's better if he stays here."

"So nobody sees him." Arlo knew what that meant. "He didn't start the fire."

"No, dear." Aunt Ginny Dee set her hand on Arlo's shoulder. "I'm sure he didn't. He couldn't have."

"Wouldn't."

"No, he wouldn't." A sob escaped Aunt Ginny Dee. "But there is fire, just the same. We should get back to Bethany and the children. They're bound to be frightened. And I need to know what's happening, where Will and the others are. Come."

Arlo didn't pull her hand from Aunt Ginny Dee's. It was the only stable thing, the only anchor. Bailey followed at their heels, as confused as they.

Outside, neighbors and townspeople gathered, whispering, praying, lamenting, watching. Mostly women huddled together, for their men had joined the battle against the fire in the cut-your-own fields. Her heart frozen in fear, Arlo felt their words run over her like water over ice, never finding a foothold.

"How did it start?"

"Nobody knows. Shame nobody was here to see it early. The family was all at church. All but the men. I think Bethany said they were out delivering trees."

"They're going to lose everything."

"Thank God it's not the houses or barn." Pastor Edwards pulled a blanket around Marley and Cooper, who, standing beside Aunt Bethany, whimpered, shivering in the cold.

It was hard for Arlo to thank God for anything. *Why didn't You stop this fire? Why didn't You keep Pa from drinking? Why did you let Uncle Luke give him that bottle and go away?*

As much as she wanted to rage and scream, as much as her body conversely shut down, there was nothing Arlo could do about any of it. She needed to close her eyes, needed to close them tight and keep them closed until this nightmare was gone, but each time she opened them the fire still raged. More fire trucks came, an ambulance arrived, and then women began setting up stations in the yard, lugging jugs of water from the kitchen.

"Arlo, I need you to take Marley and Cooper inside where it's warm. Get them ready for bed. Keep Bailey in your room upstairs. Bethany and I need to make coffee and sandwiches for the firefighters. It's going to be a long night, and I need to know you children are safe and tucked in. Can you do that? Can you take charge of Marley and Cooper for me?" Aunt Ginny Dee was talking to her, but Arlo struggled to process what she was saying.

Aunt Ginny Dee took Arlo by both arms, leaned forward to look her in the eyes. "Arlo, I know this is hard. I know you're frightened. We all are. But I need you to stand strong. I need you to help. We've all got to help. We've got to get through this together."

At that moment, the ambulance turned on its siren and headed toward the field.

"Oh no! What's happened? Who is it for?"

"Nobody knows. They just got a radio call to come."

"Pray. Everybody pray."

Arlo couldn't pray. She was afraid if she did God might turn that prayer upside down and punish whoever it was she prayed for. It was a trick.

Soon as I think it's all gonna be okay, wham! It's like being told you got the lead in the school play and then somebody rips apart your favorite costume. Only this is worse. No farm means no home. No home means on the road. On the road means they'll take Marley and Cooper and me and put us in foster homes, break us up, like before. Pa'll end up in jail again and this time he'll never get us back.

Arlo knew the train of her thoughts ran on a collision course, but she couldn't seem to stop that train, couldn't compel the brakes.

The siren wailed up and down the scale. More paramedics appeared, pulling bandages from a second ambulance and wrapping a man in a blanket.

"How can I help?" Aunt Ginny Dee asked.

"Water. Get this man some water."

Aunt Ginny Dee raced for the house, bringing back paper cups and a jug of water. While she poured, she asked, "Who was taken in the first ambulance?"

"Will Skipwith," the man with the blanket replied.

Aunt Ginny Dee dropped the jug.

"No," Aunt Bethany groaned, but Aunt Ginny Dee couldn't seem to speak, couldn't seem to move. "Which hospital?"

"Leesburg, I think."

"Burned?" Aunt Ginny Dee found her voice.

"Not sure. Smoke inhalation—pretty bad. Fool man. He's too old to be out there fighting fire."

"Bethany," Aunt Ginny Dee whispered—not, Arlo thought, because she meant to but because that's all the voice she had left. "Take care of the children. I'm going to Will."

"Don't go alone. Let someone drive you."

"No." That's all Aunt Ginny Dee said before she stumbled off.

How Arlo got in the house, how she and Marley and Cooper and Bailey made it upstairs, she couldn't think. But suddenly there were things to do.

"I can't find my pajama top," Cooper whined. "I don't want to sleep by myself."

"I need to pee but I'm afraid to go in there alone. What if there's fire in the toilet?" Marley whimpered.

Arlo stared at her siblings. She felt so helpless in the face of all that was raging outside their windows, but the fire was far enough from the house that if it got closer at least they'd have warning. Aunt Bethany would warn them, come get them, save them. *Even if Pa can't.*

Aunt Ginny Dee was right. Looking after Marley and Cooper was what she could do. She couldn't stop the fire or save Mr. Skipwith or slow the train of events that might follow, but right now she could take care of her sister and brother.

"Come on, Marley. Let's go in the bathroom together. There's no fire in there. I'll show you."

"What about my pajama top?" Cooper's eyes filled.

"We'll find it, and you can sleep with us tonight. We'll even let Bailey on the bed. Just don't tell Aunt Ginny Dee." Arlo tried to smile at her little brother, as if they shared a special secret, though she knew Aunt Ginny Dee would say they should stick together like glue.

Marley and Cooper fell fast asleep, wedged to Arlo's sides, but Arlo lay awake a long time, listening to the familiar sounds of pots shifting, water running, and grown-ups talking that came from downstairs, and the strange sounds of water rushing and men calling and the motors of fire trucks running that came from outside. Lights flashed through her bedroom curtains. What it would all mean in the morning, what would happen to Mr. Skipwith and to Aunt Ginny Dee if he died, what Pa's role in it all was, Arlo feared to think, but thinking, her brain spinning, was what she couldn't stop.

Having tossed and turned, Arlo woke while it was still dark, the faint light of dawn graying the sky. Voices drifted up from downstairs—the urgent running of women's voices overpowered by the angry, threatening rumbles of men. Arlo slipped from between her siblings and out the bottom of the bed, Bailey ready to follow. She found her shoes in the dark and closed the door behind her, careful not to wake Marley and Cooper. From the top of the stairs, the house reeked of smoke and smoldering words.

Arlo held her breath, closed her eyes, and wrapped her arm around Bailey. The fire had not been the dream, the nightmare, she'd hoped. *Real. All real.*

"What do you mean you didn't hear anything? How could five acres burn to the ground and you not know it?" Uncle Luke was shouting now. Arlo gripped the banister and eased onto a step halfway down the stairs. She didn't need to go closer to hear every word.

"Calm down, Luke. You'll wake the children. That won't help anything," Aunt Bethany whispered, but loudly.

"The children—that's all you and Aunt Ginny Dee care about. Well, I've had enough. If it wasn't for them, none of us would have put up with him. Drunk. Irresponsible. That's what you are!"

"Luke, please. You're angry, but—" Aunt Bethany pleaded.

"Angry? Why should I be angry? Pickering land burned to the ground? The farm lost for good? My brother, home from the dead, bringing us all to the grave with him? And what about Skipwith? The man who championed you? Some good you did him." Something crashed. Arlo jumped. Bailey barked. "You know what you are, brother? Trouble when you came back from Nam and nothing but trouble since. You should have been here watching those fields! You knew somebody was out to get us and yet you did nothing. No—wait, not nothing! You drank. You said you'd not touched a drop since you came here—nothing in two years. Liar!"

Arlo heard nothing from her pa.

"Luke, stop it. Stop it!" Aunt Bethany was shouting now.

"You and Aunt Ginny Dee fell for him and his 'oh, don't worry about me, I'll be fine in the barn' speech. Well, now you know why he stayed out there by himself."

"That's not—"

But Uncle Luke cut Pa off. "You never should have come back here. You can't be trusted."

"Luke! That's not fair." Aunt Bethany sounded desperate.

Arlo's heart raced. She wasn't afraid of Uncle Luke, and Aunt Bethany was right; he wasn't being fair. *You're the one who gave Pa the bottle. You know Pa can't resist drink. It's your fault as much as Pa's.*

"I didn't set the fire."

"Maybe. Maybe not. But you were too drunk to stop it. Twenty, thirty minutes earlier a phone call could have saved most of those trees. And how did it start? Somebody you cheated? Something to do with that field of weed or a bar buddy in town? None of this happened before you showed up."

Not fair. Not fair. Arlo's heart beat time down the stairs. She stood in the door of the kitchen, Bailey by her side. "It wasn't Pa found that field, it was me. I'm the one brought the trouble. Stop blaming him."

The grown-ups in the room went silent.

"None of this is your fault, Arlo. If you hadn't found that marijuana, we would never have known. We needed to know." Aunt Bethany reached for her, but Arlo pulled away.

"Yes, it is my fault. Jake warned me. I don't know what marijuana is or why it's so bad, but I didn't mean to cause trouble. And

Pa didn't plant it. He didn't do it, and he didn't start that fire. He wouldn't."

"I never said he started the fire, but he didn't do anything to stop it," Uncle Luke said. "Your pa's a drunk, Arlo, and the sooner you get that through your head, the safer you'll be. You can't trust him."

"I can't trust you! You know Pa can't keep from the drink; that's why he never has it."

"Well, he certainly had it tonight."

"Because of you!"

Shaking his head, Uncle Luke threw up his hands. "I'm done here. I'm done."

"Luke—" Aunt Bethany called after him, but Uncle Luke was through the back kitchen door and down the steps.

The sudden quiet in the kitchen unnerved Arlo. Aunt Bethany looked away. Pa sat at the table, his head down, shoulders rounded, cradling a cup of coffee between shaking hands. Arlo wanted to go to him, comfort him, but she was disgusted—disgusted and full of pity. "Pa."

He didn't look up. If anything, his head sank lower in shame.

"Mr. Skipwith?" Arlo feared asking, feared knowing.

Aunt Bethany shook her head. "We don't know anything yet. Aunt Ginny Dee is with him at the hospital. She hasn't called."

Her pa pushed both hands through his hair, then pushed back from the table. "We should never have come here. It was a mistake."

"No," Aunt Bethany, who looked dead on her feet, nearly cried. "It wasn't a mistake. The mistake was that we didn't bring in the police from the start, and that was Luke's decision. The mistake is that you drank. I thought you'd stopped."

"I had. For two years, I was clean." Pa looked up for the first time.

"Then where did you even get it?"

He looked as if he couldn't believe she'd ask that. "Ask Luke." And he left through the back door.

"What does that mean?" Aunt Bethany called after him, but he didn't stop, didn't answer.

"It was a present. Some present." Arlo let Bailey out, then turned and climbed the stairs. She dressed in the half-light, even though all she wanted to do was to climb back into bed between her sleeping siblings and stay there forever.

Downstairs, the front door opened. Arlo peeked through the curtains. *Aunt Ginny Dee.* Arlo raced down the stairs and met both aunts in the hallway, Aunt Ginny Dee just pulling off her coat.

"How's Will?" Aunt Bethany asked.

"Not good, not yet. It was close. Broken arm, far too much smoke inhalation. The doctor's keeping him a couple of days for observation." Aunt Ginny Dee's voice trembled; she sounded weary to the bone.

"Thank God he made it."

"Yes, thank God."

"You're exhausted, Aunt Ginny Dee. Go to bed. I'll watch over the children."

"No. You've been up all night too. Go home, Bethany. Is Luke back?"

"Yes, he made it back shortly after you left. He helped battle the fires."

"How bad is it? Did he say?"

"Five acres, maybe a little more. It could have been worse. It was most of the cut-your-own fields ready for harvest this year. Whoever started it knew what they were doing."

Aunt Ginny Dee rested her head against the coat she'd placed on the hook. "Yes, it could have been so much worse."

"If we can just get through this year . . . Next year there will be new acreage ready to harvest. At least all the trees for market were sent out before . . ."

Arlo caught the pitying look from Aunt Ginny Dee. Aunt Bethany was always the one to push, trying to find the bright side, determined more than any Pickering by blood to save the farm. But Arlo knew there was no bright side. Aunt Ginny Dee had said all along that the only way they could keep going was to turn a profit this year, and the last real hope to meet that goal was the cut-your-own cash crop.

"Go home to your husband, Bethany. He needs you now. I'm here with the children and I expect Mark will be coming round soon."

"He's already been in . . . shaky, but mostly sober."

"What did he say? Does he have any idea—"

"No."

"No, of course not. Go on home, Bethany. We'll be all right here."

Aunt Bethany hesitated. She glanced at Arlo, but Arlo looked away. There was nothing more to say. "Try to get some sleep, Aunt Ginny Dee. I'll do the same." She tried to give Arlo a hug, but Arlo stiffened. "Don't pay attention to the things Luke said, Arlo. He's hurt and angry, but he'll have to get over this. We all will, and your father's not to blame."

Arlo dared to breathe.

Aunt Ginny Dee watched, waiting until Aunt Bethany left by the back door. "Luke blamed Mark for the fire?"

Arlo shrugged. "He said Pa could have stopped it—called for help sooner—if he hadn't been drunk."

"Ah." Aunt Ginny Dee sighed. "That does no good now."

"You don't blame him?" Arlo felt she stood on tenterhooks.

"No, I don't. I blame whoever started the fire. They're the only ones to blame. Will has a lead or thinks he might."

"Can I fix you some tea, Aunt Ginny Dee?" Arlo would do anything for this woman.

Aunt Ginny Dee drew a breath so deep Arlo didn't know where it had come from. "Yes. That would be most welcome. I think I'll take it in the parlor, put my feet up. Chamomile mint. And some of that wildflower honey, please. Two teaspoons."

Arlo nodded eagerly. This was something she could do. She'd just set the kettle to boil when the back door opened wide and her pa stepped in.

"Arlo, get Marley and Cooper. Now. We're leaving."

"What?"

"You heard me. Let's go. Now."

"Where?"

"It doesn't matter where, we're going. Coming here was a mistake."

"It wasn't a mistake!" Arlo felt the world shift beneath her, her heart plummeting.

Aunt Ginny Dee appeared in the doorway. "No, Mark, that wasn't the mistake."

He looked stricken, straining for words. "I'm sorry, Aunt Ginny Dee. I let you down. I let you all down. I know that."

"Did you start that fire?"

"No!"

"Did you willingly let it burn out of control?"

"No, but I—I couldn't stop it. I didn't try. I was—"

"No. I told Arlo and I'm telling you, it was not your fault. The police will do what they can to find the guilty, but that is not you and certainly not your children. None of you are to blame."

"I was out . . . stone cold. I couldn't even help put it out."

"Drinking was a mistake, but not what led to the fire." Aunt Ginny Dee crossed the room and reached for Pa, but he pulled back. "We all make mistakes, Mark. I don't know what led to this one but it's over. It's done."

"Tell that to Luke."

"Luke has his own demons."

Pa turned away, bracing his hands against the sink. "Arlo, I said go get Marley and Cooper. Get dressed. Get them dressed. I won't say it again."

"But, Pa—please, no!"

"You heard me. Now. Meet me at the truck." And he walked out.

Arlo looked to Aunt Ginny Dee for help.

"Mark, I beg you for the sake of the children, don't go. Where will you go?" Aunt Ginny Dee pleaded from the door, but Pa kept walking.

Disbelieving, sick to her stomach, Arlo climbed the stairs. Marley and Cooper were still asleep. How they'd been able to sleep through all that had happened in the last hours Arlo didn't know, but she was grateful they hadn't seen, hadn't heard. She shook them, none too gently. "Wake up, you guys. Time to wake up. You have to get dressed."

"Is it Thanksgibing?" Cooper asked, rubbing his eyes.

"Yeah, sure. Thanksgiving."

Silent and grim, not trusting herself to speak, Arlo tied Cooper's shoes. She didn't bother brushing teeth or hair. She looked around the room that had become a sanctuary, a safe place for all of them over the last months. Clothes and shoes and books and toys they'd never had before . . . warm blankets, clean sheets, pillows. Bailey appeared at the door, panting. Aunt Ginny Dee must have let him back in.

Desperate, Arlo grabbed the underwear from their drawers, and socks—they'd need extra socks to sleep in the cold truck. With trembling fingers, she pulled the warmest of Marley's and Cooper's pants and shirts from the cupboard and a few of her own and stuffed them all into pillowcases. She hoped Aunt Ginny Dee wouldn't mind. She wished she could take the quilts from the beds but that wouldn't be right, and her pa probably wouldn't let her. *Travel light—that's what he always said before. That's what he'll say again.*

"What's for breakfast?" Marley wanted to know. "Muffins?"

"Maybe. Maybe we can take some muffins in the truck."

"In the truck? Where are we going in the truck?"

"Who knows. I don't. We're going."

"Arlo, why are you putting our clothes in those pillowcases? They'll get all squished and wrinkled. Aunt Ginny Dee doesn't like us to be wrinkled."

"Pa says we're leaving."

"Where? Where are we going?" Arlo saw Marley's panic rising, panic she felt too.

"I don't know. He just wants to go."

"Why?" Marley's brow furrowed and fear crept into her eyes.

"Stop asking so many questions. He's waiting in the truck." Arlo looked out the window. As if he knew, Pa blew the horn, hurrying them along. But Aunt Ginny Dee was there, too, wide awake now, with two hands on the driver's door, clearly begging him to open it. Pa was having none of it, just staring straight ahead.

"Come on, guys. Let's go." Arlo felt the weight of the world as they trudged down the stairs. She pulled their coats and hats from the coatrack and helped Cooper with the buckle beneath his chin.

"I don't want it buckled!"

"It's cold out and the heater doesn't work good in the truck. You don't want to get sick." She pushed his arms away harder than she should have and Cooper began to cry.

Aunt Ginny Dee came through the front door then, her face pale. "Arlo. I can't stop him. I tried."

Arlo looked away. "It's okay." It wasn't, but what was there to say? They'd been through uprootings before, none so painful as this.

"Wait. Let me put some food in a bag. There'll be nothing open on Thanksgiving."

"We're not gonna eat turkey?" Cooper sniffled.

"No, precious boy, but you'll have everything I can send." Aunt Ginny Dee choked back tears. The truck horn blew twice, long and angry. Arlo headed for the door. "Let him wait. You've got to have something to take with you." She stuffed pumpkin muffins and cranberry orange muffins and apples and bananas in a bag. She pulled deli ham and cheese and a loaf of bread from the fridge. She grabbed her wallet from her purse and emptied everything she had into the bag.

"He won't take that, Aunt Ginny Dee." Arlo knew her pa.

"He won't know it's there until too late if you don't say anything. You'll need it. He's earned that and so much more." Aunt Ginny Dee crushed Arlo to her chest. "As soon as he's ready, as soon as you can, come back. Please, all of you, come back."

Arlo couldn't hold it in any longer. She clung to Aunt Ginny Dee. The little ones, bewildered, cried. Bailey whimpered, eager to help, not knowing how.

They don't understand. I don't understand.

The pickup horn blew again.

"We've got to go." Arlo carried the pillowcases and food bag, Bailey on her heels. Aunt Ginny Dee took Marley's and Cooper's hands and helped them climb into the truck on the passenger's side. Arlo buckled Marley and Cooper together with the lap belt in the middle and climbed in. She couldn't look Aunt Ginny Dee, standing there so forlorn, in the eye, not again. She kept her focus on Bailey, who leaned tight against Aunt Ginny Dee's knee.

"Can't Bailey come?" Cooper asked, confused.

"No." It was all Pa said before gunning the motor and speeding down the lane.

CHAPTER THIRTY-NINE

THROUGH THE FOG OF SLEEP Bethany heard the truck horn in the distance. She didn't know what it meant but was too tired to pay it any real mind, and her husband was asleep beside her. She didn't want to waken him and didn't want to get up. Whatever it was could wait.

She rolled over. Their bedroom window gave a perfect view of the rising sun. It was one of the things Bethany had always loved about Promised Land. The windows on both sides of the house had been chosen to face the rising and setting sun. What a gift, a real gift.

Thank You, God, that the fires didn't reach the house. That loss would have been so much harder to bear. She closed her eyes. *Loss. Without those trees there's no way to pay the back taxes or repay that loan without selling the farm.*

Bethany couldn't think about that. Surely Luke and Mark and Aunt Ginny Dee and she could pull something together, couldn't they? *Is that wishful thinking, Lord? Is it wrong?*

Bethany sat up. Tired as she was, there was no more sleep to be had. She might as well go over to Aunt Ginny Dee's and get the turkey in the oven. After her night at the hospital, Aunt Ginny Dee would be in no shape to cook a turkey, and it was Thanksgiving, after all. They should muster up and do it for the children if for no other reason.

Bethany smiled. *What a gift to have these children, Lord. Just a stone's throw away.* She could stand another lean year, as long as they all had each other. They'd find a way. They had to find a way.

She looked over at Luke, sound asleep and snoring. He could be a hard man with a short fuse, too much like his pop at times, but he could also be gentle and good, and she loved him. She'd always loved him, always would. But he needed to mend fences with Mark. It would never do for this feud to go on. She'd seen what the two men could do when they pulled together. This was harder than anything they'd faced yet, but they'd have to leave the past behind and go forward together, again.

Bethany slipped from the warmth of their quilt and wrapped her robe around her, cinching it at the waist. She'd work on him, gently, hoping to calm her angry bull.

Stuffing the turkey was a ritual Bethany had always enjoyed. She would have preferred doing it in her own kitchen but since they'd be eating at Aunt Ginny Dee's it made sense to do it there. The children would love the hours-long fragrance of roasting turkey and it would give her a chance to be with them. She didn't mind giving Luke a little space at the moment, anyway. Time alone might help him cool off toward his brother.

As she walked through the orchard the stench of burned land beyond pressed through her nostrils, causing her to sigh more deeply. Passing the barn, Bethany noticed that Mark's truck was missing. *He must have pulled himself together. Didn't he plan to drag the tree trunks off the lane this morning? Why are they still here?*

Bethany remembered the horn blowing earlier that morning. For the first time it unsettled her.

She let herself in Aunt Ginny Dee's back door and stood in the silent kitchen. *Why aren't the children up yet? Maybe Mark took them out somewhere so Aunt Ginny Dee could sleep.* But that explanation did not ring true. *Something's not right.*

She checked the hall coat hooks. The children's coats were gone. Aunt Ginny Dee's hung alone. *Where are they? What's going on?*

Bethany didn't know but the least she could do was to get the turkey going. It would take several hours to roast after all, and eventually they'd all be awake and coming to the kitchen hungry.

If only that good task could drive her uncertainties away.

❦

It was noon before Luke phoned Aunt Ginny Dee's. Bethany picked up.

"I don't know where everybody is. I think Aunt Ginny Dee's still sleeping, but Mark and the children have gone somewhere. I don't know where. They should be back by now."

Aunt Ginny Dee appeared in the hall doorway, still in yesterday's clothes, her hair disheveled, her eyes haggard.

"Wait, Luke. Hold on. Aunt Ginny Dee? Are you okay?"

"They're gone. They're not coming back."

"What?" Bethany felt her spine go cold.

"They've left. Packed up and gone."

"No." Bethany shook her head, replaced the receiver in its cradle. "No, don't say that. They'll be back, surely."

Aunt Ginny Dee walked unsteadily, Bailey leaning against her, as if to prop her up. She reached for a kitchen chair and sank into it. "Mark blames himself. He thinks it's all his fault. He didn't say that, but that's what he thinks. He tore out of here."

"With the children."

Aunt Ginny Dee nodded.

Bethany closed her eyes, her heart pierced. She leaned against the woodwork as the room spun.

Five minutes later Luke ran through the back kitchen door. "What's wrong? Beth? Why'd you hang up on me? What's wrong with Aunt Ginny Dee?"

Bethany wiped her face with the tea towel she still held. "Mark's gone. The children too."

He didn't ask where. He just said, "Maybe that's for the best."

Aunt Ginny Dee moaned, got up from the table and left the room.

Bethany stared at her husband as if she didn't know him. "How can you say that?"

"How can I not?"

Bethany stood and threw the tea towel at Luke's chest. She crossed the room and pounded him there, near his heart, where hers was broken.

"Beth!" He grabbed her fists, stopped her, pulled her to him, folding her in strong arms as she poured out her hurt and fear and loss.

"You shamed him. You sent him away, with nowhere to go. And the children—this is their home, as much as it's ours. They've nowhere to go, Luke. Nowhere, and they're out there—in the cold with nothing but a truck to live in."

Luke didn't speak but held her close and let her cry, even as Aunt Ginny Dee stood in the hallway and watched.

The next morning, Bethany helped Luke by holding one side of the new sign he hammered over the old one. The old sign had been newly painted, proclaiming the opening of Wetherill Pickering's Christmas Tree Farm for the season. The new sign, big enough to cover the old, said, *Closed*. One word that changed everything.

Luke and Bethany had already cleared the lane of the trees Mark had sawed off at their bases and piled them next to the barn for now. They could be burned or mulched, but neither of them had the energy or heart to deal with that now. It was enough to put one foot in front of the other.

Aunt Ginny Dee spent her days at the hospital with Will, as if she couldn't bear to be in the house alone.

A light coating of gray ash had settled over the farm. Even inside Aunt Ginny Dee's house a pale film coated everything, making it smell as if the fireplace had burned all winter and no one had bothered to carry out ashes.

Bethany scrubbed the walls, the woodwork and counters, and mopped the floorboards. She stripped the beds and washed every sheet and quilt in the house. She cleaned the oven, which didn't need cleaning, working as if work alone might save her. At least it saved her body. It could not save her mind.

Luke had warned her not to get close to the children, but that had been impossible at the time. Now she wondered if he'd been right, but she couldn't regret loving them, caring about them, or worrying herself sick for them.

By Saturday afternoon Aunt Ginny Dee's house shone. Bethany knew she needed to tackle her own home, but it felt too close, too empty, too gray.

She wasn't ready to be closed in the house all day with Luke, and there wasn't anything he could do about the burned fields. Not now. She didn't blame him, at least not entirely, for the loss of Mark and the children. She knew he regretted the things he'd said to Mark—he'd told her so, wished he could take back his anger in that moment. But that was the thing about words—once said they were forever loosed.

She didn't blame Luke for the coming loss of the farm, either, at least she tried not to. But what she'd seen in his behavior toward Mark reminded her too much of Harold, of the control he'd exerted over Luke and her, of the knee-jerk decisions and poor judgments he'd made that set their life on a trajectory they couldn't alter. That trajectory had not changed, had shown no hope of changing, until

Aunt Ginny Dee, Mark, and the children had appeared at the farm. And now they were back to square one, below square one.

No, she wasn't going home. Instead, she tackled the barn. Mark would have left bedding and towels and who knows what else there. There'd still be more to do.

Bethany's breath caught at the small stacks of children's books on the floor and at the rows of pictures tacked along the beam over Mark's bunk—pictures the children had colored and painted for their father, love notes with hearts and flowers and renditions of what must surely be Bailey. Bethany knew Marley, who was learning to read, came often with Cooper to the barn to visit her pa and read to him.

Work jeans and shirts, washed and folded on the workbench but with that same slight film of ash, Bethany recognized as gifts from Aunt Ginny Dee. Rumpled sheets, quilts, and a pillow filled the bunk. *Mark must have flown like a bat in the dead of night with only the clothes on his back.* That he'd gone with nothing, as though he believed he deserved nothing, cut Bethany's heart.

What she'd do with Mark's clothes Bethany couldn't imagine. She hated to get rid of them. Luke wouldn't fit in them, wouldn't wear them now if he could. Perhaps they'd do for the church rummage sale. The quilts could be stored at Aunt Ginny Dee's. Another major washing should make everything usable—for someone.

She began sorting the stacks of books—some from the library and some from Aunt Ginny Dee's children's shelf. Each one she opened brought Marley or Cooper to life. Marley reading aloud, struggling through new words on the page; Cooper patiently waiting as his sister read, eager to laugh over every little thing; the songs they sang—ones they'd learned from Aunt Ginny Dee or in church and silly ones they made up on the spur of the moment.

The barn door creaked open. "Beth? What are you doing?" Bailey, a lost soul since Arlo and the little ones had gone, followed on Luke's heels.

Bethany's throat felt too thick to answer. Bailey padded over and licked her hand, a kiss of comfort that unleashed Bethany's silent tears.

Luke's arms wrapped around her. "Don't do this to yourself, honey. Please. Come home."

She shook her head. Home was the last place she wanted to be now. At least here she was closer to the children.

"They weren't ours. I knew he'd take off one day, break your heart. That's why I didn't want you to—"

She shrugged him away. "They weren't our children, but they were our family. You never got that, did you?" Bethany stood suddenly, grabbing the last stack of books, accidentally knocking the bottle hidden behind.

Luke reached for the Jack Daniel's bottle and hefted it, his jaw hard. "This is the culprit. This is the demon my brother couldn't . . ."

But Bethany didn't listen. She picked up the crumpled red tissue paper and the tag tied to ribbon and spread out the creases. Silently she read the words, tried to understand them, read them again, and finally turned to Luke.

"What? What's wrong? What's that?"

She held out the tag and waited as he read.

Time to celebrate, brother.

Luke's face registered no recognition. The writing didn't look like his to Bethany, but who else would call Mark "brother"?

She saw shades of resistance, disbelief, and understanding file across her husband's features but she didn't know what they meant. She waited.

Luke shook his head. "I didn't write this."

"Mark must have thought you did. He thought it came from you."

"I swear. I didn't."

"He trusted you."

"I wouldn't. He can't handle liquor. I know that."

"Someone else must know it too. Somebody planted this here, pretending it came from you."

"Who? When?"

Bethany didn't know, but what Arlo had said made sense. "This is why she blamed you. Remember? Arlo said, *It was a present. Some present.*"

"I thought she was just shooting off her mouth, trying to protect her pa. I didn't pay her any mind."

"No, you didn't." She turned away. "Neither did I, not about that."

Bethany closed her eyes, trying to remember, seeing the look on Mark's face, on Arlo's face. "He must have thought you were reaching out to him, wanting to celebrate all you'd done together. But in the end, he had to realize this bottle was bait. Arlo thought you'd betrayed him—betrayed them."

"I didn't. I swear. I wouldn't do that to him."

"I know that, but they don't. The horrible things you said to him, Luke—and you wouldn't listen, didn't hear him."

A long silence stretched between them. When Bethany turned to look at her husband, he'd slumped to the bunk, head in his hands, as he choked back tears. It was the first time in all this unholy mess that Bethany pitied him.

CHAPTER FORTY

GINNY INSISTED ON PICKING WILL UP from the hospital on Saturday. She would have gone to his house and stayed right there, nursing him, if half the town had not been watching.

"I'm all right, Ginny. A broken arm mends. Don't fuss." Will smiled, his remonstrance feeble and unconvincing.

"It's not your arm I'm worried about. Smoke inhalation doesn't disappear overnight. I don't think the doctor should have released you just yet. Anyway, I'm not fussing; I'm caring."

"I love that you do—care, I mean." He coughed, but his smile broadened, and so did hers, which made the heat climb up her neck. "But I don't want to go home yet."

"You need your rest. The doctor said you should take it easy for a couple of days."

"And I will, but I need to see Luke. Can you drive me out?"

"Now? Can't it wait, or can't you talk to him on the phone?"

"I need to see him in person"—Will coughed again—"and I need to talk with him—with all of you—today. You should know who was behind the fire before it comes out in the paper. Luke needs to understand it had nothing to do with Mark."

"You're right," Ginny sighed. "I know you're right and I want to know everything. I'm just worried that you'll overdo. Please don't try to talk so much. It's not good for your lungs or throat."

"Are you always such a mother hen?" he chided, tweaking her cheek.

Ginny wished with all her might that she didn't blush so easily. She never had, at least not for the last fifty years. Will Skipwith could be the most aggravating man, even when not well. Still, she mused, she wouldn't change a thing about him.

❧

Entering Christmas Lane, with no trees to line the long drive, cut Ginny's heart. The trees had never been there when she was growing up, but the way she and Bethany and the children had worked so hard to beautifully decorate them was a precious memory. The violation of that sweetness was still hard to take, a public slaying of their private love gift to one another. And now the children and Mark were gone. Nothing Will had to tell them could change that.

Will didn't speak as they neared the house, and Ginny was thankful. There weren't words for all that had been stolen from Wetherill Pickering's Christmas Tree Farm.

She'd intended to drive Will directly to Promised Land, thinking Luke and Bethany might be home by now, but as they rounded the bend in the lane the couple, their arms loaded with bedding and what looked like wrapping paper, walked out of the barn, shadowed by Bailey. "Poor dog. Without Arlo he's lost."

"I imagine Arlo's lost without him."

The lump in Ginny's throat grew.

Where are they, Lord? How are they? It's so cold at night and they're all alone. The children have to be so frightened, so confused. Is Mark okay? Did he get hold of himself or did that binge start a downward spiral? Please, God, take care of them. It was the prayer Ginny prayed countless times each day.

Before Ginny could pull her thoughts together, Will was out of the car and headed for Luke and Bethany.

"Will, it's good to see you on your feet." Luke reached a tentative hand out to the older man, who took it in a firm grasp.

"It's good to be on my feet, and I'm thankful it wasn't my right arm."

"Shouldn't you be in the hospital, or in bed?" Bethany laid a gentle hand on Will's shoulder.

"The apple doesn't fall far from the tree." Will winked at Ginny, who blushed again.

"Come in the house, all of you," Ginny ordered. "Will wants to talk with us but he needs to sit down. He hasn't got much breath yet, so please make this as easy as possible."

Luke held the door for them all. Bethany heaped the barn laundry into a corner. Ginny settled Will into the overstuffed chair in the parlor. "I'll put the kettle on. A little chamomile mint tea with honey might help your throat."

Will nodded, smiling, though it looked to Ginny as if he struggled.

"What's this about?" Luke asked, folding the piece of wrapping paper he'd held in his hand.

"Give Will a moment. Wait for the tea, Will, please." Ginny knew this was too much too soon for him.

Will nodded, leaning back, and closed his eyes.

Ginny raised her brows in Luke's direction, sending a clear warning. Luke sat back, looked away, surrender and compliance that surprised Ginny.

In less than ten minutes she was back with a tea tray, cups for all. Once Will sipped the soothing liquid, she began, "Will has news about the fire."

Luke sat forward. "Will?"

"Sheriff Tate arrested Rob Warner this morning and brought his nephew in for questioning."

"Rob Warner?" Bethany asked, but Will nodded to Luke to answer.

"Rob Warner—that guy Mark used to hang out with in high

school. Troublemaker of the first order. He's the one got Mark started drinking back then. I haven't seen him around for a while."

Will nodded and drew a shaky breath. "Lived in Atlanta until earlier this year. Evidently hooked up with a group of marijuana buyers there. Since his father passed, I've seen him and his sister in my office a couple of times for issues with their father's estate."

"You think he planted the upper field?"

"Not alone, but yes, and started the fire." Will coughed.

"Why would he set our trees on fire?" Bethany nearly dropped her cup.

"Because we plowed the field under." Luke pulled his hand down his jaw.

"Retaliation," Ginny said. "So, they cut the trees in the lane too?"

Will nodded.

"I just don't understand why they'd do that."

"The sign said *warned*, but how did you know—"

"I didn't make the connection right away, not until Arlo's Thanksgiving play. Arlo—" Will coughed again, took a sip of tea, and drew a deep breath.

"Arlo came to see me not long ago, frightened by the family's anger over the plants she'd found on the mountain. She was upset, and loud. Rob Warner was in my office that day but left before I could speak with him. I imagine he heard enough to put two and two together, realized their marijuana field had been discovered. I believe Rob's nephew, a boy in Arlo's class, is in on it with him. Who else, I don't know."

"A fourth-grade boy? I can't imagine. Is that the boy who's made Arlo's life miserable?"

"What's the matter with Arlo? What are you talking about?" Luke asked.

"I didn't say anything because I didn't see the relationship," Ginny said. "Bethany told me that a boy from school had upset Arlo, said that he knew terrible things about her father and turned some of the girls against her."

"Rob Warner is Jake Stillcoat's uncle—his mother's twin brother." Luke gripped his jaw. "Jake's been in and out of trouble since he could walk."

Will nodded.

"Aunt Ginny Dee, do you remember the day Arlo came home from school, her arm—"

"Yes. She said she'd tripped on her own feet, but I knew she wasn't telling us everything. I knew it!"

"She was terrified—stopped talking, didn't want to go back to school. Do you think he threatened her?"

"That poor child! And the nightmares! Why didn't she tell us?"

"Mark had no connection," Luke said.

"None." Will was firm.

"They must have planted the bottle too." Bethany moaned. "All of it for that stupid field."

"What bottle?" Ginny asked.

Luke unfolded the wrapping paper and tag he'd brought from the barn. "We found this wrapped around the bottle of Jack Daniel's."

Ginny took the tag and read it aloud. *"Time to celebrate, brother."* Stricken, she looked at Luke.

"I didn't write that. I'd never give Mark alcohol. I swear."

"Set up." Ginny could barely breathe. "In the worst way. They gambled that he'd be out cold before they ever set that fire."

Heartbroken over all that Arlo and Mark and the children had suffered, heartbroken over the loss of the farm for their sake and for Luke and Bethany, heartbroken over her inability to save any of them, Ginny didn't want to go to church the next morning. She didn't want to get out of bed.

But Will phoned early and asked her to come pick him up. He was going to church, and he wanted to be with her, to be with the family. She couldn't refuse him.

She hadn't imagined that Luke or Bethany would go either, but they did, and Bethany guided her husband into the last pew beside Ginny.

More surprising was that before the service began, Pastor Edwards pulled Luke from the pew and spoke to him for some minutes. Luke paled, his eyes filled, and he looked at a loss for words. Ginny couldn't imagine what the pastor was saying. Finally, Luke nodded, the men shook hands, and Luke returned to their pew.

Bethany leaned toward him, surely asking what the pastor wanted, but Luke shook his head, as if he couldn't speak, his eyes still filled. Ginny didn't know what to think.

She couldn't have said what the sermon was about. She sat with her eyes closed through most of it, opening them only to take in the words of the last verse of the last hymn.

> *"Whenever I am tempted,*
> *Whenever clouds arise,*
> *When songs give place to sighing,*
> *When hope within me dies,*
> *I draw the closer to Him,*
> *From care He sets me free;*
> *His eye is on the sparrow,*
> *And I know He watches me."*

Ginny sighed. *Are You really watching, Lord? Do you see how we're hurting, how hope is gone?*

After the sermon, before Pastor Edwards gave the benediction, he asked the congregation to stay as he shared something the Lord had placed on his heart.

"We were all here Wednesday night when the fire call came for Pickering's Christmas Tree Farm. Most of us drove out right away to help. With your help and the outstanding work of the fire brigades from Lovettsville, Brunswick, and Leesburg, we put out those fires before they ever reached the houses or barn."

Murmurs of approval ran through the congregation.

"But the acres that burned represented this year's cash crop for the family. I know they won't say, but it's hitting them hard—them personally, and their ability to keep Wetherill Pickering's Christmas Tree Farm afloat—an institution most of us here have grown up with, a place that's long been an integral part of our community, a key provider for our family Christmas celebrations. It would be a shame to see it go under."

Ginny looked at Luke and Bethany, whose faces suddenly flamed. Bethany lifted her shoulders in confusion. Luke clasped his hands and looked down.

"The Pickering family is one of our own. I have an idea how we can help them this Christmas season as well as some of our older, longtime members who are no longer physically able to meet with us—if you want to." He emphasized the *if*.

A pin could have dropped in the sanctuary as eyes locked on the pastor and ears pricked to his every word.

"I spend a fair amount of time each week in the nursing home just outside of New Scrivelsby, visiting our elderly members who can no longer attend services in person. The nursing home has been trying their best to keep monthly fees down for residents. Doing that, there's not much room for the owners to provide extras, and I've learned that some of the staff dip into their own pockets from time to time to bring a little cheer to residents, especially at Christmas. And I know that some of our older shut-in members, as well as some community members with no church, find themselves alone on Christmas. We can't solve all of those concerns, but I think we can help bring some cheer to those folks.

"The Pickerings never said, but I've learned that in addition to the fire—a couple of days before the fire was set—the arsonists cut the tops off those beautiful evergreen trees that lined Christmas Tree Lane going into the Pickering farm."

Gasps came from every corner. Ginny knew that was news to the congregation. No one would have noticed the missing trees in the dark Wednesday night with all attention on the fire.

"I stopped by the farm yesterday and saw those sawed-off treetops—only they didn't look like sawed-off treetops to me. They looked like miniature Christmas trees, just right for the small spaces in nursing home rooms, and a perfect size to hand deliver to our shut-in members and to community members who have no church affiliation. There might not be enough to cover all of those needs, but it's a start."

Louise Shellhorn's husband raised his hand. "But how will that help the Pickerings, Pastor?"

"I'm glad you asked." Pastor Edwards smiled. "I recommend each family here that wants to participate purchase one of those small trees—at full eight-foot-tall-tree price, or more if you're able to donate. But an empty tree is not much of a gift, is it? What if we hold a couple nights of ornament making, right here in the church, and bring our families together to make them? What do you say, Louise? Are you up for the organizing?"

Ginny gasped at Pastor Edwards's audacity. Louise, head of the women's ministry for the church, would not turn the pastor down for anything, even if he asked her to hang the moon.

"Yes, I guess so." She faltered. "I mean . . . yes. That's a wonderful idea, Pastor. Yes, yes, I can, and I have a suggestion." Louise stood.

"Please."

"We can make those ornaments to decorate the trees—everyone can bring their own supplies. I'll come up with a list of items to make several different kinds of ornaments and post the list of supplies needed. We could hold extra classes and make more to sell. Those funds can go to the Pickerings too."

Ginny began to feel like a charity case with Louise at the helm of that drive. She glanced at Bethany, wondering how this was for her and Luke.

"How about we make that last part optional, Louise? We don't want to stress any of our families now, but I appreciate your ideas."

Louise bristled, just a little, but sat down.

Emily shot her hand up. "Pastor Edwards? What about the rest of the trees—the part at the bottom?"

"I'm not sure we can do much about those, Emily. The way they've been cut off at the trunk they can't really be shaped into Christmas trees."

"But we could cut the branches off. I saw the wreath Arlo's dad gave to the library. We could make more wreaths out of those branches and sell them. It'd be a great project for the older kids—like me."

A youth here and there sat up straighter. Excitement buzzed through the room.

"That's a brilliant idea, Emily. Thank you." He smiled directly at Louise. "I see that those organizing genes fall close to the tree."

Louise glowed. Ginny shook her head at the many gifts of Pastor Edwards, a man she'd come to appreciate more and more.

She smiled up at Will beside her. He squeezed her hand.

The next two Wednesday nights and Saturday afternoon were designated for wreath and ornament-making. Whole families could come and choose which project they wanted to work on. "Operation Tiny Trees" would be advertised in the church newsletter, at the school, and on posters in town. The entire community would be invited to participate—another of Louise's ideas—and sales of ornaments, wreaths, and any other crafts church members would like to donate would be conducted in the church parking lot the second Saturday of December. All the funds raised would go to the Pickering family to help cover their loss.

Pastor Edwards closed the service. Ginny was overwhelmed and grateful for everyone's great kindness and enthusiasm but feared their hard work would not be enough to cover the loss. She couldn't bear for them to be disappointed. She was also fairly certain she'd never heard the church sing "We Gather Together" so robustly, a near ringing of the rafters.

CHAPTER FORTY-ONE

ARLO PULLED OPEN THE TRUCK CAB DOOR and slipped out to find a makeshift potty in the woods, doing her best not to wake Marley and Cooper. Her dad snored away, dead to the world.

It was too cold to sleep in the bed of the truck, no matter that they wore nearly every stitch of clothing they owned. There wasn't enough gas money to keep the heater going by running the truck all night. The best they could do was to pull off in the woods somewhere, hope their truck wouldn't be seen, and take turns sleeping like curled-up cats on the floor or take a stint scrunched like spoons on the bench seat, two at a time, while Pa slept sitting up behind the wheel.

Three nights in the cold was three nights too many. The food Aunt Ginny Dee had packed was long gone and the money she'd sent nearly spent. Arlo had given the cash to her pa on Friday, the day the rationed food ran out. He'd spent more than half on gas and a handful of Twinkies and chocolate milk for the little kids. He'd shared an egg salad sandwich from the refrigerated section of the Wawa with Arlo. Yesterday had been slimmer pickings yet.

"The bank opens Tuesday. I've a little money there and I can get it out then. I'll look for day work tomorrow. We'll make do till then," he'd said.

But this was Sunday and Arlo was hungry enough that her

stomach had stopped rumbling. The little kids needed something, anything. They all did.

Finished with her business, Arlo made her way back to the truck and pulled down the tailgate. She hitched herself up and lay down on the cold, frosted metal surface. Stretching out was a luxury, though she couldn't take the cold or the damp long.

The cab door opened and closed.

"It's too cold out here, Arlo. Come back inside."

She didn't answer.

"Come back in, kiddo. I don't want you catching cold."

"Then why did you bring us out here?" Arlo knew she sounded surly, angry. She didn't care.

"You know why. We couldn't stay."

Arlo sat up. "No, you couldn't stay because your pride got hurt. Because you let Uncle Luke talk to you like you're dirt."

"I let him down. I let them all down, and I'd do it again and again the first time I found a bottle. You'd best learn that now, Arlo. I want to do better, I meant to, but I—"

"You were doing great, Pa . . . until that bottle showed up."

"It was right there. I shouldn't have opened it, but I did, and then, I don't know—it sounds lame, but I couldn't stop."

"That's why you never buy it. I can't believe Uncle Luke gave that to you. Why'd he do that? Was it some sort of sick joke?"

Pa shook his head. "I don't know. I wouldn't have thought— maybe he knew. Maybe he knew I wouldn't hold back. Maybe he just wanted me gone and that was the best way to make it happen." He grunted. "It worked."

"Aunt Ginny Dee didn't want us to go. I know Aunt Bethany wants us there—all of us. She told me you'd made all the difference, helping Uncle Luke on the farm. He couldn't keep up alone. You did that, Pa. You made good things happen there."

"The fire was not a good thing."

"You didn't start the fire!"

"I didn't stop it."

"Nobody could've stopped it by themselves. You're not more powerful than God." Arlo didn't know where that came from, but she knew it was true. *Sometimes we're just so weak—like Pa with his drink—that we can't do things on our own.* It sounded like something she'd probably heard in church.

"I guess it would take God to fix this mess."

"So let Him," Arlo whispered.

"What?"

"Let Him. Stop trying to make everything right by yourself. It's not working, Pa. Ask God to help you. Talk to Mr. Skipwith. You know he'll help you figure things out. He's good at that."

"You mean go back with our tails between our legs."

"Is that all you care about? How you'll look? Marley and Cooper are going to get sick out here in the cold. Don't you care about us?"

"Of course I care. You know I do. But if I go back, I'll pull them all down with me. I'll pull you down." He hopped off the tailgate. "I've ruined the farm. Now I'm messing up for you guys. Maybe you'd all be better off if—"

"Stop it, Pa. The one you're letting down—besides yourself and us—is Aunt Ginny Dee. Forget Uncle Luke. Forget Aunt Bethany. They don't even own the farm. Aunt Ginny Dee is the one put her whole life on hold and all her savings into the farm. She gave up her trip to Scotland and maybe England to make a home for us. And now we're throwing that away and throwing all her savings away."

"We lost the crop, Arlo. There's no way to save the farm now."

"How do you know? You don't know because we ran off—like you said, with our tails between our legs! I can't believe you'd do that to her. We had nothing, and she gave us a home, made us a family. We deserted her."

"We can't take her charity all our lives."

"It wasn't charity. We all worked hard together. You worked yourself nearly to death. I saw it. It wasn't charity. It was family, and she was glad."

Her pa was silent for a long time before he leaned against the tailgate. He shook his head. "I don't know. I just don't know." Minutes passed before he took Arlo's hand in his, rubbing his thumb over her knuckles. "I messed us up . . . didn't I? I'm sorry, Arlo. I'm real sorry."

"Then take us back. Aunt Ginny Dee needs us now more than ever. Family doesn't leave family—that's what you told me after Ma cut out. She proved she wasn't family. Maybe she couldn't be, but you are . . . Aunt Ginny Dee is." Arlo pulled her hand away, took him by the shoulders, and made him look her in the eye. "Families don't run out on each other."

CHAPTER FORTY-TWO

SO MANY FAMILIES HAD SIGNED UP to buy Tiny Trees and make ornaments and wreaths for the fundraiser that Luke had stayed behind that first Wednesday night to cut a few of the younger trees from distant fields, promising to get them to the church before eight that evening. That should give the workers another full hour to work their magic.

Bethany rode in early with Aunt Ginny Dee to set up a hospitality table with coffee, cookies, muffins, and snacks. It was the least they could do for all the church and community were doing for them, and the treats would make the work time even more festive.

Bethany was glad for time alone with Aunt Ginny Dee, glad for the opportunity to thank her for the very serious talk she'd had with her and Luke that afternoon. Hearing that she had no choice but to put the farm up for sale after the first of the year had been hard, but at least they'd all looked at the books together in the light of their sudden loss.

Relief of the tax debt was only one problem. Even Luke acknowledged that he couldn't make the farm a going concern on his own, and there was no money to hire help. Luke agreed that Mark's labor had been a godsend, even with the cost of the family there. Together, before the fire and loss of the trees, there had been a chance they could make it, get on track with the loan payments and possibly begin to turn things around. Now they saw no way forward.

Bethany had imagined that nothing could ever induce her to let go of the gravesites of her babies. The prospect was daunting, but in some ways not so hard as the recent loss of Arlo, Marley, and Cooper, children she'd spent months with, children she'd come to love with all her heart. Staying on the farm without them loomed a loss so sharp, so intensely painful and lonely that she was almost relieved they'd need to move. And the idea that Aunt Ginny Dee, who'd become a true aunt to her—almost a second mother—must move on, possibly even to faraway England, opened a chasm she couldn't navigate. *Too much heartache here . . . too much loss. Starting over will be hard, but at least it means a new beginning. We need a new beginning, all of us.*

"We can't lose touch, Aunt Ginny Dee. I couldn't bear that."

"We won't, I promise." Aunt Ginny Dee took her eyes from the road for only a moment and reached for Bethany's hand. "You're the good that's come out of all this for me."

"There could have been so much more," Bethany whispered. "There was so much more."

Aunt Ginny Dee didn't reply. Bethany didn't expect her to. Tears were too near the surface for them both.

"What will you and Luke do? Where will you go, have you thought?"

"Not really. Farming Christmas trees is all Luke's ever known, ever done."

"Will you move near your parents?"

"North Carolina? I don't think so. We're not that close. My sister lives there, with her four children. Mom is so taken up with them she can't see me. Being invisible is harder than not being there."

"She's missing out."

"She doesn't see it that way."

"I've never asked this, but have you and Luke ever thought of adopting?"

Bethany's breath hitched in her chest. "Once. We even began the application process."

"What happened?"

"Harold. He wouldn't have children who were not Pickering blood on his land, and it was all his land . . . or so we thought."

"Because of the way he viewed Curtis, I imagine . . . as an inter-loper." Ginny shook her head. "That's so different from the way Mama and Daddy looked at things. I'm so sorry for all Harold put you through."

Bethany looked out the side window. "Me too. But maybe now . . . maybe we could try again."

"You'd make a wonderful mother. I saw how you were with Mark's children. Any child would be so blessed to be claimed by you, loved by you."

Bethany was grateful for the dark, grateful that the tears that fell could not be seen. She swiped them away. *She's right. I'd make a good mother. I can be a good mother.*

By the time they pulled into the church parking lot it was nearly full. They'd expected to be the first there, but lights already blazed from the sanctuary and hospitality room, creating a warm welcome.

"Ready?" Aunt Ginny Dee asked, clasping Bethany's hand.

"Ready as I'll ever be." Bethany drew a deep breath and forced a bright smile.

Inside, Christmas carols poured from a boom box in the back of the room. Construction paper, glitter, glue, tape, red and green yarn, colorful sheets of foil, pine cones, paint and brushes, small silver jingle bells, and every color of ribbon covered tables on one side of the room, ready for eager crafters.

Boughs of evergreen, remnants Luke had cut from the decapitated tree trunks the day before, were piled against the wall on the opposite side of the room and filled the air with the fragrance of Christmas. Families were already gathered, having brought their own clippers. The hardware store had donated metal wreath frames. The local flo-rist had donated thin green wire. Large red, velvety bows from the fabric store and a collection of sprayed pine cones and Christmas balls heaped yet another table.

Pastor Edwards met the women at the door and helped them unload their boxes and baskets of treats. "Festive, isn't it?" He beamed. "A true party in the making."

"Pastor—so many people already here. I didn't expect so many." Aunt Ginny Dee looked overwhelmed.

"I believe the newspaper article about the fire and the arrest brought more people out. The fire was tragic enough, but when we all realized what had been done and the terrorizing of young Arlo, well, I think folks understood it could have been any one of our farms, any one of our children, our families. We need to pull together in times like these."

"That's right." Louise appeared from behind Bethany. "I have to say that until I read about that Rob Warner and until Emily told me about the Stillcoat boy in her class, I'd blamed Mark Pickering as well. It sounds like Rob was the ringleader, though I guess there's still questions Mark needs to answer."

"What questions? Mark had nothing to do with it." Aunt Ginny Dee looked horrified.

Louise leaned forward conspiratorially. "Considering his relationship with Rob. Those boys were thick as thieves in high school, always getting into trouble, if you know what I mean. Well, you wouldn't. You weren't here. But I don't know that anything's really changed since Mark came back from the war—Harold's own prodigal son. Once a bad penny . . . Well, they turn up again and again, don't they?"

"Mark's not a bad penny. He's not even a prodigal . . . not anymore, no matter what he went through. War is hard on men, Louise. It changes them in ways they can't always help, can't always get over— ways you and I can't imagine. Mark worked hard on our farm—his farm too. He's a valued member of our family. I just wish he'd turn up again."

Louise's brows rose. "I'm sorry, Ginny. I hope you're right. I guess we'll see, won't we?"

"I beg your pardon?" Aunt Ginny Dee's ire was up.

"Mrs. Boyden?" Emily interrupted on the heels of her grandmother. "I just wanted to say I'm sorry . . . about everything . . . and I wonder, do you think Arlo will come back to school?"

"No, Emily. She's not here . . . and I don't think she was very happy in school."

Bethany could not resist speaking up for Arlo, could not resist poking a finger at the likes of Emily and her grandmother. "She wasn't treated very kindly—by some."

Emily flushed. "I know. I was one of those, Mrs. Pickering, and I'm sorry. I believed Jake Stillcoat when he told us bad things about Arlo and her dad. I know now that he lied—about lots of things. I just wish I could tell her sorry."

"It's a little late now."

Aunt Ginny Dee laid her hand on Bethany's arm as she spoke to Emily. "It's never too late to ask God's forgiveness, to make the amends we can, even if we can't ask the person. You might never see Arlo again to tell her, but if you're truly sorry, Emily, you'll take this lesson with you in life. Next time, reach out to girls who are new, and don't be quick to believe everything you hear."

"Yes, ma'am." Emily looked miserable, but relieved at the same time.

"I wouldn't worry too much," Louise interjected. "I imagine you'll get your chance sooner than you think."

Bethany didn't know what she meant; she only knew that Louise irritated her more than she could say. "Let's get these refreshments set up, Aunt Ginny Dee."

"Want some help?" Emily asked. "Please?"

Aunt Ginny Dee looked momentarily conflicted, but smiled and handed Emily the tablecloth. "Yes, let's get this spread first."

Bethany turned away, bit her lip, and closed her eyes. She needed to get hold of herself. If Aunt Ginny Dee could forgive so quickly, why couldn't she? Something inside made her want to punish Emily, punish Louise, punish all those who'd given Mark and his precious children a hard time, as if they'd had something they needed to prove to be accepted . . . as if they could ever be accepted by such judgmental people.

She set out plates of the cookies Arlo and the children had made, the ones they'd frozen, anticipating the opening day of Christmas tree sales. She arranged a pyramid of cranberry orange mini muffins and helped Aunt Ginny Dee arrange a Christmas centerpiece made from one of the wreaths Arlo had fashioned before the fire. Each and every memory of the children broke Bethany's heart in fresh places. Each reminder increased her fear and worry over where they were, how they were.

When the refreshments table was ready and the coffeepots were percolating, Aunt Ginny Dee joined Emily and her friends at the wreath-making table, but Bethany could not.

How can she smile and celebrate and work with those girls when they rejected Arlo? When they turned their noses up at Marley and Cooper? When Emily's grandmother treated Mark like dirt? If Mark and his children had been welcomed as equals by people like Emily and Louise— by Luke—would things have gone the way they did?

If ever Bethany felt her heart grow hard, it was then. She'd never stood outside her church family and refused to participate in anything, but now, despite all they were doing, despite how sorry Luke was and all he was doing to help . . . how could she pretend everything was okay, forgiven, forgotten? Wasn't it all too little too late?

"Bethany?" Aunt Ginny Dee placed a hand on her shoulder. "Are you all right? Why don't you come help with the wreaths? We need some of your bow-tying skills."

Bethany shook her head. "I'm not sure I can." She looked at Louise, so full of herself, bustling around the ornament-making table, instructing the children to do things her way, totally in her element.

"You need to forgive them," Aunt Ginny Dee whispered. "They can't change what they don't see. God will work in them just like He's working in each of us . . . in His time, His way—not ours."

Bethany drew a deep breath. "That's hard to do."

"We're made for hard things."

She knew Aunt Ginny Dee was right, but Bethany needed to change the subject or she'd cry, right then and there. "Where's Will? I thought he'd be here." *At least he's a supportive soul. He cared about Mark and the children, tried to help them, welcome them, right from the start.*

"I don't know. I thought so too. He might have gotten waylaid at work, or maybe his arm's giving him trouble. I'm sure it aches more than he lets on. Besides, I don't imagine he'd be much help at wreath or ornament making just now." Aunt Ginny Dee tried to make light though Bethany knew she, too, craved Will's presence and moral support. "Come on, let's work on the wreaths together. We'll bolster one another."

❧

Halfway through the evening everyone took a refreshment break. Pastor Edwards led the group in prayer that their labors on behalf of the Pickering family would produce necessary fruit for them and for all the recipients of the Tiny Trees.

Louise manned the punch bowl. Bethany thought that a bit presumptuous, but Aunt Ginny Dee looked too weary to care. Despite the brave face she put on, Bethany knew the last several days had taxed the older woman's endurance and resolve. She imagined Aunt Ginny Dee kept sleepless prayer vigils for Mark, Arlo, Marley, and Cooper, just as she did.

Louise poured a glass of punch and handed it to Bethany. "You look as if you could do with this."

"Thanks." Bethany attempted a smile but still couldn't look Louise in the eye.

"Don't look so glum. If Ginny Dee is right about Mark, I'm sure Will Skipwith will sort things out. Even Emily might get her chance to apologize, though for what exactly, I can't imagine."

"What do you mean?"

"Assuming they stay, and Arlo returns to school—Emily can see her then. That's also assuming this fundraiser brings in enough money to save your farm. And I hope it does, Bethany. I mean that. It's awful what you've all been through."

Bethany shook her head. "Mark and the children aren't coming back."

"But they have. I'm sure that was Mark's truck I saw outside Will's office this afternoon."

"What? Today? Are you certain?"

"Ancient red pickup with enough dents to call it a piñata? I don't think there's another like it anywhere."

Bethany nearly dropped her punch glass. "Aunt Ginny Dee! Aunt Ginny Dee!" Bethany pulled her away from a conversation with another of the women. "Louise just told me she saw Mark's truck outside Will's off—"

But Bethany was cut off the moment the outside door to the community room opened, bringing in a rush of cold air, a swirl of leaves, and Mark, Arlo, Marley, and Cooper, followed by a smiling Will.

"Aunt Ginny Dee!" Marley cried out first and, drawing Cooper by the hand, raced across the room.

"Mark!" Aunt Ginny Dee shoved her paper plate into Bethany's hands and rushed toward her nephews and nieces, scooping the three youngsters into a quick hug before reaching for Mark with open arms. "You're home!"

"Aunt Ginny Dee," Mark began, clearly all too aware that all eyes were on him and his disheveled entourage, "I let you down. I know I shouldn't—"

"It doesn't matter. Nothing matters but that you're here now. You're home." She framed his face between her palms and pulled his head down to kiss his forehead. It was a moment so private, so precious, Bethany turned away.

She heard their conversation as background to the hugs and kisses she poured out on and received from the three children she knelt before. She couldn't stop the tears—happy tears—or the laughter that bubbled from the sudden pang of relief.

Cooper reached up and wiped her face with his palm. "Don't cry, Aunt Bethy. Don't cry."

Bethany laughed and cried more.

"Aunt Bethy." Marley tugged her sleeve and pointed. "Are those our cookies over there?"

"They are, sweetheart. Want some?"

Marley nodded. "I'm hungry. Cooper's hungry too."

"I'm sure you are. Let's go fill a plate, shall we? Arlo? Coming?"

Arlo nodded. "Can we give some to Pa?" she whispered. "He hasn't eaten since yesterday and I don't think he feels so good."

Bethany's heart constricted. *When did any of you eat last?* "Right away."

Bethany had just settled the trio with food and drink and convinced Aunt Ginny Dee to release Mark long enough to let him sit and eat when the outside door opened again, bringing with it an icy wind this time, and Luke, loaded down with evergreen limbs.

He entered warily, his eyes searching the room, Bethany knew, not only for her. He would have seen Mark's truck in the parking lot. The brothers' eyes connected.

Gently, Bethany pushed Cooper from her lap and crossed the room, ready to meet her husband, to urge him to see the hope in Mark's returning, but Aunt Ginny Dee reached him first and wrapped her arm around his shoulder. Luke shrugged it off.

"Luke," Aunt Ginny Dee began, "I'm glad you're here. Come, celebrate with us. Mark's home." She waited.

Bethany held her breath.

"For how long?"

"To stay, I hope—as long as any of us can. He's offered to help with the cleanup."

Luke still clutched his load of evergreen boughs.

Bethany embraced her husband, whispering, "Remember that

note, that bottle. It wasn't from you. He thought it was. This is your chance to mend fences."

"None of us make it on our own, Luke," Aunt Ginny Dee spoke softly. "Not you or Mark or me, not one of us. We need one another, now more than ever. Mark made a mistake. You made a mistake when you blamed him. We all make mistakes, but we don't have to live in them forever."

Luke stared at his aunt, his eyes clouded in conflict. From across the room Bethany saw Mark stand, facing them. *Too many eyes, Lord. Too many eyes. Please, help.*

Will stepped up. "Can I relieve you of some of those limbs, son? Got more in the truck?"

It snapped Luke to the moment. "Thanks, but I don't think you're up to that." He nodded toward Will's cast.

"One-armed bandits are still bandits." Will winked and reached for what he could. Bethany barely caught the words Will whispered to her husband. "Forget those things which are behind; press forward . . ."

Luke jerked, almost imperceptibly, as if someone had slapped him awake.

"Let me, Will." Mark stepped between them, reaching for Luke's load. "Luke? I can help."

It was a peace offering, a plea, a bend toward grace and, Bethany hoped, forgiveness. *Please, God, open Luke's heart.*

Time seemed to stand still, far too long, before Luke gave a half nod and released his load into Mark's arms. Mark carried the branches to the side of the room where the wreath making was ostensibly going on, though much more quietly than before while friends and neighbors watched the brothers from the corners of their eyes.

Bethany squeezed Luke's arm in appreciation. *Thank You, Lord. Thank You for answering, and so quickly.*

Luke's jaw tightened and released, tightened and released, his eyes following Mark, taking in Marley and Cooper happily gobbling cookies and Arlo, whose eyes challenged him, protective of her pa. Luke's chest visibly rose and fell. He squeezed Bethany's hand.

It wasn't a guarantee that everything—anything—was settled, or that things would move forward smoothly. A hand squeeze was so little, but it gave Bethany hope, and hope had been a long time coming.

"Got any more evergreen out there?" Pastor Edwards asked. "We've got lots of men to help unload tonight."

Luke nodded again and headed out into the dark, Mark on his heels.

CHAPTER FORTY-THREE

THE NEXT SEVERAL DAYS PASSED without Luke stepping into Ginny's kitchen. He drove out first thing in the mornings, picking up shifts at a couple of local Christmas tree stands, where he was helping to sell trees he'd delivered before the fire. Ginny didn't blame him, in fact was glad he'd found some work, albeit temporary. He had no reason to invest more of his labor in the farm now; he needed to be putting away all he could in anticipation of their move.

She could count on one hand the minutes it took Bethany to make her way over to the farmhouse and the children once Luke left. Bethany didn't confide what went on behind closed doors at home and Ginny admired her discretion. She just prayed that all was well with the couple.

Mark, at Ginny's insistence, had finally moved to share the upstairs bedroom with Cooper, much to Cooper's delight. Mark had been meeting with Will every evening, though neither of them had made her privy to their conversations. During the day, he busied himself cleaning up the burned field, pruning the orchard, and sprucing up the barn and grounds near the house—whatever he could find to do that might help with the sale of the farm, for surely that was coming.

Ginny saw that this work was somehow therapeutic for Mark and figured he believed he needed to earn his way for room and board. She appreciated his efforts more than she could say, though it made her sad to imagine where he would go, what he would do once the farm sold. She wanted to do something for Mark, something that would let him know how much she cared for him, valued him as a member of the family, something for him to hold on to. She wanted him to remember his time at the farm as a healing time, however long or short that might be.

During those evenings when Mark was out with Will, Ginny worked on a botanical treasure. It was the largest framed picture, the most intricate and impressive work she'd ever created. Made of pressed flowers and leaves and bits of evergreens she had saved from her pressings to take with her to England, she included everything from the farm she could imagine. Beneath it she carefully lettered words from Moses' song in Exodus, words she hoped would remind Mark where to find his strength in future days: *The Lord is my strength and song, and He is become my salvation. Exodus 15:2.*

It would be her legacy gift to Mark, something portable he could take with him, something that reflected the farm in every way she knew and yet was a reminder of his true foundation. She hoped the gift would also remind him and his precious children of her long after she was gone to England, and of her love for each of them.

The night she finished, Mark was out with Will, and the children were fast asleep in bed. She wrapped the heavy frame in white tissue paper and tied a wide, red ribbon around it, leaving a note for Mark, saying all she wanted to say, all she had the heart to say. Even as she penned the words, she knew that a part of her was remembering Curtis, wishing she could have shared the strength of the Lord with him as she was doing with Mark. She didn't know if it would have made a difference, if Curtis could have understood when he came back from the war. She hadn't known how to do that, not then. She drew a deep breath. *I can do this now.*

She placed her note atop her gift on the kitchen table where Mark would surely see it when he walked through the back door. She hadn't quite known how to give it to him; it was that personal. *Better that he has time alone with it first.* She'd see him in the morning.

Saturday morning dawned bright and beautiful, with the snow-laden skies of December reverting to a perfect October blue. Still, just as cold, Ginny, Mark, Bethany, and the children all bundled up in layers to attend the sale and take shifts in manning the booths.

Mark helped load the cars with baked goods for the sale. He'd avoided Ginny's eye and never mentioned her gift through breakfast, though she'd made every effort to be near him. Just before she slid behind the wheel of her car, he drew her into his arms, hugging her long and hard, and whispered, "Thank you, Aunt Ginny Dee. Thank you for everything."

It was enough and more than enough.

"What was that about?" Bethany asked, giving Mark a backward glance as the women and children drove down the lane.

Ginny simply shook her head. Bethany's brows rose, but she didn't pry, and changed the subject.

"Doesn't it seem strange that we're part of selling on the day that the funds taken in will benefit the farm?" Bethany asked.

Ginny lifted her hands. "Louise asked if we'd help. For as odd as it feels, I didn't think we could refuse."

"I imagine she thinks having the children there will make people take pity on us. That's hardly fair to them."

"No, but being homeless is hardly fair to them either. Let's do what we can and leave the results in God's hands."

"You're right. That's all we can do."

"That's all we can do, all we need to do." Ginny spoke with conviction but prayed for help in her doubts and fears.

"Aunt Ginny Dee," Cooper whined, once they'd set up their table in the church parking lot, "I'm hungry. Can I have a cookie—one of those Surprise Cookies with the chocolate chips and cherries?"

"Me too?" Marley asked. Arlo raised her eyes in hope. Ginny couldn't turn them down and pulled out her purse.

"Business had better pick up soon or our darlings will eat the profits," Bethany huffed.

Ginny was past caring about profits.

"Aunt Ginny Dee, the way things are going, we might still stand a chance—don't you think?"

Ginny shrugged. "I'd like to think so, Arlo, but I can't see how."

"If we truly sell the farm, what will you do? Will you go to England after all?" Bethany asked when the children were out of hearing.

Ginny had thought of little else. England—tending the gardens of her ancestral Scrivelsby Manor—had been her dream for years. Now the idea of leaving the gardens she and her mother had started, saying goodbye to the patch of ground crowned Promised Land, even though she was yet to walk it, and most especially losing the family she'd come to love smacked of defeat, loss, portent to grief. "I don't know what else to do."

"What about Will? I thought, possibly . . ."

Ginny shook her head. They'd made no promises, and since the fire he'd been more remote, perhaps busier than usual . . . perhaps not. "We're friends. That's all." *That's all. I'd hoped for more. Foolish, foolish me.*

Noon brought a crowd in search of food and Christmas shopping, as well as new deliveries of items donated for the sale—a log cabin quilt handmade by the quilting ladies of Stitch in Time, the fabric, yarn, and embroidery store in town; boxes of chocolate milk from the dairy, and milk and dark chocolate from the local confectioner's; an entire table of used books from the local library, thanks to Louise.

Pastor Edwards rushed in at the last minute, tipped his hat to Ginny, and directed several church members in picking up the decorated Tiny Trees that had been pre-purchased for nearby shut-ins and residents of the nursing home.

She'd hoped to speak with him about her decision to sell the farm, but between her wreath and cookie sales and his directing, there wasn't time. The first moment she had a break in customers she saw Pastor Edwards headed toward his car, parked across the street. By the time she reached him he was pulling away. He didn't make eye contact but gave her a quick wave, never slowing. As he drove by, she saw that his seats, front and back, were loaded with her botanical pictures.

I thought Mark sent those with Pastor because we were going to sell them here today. Why is he driving off with them?

"Aunt Ginny Dee! We need you over here!" Bethany called, clearly swamped with customers.

Wreath sales picked up, faster than Ginny and Bethany could keep up with. She was glad not to be the one manning the cashbox. That lid went up and down faster and more times than Ginny could count, though most of it was for nickels, dimes, quarters, and small bills. By two o'clock her head was splitting, and she and her smile were frozen through.

She'd had Bethany take the children home where it was warm just after one. Louise or no Louise, she wasn't going to risk them catching colds.

Will appeared at three and met her behind the wreath table. "Ginny Dionysia Pickering Boyden, you look ready to drop."

"Two more hours before we shut down. I can make it."

"No, you can't. Time to go home."

"I can't."

"Yes, you can. There are enough others here to help. I'm here; I'll man your booth, m'lady." He winked, but she saw concern for her in his eyes, and perhaps something more. That confused but bolstered her more than any amount of coffee loaded with sugar and heated cream had all day.

"I sent Bethany with my car to take the children home. It was too cold for them to stay."

"It's too cold for you. I'll be right back."

He was gone two minutes before returning with Pastor Edwards, who was back from his rounds.

"I'm here to rescue this lady in distress." Pastor Edwards grinned, stomping his feet to keep warm.

"I'm not in distress, really."

"Be that as it may, I'll drive you home, Ginny. It's time to call it a day. We've plenty of help to wrap things up here."

"Will, you shouldn't have bothered Pastor." *Why don't you take me home?* That's what she wanted to say.

"It's no bother—and a perfect excuse for me to get out of this cold before my feet freeze. Please don't take away my blessing."

There was nothing she could say to that. Careful of his cast, Will lifted her backpack from beneath the table. "Anything else?"

"No. Bethany carried everything else."

"Good. I'll see you soon." Will smiled, fitted the backpack to Ginny's shoulder, and gave her arm a squeeze.

Ginny nodded, too confused by her headache and his mixed messages to think.

Halfway to the farm, Pastor Edwards glanced at Ginny, then kept his eyes on the road. "This project—Operation Tiny Trees—and all that we're doing here has really brought the church together in a way I haven't seen . . . maybe ever, certainly not during my time here. I know this has been hard, has required a lot from you, Ginny, but I want to thank you for accepting this effort, and for helping."

Ginny almost snorted. "The church members are the ones helping, doing so much, so generously. Honestly? I feel guilty, Pastor. Everyone putting out their time and money and energy here, just before Christmas, when they have their own families to tend to. And all the while, what they're doing won't be enough for me to keep the farm. I have to sell. There's simply not another way forward. I'm afraid it's going to be such a disappointment, will seem like such a failure to them. I feel worse about that than anything."

"Anything?"

Ginny looked down, knotted her fingers. "No. I feel the very worst about losing the farm for Mark and the children, for Bethany and Luke. I really thought we could turn it all around, if we could just get through the season and get on board with the payment of that debt. We calculated it all so carefully. We even hoped there'd be enough to make it through another year. But we didn't count on the fire." She sighed, weary from the depths of her soul. "I guess keeping the farm wasn't in God's providence."

"I don't believe God's providences are always clear to us, Ginny."

"True enough."

"Sometimes I think we're too deep in the forest to see the trees, so to speak." He smiled but kept his eyes straight ahead.

"What do you mean? You think there's something I'm not seeing?"

"Oh yes." He didn't elaborate.

"What? What am I not seeing?"

"The bounty. Luke and Bethany, for one. You didn't know them before you came. They lived under Harold's thumb a long time. They lost three children, you know . . . three tiny babies at different stages of Bethany's pregnancies. Those losses nearly killed her. But she hung on, even nursed Harold, though he made their lives miserable. And then you came."

"I came to sell the farm they'd thought was theirs. That's not exactly a gift."

"But when you came, Mark and his children came, too, and that is a gift—a gift to Mark and the children, certainly."

"Mark needs more help than I can give him, Pastor. He's trying, he tried so hard, but his addiction—"

"Will told me something today. He and Mark have worked it out for Mark to go to AA meetings in Brunswick and to see a counselor in Leesburg. He's still got a lot to work through."

"I didn't think Mark was open to that."

Pastor Edwards nodded. "I think this recent episode scared him. He's willing to do anything to make sure he doesn't lose his children or their home together."

Ginny choked back a sob of regret. "They'll have a home here as long as I do. But I don't know how long they'll be able to stay together. If the farm sells quickly—"

"His work on the farm is a help in the meantime, isn't it?"

"Yes, absolutely. Even Luke has softened a bit toward him now, but I don't know if that will last, or even where any of them will go."

"I think Luke's beginning to realize the good of Mark and the children being here—good that he didn't see before. Some things he might not see until later."

"I hope you're right; I'm just afraid there's not going to be a later."

He was quiet for a moment as he turned down the lane to the farm. "When you first came to church, Ginny . . . slipping into the last pew once the service had started and out of the sanctuary before it ended. Do you remember? Week after week, you sat alone. Seldom have I seen a sadder face while preaching."

Ginny looked out her side window. "Coming back here was hard. I still don't know if my being here is going against my mother's wishes."

"Surely you don't doubt your mother would have welcomed you home?"

"Like your 'running father'? I don't know. I want to think so, but I'll never know for sure. Not knowing made it harder to come back than learning what Harold had done."

"But you did come back, and now you don't sit alone. Your pew is filled to overflowing with family. Have you looked in the mirror lately? When you smile, you're radiant. And I don't know if I've ever seen this much energy or light in Will Skipwith's eyes."

Will was too hard, too painful and uncertain a topic for Ginny to address.

"You've made a home here, a real haven out of your parents' farm for yourself and all your family, though I think you might consider changing the name."

"Excuse me?"

Pastor Edwards brought the car to a stop in front of the house.

"It's not really Wetherill Pickering's Christmas Tree Farm anymore, is it? You've made it your own. Might be good to give yourselves a fresh start."

"Pastor Edwards, you're not listening. I can't keep the farm. I want to, but I can't. Even if I sink the rest of my savings into it and whatever this very generous fundraiser brings in, there's not enough to pay the taxes and make the farm an ongoing concern. The bank won't wait much longer and there are taxes to pay. So much would need to be reinvested now, since the fire. It's not only about losing this year's crop, which is devastation enough, but all those acres need to be cleared—stumps pulled and planted new. The buildings all need more work. There's no miracle of loaves and fishes here. I know you mean well, but—"

"You're looking at this in your own strength, Ginny—what you can do, what you can afford, what you can make happen. You're worried about many things. Let God finish His work. Let Him finish what He's begun and see what happens."

You're worried about many things—that's what Jesus said to Martha when she kept serving, serving, while her sister sat, listening, at Jesus' feet.

Ginny climbed out of the car, unsure whether to slam the car door in frustration or fall to her knees in repentance. She did neither, but with her hand still on the door said, "I'd hoped for a happy ending, but I can't go on believing in fairy tales. And even if I did, the original fairy tales often held tragic endings."

"True, Ginny. But miracles . . . that's another thing."

🌹

Ginny couldn't argue with Pastor Edwards. He was right in saying that she believed it was all up to her. She'd operated that way all her life, believing that God helped only those who helped themselves and that mountains were moved one small stone at a time.

It might not be scriptural, but she'd done what she could until she couldn't do more. She'd taken care of Curtis as long as she could, but then she'd quit, even before he had, if only in her heart. These last months she'd given up her tour of Scotland, Ireland, and Wales to try to make a go of the farm, to provide a home for Mark and the children and the possibility of a future for Bethany and Luke, her stubborn, stubborn nephew. She'd postponed her move to England. Who knew if the Dymokes would even allow her to come now? She'd done all she knew to do but still it wasn't enough. Now, to ask God to intervene, to create something from nothing—how could she? What right did she have?

Bailey trotted out from the barn. When he saw her, he bounded toward her, happiness on four black feet and a white chest patch. "Good boy, Bailey. Good boy." She gave him a good scratch behind his ears, one ear hiked straight up and the other bent down, true Bailey fashion. "What will happen to you, my friend, when we all go? Where will you find a home?"

Ginny looked up, and in the gathering dusk she saw the light come on through the kitchen window . . . her mother's kitchen window. Bethany was pulling on an apron, Arlo at her side, looking up, asking something. The top of Marley's head bobbed up and down. They must have received the answer they wanted for the girls high-fived and disappeared.

Content. That's how they look . . . content. How far they've all come, Lord. Pastor Edwards was right about that.

It was cold and Ginny needed to go inside, but she didn't want to just yet. She wanted to watch the film in the window play out. She walked with Bailey to the woodpile and took a seat on an old maple stump, wrapping her arms around her torso to stave off the damp.

The back screen door slapped shut. Luke appeared in the window behind Bethany, who was doing something at the sink, maybe scraping carrots or washing dishes. Luke seldom came into Ginny's kitchen. He must be wondering where his supper was, when Bethany was coming home. But he didn't look vexed. He nuzzled the back of Bethany's neck, something Ginny had not seen him do.

Bethany smiled and turned to face her husband. She stroked his cheek. He smiled in return and kissed her, long and lingering.

What's happened? Ginny felt she was watching a foreign film, one that she'd never seen. Captivated as she was, she knew she shouldn't watch their private moment, so she turned away. "Come, Bailey." She scratched behind his ears again. "We'll go in the front door." She made enough noise upon entering to alert the cavalry, just in case.

By the time Ginny reached the kitchen, Luke was gone, and Bethany was smiling, humming. Ginny could not imagine what had changed. *Perhaps miracles do still happen.*

❦

Church the next day felt awkward to Ginny. People kept congratulating her on the very successful fundraiser, saying what a great event it was and how much they'd enjoyed it and maybe they could all do another one for someone else in the new year.

Pastor Edwards commended the congregation for a job well done in Christian love, emphasizing the joy of laboring together to bless one another through giving. He told of the delight of the nursing home patients and shut-ins upon receiving their beautifully decorated Tiny Trees. He praised the youth for the wreaths they'd made to sell and celebrated the fact that Pickering wreaths were now adorning most of the storefronts and many of the homes of New Scrivelsby.

Will slipped into their pew after the service started and out again just before the benediction, whispering, "I need to speak to Pastor Edwards right after the service. I'll call soon." He seemed distracted, preoccupied, leaving Ginny only to nod noncommittally.

Outside the church, Bethany stopped Mark and Ginny. "We want you all to come to our house for Sunday dinner, say one o'clock. Okay?"

Ginny felt her eyes go wide. She'd never been invited into Bethany and Luke's house, and as far as she knew neither had Mark, even though the children had gone back and forth. "You do?" Ginny glanced at Luke, expecting his standard frown.

"We both do," Luke said, wrapping his arm around his wife and looking Ginny in the eye.

Mark shifted his feet.

"You, too, Mark—you and the kids." Luke reached his hand out to his brother.

"Yay!" Marley jumped up and down. Cooper followed suit. "Arlo! We're going to Uncle Luke's for dinner! What's to eat, Aunt Bethy? Can we have chocolate milk?"

Luke's hand was still extended. "I mean it. We want—I want you to come."

Mark glanced at Ginny, but Ginny held her breath, refusing to look either nephew in the eye. This was between them.

"Go on, Pa," Arlo urged, even as she eyed her uncle suspiciously.

Tentatively, Mark reached out his hand. Luke pumped it once, a firm grip, and dropped it. It wasn't long, but it was enough.

CHAPTER FORTY-FOUR

OF ALL THE THINGS Ginny expected to happen that day, she'd not imagined stepping foot into Promised Land. Her Promised Land. Only it wasn't hers. It wasn't the little house with the white picket fence her young heart had dreamed of for her and Curtis. It wasn't surrounded by pink roses and blue hydrangeas. The back garden wasn't filled with roses and winding paths through perennials and wildflowers, each planted not only for its color and bloom time, but for its meaning. The front porch wasn't draped in purple wisteria, scenting the air with a little bit of heaven. It was winter, after all, when none of those things bloomed, but Ginny could tell that they were not part of the package—not even in summer—and had never been.

It was a house she could well imagine her older brother building—straight, even lines, very utilitarian, "no froufrou," as Harold would have said, and no landscaping to speak of except a couple of holly bushes kept trimmed beside the front porch. Mama would have cringed at the austerity. But it wasn't Harold's any longer and Ginny wondered what Bethany thought of it, for she, after all, was the woman of the house.

Ginny drew a deep breath and stepped from her car.

Thankfully, Marley slipped her hand inside Ginny's. "Come on,

Aunt Ginny Dee! Aunt Bethy said she made roast beef and some funny kind of pudding, just for you!"

"Yorkshire pudding," Arlo intervened, "and it's not funny—it's just not sweet. She said you put gravy on it."

"Eew! I'll never put gravy on my pudding!" Marley exclaimed.

"I don't want gravy on my pudding either," Cooper lamented, in tandem with Marley.

"Yorkshire pudding? That's very thoughtful of Bethany. She must know they eat that in England." Ginny pasted a smile on her face, determined to be gracious. England was her future, a future she needed to embrace apart from this family. Promised Land was the dream of her past. It belonged to Bethany and Luke, at least for now. Neither of them was responsible for the pain of her loss.

The front door opened, and Bethany stretched her arms to enfold Ginny. "Welcome to Promised Land, Aunt Ginny Dee."

Ginny swallowed the lump in her throat, so near the surface.

"I know this land, this house was promised to you," Bethany whispered in Ginny's ear. "I'm sorry for the way things happened. I'm sorry it's taken so long for us to invite you, but I love you and want you to feel at home here."

Ginny nearly sobbed, knowing Bethany would have invited her sooner. But Luke hadn't been ready. That he was ready now—for her and for Mark—said wonders. Ginny closed her eyes, praying as Bethany took her coat, for strength, for the Lord to help her be what and who He wanted her to be. When she opened them, she turned to see the living room and involuntarily gasped.

"Since Luke's dad passed, I've been trying to make it a little cheerier, more our own. Luke helped me paint." Bethany seemed nervous, clearly wanting Ginny's approval. "The curtains are new—I made the slipcovers on the sofa to go with them."

"It's lovely, Bethany." Ginny meant it. The walls were a mild and welcoming yellow that caught the midday sun. The curtains, pillows, and slipcovers bloomed a garden of blues and yellows and whites— everything sunny and lovely that was Bethany. The furniture wasn't new, but it had been lovingly recovered—a perfect bit of summer in the midst of winter. A Christmas tree, modest but decorated top to bottom in cutout snowflakes, white lights, and a few scattered ornaments, stood in the front window.

"We'll get more ornaments sometime." Bethany looked embarrassed. "Luke's promised."

"It's beautiful, and creative." Ginny's heart warmed toward her niece. "Harold wasn't much for Christmas, was he?" The irony of running a Christmas tree farm and not celebrating was almost too much.

Bethany shook her head. "This is the first tree we've had in the living room since we've been married. But enough of that. The roast is done. I had it in the oven before church. We're almost ready to sit down."

"Can I help you?"

"Not a bit—you're our guest of honor." Bethany smiled the smile of a girl much younger and left Ginny to follow her to the dining room. "Arlo, help me bring out the food."

The table was set with the remains of Ginny's mother's Haviland china, a blue-floral-patterned wedding gift from relatives in England. That, too, had been promised to Ginny. Little wonder that Harold claimed Mama's best china. Well, now it's where it was meant to be, on the table of Promised Land.

Bethany set the platter of mouthwatering roast beef, surrounded by puffs of golden-brown Yorkshire pudding, on the table. Arlo flanked the roast with bowls of steaming vegetables, stepped back, and bowed with a flourish. The group grinned, looking to Luke and Bethany to know what was next.

"Sit by me, Aunt Ginny Dee," whispered Cooper.

"And me!" Marley declared.

"That's fine. Everybody take a seat and let's join hands." Luke nodded to his brother. "Mark, will you pray for us?"

Another surprise. *This day is full of them.* Ginny clasped hands with Marley and Cooper and bowed her head. Mark took a moment to breathe. Ginny wondered if he'd ever been asked to pray in public.

"Lord," Mark began shakily, "we're here as a family to say thank You. Thank You for keeping us safe, for bringing us together. Bless this home and this good food, Lord, and the hands that have provided and prepared it." A long moment passed. "And thank You, Lord, for forgiving us, for helping us, and for never giving up on us, even when we deserve it. In Jesus' name, amen."

Ginny tried not to notice the wells that filled the grown-ups' eyes, or the almost imperceptible nod of something unspoken that passed between the brothers.

"Where's the funny pudding?" Marley asked.

"Funny pudding?" Bethany raised her eyebrows. "I beg your pardon, Miss Marley, this is Yorkshire pudding—these golden puffy things."

"That's not pudding. Those look like lumpy muffins."

"They go with the roast beef, and I know you're going to like it."

Marley and Cooper exchanged a skeptical glance as Luke carved the roast.

"I'll try one first and show you," Arlo informed, leader of her siblings to the last. "Mmm!" she pronounced after her first bite.

Marley and Cooper bounced in their chairs, ready to follow their sister. Luke grinned, ladled on the gravy and passed their plates.

A bowl filled with roasted potatoes, carrots, and onions was chased round the table by another of minted peas and a boat of rich brown gravy.

Ginny couldn't keep up with the multiple conversations, the bubbles of laughter amid the chewing and encouragement to do that with closed mouths.

Family. Her heart filled nearly to overflowing as she listened and watched them, one precious, treasured face after another in the generations before her.

She almost laughed aloud to think of her anger when she'd first realized that Luke and Bethany were living at Promised Land. She'd been so focused on her little green apple that she hadn't seen the ripe, red, luscious one the Lord held out to her, to them all.

Pastor Edwards was right. It's time to change the name. It's all Promised Land—all of Wetherill Pickering's Christmas Tree Farm is Promised Land! I'm sorry, Lord, for not seeing the bounty of Your gift from the start.

🌹

The morning of December 15, shortly after Arlo had left for school, while Ginny was nestled between Cooper and Marley on the parlor settee reading *Goodnight Moon* aloud for the third time, Pastor Edwards phoned. Ginny had been expecting his call.

"I wanted to make sure the checks we received cleared before I called, Ginny, so there's no mistaking the total. The church raised nearly five thousand dollars in sales and donations."

Ginny sobbed, pushing her hand to her mouth.

"I realize that's not enough to turn the farm around, but—"

"That's not it, Pastor. That they worked so hard for us, gave so much . . . it's incredible. I'm overwhelmed. I'm grateful, just overwhelmed."

"It's the church at work, Ginny, the hands and feet of Christ doing for one another. I wish we could have made the difference you need."

By the time Ginny hung up, she'd nearly pulled herself together.

"Why are you crying, Aunt Ginny Dee?" Cooper pulled her back to their nest on the settee.

"Because people have been so kind to us, so generous."

"That's not a reason to cry," Marley objected. "They want to help us keep the farm, that's what Pa said."

"Yes, that's what they want, but I'm afraid it's not possible. The money we need to keep the farm is too much."

"Does that mean somebody's gonna take the farm away?"

Ginny nodded, her throat too tight to speak.

"Will we have to move again?"

It took Ginny a moment, but she needed to answer, to be honest with the children. "I'm afraid so. Not right away, but soon. I'm so sorry." She would give anything to have a different answer.

"I don't wanna live in the truck again. Not now. Christmas first!" Cooper declared.

"Yeah," Marley agreed. "Christmas first."

"You won't have any place to live if they take the farm away." Cooper's brow furrowed with the new thought.

"'Course she will," Marley chided. "Aunt Ginny Dee, you come live with us."

"Where?" Cooper asked.

"Wherever we live. Even in the truck—or anywhere. It doesn't matter, Aunt Ginny Dee, you stay with us." Marley spoke as though it was all so clear, so simple, so much a done deal.

Ginny wrapped her arms around both children, pulling them close. *If only that were true.*

When Marley and Cooper went out to play, Ginny phoned Bethany with the news.

"It was a valiant effort and so generous of everyone, but it barely puts a dent in the debt, and I don't have enough to make up the difference. I see no alternative to selling."

Bethany was silent on the other end of the line.

"I'm so sorry, Bethany."

"We need to make this the best Christmas ever."

"I don't feel much like celebrating."

"Not for us, for the children. This may be the only Christmas they've ever had in a real home. I don't want to think it, but depending on how things go with Mark and if he's able to get solid work, it might be the only one they'll all be together."

Ginny closed her eyes. Separation of the children was the thing she hoped would never happen, but it could. It had happened before. "Pastor Edwards said that Mark's getting help. I hope that means—"

"Yes, he told Luke about going to AA and counseling."

"He told Luke?" Ginny could hardly believe that.

"For the first time since they were kids, they're becoming like brothers—real brothers."

"I can hardly imagine it. Sunday, I saw Luke reaching out, but I thought that was your doing."

"Partly, at first. But Luke is sorry for the hateful things he said to Mark that sent him off with the children. He knows Mark believed that bottle really came from him—that Mark had started to trust him and then felt betrayed."

"Mark is too easily swayed."

"Yes, he is, but Luke won't hurt him, not again. This is the first time Mark's gone for help with his drinking on his own. The other times it was forced on him—by the Army, by the courts—but now he's scared. He doesn't want to lose his children, and if Luke and I can help prevent that, we'll do whatever it takes. We're family, and at last we're all in this together."

Family, the one thing I've always wanted . . . and now we'll be family without a home.

Ginny marveled when Luke and Mark, trailed by Arlo, Marley, and Cooper, all laughing as if they'd done it all their lives, dragged into her front parlor the biggest Christmas tree the room could hold. "Where should we put it, Aunt Ginny Dee?"

She automatically pointed to the space between the front windows, where her parents had always set their tree. It felt like the hands of time swinging backward.

"It touches the ceiling!" Marley clapped.

"We'll cut a little more off the bottom so there's room for a star," Luke promised. "Come on, Mark, let's pull it back onto the porch to cut that trunk off a few inches, maybe a foot."

"We should've measured," Mark countered.

"Yeah, well, we didn't." But it wasn't a snide remark. It was confession of a shared omission.

"Are there ormanents, Aunt Ginny Dee?" Cooper asked. "The Tiny Trees had ormanents."

"Ornaments!" Marley corrected.

"Well, no, I don't . . ." Ginny stopped. Once upon a time there had been ornaments—fragile Christmas balls and globes and little urns, beads, glass birds . . . and lights, and a star. *What happened to them?* "Luke, did your father take Mama and Daddy's Christmas ornaments to your house?"

"None there. Pop never put up a tree after Mom died. Bethany and I bought the only ornaments we have after we got married."

"We put a tree up in our room. Harold wouldn't have one in the main part of the house." Bethany spoke quietly.

"No Christmas tree on a Christmas tree farm?" Arlo couldn't believe it. "Pa, you never had a Christmas tree either?"

Mark shook his head.

"The attic. Maybe there are some in the attic. I haven't been up there, but that's where Mama stored them. Arlo, come with me. Let's go see. If there are some, you can help me carry down the boxes."

"Me too!" Marley jumped up and down, clapping. Cooper did the same.

"No, those stairs are too steep. Marley, I need you to stay downstairs and make sure Cooper doesn't try to climb them. You both might fall."

"But I want to—"

"Marley, Cooper, come with us," Luke broke in. "Your pa and I need some help with this tree. It's awful heavy. Can you help us push it back outside?"

Ginny wondered where this new Luke had come from, what he'd done with the old one. But there wasn't time to ponder.

Arlo grabbed her hand and headed for the attic stairs. "Is there a light, Aunt Ginny Dee?"

"A string, hanging at the top of the stairs, and one farther back, near the roof's slope, if the bulbs haven't burned out. Be careful on these stairs, now." But it was Ginny who struggled with the stairs. Arlo ran up them like a gazelle.

"Wow! Look at all this stuff. What's in these trunks and boxes?"

"I've no idea. But the Christmas boxes should be there"—she pointed—"under the eaves."

Arlo ducked beneath the slope of the roof and, grunting, pulled out boxes and a small trunk. "Look, here's some lights!"

"I don't know if they'll be safe. If these are really from the 1940s and they've been up here in the heat all this time, the wiring may not be much good. They might be a fire hazard."

"There's lots of other stuff."

"Well, let's bring it out and see what we have." Ginny's heart thrummed. She'd not seen her parents' ornaments since she was a teen. *Surely Mama never imagined it would be me unpacking her ornaments. I'm so sorry, Mama. I wish I could tell you. I wish we could share one more Christmas.*

Arlo pulled and pushed and finally had all the boxes dragged to the center of the attic floor. She lifted the lids on two. "There's not enough light to see them real good."

"But these are the ornaments. Why don't you go get your pa and Uncle Luke? I think we'll need help to carry these down. Wait—what is that trunk in the back? Can you pull that out?"

"This is like a treasure hunt!" Arlo crawled back under the eaves, took hold of a cracked leather strap, and pulled the small trunk to Ginny.

"Mama's treasure chest," Ginny whispered, the memory and the moment sacred.

"Treasure chest?" Arlo's voice rose with the joy of a girl detective on the trail of a great discovery.

"More like a memory chest. Mama kept things passed down from her family in England and things from her life here, things she didn't want to forget . . . nothing of monetary value, if that's what you're thinking. Just things that brought her pleasure." *Except for*

Grandmother's ring, the one treasure that you kept in your jewelry box, the one you meant to give me on my wedding day, the one I took and sold.

"Open it and let's see."

"Not just yet. Go see if your pa and Uncle Luke can come help, and be careful on those stairs."

Arlo hesitated, frowning, clearly wanting to open the chest, but she obeyed.

Ginny needed a moment alone. She wanted to open the chest, too, to see what was there, but part of her was afraid. She'd violated her mother's trust once. *What if Mama took out every memory of me? What if I really was dead to her, as Harold said I was? Dear God, I don't think I could live with that now, not on top of losing the farm. Is knowing supposed to bring closure, to make certain I move on?*

"Aunt Ginny Dee?" Mark was at her elbow. "Are you all right? Arlo said you need some help."

Ginny hadn't realized she was crying. She swiped her cheeks with her sleeve. "Sorry. We just need help carrying these things down. There are Christmas ornaments in those boxes, and I think the stairs are too steep for us to carry them."

"Sure, no problem. Want me to take this chest too?"

Ginny laid her palm on the chest again, not sure if it was better to know or not know, then took her hand away. "Yes, please, but put this in my room. The other boxes can go in the parlor. You and Luke and the children can go through them for the tree, but please be careful. Some of those ornaments are very old and fragile. Mama— your grandmother—some of them came from her family's home in England."

Mark nodded, but his eyes held concern. "We'll get everything downstairs. First, let me help you."

"I'll be okay, just bring this. Now, please."

"Right, I can carry it. I'll go first on the stairs, but I want you to give me your hand going down."

Ginny looked at him, surprised, not for the first time, by his caring. There was something of her father in Mark, and something of her mother in his eyes, more than there'd been in his own father, Harold. *He treats me as Curtis treated Mama, as he treated Daddy.* Ginny choked back a sob.

"I think you need to lie down, Aunt Ginny Dee. We'll take care of all this. No worries. No more worries for you, you hear?"

Ginny could only bite her lip, nod, and let him lead her down the stairs.

꽃

Ginny closed her bedroom door and lay down, spreading her favorite pink-and-lavender patchwork quilt over her feet, the one her mother had made. She pulled it up to her chin.

Merriment reigned in the front parlor. It came as muffled oohs and ahs from Arlo and squeals of delight from Marley and Cooper as they tore into the boxes of ornaments. Ginny prayed that Mark and Luke were helping them, that the children wouldn't break them, but she was too tired to check.

It was dark by the time Ginny woke. The house was silent, no young footsteps running through the rooms or hallway above her, no chatter coming from the kitchen. She switched on her bedside lamp. Seven thirty. She'd slept through supper. *Did Bethany take the children to Promised Land to eat? That's good. They can manage without me.* The thought relieved her of the weight of responsibility but gave her uncomfortable pause.

Ginny sighed and sat up. She slipped on her shoes, smoothed her blouse and skirt, and combed her hair. She set down her comb beside the small chest Mark had left on her dressing table. *Now is the time. If I'm going to open it alone, now is the time.*

Ginny heard a cough and a soft giggle from the parlor. *Ah, they are there.* Still, she was alone and quiet, for now. She lifted the lid, preparing to step into her mother's past.

Only it wasn't her mother's past, not entirely. Ginny's breath caught.

She lifted a tissue-wrapped package, which she knew by its feel to be the Christmas star that had always sat atop their tree, the one that had come from England and been in Mama's Dymoke family since Victorian days. Each year, as her daddy set the star in place, before he'd turn on the electric tree lights, they'd each make a wish on the star.

What was your wish that Christmas, Mama, the one after Daddy passed and I left? Did you wish me home? Did you think of me? Ginny wished she knew. She set the star aside. She'd open that later so they could place it atop the tree. Maybe they could each make a wish. Beneath the star there were other things, one she recognized immediately.

She lifted out the small snapshot, the black-and-white prom picture her daddy had taken with his 35mm camera. Curtis, standing so proud in his navy suit, the one he'd saved every penny to buy. Ginny in her pale pink organdy dress, the gardenia corsage he'd given her pinned to her shoulder. *Curtis and me. Mama kept it. In her treasure chest.* Ginny could hardly breathe.

Beneath that she found two more packages wrapped in tissue: a tiny white baby sweater, embroidered with pink rosebuds, and another, a blue one, embroidered with tiny yellow ducklings. These were not garments that had belonged to either her or Harold, she was quite sure. *They look new, as if they've never been worn. Did you lose children I never knew about, Mama? Or were these hopes for grandchildren—grandchildren you never saw?* Her heart clenched to think of those years for her mother, years Ginny'd never known.

The remainder she recognized, remembered seeing. *Your and Daddy's wedding picture; newborn pictures of Harold and me; two pairs of booties—one mine, one Harold's; Harold's and my first baby shoes; two baby teeth—the first ones we lost; the scarf Daddy bought you the year of the good harvest; dried petals from sometime, something you wanted to remember. Bits and pieces of your woman heart, tiny treasures, things known only in your depths, Mama.*

Ginny packed the bits and pieces away, all except the picture of her and Curtis. She might keep that out, might try to remember the good times, the good days. She breathed deeply and closed the box, then set it on a shelf in her closet. She didn't want the children rummaging through it, and she knew they would, ever in search of hidden treasure.

She picked up the tissue-wrapped star and carried it to the parlor. Even before she entered the room, she saw colorful lights reflected in the window.

"Aunt Ginny Dee! You came to see. Isn't it beautiful?" Marley asked.

"You've decorated it all—yes, it's beautiful!"

"You don't mind that we didn't wait for you, do you?" Mark asked, pulling himself up from the floor where he'd been playing cars with Cooper.

"No, not at all, but I'm concerned about those lights. They must be ancient and the wiring—"

"Mr. Skippy brought us new ones!" Cooper threw his arms around Ginny's legs in a giant hug.

"Will was here?"

"Is here." Will walked in from the kitchen with a tray of reindeer and snowflake cookies in one hand, balanced against his cast. "You're just in time to celebrate. I hope you don't mind my crashing the party."

"You didn't crash, Mr. Skipwith. Pa telephoned you," Arlo said, stuffing ornament wrapping paper into the empty boxes. "Pa wanted to give you that picture. Anyway, all our family should be here. Aunt Bethany and Uncle Luke just went home."

Family. Is Will family? To Arlo he is. What Ginny said was, "Picture?"

Mark's face flamed. "I gave Will the framed botanical you gave me. I hope you don't mind."

"You know, Aunt Ginny Dee, the one with all the plants from the farm." Arlo spoke as if that was the most normal, easy to come by thing in the world.

Ginny froze. *That was my legacy picture to you, Mark. The farm's legacy.*

Will and Mark exchanged glances and quickly looked away.

Is Will embarrassed for accepting such a gift? He should be. Ginny stared at the tree, not wanting to reveal what the picture had meant to her, what it meant to create it from the very nature of the farm and to give it to Mark. It was the largest, most beautiful work she'd ever done and was meant to be his family heirloom.

"What's that, Aunt Ginny Dee? Is that a present?" Marley was fixated on the tissue paper in Ginny's hand.

"No, no, it's a star—our family Christmas star." Ginny mustered her courage, her hospitality, and did her best to smile. "My mama brought it here from England after she visited there as a girl. She and Daddy—your great-grandpa—put it on the top of our tree every Christmas. When Daddy placed it on top, we'd each make a Christmas wish—a secret wish. I thought we could put it on this one."

"And make wishes!" Marley sang.

"And make wishes," Ginny agreed.

"I wish we could stay here forever," Arlo said.

Ginny's breath caught. *I wish the same.*

"It must be really old!" Cooper looked so serious.

"It is. I think it was in the Dymoke family since Victorian times. Here, Arlo, why don't you do the honors since you found the ornaments in the attic? Be careful with it, please."

"Pa, you'll have to lift me up."

"My pleasure, Miss Pickering."

Marley and Cooper giggled. Arlo glowed, and gently pulled the tissue paper off the cut-tin punctured star. A little paper the size of a recipe card fell to the floor. "It has some writing on it." Arlo picked up the paper.

"What?" Marley asked. "What does it say?"

"It says, *December 25, 1942. For Ginny Dee and Curtis. May your love shine bright as our Christmas Star. All my love, Mama.*"

Weak in the knees, Ginny felt her heart triple-beat. Mark caught her before she stumbled, guiding her to the settee. Still, Ginny held out her hand for the paper. "1942."

Will set his tray down and took a seat on the other side of Ginny. He placed a hand on her back. "The year you left, the year you married. It must have been your mother's Christmas wish."

Ginny could only stare at her mother's handwriting.

"She loved you, Ginny. And Curtis. She understood." Will spoke softly, rubbing the tender place on the back of her neck, just below her hairline.

Ginny choked back a sob.

"Why are you crying?" Arlo looked confused. "Are you happy or sad?"

"Yes." Ginny nodded, almost laughing but not quite. "Yes, I'm happy . . . and sad." She looked up at Will, the only one who'd remember that time, the only one who'd known Curtis or her mother or father.

"Can I hang up the star now?"

"Yes, turn off the lights first," Mark ordered.

Marley pulled the plug; instantly the room was dark, except for the light from the fire.

Mark squatted, letting Arlo climb onto his shoulders, and stood so that she had to bend lest her head scrape the ceiling.

"If you set it just in front of that top white light, it will glow all over the room, making great pictures on the ceiling," Will said.

"How did you know that?" Ginny was surprised.

"I remember it from the time your parents invited my family for a Christmas party. I was in high school then, the year before you and Curtis . . . I saw your dad smile and wrap your hands around this star. Then you climbed on a chair to place it on top of the tree. You were so happy, eyes brighter than any star, and then when he plugged in the electric lights, it was as if two stars exploded, filling the room."

"I can't believe you remember that, or that it was quite that way."

"It was. Exactly." Will took her hand and looked into her eyes. "As for remembering, I remember everything about you, Ginny Dee Pickering."

CHAPTER FORTY-FIVE

"CHRISTMAS WAS SPECTACULAR AMAZING," Arlo said over and over to herself and anyone who would listen.

"Christmas was the best ever in the history of the world," Marley declared.

"I want Christmas every day," Cooper decided. "Let's do it again."

Ginny couldn't agree more. It was an entire season to remember. Bethany and Ginny had outdone themselves in the kitchen, until both houses rivaled candy shops and bakeries. Carols around the piano, old records on the stereo and tapes on the player, old-fashioned taffy pulling, snow cream with maple syrup the day it snowed, board games in front of the tree at night . . . It was the last Pickering Christmas they'd likely all be together, and now that she knew her mama had never stopped hoping for her, Ginny felt like she was truly home in every way, where she'd longed to come, where she belonged . . . just in time to leave. Like Cooper, she wished it would never end.

With the week after Christmas came a letter from across the pond, from Lord Dymoke, needing a firm date for Ginny's arrival. The nephew of one of the gardeners had applied for the apprenticeship. Mr. Longwood should consider him if Ginny had decided not to come. *Someone younger and strong, surely.* Ginny knew that Lord Dymoke and Mr. Longwood had extended her courtesy beyond reason. She couldn't keep them waiting longer.

She needed to meet with Will, not on a friend or "family" basis, but on the business of selling the farm. She'd need to put the sale into his hands, making sure he took his rightful commission. She couldn't negotiate all of that from England, and in truth, she didn't want to. Leaving would be so very hard; selling the farm to strangers would be killing. She needed to go soon, to find new purpose, ground herself, engage in the physical work of greenhouses and gardens, and turn the soil of a new life. *Gardening. It's the thing that's kept me sane. It will again. It must.*

There was no way to know how long it would take to sell the farm. Mark and the children could live in the house until then, and Luke and Bethany at Promised Land. Where they would go or what they would do after the sale, even with whatever of the proceeds Ginny could award them, she didn't know, and that made her heart ache all the more.

She hadn't heard from or seen Will since the night she'd discovered the star, which confused her. She'd hoped he'd spend Christmas Day with them. She'd invited him and thought he meant to come. But he never showed and never phoned. Luke had simply told her not to expect him.

She wasn't a vain woman, but she'd felt certain after what he'd said, the way he'd looked into her eyes the night they'd hung the star, that he was interested in some romantic way, or at least tended in that direction.

She'd seen him in church the last two Sundays, but he hadn't sat with them. Yesterday he'd sat near the front with a well-dressed man and woman—visitors, apparently.

Bethany had leaned toward her. "I heard that's the governor and his wife. Can you imagine? In New Scrivelsby?"

Ginny hadn't wanted to seem to be hanging around, waiting or hoping for Will's attention. But it hadn't mattered. The group waited near the front as the congregation filed out. From the parking lot, Ginny saw Will introduce the couple to Pastor Edwards as they shook hands with him at the church door. Pastor Edwards huddled with them, as if longtime friends, nodding and smiling broadly. He'd cast a furtive glance in Ginny's direction, seemed to indicate a willingness to move the group toward her and her family, but Will had stepped forward, blocking the pastor's view and apparently declining. Then the group had gone out together.

Ginny had tried not to mind. After all, she reminded herself, Will had his own friends and longtime connections. What he did and with whom he spent time were none of her business.

With the arrival of the letter, though, she phoned Will's office to make a business appointment, hopefully for that day.

"I'm sorry, Mrs. Boyden, he and Mark left this morning for Richmond to finalize things with the governor—you know. Wasn't it exciting that he and his wife came to our church?" Sheila said, a smile evident in her voice.

"What?" Ginny was confused. "No, I didn't know."

"Really?" She sounded puzzled. "Mark said—I mean, oh . . . Mr. Skipwith said he wants to see you on Monday—the fourth, that things should be settled by then."

"Settled? The fourth is a full week from now."

"Yes, Mark told me he—well." Now she sounded flustered. "What time would you like to come in on Monday? Our office opens at ten."

"Ten will be fine, thank you." *What does "settled" mean, and why did Mark go with Will to see the governor today?*

Come to think of it, Ginny had seen very little of Mark lately except on Christmas Day. He'd been gone long hours. It hadn't bothered Ginny; she'd assumed he was looking for work, or perhaps attending counseling sessions. She loved having the children, and with Arlo being out of school for the holidays, they'd spent at least as much time at Bethany's and Luke's as they had her house. Still, if he was going as far away as Richmond, he should have said.

Ginny didn't want to think about that now. She wanted to make the most of her days with the children while they were all home with her. *Make every moment count while we can.* There was one more tradition she wanted to share with the children before she left for

England, before they were no longer together, something she hoped they would tuck away in their book of memories from the farm and perhaps carry into their future. Snow was predicted again for Friday, New Year's Day.

After a pumpkin-and-raisin pancake breakfast to celebrate the New Year, for which Mark was noticeably absent, Ginny pulled a bag of suet from the freezer. "With more snow coming we need to make certain our feathered friends have all the provisions they need—food, water, shelter."

"Pa and I filled the bird feeders yesterday."

"Excellent, Arlo! But I think the birds need a bit extra. When I was a girl, in the days after Christmas, when our work died down for a while, my parents always decorated a tree outside for the birds."

"You mean we have to take the ormanents off our Christmas tree?" Cooper wailed.

"Or-na-ments!" Marley corrected, emphasizing each syllable.

"No, nothing like that," Ginny laughed. "We'll make our own ornaments—food ornaments for the birds. I'll show you how and we'll make them together."

They spent the morning cutting orange slices, stringing popcorn and cranberries, making suet balls rolled in birdseed, and slathering pine cones in peanut butter, then rolling them in sunflower seeds. They used red string to create hangers for all they'd made, string the birds would use for nest building come spring. Finally, their basket of goodies was filled. Ginny had hoped Mark would join them for their celebration but his truck was gone and he never appeared, not even for lunch.

It was late afternoon when the troop made their way to the front yard to hang their treats from branches of the maple and dogwood trees, there no longer being evergreens standing along the drive to decorate. It was a happy time, a merry time. All three children danced with the joy of their work, each vying for the best place to hang their treats, each hoping to be the first to glimpse their feathered friends partaking of their smorgasbord.

By the time they'd finished, the sun was just going down, cheeks and fingers were frozen bright pink, and the first light flakes of snow had begun to fall.

"Pa said there's a sled in the barn! We should get the sled out!" Marley shouted.

"There's not enough snow to sled yet, stu—" At Ginny's raised eyebrow, Arlo stopped before saying the forbidden word.

"Tomorrow morning will be the time," Ginny said. "Maybe your pa will be home and go with you then. There's a wonderful hill over by . . ."

"By where, Aunt Ginny Dee?"

"By Promised Land, by Aunt Bethany and Uncle Luke's house." Ginny breathed. She could say the name of that dear place and give it to its inhabitants unreservedly now.

Ginny's thoughts were interrupted by two vehicles coming down the lane, faster than normal—Mark's truck followed by Will's car. *What now?*

Mark was first out of his truck, grinning from ear to ear.

"Pa!" Arlo shouted. "Come see what we're doing!"

"We're feeding the birds!" Cooper ran for his pa.

Mark didn't stop to pick up his son but headed straight for Ginny, lifted her from the ground, and swung her round and round until she was breathless.

"Pa!" Marley sang, delighted. "Swing me too!"

Mark set his aunt on her feet. "This swing is for Aunt Ginny Dee!"

Ginny couldn't catch her breath.

Will was out of his car by then, his smile just as broad as Mark's.

"What in the world is going on with you two?" Ginny felt her face flush. She pulled the hat that had flown off her head back over her ears. "You're both grinning like Cheshire cats!"

"Will, you should say; it was your and Pastor Edwards's doing." Mark looked like he might explode if Will didn't speak soon.

"The governor bought your botanical." Will grinned.

"What?"

"Last Sunday—while he and his wife were visiting. Charles—Pastor Edwards—and I took them to lunch at the diner. Charles told the governor about the fire and the fundraiser the church hosted. The governor asked what else was being done to help and we showed them one of your botanicals Rosemary had hanging for sale in the restaurant. Charles has been working to sell some of your other ones."

"The ones he took during the fundraiser. I'd all but forgotten about them with everything going on." Ginny felt the world spinning.

"It was the governor's idea to auction a bigger piece at his New Year banquet. That's when I showed him a photograph of the legacy work you'd created for Mark."

"I didn't think you'd mind about the picture, Aunt Ginny Dee—not if it helped save the farm. I'd already asked Will if he thought it might help if we tried to sell it." Mark looked a little nervous and ecstatic all at once.

"The governor insisted on buying your botanical for ten thousand and silent auctioned it for fifty at his New Year banquet. The rest of your pictures are selling too—outright."

"Fifty dollars?"

Mark laughed. "Aunt Ginny Dee! No, fifty thousand! He's donated the entire sum to help clear the tax debt, and Pastor Edwards received pledges for the rest."

"What? I don't believe it! Why?"

"Why?" Will asked. "Because the Dymokes founded New Scrivelsby. Because Wetherill Pickering's Christmas Tree Farm is a Virginia institution. And because—"

"Will and Pastor Edwards are friends with the governor, who is friends with money across the state of Virginia."

"That's an overstatement, Mark," Will chided.

"This is what you two have been up to?"

"For the last couple of weeks, Ginny." Will stood close. "I'm sorry we couldn't tell you sooner. We wanted to make sure it would work."

Ginny couldn't think. "What does it mean?"

"It means there'll be enough to pay those back taxes and take a chunk out of that bank loan! Will talked with the bank, and they're willing to work with you on the rest of the loan as long as regular payments can be made," Mark crowed. "It means we can—you can—keep the farm! We can all stay!"

"If you want to, Ginny. Only if you want to," Will countered. "There'll no longer be a tax lien on the title and the debt will be reduced. There will still be the loan to repay, but those payments can be reduced and spread over a longer time. You're still free to sell. Proceeds from the sale of the farm would clear that debt with money besides. You're not obligated in any way. It's up to you, but it's possible."

Ginny was aware that all eyes were upon her. Arlo clasped her hands, as if in prayer. Marley grabbed Cooper's hand. Mark waited on tenterhooks.

But it was Will she looked to, waiting for him to say something more. Yes, she wanted a family—her family. But was it enough? The children would grow up and move on. Perhaps Luke and Bethany would stay, but would Mark? *Is that enough, Lord? It's what I thought I wanted, but is there something more? Someone more?*

"I need to think, Will. I appreciate all you've done, but that ten thousand from the governor should be your money. Mark gave you the piece. You sold it."

"No, Ginny, I—"

"I need to think . . . and talk with Mark and Luke and Bethany. It's—it's too much all at once." Ginny turned away, walked toward the house, and left them there.

Ginny spent the evening staring at the letter from Lord Dymoke, then into the dark window of her room.

Long after the children should have been asleep, Mark knocked on her door. "Aunt Ginny Dee? Can I come in?"

"Yes."

"Are you okay?"

"Yes."

"Maybe we shouldn't have taken matters into our own hands. We should have talked with you first, asked you. I'm sorry."

"It isn't that. I appreciate what you and Will and Pastor Edwards have done, more than I can say. I'm overwhelmed. And I want there to be a home here for all of you. I won't sell the farm but I don't think I'll stay." The words thickened in her throat.

"What?" Mark sat on the edge of the bed and took her hand. "Why wouldn't you stay?"

"You need to live your own life, Mark—you and the children, Luke and Bethany. And I need to find mine."

Mark rubbed his thumb over her knuckles, in much the same way Will had once done. She clamped her lips shut to keep them from quivering.

"I thought maybe, Will thought . . . he might be enough. We might all be enough."

Ginny shook her head. "Will's never said that. He's been a friend in every way, but I don't think—"

"You think too much, Aunt Ginny Dee. Give him a chance."

"He's had opportunity if he was interested in that way, Mark. I don't want to make a fool of myself."

"I can't believe you wouldn't—"

They both jumped when the phone rang.

"Get that, before it wakes the children . . . please."

Mark sprinted for the hallway but was back a minute later, before Ginny shut her door.

"It's for you." He grinned. "Will."

Ginny hesitated.

"He's waiting, Aunt Ginny Dee. Listen to him, just listen."

Before picking up the phone Ginny sighed, not from weariness, but from uncertainty, an unknown amount of fear and of anticipation she couldn't clarify in her own mind. "Hello?"

"Ginny, it's Will."

"Yes."

"I didn't get a chance to apologize for jumping ahead of you, for taking your beautiful botanical and selling it. It's no wonder the governor loved it—it's a masterpiece. I wanted to surprise you. I got carried away when he wanted to buy it, but I should have thought how important that picture was to you. It was a legacy work from the farm that you'd given to Mark, for him and his children."

Ginny started to interrupt, but he rushed on. "Let me finish, Ginny, or I'll lose my nerve."

She waited.

"I'm sorry for running ahead, for not asking you first."

"It was Mark's picture to do with as he liked."

"But I pushed it. All I could think of was finding a way for you to stay, hoping you would stay, and I never even asked you if that was what you wanted."

"You knew I didn't want to sell the farm."

"I knew you didn't want to sell the farm for the sake of Mark and the children, for Luke and Bethany . . . but I never asked if you wanted to stay."

No, you didn't.

"I'm asking now. Will you stay, Ginny? Will you stay here in New Scrivelsby, with me?"

Ginny held her breath. "With you?"

"I've not been brave enough to court you, not until I knew I could help save your farm for you. I know we haven't . . ."

"Courted?" She smiled at the old-fashioned word.

"Yes, but I want to do that now, if you'll let me. If you'll have me." Will hesitated. "My intentions are honorable, Mrs. Boyden. If your father were here, I'd ask him for permission. Since he's not, I've asked Mark and Luke."

"You what?" Ginny almost laughed.

"Next of kin, the men in your life. They both said yes. Arlo's ready to call me Uncle Will or even Grandpa. I told her only if you say yes—to me, not to her. Will you?"

"Hmm. So you've asked Arlo? And you think her vote will help persuade me?"

"And Marley's and Cooper's. I'm counting on it." She heard the hope in his voice.

Hope—a gentle, fragile thing . . . Wings of hope, like the butterflies that landed among Mama's roses.

"Dare I hope, Ginny?"

She swallowed back tears. "Yes, Will. Dear Will. There's room for hope, for both of us, I think."

Minutes later Ginny set the phone in its cradle and dropped the letter from Lord Dymoke into the fire.

Epilogue

Ginny pulled the turkey roaster halfway from the oven, gave the twenty-five-pound bird a final basting, and pushed it back into the oven to finish roasting to a rich, golden brown.

"Mmm, that smells heavenly, Mrs. Skipwith. All the fragrances of home." Will wrapped his arms around Ginny's middle and nuzzled the back of her neck as she stood.

Ginny didn't protest.

"What do you think? Can a hungry husband get a turkey sample before dinner?"

Ginny laughed. "Possibly. In about a half hour . . . if he fetches a gallon of apple cider from the root cellar for me."

"Consider it done." He pulled her closer.

A gust of cold air whipped through the kitchen as Bethany, loaded down with apple and pumpkin pies, burst in the back door, Bailey at her heels. Marley, Arlo, and Cooper followed in her wake, their arms filled with bouquets of late orange and golden roses, fragrant spearmint, burgundy chrysanthemums, and wild feathering weeds, each laughing and singing at the top of their lungs, "Over the river and through the woods, to Aunt Ginny Dee's we come!"

"Welcome! Welcome!" Ginny laughed. "Happy Thanksgiving! Where on earth did you find those roses? They're gorgeous!"

"They're the last from that bush outside my back door—on the south side of Promised Land, where it's still warm. I've been protecting them against the frost, hoping there'd be blooms for today. The children came over for breakfast and flower gathering." Bethany's joy rang triumphant.

"An entire family of brilliant horticulturalists!" Will smiled while opening his arms to the children. "And look at those maple leaves, Marley!"

"I found them by the creek—still pretty."

"They're red," affirmed Cooper.

"Yes, they are—and beautiful!"

"Enthusiasm, energy, passion—that's what orange roses mean," Arlo stated, matter of fact.

"Is that so?" Will asked. "Well, let's see, I'm enthusiastic about having all our family home for Thanksgiving. You and Marley and Cooper fill the house with energy each and every day. And I'm passionate about—"

"Aunt Ginny Dee!" Marley hopped up and down. "You're passionate about Aunt Ginny Dee, we know!"

"Yeah!" echoed Cooper.

Bailey gave a woof.

"And by the way, dark red chrysanthemums mean love and passion!" Arlo waggled her eyebrows, waving her bouquet in Ginny's face.

"That's enough, Miss Arlo." Ginny barely suppressed her smile, knowing she'd get nowhere trying to stop the girl.

"Brilliant." Will grinned.

"What can we do to help, Aunt Ginny Dee?" Bethany tied an apron round her slightly thickened waist.

Ginny looked away. It was not the first time she'd believed Bethany's gain might mean more than the consumption of Halloween's candy apples, November's cranberry pumpkin bread, apple pie with crumble topping and homemade ice cream, pre-Thanksgiving pumpkin custard with whipped cream, and the dozens of ginger cookie cutouts they'd baked, decorated, and frozen in anticipation of their Christmas shop. Ginny knew she'd struggled with an extra five pounds herself. But she wouldn't ask just in case it wasn't what she hoped for her.

Still, Bethany had seemed more determined and energetic and a good bit happier lately, even more than she'd been since Ginny and Will's wedding last Easter—a resurrection celebration and new beginning for the family in every way. Several times in the last month or so Ginny had seen Bethany smiling, heard her quietly humming. Come to think of it, some of those melodies had been nursery tunes . . . ones she sometimes sang to Cooper, even though he was outgrowing them.

"What about Luke and Mark?" Will asked, breaking Ginny's train of thought.

"Luke said they should be finished by eleven thirty. They wanted to get the Christmas tree stand outside the barn well supplied with cut trees before tomorrow. Big day."

"Very big day," Ginny agreed. "I think we have plenty of cookies to offer alongside the wreaths and botanicals we'll sell, but we'll need to get an early start on the mulled cider and hot chocolate."

Bethany nodded. "With all the advertising this year I'm thinking folks might show up at the crack of dawn."

Ginny hoped so. They'd skated through the year on thin financial ice. If it hadn't been for Will's continued investment, they wouldn't be standing on the threshold of hope. A good tree-selling month should put them firmly in the black for the new year.

Marley stood at Ginny's elbow and whispered, "You said I could decorate the table, me and Cooper."

"Yes, that's right. I remember. Do you have a plan? Are you ready?"

Marley's pearly white milk teeth shone, and she nodded enthusiastically.

"Well then, go ahead. Do you want Arlo to set the turkey plates around?"

"No, I want to do everything . . . except maybe the silverware. Arlo can do that. Cooper can fold napkins."

CATHY GOHLKE

"I brought cloth napkins and rings for today," Bethany said. "Cooper can push the napkins into the rings. Here you go, Cooper. I'll show you how."

Ginny's heart warmed. *Everyone with a job. Everyone doing their special things to contribute to this day.*

By the time Ginny spooned the stuffing from the bird and Bethany whipped heated milk and butter into the mashed potatoes, everything was ready. Between Marley's array of scarlet maple leaves, pine cones, acorns, and tiny pumpkins and Arlo's vases of autumn roses, Ginny and Bethany set bowls of steaming vegetables. Bounty from their summer garden, canned or frozen in August, and root vegetables that had nestled in the cool of the cellar covered the table.

At the last minute Mark and Luke, ruddy cheeked and laughing, burst through the back door, feigning starvation.

Scents of fresh air and pine mingled with rosemary, sage, and thyme, filling the house with all the fragrances of Thanksgivings from Ginny's childhood.

As the family gathered round the table and bowed their heads to pray, Ginny was struck with memories past, of the last Thanksgiving before her father had died, of the day she and Curtis and Harold had sat at that very table, holding hands with her parents as her father prayed. *How Mama and Daddy would have loved this—this bursting-at-the-seams house, this family with all its generations.*

"Luke, would you pray?" Will asked.

"It's your home. You're the spiritual leader of your home, Uncle Will," Luke countered. A smile of recognition that Ginny didn't understand passed between the men.

Will bowed his head. "Father in heaven, we thank You for the bounty of this table, for the loving hands that have prepared this feast, and for the wonderful family gathered here." Will's voice caught. Ginny squeezed his hand in understanding and solidarity. "You've blessed us, Lord, each and every one. A year ago today we didn't know if we'd have a family or a home or a farm. We couldn't have imagined this thriving work where we all pull together. You've blessed us with all these things, Lord, and especially with each other. We're so very grateful. Help us pour out the blessing to others that You have to us, Father. Help us to see needs and fill them. Make us Your hands and feet. We pray, and thank You, through Jesus Christ our Lord, amen."

"Amen" echoed round the table.

In the moment of silence that followed Will's prayer, Ginny spoke. "Your grandparents"—Ginny looked at Luke and Mark—"kept a Thanksgiving tradition in our home all the years I can remember. I'd like us to keep that now."

"What?" Arlo asked.

"As we pass the food, each person says what they're most thankful for today."

"Turkey! And pie!" Cooper shouted. "Can I eat now?"

"Yes," Ginny laughed. "Marley, what about you?"

"I'm thankful for flowers and red and yellow leaves and for Bailey—and that tomorrow we're gonna sell cookies."

"We're gonna give away cookies—and cider and hot chocolate," Arlo corrected. "I'm thankful that the girls at school are nice to me this year, and that we can all stay here together, that we'll never have to move—ever again." She looked to her pa for affirmation, daring him to offer anything less.

Mark nodded. "Me too. I'm thankful, Aunt Ginny Dee, Uncle Will, that you've taken us in, made us part of this family. This year is the first time the farm's felt like a real home to me." He hesitated. "And I'm thankful for my brother, and for the work we're doing." He spoke the words without looking at Luke, whose face reddened in some mixture of embarrassment and pleasure.

Ginny's throat thickened.

"Yeah, well, I'm thankful for you, too, bro." Luke tried to make light, but his voice came out husky. "More than I can say. And I'm thankful we can keep the farm and the business going. There's no place I'd rather raise my family." He looked at his wife.

All eyes landed on Bethany. Ginny's heart double flipped.

Bethany laughed. "I guess that means it's my turn." She looked at

Ginny. "I know you've wondered, Aunt Ginny Dee. Thank you for not asking." She drew a deep breath and smiled, glowing. "The answer is no, I'm not pregnant, but yes, we're expecting a new little Pickering come sometime next year." She sobered and quickly added, "We've applied for adoption and have been accepted. We're not counting our chickens—or child—before time, but we're hoping . . . with all our hearts, and we want you all to pray . . . please."

"Congratulations! That's wonderful!" Will was the first to speak.

"Bethany, Luke!" It was all Ginny could say.

"Does that mean I'll be Aunt Marley?"

"Not exactly," Bethany laughed, "but close enough."

"Cousins. He'll be our cousin," Arlo stated flatly.

"Him? I want a girl baby," Marley insisted.

"Well, it'll definitely be one or the other." Luke grinned and wrapped his arm around his wife. "Either one will do."

Will grasped Ginny's hand beneath the table. "One more seat at the table. And so the family grows."

Oh, Mama, Daddy, if you could only see this family. What you started, what the generations before you started.

"I'm thankful for the love of my wife, for each one of you, that you've all welcomed me without reservation." Will's grip on Ginny's hand tightened as he spoke.

"You're like our grandpa," Marley said. "Aunt Ginny Dee, you're like our grandma. We don't have any so you guys can be it."

Ginny's heart overflowed.

"Your turn, Aunt Ginny Dee. What are you thankful for?" Arlo wanted to know.

Ginny shook her head. How could she speak after all of that? "You, Arlo. And you, Marley, and you, Cooper, and Mark and Luke and Bethany—and the blessing on the way—and—" Ginny couldn't stop the tears as she looked at her husband. "And you, Will. You've no idea how thankful I am for you."

Will lifted Ginny's hand to his lips and smiled. "I have an inkling."

"Time to eat!" Cooper and Marley shouted together.

Late that night, once all the family was tucked in bed, Ginny and Will, wrapped in coats and hats and mufflers, snuggled beneath a quilt on the porch swing with mugs of hot cocoa. Ginny laid her head against Will's shoulder, cozy in the comfort of his arm around her, and gazed at the night sky, alive and dancing in flaming points of light.

"What are you thinking, Mrs. Skipwith?"

"I'm marveling at how content I am in this moment, Mr. Skipwith, how I never in all my life expected such contentment, such peace."

"Not missing those gardens in England, then?"

Ginny chuckled. "I saw them on our honeymoon, remember?"

"I certainly remember our honeymoon." He tickled her cheek.

"No, I don't miss those gardens. But I confess I'm eager to get my hands in the soil again come spring. I have some great ideas for borders outside the church. I think Pastor Edwards will be pleased."

Will pulled her closer. "I'm sure he will."

Ginny sighed happily. "I don't miss England, but to think I almost missed out on this—all of this."

"But you didn't. We didn't."

"No, we didn't. I was thinking today, as we sat around the table, that we've all come home, haven't we? Prodigals and naysayers, every one of us."

"That wouldn't have happened if you hadn't opened the door for Mark and the kids, for Bethany and Luke, for me."

"That couldn't have happened if you and Pastor Edwards—and even the governor—hadn't made it possible," she countered.

"I don't think it was our doing."

"That's true. God made it possible. He prepared the feast ahead of time—ahead of all of us. We just didn't realize it. We only needed to walk through the door."

A Note from the Author

My brother, Dan Lounsbury, loaned me his copy of Timothy Keller's book *The Prodigal God*. Reading it may have been the first time I recognized myself in the role of the wayward and desperate Prodigal Son, as well as the older, jealous, judgmental, and unforgiving son from Jesus' parable in Luke 15. Keller's book woke in me the realization that we all hold traits of both brothers, and a desire to remain neither.

I determined to face and own my mistakes seen in the extremes of both sons by better understanding how each had failed their loving father, how each came to take the path he'd chosen, and how each stood on the threshold of response to his father's entreaty and love.

The questions ultimately became: Can I repent and accept my heavenly Father's welcome and forgiveness? Can I live joyously within my Father's house as an obedient and treasured daughter without judging others?

Such questions led me to other writers who had explored this quest—Henri Nouwen in his book *The Return of the Prodigal Son*; Kenneth Bailey in his book *The Cross and the Prodigal: Luke 15 Through the Eyes of Middle Eastern Peasants*; Kristi McLelland in her online course "The Running Father."

Each enriched my understanding of what the parable meant to those who first listened to Jesus as well as the culture in which they lived and moved. Each grew my appreciation for the economy and genius of the three parables in Luke 15 as Jesus' response to criticism, and what each of those parables could mean in my life.

I especially appreciated Kristi McLelland's Middle Eastern understanding of the Running Father, who represents God the Father. I remain amazed at the extent of his willing sacrifice on behalf of his children, and of the enormity of his great love for both of his wayward sons.

The realization that we, like Ginny, Curtis, and Mark, are all at one time prodigals who've "left home" and are in desperate need of returning is the first and primary focus of my story. Ginny's dawning realization that she'd also lived the role of the older judgmental son in her feelings toward Curtis, Harold, and Luke helps her realize she wants to change. In helping Mark and his children, Ginny finds not only a second chance for herself but an opportunity to grow, following in the steps of the Running Father.

Some notes about historical aspects of the story:

The town's name, New Scrivelsby, the original Scrivelsby Manor, and the family names of Dyonisius, Dymoke, and Skipwith all came from genealogical research my brother, Dan, had done. The Dymoke family of Scrivelsby Manor in England has held the position of the King's or Queen's Champion since 1066.

Curtis's character was inspired by a teen who entered the foster-care system during the Great Depression and lived and worked with my father's family on their farm in western New York. Curtis was dearly loved as a brother to my father and aunts and as a son to my grandparents. The real Curtis actually did wash the feet of my hardworking but weary and infirm grandfather, inspiring that scene, though other aspects of his backstory are fiction: Curtis never went to war, never suffered the consequences or perpetrated any of the postwar actions I've portrayed. Sadly, Curtis died as a teen from peritonitis as the result of a burst appendix. My brother, Dan, was given Curtis's name as his middle name.

Writing about Ginny and Curtis, before and after the war, reminded me of the challenges young couples faced during WWII. Some waited to marry until after the war, as Ginny's parents dictated. Many, however, opted to marry before men went off to war, not knowing what life would be like afterward. Because of the draft, couples often had quick weddings. Elkton, Maryland, known as the Marriage Capital of the East Coast at the time, was a favorite spot for elopement as no waiting period or blood tests were required before tying the knot.

Sometimes loved ones returned home to lead full and productive lives postwar. Taking advantage of the new G.I. Bill helped push many American families out of poverty and into the middle class.

Sometimes, however, like Curtis and Mark, returning soldiers dealt with physical, mental, or emotional scars from the war for the rest of their lives. We owe understanding, support, and a tremendous debt to those who've risked their lives, their futures, and their families to protect us—a debt too often overlooked and not paid by merely saying thank you or clapping after ceremonies of recognition.

Story seeds come from many places. Not all of them germinate or grow, but I'm always searching for those golden nuggets of promise. Some of those from this story include:

The character of Pastor Charles Edwards was named in honor of Pastor Charles Edwards, emeritus, of College Park Baptist Church, in Winston-Salem, NC, who married my husband and me over forty-two years ago. As I write to him and his wife, Judy, in my Christmas card each year—*The knot you tied still holds!*

The name Wetherill Pickering's Christmas Tree Farm came from a sign I read over fifty years ago—actually, a sign I misread. It stuck in my mind as an imaginary place where I wanted to someday set a story.

The mountain farm was inspired by Milltown Creek Tree Farms

in Lovettsville, Virginia (a town originally settled in the 1700s by German folk rather than English), a family-owned Christmas tree farm set amid beautiful rolling hills not far from my home. We found and cut our Christmas tree there for the last few years and plan to return year by year.

The idea for cutting off the tops of Christmas trees came from a picture I saw in a newspaper, possibly in the 1980s, of a "prank" played on a local Christmas tree farmer in Maryland. At the time I wondered what could be done to redeem such cruelty, a question I enjoyed answering in this story.

Years ago, my husband and I bought acreage in Elkton, Maryland, much of it wooded, to build a home. In exploring the woods, my husband discovered a small patch of marijuana and alerted the authorities, who sent officials from a specialized department to deal with it. We never knew who planted the patch or how long it had been growing there.

More recently came the inspiration for creating and selling pressed botanicals. A friend, Sara Edi Boyd, creator and owner of Sweetgrass Botanicals, introduced my brother, Dan, and me to the fascinating process of pressing and preserving flowers and leaves to create beautiful works of art. I saw this as a project I'd love to do with my grandchildren. My brother saw it as an enjoyable creative process with business possibilities he could pursue for years to come. I've planted flowers, roses, and other botanicals in my home garden that I hope he'll find useful and that will produce hours of creative fun with my grands.

I hope you've enjoyed *This Promised Land*, and that you take with you the heart of Jesus' parables in Luke 15. In truth we are all lost sheep in need of being rescued; we are lost coins in need of being found; we are all prodigals who've gone our own way, who desperately need to return to our Father; and we are all easily offended, judgmental children in need of welcoming our brothers and sisters and joining the feast and celebration our Father has prepared. May each of us turn, run to Him, celebrate with Him, and welcome one another Home.

I'd love to hear from you. Know that I am praying God's great blessings for you,

Cathy

P.S. If your book club has enjoyed this or any of my books, know that I'm happy to meet with your group virtually. You can reach me through my website at cathygohlke.com.

Acknowledgments

I'm especially grateful to my brother, Dan Lounsbury, for introducing me to Timothy Keller's book *The Prodigal God* that started me on this journey.

Many thanks also to Henri Nouwen for his book *The Return of the Prodigal Son*; to Kenneth Bailey for his book *The Cross and the Prodigal: Luke 15 Through the Eyes of Middle Eastern Peasants*; and to Kristi McLelland for her online course "The Running Father."

Special thanks to Sara Edi Boyd of Sweetgrass Botanicals for introducing my brother and me to the wonders of collecting, pressing, and creating art forms from flowers, herbs, leaves, and all manner of natural lovelies.

Thank you to my longtime literary agent, sister in Christ, dear friend, and champion, Natasha Kern. We've traveled many literary, heartfelt, and gardening miles together. You are a rare treasure to me.

Libby Dykstra, Senior Designer, I love the cover you've created for *This Promised Land*. You've captured generations and the mountain's morning light amid towering trees and wildflowers—I'm so pleased.

So much appreciation for Stephanie Broene, Sarah Rische—my amazing editors—and for all of my wonderful Tyndale Fiction team. Thank you for your years of support and encouragement through stories dreamed and written, and through this topsy-turvy journey we call life.

Thank you, dear friend and wonderful author Terri Gillespie, for reading an early copy of this manuscript and for offering your critique and insights. Our friendship is a precious gift to me. I treasure our talks and journey together.

Thank you, Carrie Turansky, sister historical fiction author and dear friend, for all your encouragement and support. We've traveled through years of life and inspiring stories together. I count each step of that journey precious.

Special thanks to my family—my husband, Dan; my son, Daniel; and my daughter, Elisabeth, son-in-law, Tim, and your three precious children from whom I drew much inspiration for the children in this story. You are all the wind beneath my wings.

Thanks always to my uncle, Wilbur Goforth, who encouraged me to ask in my service for the Lord, "Do I have joy? Is this yoke easy? Is this burden light?"

I have learned through studying the parables in Luke 15 that in the time of Jesus, His hearers would have understood Jesus' word *yoke* to mean His teaching. So now I ask this question with new insight: Does Jesus' teaching in this parable give me joy? *Yes!* Is this teaching of Jesus easy to bear, is the burden of it light? *Yes, it breaches boundaries I hadn't understood. It's given me new insights, greater freedom to run Home to our heavenly Father unfettered, and it makes the writing of this story the joy of my heart.*

Last but never least, always most—I thank my heavenly Father and Lord Jesus Christ for gifts of life and salvation, for love, for understanding, for family. This gift of writing and story comes directly from You, Abba, and I am eternally grateful. May this book glorify Your holy Name. May it encourage all who read it to run home into Your open arms.

Discussion Questions

1. Ginny wants closure before moving to England. Do you think it is realistic for her to expect that from visiting her parents' graves? What do you think might have happened had she never gotten that letter?

2. Discuss Ginny's regrets about her parents. What still haunts her, and why?

3. Why do you think Harold might have misled both Ginny and eventually his sons about the ownership of the farm? What made him so bitter? How did that affect the choices and lives of each of his sons? How did it affect Bethany?

4. Why do you think Will Skipwith never remarried after the death of his wife? Did that have anything to do with his attraction to Ginny?

5. Explain the parable of the Prodigal Son and Running Father in Luke 15 from Pastor Edwards's point of view. Do you agree with him? Do you see yourself in the roles of any/all of the characters in the parable? Why or why not?

6. What do you think of Arlo's idea to help save the farm through the sale of pressed botanical works of art? Why does Will support her immediately? Why is Ginny reluctant at first? What does this difference in reaction say about each of them?

7. If Will had not been able to help save the farm for Ginny, do you think he would have spoken up, asking her to stay? Did his courtship depend on success in this way? Should it have?

8. Explore Luke and Mark's relationship from each character's point of view. What tore them apart? What brings them together?

9. Arlo finds trusting adults very difficult. Discuss the various reasons for that. How is her trust built?

10. Each of the characters in the story has needed and longed for family. Discuss how that need affected each of their personalities and life choices, and how those needs are fulfilled in the story.

About the Author

Bestselling, Christy Hall of Fame, and Carol and INSPY Award–winning author Cathy Gohlke writes novels steeped with inspirational lessons, speaking of world and life events through the lens of history. She champions the battle against oppression, celebrating the freedom found only in Christ. Cathy has worked as a school librarian, drama director, and director of children's and education ministries. When not traveling to historic sites for research, she and her husband, Dan, divide their time between northern Virginia and the Jersey Shore, enjoying time with their grown children and grandchildren. Visit her website at cathygohlke.com and find her on Facebook at CathyGohlkeBooks; on Bookbub (@CathyGohlke); and on YouTube, where you can subscribe to Book Gems with Cathy Gohlke for short videos of book recommendations. Cathy welcomes invitations to virtual book club meetings through the Connect page of her website.

CONNECT WITH CATHY ONLINE AT

cathygohlke.com

OR FOLLOW HER ON

@CathyGohlkeBooks

@cathy_gohlke

@Cathy_Gohlke

@CathyGohlke

TYNDALE HOUSE PUBLISHERS IS CRAZY4FICTION!

Become part of the Crazy4Fiction community and find fiction that entertains and inspires. Get exclusive content, free resources, and more!

JOIN IN ON THE FUN!

 crazy4fiction.com

 Crazy4Fiction

 crazy4fiction

 tyndale_crazy4fiction

 Sign up for our newsletter

FOR GREAT DEALS ON TYNDALE PRODUCTS, GO TO TYNDALE.COM/FICTION

CP0021